Mr. Infuriating

The Mister Series

Tess Summers
Seasons Press LLC

Published: 2025
Published by Seasons Press LLC.
ISBN: 978-1-966869-02-3

Edited by Maggie Ryan.
Cover by Star Child Designs.
Page edge design by Painted Wings Publishing Services.

This is a work of fiction. The characters, incidents and dialogues in this book are of the author's imagination and are not to be construed as real. Any resemblance to actual events or persons, living or dead, is completely coincidental.

This book is for mature readers. It contains sexually explicit scenes and graphic language that may be considered offensive by some.

All sexually active characters in this work are eighteen years of age or older.

No AI was used in writing this book.

Mr. Infuriating

A steamy, single dad romance...

Before we'd even met, Gretchen–the beautiful and newly divorced customer of my cabinet shop–called me the "Infuriating Jerk of the Year".

Fair enough. When she called to cancel her custom cabinet order, I may have suggested I would allow it only if she rode my... appendage. But in my defense, I didn't know my foreman hadn't put her on hold.

When we crossed paths flirting at my brother's bar later, she had no idea Mr. Infuriating and I were one and the same.

Full disclosure: I came clean before things went too far.

Fuller disclosure: We put aside our differences for one night only, but we agreed it couldn't go any further.

But when her kitchen springs a leak during installation, I insist she and her son move in with me and my kids until I finish. Of course, the second I have her under my roof, she ends up back in my bed.

So, we make a deal–it's only until her cabinets are installed, or she finds Mr. Right–whichever comes first.

But what if she wants *me* to be Mr. Right. Or worse yet, what if she doesn't?

Table of Contents

Mr. Infuriating iii

Prologue.. 1

Chapter One..6

Chapter Two 15

Chapter Three..25

Chapter Four..32

Chapter Five 36

Chapter Six 38

Chapter Seven..49

Chapter Eight..59

Chapter Nine..66

Chapter Ten 70

Chapter Eleven 74

Chapter Twelve..77

Chapter Thirteen 84

Chapter Fourteen.. 91

Chapter Fifteen..96

Chapter Sixteen 102

Chapter Seventeen...106

Chapter Eighteen...112

Chapter Nineteen... 118

Chapter Twenty 132

Chapter Twenty-One 140

Chapter Twenty-Two...146

Chapter Twenty-Three 151

Chapter Twenty-Four...156

Chapter Twenty-Five... 160

Chapter Twenty-Six...163

Chapter Twenty-Seven 166

Chapter Twenty-Eight 171

Chapter Twenty-Nine...177

Chapter Thirty.. 183

Chapter Thirty-One.. 186

Chapter Thirty-Two..191

Chapter Thirty-Three 198

Chapter Thirty-Four...204

Chapter Thirty-Five... 207

Chapter Thirty-Six 213

Chapter Thirty-Seven 222

Chapter Thirty-Eight... 227

Chapter Thirty-Nine...231

Chapter Forty 241

Chapter Forty-One 247

Chapter Forty-Two 250

Chapter Forty-Three 256

Chapter Forty-Four 261

Chapter Forty-Five... 269

Chapter Forty-Six 274

Chapter Forty-Seven 278

Chapter Forty-Eight 284

Chapter Forty-Nine 289

Chapter Fifty...294

Chapter Fifty-One... 300

Chapter Fifty-Two 305

Chapter Fifty-Three 310

Chapter Fifty-Four... 316

Chapter Fifty-Five.. 321

Chapter Fifty-Six 326

Chapter Fifty-Seven...330

Chapter Fifty-Eight..337

Chapter Fifty-Nine...343

Chapter Sixty 344

Chapter Sixty-One 349

Chapter Sixty-Two 352

Chapter Sixty-Three 355

Chapter Sixty-Four...358

Chapter Sixty-Five... 361

Chapter Sixty-Six...363

Chapter Sixty-Seven 373

Chapter Sixty-Eight 376

Chapter Sixty-Nine 380

Chapter Seventy 384

Chapter Seventy-One 388

Chapter Seventy-Two 390

Chapter Seventy-Three 395

Chapter Seventy-Four 403

Chapter Seventy-Five 407

Chapter Seventy-Six..414

Chapter Seventy-Seven 418

Chapter Seventy-Eight 421

Chapter Seventy-Nine 425

Chapter Eighty 431

Chapter Eighty-One 438

Chapter Eighty-Two 442

Chapter Eighty-Three...445

Epilogue 455

Thank you..457

Acknowledgments 458

Breakfast Is Served...459

San Diego Social Scene 460

Agents of Ensenada...461

Boston's Elite series 462

About the Author..463

Contact Me! 463

Mr. Infuriating

Prologue

Gretchen

"*No!*" I screeched when my computer screen went black at the same time all the classroom lights shut off.

I dropped my head to my desk and willed myself not to cry in frustration as the silence of the dark room filled the air. Even if the power did come back on, the old software on my classroom desktop didn't update my work constantly like my personal laptop did. I knew when I turned the dinosaur back on, everything would be lost.

Administration had decided to schedule school building maintenance during the teachers' planning day. Kids were dismissed at noon, and we were supposed to use that time to work on our curriculum. But the last hour I just spent on lessons might have been in vain.

There was nothing that annoyed me more than having my time wasted.

I really should bring my laptop to work with me and use that.

Except it would be just one more thing I needed to remember in the morning, and the last thing I needed was to add another item to my morning checklist.

I barely made it to work on time as it was. Between getting Jake, our eighteen-month-old son, up and ready in the morning and getting him to daycare, plus remembering my lunch, his diaper bag, and my satchel of student work, my mornings were hectic enough.

My classroom door opened and Samantha McClung, my principal, stuck her head in my room.

"Hey. It looks like we're going to be without power for a while. Feel free to get out of here."

"Okay, thanks for letting me know." It was on the tip of my tongue to ask what happened, but then I realized I didn't care. "Have a good night."

"You too, Gretchen."

I decided to take advantage of this new-found free time and do something nice for my husband. I could swing by the grocery store and pick up ingredients to make his favorite, lasagna, and get it prepped before heading out to pick up Jake from daycare.

The question was, would Troy be home to enjoy dinner while it was hot? He'd been working so much lately.

Me: Hi, babe! Do you think you'll make it home for dinner tonight?

He answered right away, which I hoped was a good sign.

Troy: Sorry, hun. Probably not. I'll try not to wake you when I get home. Give Jake a kiss for me.

It had to be killing him to only see his son on Sundays. He rarely made it home before I put Jake down for bed, and he didn't wake up until after we'd left for daycare and work. When I suggested he take Jake to daycare in the mornings, he said he didn't want to disrupt our son's sleep schedule.

I guess that made sense.

Not five minutes later, Stacy McCartney, the sixth grade English teacher from across the hall walked in with her backpack slung over one shoulder.

"Studies have shown one-strapping is bad for your back," I admonished as I grabbed my lunch bag from the little minifridge under my desk.

"I know, but old habits die hard. The cool kids one-strapped it when I was in high school twenty years ago."

"I'm glad that trend died before I got to my freshman year. My back hurts enough now as it is."

"It's because you carry a thirty-pound human everywhere. And thankfully, I do yoga three days a week to counteract any effects one-strapping might be having. Speaking of... I'm headed to an early class now, wanna go with me?"

Yoga would do me good. Maybe it'd even help with the remaining baby weight that had been lingering on my hips. But not today, I had an idea.

I looked at the folder of essays to be graded as I draped my satchel over my body and hemmed about whether to take the file home.

Zipping up my bag while leaving the essays on my desk, I replied, "I think I'm going to take advantage of this early out and surprise Troy with an office picnic."

It'd felt like Troy and I were drifting apart, and I desperately wanted to rectify that. I couldn't even remember the last time we'd been intimate.

I'd thought with me being off for the summer break, we'd have more time together, but my poor husband worked six days a week and rarely got home before eight or nine in the evening. I could count on one hand the number of times we'd shared a meal in the last six months.

But today it wouldn't matter. I'd come to him.

Maybe there was a bright side to this power outage after all.

~~

I felt like Dorothy from the *Wizard of Oz* as I practically skipped up the sidewalk leading to Troy's office building with the picnic basket tucked under my arm. My heart raced as I waved to the receptionist and walked to the elevators.

Rarely did I get to see Troy in his element. Although he always looked handsome when he walked in the door at night with his tie loose around his neck, it wasn't the same as seeing him behind his desk. I hoped he'd be surprised to see me.

And that he'd know how much I loved him. It felt like I hadn't had a chance to show him in a long time.

It worked perfectly that his assistant Cora wasn't at her desk that sat just outside his office. Her not announcing me only added to the element of surprise, and I'd get to see his genuine reaction.

I hesitated outside his closed door. Should I knock? What if he was meeting with clients?

Surely, they'd forgive an intrusion by his wife.

I opened the door with a big smile that quickly fell when I saw Cora bent over Troy's desk, ass up, while he nailed her from behind.

The sound of the contents of the picnic basket rattling as it crashed to the floor echoed in my brain when my eyes met his shocked ones. I knew in that instant, my beautiful little life had ceased to exist.

Chapter One

Six months later

Gretchen

"Mrs. Wainright?" a young woman's cheery voice asked when I answered my cell phone.

I replied, "Yes?" immediately.

Although I had ceased being *Mrs.* Wainwright three days ago in a Boston courtroom, I wasn't going to change how people addressed me in the middle of the school year. I'd start over with Ms. Kelly next fall.

"Hi, it's Shelly from Mitchell Cabinets and Woodworking. How are you today?"

I instantly closed my eyes tight.

Fuck.

I'd completely forgotten about the custom kitchen cabinets we'd ordered seven months ago. One month before my world turned upside down.

Finding Troy fucking his assistant over his desk had been so cliché, it was gross.

He'd even run after me, tucking his dick in his pants as he yelled, "It's not what it looks like."

And seriously, they hadn't even bothered to lock the door? What the fuck? It was like they'd wanted to get caught.

Or maybe everyone in his office already knew, and I was the laughing stock of his company.

He hadn't come home that night, and I knew then I'd be the only one trying to save our marriage and our family. That wasn't something I could do alone.

The divorce had taken its toll, so the kitchen renovation had been the furthest thing from my mind. In fact, I'd forgotten all about it.

"Hi, Shelly. I hope you're calling to tell me that you can't get the materials, and you need to cancel."

I remembered the salesman had pushed our date to cancel with a full refund to until they began work on the project because they were having trouble getting the walnut wood that Troy had insisted on.

"No! Great news! Your cabinets are finished, and I'm calling to schedule your installation."

I bit back a sigh. They must have notified Troy they were starting the work, and the bastard "forgot" to tell me. How convenient they were finished right after we'd signed our papers.

"Shelly, I'm hoping you can help me out." I decided to be vulnerable—woman-to-woman, with hopes she'd take pity on me. "My husband was the one who wanted the kitchen renovation, and well, I caught him cheating on me with his assistant not long after we placed our order with you, and he moved out. Needless to say, during the divorce proceedings, I completely forgot about the cabinets, and now it's just not in my budget. Is there anything you can do? I mean, I understand if there's a penalty or something, but I'd like to cancel the order."

"Ohhh."

That didn't sound promising.

She was silent a beat before continuing. "I'm so sorry about your divorce, but the cabinets are *done*. They're custom-built, specifically for your kitchen."

"I know, but surely they could be used for someone else's project?"

I was willing to take a hit, but not a forty-thousand dollar one. Especially since now that the divorce was final, I couldn't even get Troy to pay for half of the cabinets I hadn't wanted in the first place.

"Let me put you through to a supervisor."

"Thanks."

I let out a long exhale, steeling myself to have to retell my tale of woe to a new person. And not to be sexist, but woodworking was a male-dominated industry, so I prepared for a man's voice to come on the line. He probably wouldn't give two shits about my problem.

Not that Shelly really had either.

"This is Rick."

I took another deep breath and recounted my story, complete with all the embarrassing details.

He was sympathetic to my plight.

Sort of.

He exclaimed, "oh, no!" in all the right places, offered his condolences, and told me I was better off without Troy.

Then he said, "If only you would have called when you found out. We would have been able to cancel the order with no problem. But as it stands... the cabinets are done." He tried to insert some pep into his tone when he added, "The good news is they'll increase the value of your home."

That wasn't what I wanted to hear. I had no intention of selling my house, so I couldn't care less about increasing the value.

"Please, Rick. My divorce was finalized *three days* ago, and the cost of the cabinets wasn't included in the settlement. Isn't there something you can do?"

"I'm afraid not."

That made my spine stiffen. I wasn't trying to be an entitled bitch. More like a desperate one. I'd made a lot of concessions to keep the house in the divorce because I wanted Jake to grow up in Lancastle, with my family nearby, and go to school in the Lancastle district. With the skyrocketing cost of housing, there's no way I'd be able to afford even a "starter" home here now.

"What if I just don't schedule a time for your installers to come."

Yeah, I'd lose the ten percent deposit, but really, what else could they do? Although, four thousand dollars was no meager sum for someone on a teacher's salary.

"We'll take you to court. And based on past experiences, you'll lose. Our contract is air-tight, so you'll be out the cost of the cabinets, plus the cost of the lawyers—plural. The contract spells out that if we go to court, the losing party pays all attorneys' fees."

I didn't remember that little tidbit.

"Look, I'm desperate. I can't afford the cabinets, and I seriously doubt they'll improve the value of the house enough to cover the cost. Isn't there someone you can talk to?"

"I can talk to Gabe, the owner, but I don't think he'll budge. He's the guy who spent the last two-and-a-half months making them."

I had a feeling Rick was ready to get rid of me and just wanted to pass the buck, but I still said, "I'd appreciate anything you can do."

"Hold on."

He punched a couple of buttons; except he didn't put me on hold. I wasn't sure if he realized I could hear him humming a tune while he walked along a hallway, then through a door into what I assumed was a workshop based on how much echo his footsteps started to make and how the sound of machinery grew louder.

I heard him call, "Hey, boss?" and the machine noise stopped.

"Yeah?" a deep, gruff voice replied from a distance.

"About those cabinets for the Wainwrights—"

"When are they getting the fuck out of here? They're taking up too much room. Did you schedule the installation?"

"Uh, about that—"

"What about that?" the other man snarled.

"Apparently the Wainwrights got divorced after they ordered the cabinets."

Gabe snorted. "I could have seen that coming. She is way out of his league."

My ego welcomed his assessment, especially since it'd taken such a blow when my husband decided to throw away our family for a woman probably ten years younger than me. I wasn't even sure if she could legally drink. But I wondered how Gabe could say that about me since we'd never met. Maybe he'd been there when we went into the showroom, and I hadn't realized it.

"I guess she caught his secretary riding his dick."

I heard him wince. "What a moron. That chick is hot with a capital H, and he cheats on her? He was probably neglecting her at home, too."

Again, the ego boost was appreciated, and he wasn't wrong about me being neglected.

"Yeah, well… she doesn't want the cabinets anymore—"

"*What?*"

"And is wondering if there's something you can do."

"They're *custom* cabinets, what the fuck does she think I can do for her? Tell her unless she wants to ride *my* dick, she's out of luck. We have a contract."

"*Excuse me?*" I shouted into the phone.

I heard Rick mutter, "Oh, shit," before the line went dead.

****

Gabe

I looked at Rick's mortified face as he punched a button on the phone, then dropped it on the nearest surface like it was burning his hand, and I realized what had just happened.

"You are fucking fired," I growled.

"Damn, Gabe. I'm sorry. I thought I'd put her on hold."

"Obviously not, dumbass."

Pinching the bridge of my nose, I let out a deep sigh.

How the hell am I going to fix this?

I had no clue.

What I did know was that I didn't need this shit today. Becky had called earlier that morning asking me to bring our daughter Brittany's school sweatshirt to our son Brayden's first lacrosse game of the season later that afternoon.

When I explained that wasn't feasible since I didn't have time to go home before his game, she threw a tantrum like only my ex-wife could.

"She needs that sweatshirt, Gabriel."

I bristled at her use of my government name.

"She's staying with me this weekend, *Rebecca*. She can get it then. Obviously, it's not that important or she wouldn't have left it in the first place."

"So, you're okay with our daughter waiting for the bus in forty-degree weather in the morning without a sweatshirt."

"And you're telling me that my daughter has no spring jacket or any other sweatshirt in her closet? It has to be the one sweatshirt she left at my place."

I deliberately called Britt *my* daughter because I knew that would piss Becky off. Yeah, it was petty, but the woman was picking a fight with me over a goddamn sweatshirt.

"None that she'll wear!"

"Then she must not be that cold in the morning."

"I can't believe that you're being so difficult about this."

"I'm not the one being difficult. If I had time to go home before Brayden's game, trust me, I would."

If for no other reason than to shut you the hell up.

I left that part unspoken.

"Fine. I'll handle it, like I always do."

Without another word, she ended the call.

I closed my eyes and threw my head back with a loud sigh as I set my phone on my desk. Becky was going to make me pay for not doing her bidding, of that I was certain.

Fortunately, I now had the option to simply walk away and ignore her.

I'd take the kids shopping this weekend and buy them ten damn sweatshirts each if I thought that would placate my ex-wife. But I knew it wouldn't, because she'd find something else to be upset with me about next week. That had been par for the course since our divorce was finalized five years ago.

Actually, pretty much since Britt turned four and our world fell apart. We just didn't get divorced for another two years.

In some ways it'd been a blessing, but I did miss being with my kids every night.

And now, thanks to fucking Rick, I had another woman pissed off at me.

Granted, this one had every right to be, but I had no idea how to fix it. I wasn't in a position to give Gretchen Wainwright what she wanted. I'd spent the last ten weeks working on those cabinets, not to mention the cost of materials, I couldn't just eat that, even if I wanted to.

Besides, my brother, Maverick, would have my ass if I did. He was supposed to be my silent partner, but he was hardly silent. Which, I had to begrudgingly admit, was a good thing. His business savvy had allowed me to turn what had once been my side-hustle into a full-time gig, complete with ten employees.

He'd also been the one to have a lawyer draw up our contract. And he was the one who insisted we take people to court if they breached said contract—something we'd only had to do twice, fortunately.

I could picture how this one would go.

"So, Mr. Mitchell, did you really suggest my client ride your... appendage in exchange for terminating the contract for her custom kitchen cabinets?"

Headlines flashed in my head. "*Contractor Demands Sex From Clients*" or some shit like that.

That would not be good for business. Not to mention, the Yelp reviews would probably be scathing.

One thing was certain—Rick was going through training on how to work the damn phone.

Chapter Two

Gretchen

Instead of grading the papers I'd stayed after school to work on, I found myself pacing my classroom floor, absent-mindedly straightening students' desks and picking up the stray trash on the floor as I fumed.

The nerve of that man!

I mean, obviously he hadn't known I was listening, but still! I didn't want his stupid misogynistic cabinets in my house.

Screw that guy.

Surely his rude comment was grounds to cancel the contract. I'd have to call my brother, Andrew, and see what he thought. He was an attorney of whom I'd asked way too many favors in recent months.

Even though family law wasn't his specialty, he'd had someone from his fancy law firm represent me in the divorce, yet I still received the discounted family rate. I was positive it was because of my lawyer that I'd managed to get the house outright, although in hindsight, Troy might have thought it was a small price to pay to walk away from his responsibilities to his wife and son.

I guess Cora's vagina must be magical. Or maybe mine was just that bad after having Jake.

I decided not to bother my brother until our monthly family dinner and casually mention it then.

Realizing I was not in the right frame of mind to grade my seventh grader's essays—right now they'd probably all get Ds—

I decided to pack up and take the papers home to hopefully work on later that night.

My phone dinged with an incoming text, and I cringed internally, thinking it was Laura, my BFF, asking me *again* to go to happy hour and "celebrate" my divorce. I suspected "celebrate" meant get me drunk and try to find me a one-night stand.

I wasn't ready to celebrate yet. And one-night stands had never really been my thing, even when I was young and carefree. I was a mom now; they definitely couldn't be my thing.

My vibrator had been scratching my itch for quite a while, it could continue doing the job until I figured things out.

Reluctantly, I opened my text app and found an unread message from an unknown number.

Unknown numbers weren't unusual—I gave my students' parents my number at the beginning of the year with directions to use it if they had questions or concerns.

Clicking on it, I scowled at the words.

Unknown number: Ms. Wainwright—it's Gabe Mitchell. I owe you an apology for my crude response to my foreman, Rick, when he asked a question on your behalf. Please know I'm embarrassed and never meant any disrespect.

Never meant any disrespect?

I wasn't letting him off the hook that easily.

Me: So, suggesting I ride your dick was meant to be respectful?

The bubbles that indicated he was replying started and stopped and didn't restart again, so I put my phone in my purse, grabbed my satchel with my students' papers and walked out my door.

On my way to the parking lot, I felt the phone's vibration. Part of me wanted to make the asshole wait before I read his reply, but the worrier in me wanted to get this cabinet situation resolved or I knew I'd fret until it was.

Gabe Mitchell: What I said was crude and out of line. In my defense, I was sweaty and grumpy, and I thought I was only talking to my foreman. I would never knowingly speak that way in front of any woman. Please accept my apologies.

Me: I'll accept your apology if you'll cancel my order.

Gabe Mitchell: You know I can't do that, ma'am. I've spent the last ten weeks working on your cabinets—made specifically for your kitchen. Not to mention the expense of your specialized wood choice.

Did he seriously drop a *ma'am* on me? I was disliking this guy more and more.

Me: I have a hard time believing my kitchen is so unique that those cabinets wouldn't work somewhere else.

Gabe Mitchell: They probably would. If someone came in with a similar layout to your kitchen and wanted that exact wood. But the chances of that happening are slim. And I'm sorry to have to remind you, we have a contract, which I've upheld my end of. Now I need you to uphold yours, so I don't have to take legal action. When can we schedule an installation?

Ugh.

I wasn't sure how long I could avoid Mitchell Cabinets and Woodworking, but I knew I could get away with it at least until next week.

I shoved my phone back in my purse without replying and started my little Honda Accord—I'd decided against getting a minivan until I had Kid Number Two, and it didn't look promising that was ever going to happen.

I don't want a minivan anyway.

My phone buzzed again, and I pulled it out of my purse. Only this time it was from Laura.

Laura: Happy hour tonight?

Me: I don't think so.

Laura: Come on; Thursday night is ladies' night! You need to get out and embrace your new found freedom! You're officially single! It's time to start acting like it!

Me: Um, I have a *child*. I can't just go to a bar on a whim.

Laura: I know for a fact Carrie would love to watch him.

Me: How do you know "for a fact" my sister would love to watch him?

Laura: I already asked her for you. She'll be at your house in 30 minutes.

Of course she had.

I never thought I'd find myself single again at the age of thirty-one. It hardly felt like something I wanted to embrace. Although, "marry a cheater who abandoned his family" hadn't exactly been on my bingo card, either. Yet here I was.

Maybe Laura was right—I should welcome my new marital status.

Yet the second I thought it, it still didn't sound appealing.

Power through, Gretchen! my inner voice chided. *You're lucky to have people who love you and are willing to support you!*

I decided to compromise.

Me: I'll come for one drink.

Laura: I'll meet you at Flannigan's in an hour.

With a sigh I put my car in drive. If I hurried, I could pick up Jake, go home and help Carrie with dinner, change out of my teacher clothes and into something more bar-worthy, freshen up my makeup, and only be a few minutes late.

I could at least look the part of an available woman. Maybe I'd even get a free drink because, thanks to Gabe Mitchell, I wasn't sure I'd be able to afford anything more than water or maybe a soda.

Screw you, Troy.

And screw you, too, Gabe Mitchell.

And while I was at it—screw the asshole at the electric company who charged me a setup fee to remove my ex's name from my utility bill.

I was still sore about that one, too.

Getting divorced wasn't for the weak. Or poor, as I was quickly finding out.

****

Gabe

I thought about Gretchen as I drove to Brayden's game. I didn't want her to think I was a creep.

I mean, I had been crude—no doubt. And I was embarrassed as fuck about it. But I'd apologized, dammit. She should have accepted my apology.

Why should she? my inner voice asked.

Because I really was sorry!

I was also sorry we were going to have to sue her if she didn't pay up.

I didn't want to do that—especially if she was tight on money like she'd told Rick. Going to court was going to double her bill. Not to mention I was going to have to charge her for a storage unit if she didn't schedule the installation soon.

Hopefully, she had someone in her corner who would help her realize it was in her best interest to just have the cabinets installed.

While I waited at one of the few stoplights in town, I noticed a sign announcing the opening of a new clothing store and decided to stop. Maybe if I showed up with *a* sweatshirt, that would placate my ex-wife.

I doubted it, but I might as well try. Get back into one woman's good graces at least.

~~

I approached where Britt was sitting next to her mom and tossed her a yellow bag containing the new sweatshirt.

"What's this?" she asked with furrowed brows as she peeked inside.

"Your mom said you left your sweatshirt at my house, and I figured you might be cold today."

She pulled out the pink hoodie with some logo I wasn't familiar with, and I held my breath. I didn't know if this brand was fashionable, or if I'd be taking it back on my drive to work tomorrow.

"Dad!" she shrieked before quickly pulling it over her head. "I love it! Thank you!"

Becky, on the other hand, glared at me.

Nope. Not placated.

Apparently, I was supposed to go home and get the one she'd specifically asked for.

"If you had time to stop at the store, why didn't you have time to go home?"

"Because the store was on my way. My house would have been another thirty minutes round trip."

She rolled her eyes and shook her head.

"*Thirty* minutes, Gabriel? Exaggerate much?"

There she went with my government name again. She'd never once called me Gabriel during our ten years of marriage.

I didn't have the energy to argue with her, so I just gave her a *fuck you* smile, kissed Britt on her forehead, and walked to the opposite end of the field to find a space next to the parents of some of Brayden's friends.

Brayden's best friend's mom stood and greeted me with a hug. "Hey, Gabe! How have you been?"

"Hi, Missy. You look as beautiful as ever." I shook her husband's hand. "Good to see you, Bryan."

"You too, Gabe. Pull up a chair."

I unfolded my camping chair just as Missy said, "So, Brayden told Will you're still not dating anyone…"

I only faltered a little as I set the chair up. *Here we go…*

"Whoever you know who would be perfect for me, I'm not interested."

"I told you to leave it alone, Miss," Bryan grumbled.

"But she really would be perfect!"

"Oh yeah?" I said with a mischievous smile as I plopped into my chair. "Why's that."

I was dying to hear what Missy thought made a woman perfect for me.

"Well, she's newly divorced."

"That's good. I would hate to think you wanted to set me up with a married woman. Hopefully she's straight, too."

"Of course, silly."

My teasing was lost on the woman.

"So, single and straight… I'm not sure that qualifies as 'perfect for me'."

"She's funny and smart… and she wants to have children."

I choked out a laugh.

"I'm afraid that instantly *disqualifies* her. Britt and Brayden keep me plenty busy. I have no interest in having more kids."

It'd taken a while to come to terms with that, but now that I had, I embraced it.

Missy waved a hand at me. "Oh, you say that now."

"And I'll keep saying it."

"Just meet her. I know you'd really like her."

"I appreciate you thinking of me, but really, I'm not interested in being set up."

She let out a dramatic sigh.

"You won't even think about it?"

"Nope. Thank you, though."

With pursed lips, she grumbled, "You're no fun."

I burst out laughing. "Then why would you want to set me up with your friend?"

"It's not her friend," Bryan chimed in. "It's her sister."

"Who's also my friend," Missy shot back.

"Again, thank you for thinking of me. I'm honored you think I'm worthy to date your sister, but I really don't want to date anyone right now."

Although I wouldn't mind a roll in the hay with someone.

Definitely not with Missy's sister though. There wasn't a doubt in my mind that wouldn't end well. Not to mention me fucking my son's best friend's aunt once and not going back for a second date would be a disaster for Brayden.

Maybe I'd visit my little brother's bar soon and see what that scene had to offer. Derrick seemed to get laid a lot without any strings; he said it was a benefit of being an owner of not one, but two Flannigan's. He'd just opened one in Lancastle, our little coastal town in Massachusetts, and decided to name it after the original one he and Maverick owned in Boston.

But just having a brother who owned a bar appeared to do the trick when it came to getting women. Every time any of us stopped by, we usually ended the night with a proposition from a woman wearing beer goggles. Beau was only a year older than Derrick and visited him often, taking full advantage of the brother/bar owner angle. I'd only left with someone once. And the one-time Mav had taken a woman home from the bar, he ended up marrying her nine months later when he found out she'd had his baby.

The idea made me shudder. Which, I had to admit, was ironic.

My kids were now thirteen, eleven, and forever two. While I'd once been devastated at the idea of not having more, I couldn't comprehend starting over now. Maverick's boys had already graduated high school, with Nick in college and Nash in the Navy when little Sawyer was born.

Fuck. That.

Again, the irony wasn't lost on me.

Although, I had to admit, I'd never seen Maverick happier, and my nephew was a pretty damn cute baby. I enjoyed spending time with him. But I was always glad that I could hand him back when he got fussy or needed a new diaper.

Still, Missy was not going to be deterred.

"Well, if you change your mind…"

The whistle blew to start play, so thankfully she let it go when I told her again, "I appreciate it, but I'm really not interested in dating right now."

If you know anyone who'd be up for one night, however, give her my name.

Obviously, I kept that to myself.

But now that the idea was in my head, I made a mental note to visit Derrick at the bar soon. Maybe even tonight after the game.

Chapter Three

Gretchen

Even though I'd arrived past our agreed-upon time, I still beat Laura to Flannigan's, so I took a seat at the bar where I could see the TV and the door.

"What can I get you?"

The bartender was hot, and judging by his flirty grin, he knew it.

"I'll just have a Coke until my friend gets here."

"Are you waiting for a guy or a girl?" he asked as he scooped ice into a glass.

"Does it matter?"

"Not to me. I just wanted to know who to keep an eye out for."

"My best friend, Laura."

His flirty grin turned mischievous as he pressed a button on the bar gun and shot soda into the tumbler. "You girls gonna paint the town red tonight?"

"Honestly," I glanced at his name badge and continued, "Derrick, I'll be lucky if I make it past nine o'clock."

He pushed a black straw into the ice, then set the drink in front of me. "Long day, huh?"

"A hundred seventh graders have a tendency to drain your energy."

"I'll take your word for it," he said with a laugh. "My nephew is in seventh grade, and he's a cool kid. But I couldn't imagine a hundred of him, all day, every day."

"It can be challenging. Fortunately, I get them in chunks of twenty at a time. But honestly, I wouldn't want to do anything else."

He smiled thoughtfully at me.

"You found your calling."

"I found my calling," I agreed before taking a sip through the straw.

Derrick filled drink orders while he chatted with me. I didn't get the impression he was hitting on me, and he definitely wasn't angling for a big tip considering I'd ordered a four-dollar soda. He genuinely seemed interested in talking to me. I found I enjoyed his company, too, and it wasn't until my phone buzzed that I realized I'd been waiting a while for my friend.

Laura: Please tell me you haven't left your house yet.

I glanced at my watch.

Me: I've been at Flannigan's for thirty-five minutes. Where are you?!

Laura: I am so sorry! I'm still at work! My boss came in just as I was getting ready to leave and dangled a chance to be part of a big project in front of me if I helped him with the presentation. It's taking longer than I thought it would. I think I can probably get out of here in an hour.

Me: I don't want to wait an hour. We can do this another time.

I was a little miffed at my BFF for making me come out for nothing and miss dinner with Jake but decided to give her a pass. She didn't have kids yet, so she didn't understand. I knew she wasn't intentionally being thoughtless.

Laura: How about two weeks from tomorrow? I'll pay for a sitter if Carrie or your parents can't watch Jake, and I promise I'll be there before you, and drinks will be on me. Plus, you'll have all weekend to recover.

Again, she didn't understand that just because I wasn't working, didn't mean I had no other responsibilities. Keeping a two-year old alive was no simple feat. Not something easily done hungover.

Me: It's a soft yes.

Laura: Again, I'm so sorry, and I apologize for not texting sooner. I feel awful making you wait by yourself.

Me: It's okay. I've been chatting with the bartender, Derrick.

Laura: He's not the bartender. He's the owner. I think Vicky fucked him last year.

Me: I don't want to sleep with him, but he's been really nice. It makes sense, knowing he's the owner.

Laura: Maybe he has a brother.

Me: Maybe. I'll talk to you this weekend. Don't work too hard.

Laura: Love you. Thanks for understanding.

Me: Love you, too.

I set my phone on the bar and slipped my purse off the back of my chair as I smiled at Derrick.

"Well, my friend isn't going to make it, she has to work late, so we're going to try again two weeks from tomorrow." I pulled my wallet from my purse. "What do I owe you?"

"Aw, I'm sorry she couldn't come," he waved his hand. "The soda's on me. Thanks for keeping me company."

"Likewise," I said as I slid off the barstool. "Thanks for the Coke."

"Are you guys meeting here when you go out again?"

"I think so."

"Good. I hope to see you then. Have a nice night."

"You, too."

I left with a smile. Even though the evening had been a bust, I was glad I'd gone out. I proved to myself that I could be alone, and I'd be okay.

Staring at the hunky bartender had helped.

It was true what I told Laura. I didn't want to sleep with him. Especially now, knowing he'd been with our friend, Vicky. She was a trainwreck. A sweet trainwreck, but a hot mess, nonetheless. Derrick obviously didn't have very high standards about who he slept with.

But he'd managed to make me feel good by taking an interest in me, and my still-bruised ego appreciated that.

****

Gabe

After Brayden's game, I decided to swing by and say hi to my brother and see what possibilities were at Flannigan's tonight.

I took a seat at the bar, and Derrick greeted me with a big smile and set a coaster down in front of me.

"Hey! Was your spine tingling? 'Cuz I was just thinking about you!"

I eyed him warily while he pulled a frosty mug from the cooler and filled it with my favorite draft beer.

"Oh yeah?"

"Yeah. You just missed meeting your soulmate by twenty minutes."

I snorted when he set the beer in front of me. "Looks like I dodged a bullet."

"I'm serious, man. I talked to her for like, forty-five minutes, and the whole time I was thinking how great you two would hit it off."

Some matchmaking dust must be in the air tonight or something.

"Okay, I'll bite. Why do you think we'd hit it off?"

He shrugged. "I can't explain it. She just had the same energy as you. I could see you two getting along and talking all night."

"Well, hate to break it to you, little brother, but I'm not really interested in *talking* with a woman all night, if you know what I mean."

"Oh, she was hot, too. In a naughty librarian kind of way. She teaches seventh grade."

I tried not to choke on my beer.

"That's just what I need—a date with Brayden's teacher. Becky would hand me my balls on a paper plate."

Derrick looked dejected when he replied, "Hadn't thought of that. I just thought your kids would like her since she hangs out with middle schoolers all day and probably would know how to relate to them." He seemed lost in thought as he pulled a ticket from the printer, set it in front of himself, and prepared a drink order. "Did I mention she's hot? And really sweet."

"I'm not looking for sweet."

"Oh, yeah. I forgot you like those dramatic, crazy bitches."

"Nope. I divorced crazy and dramatic, and I like my freedom, thank you very much. I'm not looking for anyone who wants something more from me than one night."

"You never know. That might be what she's looking for, too. She was supposed to be meeting her friend, and I got the impression they were going on the prowl."

"Where'd they go?"

"Her friend ended up working late, so I think she just went home. Good news is, they're meeting here in two weeks to try again on a Friday night."

That could actually work. Becky and I had switched weekends, so I had the kids two weekends in a row and would be available in two weeks.

I gave my brother a noncommittal grunt, and he continued his sales pitch.

"You should drop in, see what happens. No harm in meeting her if you both just happen to be sitting at the bar."

"Yeah, maybe." I glanced around the room, trying to determine if there was anyone worthy of "meeting" tonight while I was already there.

Derrick noticed me surveying the prospects, of which there were few.

"You're too early, man. You gotta come in after eleven if you're looking for a hookup."

"*After eleven? On a Thursday night?* I'll be home in bed, sound asleep by then. Some of us work all fucking day and are tired by ten."

My little brother chuckled as he mixed alcohol and soda in a glass. "Maybe you should try a dating app for old people."

"Fuck you. I'm thirty-nine."

"You act like you're seventy-two."

I took another swig of beer and set the mug on the coaster with a sigh.

"Sometimes I feel like I'm seventy-two."

Even though it wasn't completely empty, Derrick picked up my glass and set it under the tap to refill it.

"You need a pretty little thing to keep you young." He put the beer in front of me. "I'm telling you—two weeks from tomorrow, around seven…"

I shook my head when I remembered I already had plans.

"Brayden has a tournament that weekend. His Friday game won't be done by then."

"Well, then come as soon as it's over; I'll stall them until you get here."

With a raised eyebrow, I paused as I lifted the mug to my lips. "How would you do that?"

"Dude, I'll just give them the Mitchell charm. Works every time. You should probably polish yours off."

"Yeah," I snickered. "Mine does need work." I thought about the conversation Gretchen Wainwright had overheard.

"Just think about it. What's the harm in stopping by on a Friday night for a drink with your little bro?"

"There's not, I guess."

Famous last words.

Chapter Four

Gabe

I walked into my shop Monday morning, flipped the lights on, and immediately felt a frown crease my eyebrows.

The Wainwright's cabinets were still lined against the wall, taking up too much space, and I was reminded of the events that took place last week.

I was over being embarrassed—shit happens, but I did feel bad about offending her. I didn't ever want to offend a customer. Especially one who looked like her.

How her pencil-dick husband had landed her in the first place was beyond me. But to then fuck around on her? Further proof the dude was, to borrow a term from across the pond, a wanker.

If she were in my bed every night, I'd fucking worship her. Well, after tying her up and teasing her, along with maybe some light spanking, if she were into that sort of thing. I sure as fuck wouldn't cheat on her.

I remembered when she came into the showroom on a warm day in late September, and I about fell out of my chair as I watched her from my desk. She'd been wearing black yoga pants that showcased her round ass nicely, along with black flipflops and a baby-pink t-shirt that dipped just enough in the front to offer a glimpse of cleavage.

I hadn't been able to take my eyes off her and moved to stand and leave my office to greet her personally—something I usually avoided like the plague—when Matt, our twenty-two-year-old apprentice who doubled as a salesman when necessary, approached her and struck up a conversation.

I'd leaned back in my chair and admired her from afar. Her long blonde hair had been piled on top of her head in a messy bun with loose strands framing her heart-shaped face. Her bright blue eyes reminded me of the sky on a clear summer day, and her button-nose when she scrunched it up had made me want to wrap my arms around her and pull her against me. Then she threw her head back and laughed at something the kid said, and I was left wondering what her neck would smell like if I buried my face in the crook of it.

Five minutes later, a pasty dude with slicked back brown hair walked in, and her face lit up with a smile. I don't think anyone had ever looked at me like that—not even when Becky and I were in our honeymoon phase. For a moment, I imagined it was me Gretchen Wainwright was staring at starry-eyed.

I remember again thinking, if she were mine, she would be worshipped. Daily. In and out of bed. Something her fuckhead husband obviously wasn't doing. He barely acknowledged her after he walked in.

I'd only been half-kidding when I'd told Rick if she wanted to ride my dick, I'd strike a deal with her.

Of course, in addition to overhearing my rude ass comments last week, I'd also threatened to sue her in a text message, so it was a safe bet that she wouldn't be riding my cock anytime soon. Or ever.

Which was probably for the best. I couldn't afford to eat those cabinets. I'd spent a lot of time and care on them. I took pride in all my work, but I might have been extra meticulous with hers. Part of me hoped she'd appreciate the craftmanship, even if she never met me.

Rick came into the shop thirty minutes later, and I shut the saw I was using down and gestured to the offending cupboards.

"These need to go. Your mission this week is to get that installation scheduled and get these the fuck out of here."

"I'll have Shelly call her again today."

I shook my head.

"No, I'm not going to have the former Mrs. Wainwright take her wrath out on poor Shelly for your fuckup. *You* call her."

"I wasn't the one who suggested she ride my dick," Rick grumbled under his breath as he opened a toolchest drawer.

"No, but you're the asshole who doesn't know how to put a damn call on hold. Speaking of... remind me to have Shelly give you a refresher training on how the phones work around here."

"I *know* how the phones work, Gabe. I just fucked up one time and didn't put the call on hold like I thought I had."

"Whatever," I grumbled. "Just get the installation scheduled, and I'll *consider* letting it slide—this time."

He pulled the tool he was looking for from the drawer, gave me a mock salute, and said, "On it, boss," before walking out the shop door back toward the showroom.

I turned the table saw back on and got back to work. As I ran a board through the blade, I realized I was pissed that Gretchen Wainwright had refused to accept my apology.

~~

Early morning a week later when I turned the shop's lights on, the Wainwright's cabinets sat staring at me. I wondered if Rick had gotten something scheduled with Gretchen. If not, we were going to have to rent a storage space and add that expense to her bill.

She was really going to hate me.

Eh, she won't be the first woman. She'll get over it.

Or not, if my track record was any indicator.

Rick walked through the door at eight o'clock on the dot.

I nodded toward the walnut cabinets. "What's going on with those? We've got a lumber shipment coming, and I have no place to put it with these in the way."

"She's not answering my calls or texts. I've tried her like four times a day all week. I've also emailed her every day."

"Maybe you need to stop by her house on the way home tonight."

"You don't think that'd be kind of creepy?"

"Probably. But she needs to know these are going into storage, and she's paying for it. And that our next step if she doesn't take possession soon is filing a lawsuit."

"And you want *me* to tell her all that?"

"No, jackass. What I wanted was *you* to schedule the installation, but you haven't done that."

"I can't make her respond to me, Gabe."

"You're a smart guy. Figure something out." I put my safety goggles on and grinned at my foreman. "You get that refresher phone training done yet?"

He scowled at me then headed into his office—hopefully to try the elusive Ms. Wainwright again.

Chapter Five

Gretchen

I looked around my classroom Friday afternoon once all my students had gone home for the weekend and let my shoulders sag in relief that I'd made it through another week.

I was ready for a few days off, but I wasn't sure I wanted to go out tonight.

No, that wasn't true. I was *definitely* sure I *didn't* want to go out tonight. Laura had texted me every night this week though, apologizing for standing me up two weeks ago while saying how excited she was to hang out and promising to buy all our drinks. She'd even offered again to pay for a sitter, but that wasn't necessary since my parents were picking Jake up from daycare and keeping him until Sunday.

My family had really stepped up to make sure my son knew he was loved and wanted.

I couldn't cancel now.

In addition to Laura's daily texts were Rick's from Mitchell Cabinets and Woodworking. Last week's had started polite enough, along with his voicemail and email. By this week though when I still hadn't replied, the tone had gotten a lot more curt.

Oh well. Tell your owner not to be an asshole.

I still needed to talk to my brother about what my options were to cancel.

A problem for next week's Gretchen to deal with.

My classroom phone rang, and I hesitated. Hopefully it wasn't a parent who wanted to chat for forty minutes about all the reasons his or her child should be allowed to do extra credit or turn in assignments from last quarter.

"This is Ms. Wainwright."

"Hey, Gretch. It's Lisa in the front office."

"Hi, Lisa. What's going on?"

"Hey, a letter just came for you by courier. It looks important."

Courier? Was that even a thing anymore?

"Does it say who it's from?"

"No, it's just one of those white, nondescript cardboard envelopes, but he made me sign that I received it on your behalf. I know you're going through a divorce. Maybe it has to do with that?"

"Maybe," I replied. Although it didn't seem likely. That had been wrapped up earlier this month. Troy better not be trying to pull some bullshit after the fact. Just the thought made my spine stiffen. "I'll be right there," I said, then hung up the phone and grabbed my keys from my desk drawer.

As I walked to the office, I wracked my brain trying to figure out what this could be about but kept coming up short.

I certainly wasn't prepared for what I found when I pulled the tab to open the envelope.

Chapter Six

Gretchen

"They sent what?" Laura exclaimed when I sat down on the barstool next to her at Flannigan's.

"A notice of intent to sue."

She slid one of the two Cosmopolitans in front of her to me, then took a sip of hers.

"That's kind of bullshit, don't you think? I mean, they just notified you what, like, two weeks ago your cabinets were done? I'd think that, legally, they'd have to give you a little more notice than fourteen days."

"From what the foreman's texts (okay, texts, voicemails, *and* emails) said, they're taking up too much space in their shop, so they're going to have to put the cabinets in storage. Which means they're going to try and charge me for that, too, so they're giving me one more chance to take possession before going that route."

"What did Andrew say?"

I shook my head as tears filled my eyes. I couldn't repeat his advice out loud. Hearing it in my own voice would make it too real. I'd poured my heart and soul into that house while imagining my son growing up in it. The idea of losing it was more than I could bear right now.

Laura wrapped an arm around my shoulders and touched her forehead to my temple.

"Come on. What did he say?"

Taking a deep breath through my nose, I squared my shoulders and sat up taller.

"A couple of things, some good, mostly bad. He'll do what he can, but thinks if it goes to court, I'll lose. *But,* just because we're divorced doesn't mean Troy is off the hook, since he signed the contract, too, and it was never spelled out in the divorce decree that he's not responsible."

"Well, that's good news, right?"

"Not really. I called Troy, and he said, 'Let them take me to court,' so he's not going to be any help. But Andrew suggested I have the cabinets installed and have them put a contractor's lien on the house."

"A contractor's lien? Isn't that only good if the house sells?"

One tear trailed down my cheek as I nodded once, then gulped down half my drink.

"No! Gretch, there's got to be something you can do!"

"I don't know what. I can't afford the interest rate on a credit card, and I'm not going to ask my parents for the money."

"What about a home equity loan?"

"Maybe. But between my student loans and daycare costs, I'm not sure the bank will think I'm a good risk."

Laura spun her barstool to face forward and took a drink from her glass.

"I fucking hate Troy. You should not have to struggle and do this alone."

"I'd rather it be this way than have to worry about fighting him for custody someday."

"Maybe you could work out a payment plan with the cabinet company?"

I cocked my head. "I hadn't thought of that."

Laura shrugged. "You never know until you ask..."

"I guess. But they're still going to have to put the cabinets in storage because I'll have to wait until summer break before I can have them installed."

"Maybe if you schedule it, they won't charge you."

"Maybe, but I doubt it. Their attorney's letter was pretty aggressive."

In fact, it'd made me wish I was rich so I could have their stupid cabinets delivered, then smash them with a sledgehammer and send them back to Mitchell Cabinets and Woodworking in little pieces. Because fuck them. They hadn't needed to escalate things so quickly.

"Okay, you're going to ask the Universe to fix it, then you're not going to think about it for the rest of the night so the Universe can do its thing."

I looked at her skeptically but muttered, "Universe, fix it," because I had to begrudgingly admit her woo-woo had worked on more than one occasion. "I'm not so sure I can just quit thinking about it, though."

My BFF shot me a grin. "That's what alcohol is for."

I downed the rest of my drink just as Derrick, the hot bar owner, appeared.

"Hey! Good to see you!" He nodded toward my glass. "I see you're going with something stronger than Coca Cola tonight."

"Yep," Laura answered for me. "And they're all on me, so make sure her glass is never empty."

I shook my head. "Don't listen to her. If I drink more than four of these, I'll be dancing on the bar."

"So, we're shooting for five, then," he said with a wink as he scooped ice into two tumblers then filled them with water and set them in front of us. "But you should be drinking water, too, otherwise you'll really hate me in the morning."

"Thanks," I replied and gratefully took a sip while he poured the ingredients for another Cosmo into a cocktail shaker.

As he shook the metal container, he looked over at me with a grin. "I'm assuming you're not driving?"

"No, I'll take an Uber home if I need to. I could lose my teaching certification if I got a DUI, so there's no way I'd risk that."

He set a cold fresh martini glass in front of me, then placed a strainer over the shaker and emptied the pink contents until my glass almost overflowed, then added a lime slice to the rim. Without asking Laura if she wanted more, he poured the rest of the shaker's contents into her drink.

"Thanks," she told him with a flirty smile.

"My pleasure."

Just then, my stomach growled—loudly, making Laura laugh as she told him, "I think we need menus, too."

No sooner did she say it than two laminated menus appeared in front of us.

I looked at the selections on the front before flipping it over to peruse the back.

"What do you recommend?"

"Their fries are amazing!" Laura offered, and Derrick looked at her with a big smile.

"Thanks. The secret is the beer batter." He pointed to the section with their burgers. "But you need more than fries. Get a cheeseburger, too. My favorite is the Western Burger."

I read the description and handed him the menu.

"Sounds perfect."

"And what are you having, beautiful?" he asked Laura with a mischievous smile.

She took her time surveying him up and down and biting her bottom lip in the process. She left him no doubt what she was thinking.

Damn, I wish I had her moxie.

Finally, she told him, "Well, since I don't see sexy bar owner on the menu, I guess I'll have the sliders with fries."

He returned her stare with a cocky grin.

"We have a special menu for my favorite patrons. I'll have to show you that one later if you're interested."

"Oh, I'm interested."

"Good." He gave her a wink. "Let me put your food order in," then he moved to the other end of the bar to stand in front of a touchscreen where he proceeded to press buttons.

"I thought you said he slept with Vicky?" I hissed.

Laura shrugged. "That was last year."

"Okay, but still... he slept with her. I get the impression he doesn't go home alone a lot."

My friend seemed undeterred.

"I just want to fuck him, I don't wanna marry him." She took a drink, then set her martini glass down with a smirk. "You should try it."

I shook my head. "That's not my style."

"Maybe it's time for a new style."

"Well, I'm definitely not fucking him after you *and* Vicky."

"I didn't mean him."

I could tell Derrick was coming back, based on the way Laura sat up straighter and pushed her boobs out.

"Hey," she called to him. "Do you have a brother you could introduce to Gretchen? She's newly single and ready to mingle."

He raised an eyebrow while I knew my cheeks were beet red.

"*Newly* single, huh?"

"Her divorce was final earlier this month. But she kicked him out almost six months ago, so while she's *officially* newly single, she actually has been for a while. So, do you have any brothers you could set her up with?"

I shook my head. "I'm not ready to date, yet."

"Who said anything about dating? You just need to get laid."

I felt my brows rise when I turned to my friend to find her finishing her drink with a smirk on her face.

"How many of those have you had?"

"Just two."

"Well," Derrick interjected. "I have three brothers, but one is married. Either of the other two would be happy to show you a good time, if that's what you're looking for."

His face broke into a wide grin as he looked past us toward the door.

"In fact, here comes one of them now."

Maybe it was the effects of the alcohol on my empty stomach, but when I turned to see who he was looking at, I felt my breath hitch in my chest.

Walking toward us was the best-looking man I'd seen in a long time. And considering Derrick had been keeping us company for the past thirty minutes, that was saying something.

The grey at his temples suggested he was Derrick's *older* brother, and although his hair was darker than Derrick's, I could see the resemblance. They definitely shared the same swagger. But instead of the black, nonslip shoes that Derrick had on behind the bar, this guy was wearing tan work boots and tan Carhartt pants, and his broad chest nicely filled out the maroon Henley he was wearing. He looked like he'd just come from working all day with his hands. I could picture a tool belt slung low on his waist.

Damn.

Was there anything sexier than a man who worked with his hands?

As I watched him come closer, I concluded, *no, no there was not.*

He must have thought I was a crazy lady when he caught me staring at him, because he stopped short, as if trying to determine if it was safe to proceed to the bar where his brother was.

I offered a small smile to hopefully convey I was harmless, and he cocked his head, like he was still unsure, then finally continued toward us.

"Hey!" Derrick said with a big grin. "Good to see you! How was Brayden's game?"

His brother glanced in my and Laura's direction before answering, "Great. They won. He scored the winning goal."

"That's awesome! First round's on me."

The way his brother laughed out loud made me wonder if that was an inside joke.

"Thanks, man."

Even though the barstool next to me was vacant, he didn't sit down, instead, he looked over at me like I might try to kiss him unsolicited or something if he sat by me.

I mean, the idea had merit, but still... I would never do such a thing.

"You can sit down," I said with a grin. "I don't bite. I promise."

"Unless you want her to," Laura chimed in.

The corner of his mouth hitched and the lines around his blue eyes crinkled as he sat down. "Good to know."

"I'm Gretchen," I said as I offered my hand. "This is my friend, Laura."

He nodded at my friend with a smile then took my hand in his calloused one. "Gabriel."

"It's nice to meet you, Gabriel."

His eyes twinkled like he had a secret as he studied my face for a beat before it seemed like his whole body relaxed, and he replied, "The pleasure is all mine, Gretchen."

****

Gabe

She doesn't know who I am.

That much was obvious by the way she was smiling at me.

I caught Derrick's eye as he pulled my beer from the tap, and he quickly pointed to Gretchen and mouthed, "That's her!"

What were the fucking odds? I was sitting next to the woman who, not more than two hours ago, sent me a text telling me what an infuriating jerk I was and that her attorney would be in touch, and now she was flirting with me.

The same woman I'd been unable to tear my gaze from the first time I saw her. Tonight wasn't faring much different.

She was even prettier up close. I could see the freckles across her nose and cheeks, and the floral scent of her perfume sent my olfactory receptors into overdrive.

I knew I should come clean right then and tell her who I was, but I liked the way she was looking at me too much. If she knew I was *Gabe Mitchell*—infuriating Jerk of the Year (her words—not mine) her playful smile would surely morph into a scowl, maybe even a right hook. I didn't want that, at least not yet, and I definitely didn't want the punch.

I decided I'd enjoy my time with her while it lasted, but I knew I needed to fill my brother in with the CliffsNotes version of what was going on with her, so he didn't blow my cover.

"Hey, Derrick—did you bring that card for Mom for me to sign?"

That was a code we'd been using since we were kids. Fortunately, he didn't miss a beat.

"Yeah, it's in my office. Why don't we go back there; it's less likely to get something spilled on it if you sign it on my desk."

I gave Gretchen a wink as I slid off the barstool and told her, "Save my seat for me."

"Of course. Hurry back so I don't have to fight anyone for it."

"I won't be long, darlin'."

Did I just call her darlin'?

Yeah, I did. It had come out without a second thought.

I was going to need to be on my A-game around her, so I better nurse my beer.

"What's going on?" Derrick asked once we walked into his office, and he closed the door.

"That Gretchen chick? Yeah, she's a client, and she tried to cancel her custom cabinet order—*after* I finished them."

"Oooh, not good. I'm assuming you told her no."

"Yeah, but... she... well, she heard me tell Rick that unless she wanted to ride my dick there was no way that was happening since we had a contract, and they were already finished."

"Oh shit!"

"Yeah, it, uh, gets worse."

"It gets worse?"

"Our attorney served her with an intent to sue today."

My brother started laughing. "Ohhhh, fuuuuck."

"Obviously she doesn't know I'm *Gabe Mitchell*, so, let's keep it that way. Don't mention what I do, or what our last name is."

"I wondered why you introduced yourself as Gabriel. I thought maybe you were trying something new."

I chuckled. "Nope."

"You know she's going to want to know what you do for a living. That's like the second question people ask when they meet someone."

I sighed. I really didn't want to outright lie to her. Omission was one thing, but lying was next level.

"Maybe you could run interference for me if she asks?"

"Yeah, I can do that."

"Thanks."

Derrick's face split into a big grin.

"I was right though, huh? She's exactly your type."

"Yeah," I chuckled. "I mean, minus the whole hating my guts thing, and possibly suing her, I could see myself wanting to get to know her better."

"Stranger things have happened."

"Don't get any ideas, little brother. Once she finds out who I really am..." I shook my head. "Ain't happenin'."

"So, why don't you just tell her now?"

Because I like how she's looking at me.

I shrugged. "I don't want to ruin her night. She seems to be having a good time with her friend. If she knew who I was, she'd want to leave, and then I'd feel bad."

"But you don't feel bad for suing her?"

"I'm hoping she comes to her senses, and I don't have to sue her. Her cabinets are fucking beautiful. If she'd just agree to get them installed, she'd see that for herself."

He clapped his hand on my shoulder and squeezed.

"Well, bro, I hope she does, too. In the meantime, your secret is safe tonight."

"Thanks."

"Now, get back out there and charm the pants off her. Maybe you could even get her to come around and get her cabinets installed so you don't have to take her to court."

Or maybe she'd ride my dick, and we could strike up a deal.

No!

That wasn't an option!

But looking into her cornflower blue eyes, I conceded, I'd be willing to think twice about it. It might even be worth Maverick's wrath.

My bank account on the other hand...

Chapter Seven

Gretchen

"Oh. My God!" Laura squealed once Derrick and Gabriel disappeared down a hall at the end of the bar. "He is so hot! And he was totally checking you out."

"No, he wasn't."

"Uh, yeah, he was."

A small smile escaped my lips, and I whispered, "He was, wasn't he? I thought maybe it was just wishful thinking on my part."

"No, babe. That man was looking at you like you're a snack, and he's starving! I'm pretty sure he was envisioning peeling off these cute jeans you've got on."

The feeling was mutual.

Still, I shook my head.

"He's probably a player like his brother."

"So?"

"So, I don't think I could have a one-night stand."

Laura grabbed my arms and turned me on the barstool, so I was looking at her directly.

"You haven't had sex in over a year. You owe it to yourself to have a freaking fling! If not for you, then for your poor neglected vajayjay."

"It's not that neglected," I grumbled as I spun back to face the bar and pick up my drink. "I have toys."

"Toys are no substitute for the real thing."

I let out a sigh. "No, probably not."

"Exactly. Now, go into the bathroom, push your boobs up, put on some lipstick, and when you come back out here, you better be ready to get your flirt on."

I looked at her with pursed lips, and she gestured to the restrooms and barked, "Go!"

Reluctantly, I moved off the barstool and grabbed my handbag with my lipstick in it.

"Fine. But I'm not having a one-night stand."

"Oh yes you are! When he wants to take you home tonight and do dirty, dirty things to you, you're going to say yes!"

"I *might* be willing to give him my number, but I'm not going home with him."

"We'll see," she said with a smirk. "I'll order you another drink when Derrick gets back."

I can't go home with a stranger, I thought as I made my way to the ladies' room.

But if you get to know him tonight, he won't be a stranger, the devil on my shoulder reasoned as I pushed the bathroom door open.

I'm a teacher! A role model!

The little tipsy bastard on my shoulder wouldn't shut up. *You're also a woman with needs. And that man is hot. You'd be a fool to turn him down.*

I mean, it was hard to argue with that logic.

I doubt he's even attracted to me, I told myself as I pulled the lipstick out and applied a fresh coat. *He's probably just a giant flirt like his brother but isn't really interested. It's all just harmless fun.*

Harmless fun. Yeah, I was going with that, I decided as I reached inside my bra and pushed my boobs up so my cleavage was on-point.

After the month I'd been having, I deserved a little alcohol-infused, harmless fun.

****

Gabe

Gretchen's barstool was empty when Derrick and I walked back into the bar, and for a second, I felt disappointed, thinking she'd left. But her friend was still there, and Dan—Derrick's full-time bartender—set a fresh martini glass filled with some pink concoction in front of Gretchen's seat next to my half-empty beer mug.

"Is it your mom's birthday?" Laura asked when I sat down.

I blinked at her. "What?"

"The card, for your mom that you needed to sign. Is it her birthday?"

"Yeah, it's coming up."

In two months.

Didn't everyone get a card for their mom's June birthday in April?

"Where'd your friend go?" Derrick asked from the other side of the bar.

"Gretchen, right?" I asked.

If I was going to play dumb about who she was, I was going to try and sell it.

Laura smirked, like she wasn't buying my sales job.

"Yeah, Gretchen."

"Derrick said she just went through a divorce?"

"It was finalized a few weeks ago." Before I even asked, she offered, "And she's not seeing anyone."

"I'm surprised. It seems like men would be lining up to date a beautiful woman like her."

"Are you angling to cut to the front of the line?"

I chuckled at her bluntness.

"I don't think I'd have much to offer."

"Maybe she's not looking for anything more than a good time."

That got my attention, but I quickly gave myself an internal shake. It was one thing to flirt with her at a bar while withholding who I was. It'd be another to take her home and do the things I'd been thinking about without coming clean.

Her feisty texts earlier today had made my dick move. Probably not the reaction she'd been shooting for.

I noticed Gretchen walking toward us and tried not to stare. It looked like she'd fluffed her hair and reapplied her lipstick, and I had a sudden urge to kiss it off her.

Laura should not have told me Gretchen was only looking for a good time. Now that's all I was going to think about as the beautiful woman sat next to me.

I greeted her with a smile. "There you are."

She returned my smile. It reminded me of the time in the showroom when she'd smiled at her husband, and I had let myself imagine it was me she was looking at like that.

"Here I am."

"I got you another drink," Laura said as Gretchen perched on the barstool, giving me the perfect view of her peak-a-boo cleavage teasing me.

Fuck, she had perfect tits.

I glanced up and found Derrick grinning at me like he knew exactly what I was thinking. He nodded toward my beer.

"You ready for another?"

"Nah, not yet."

My brother pulled glasses from a green rack that looked like they'd just come out of a dishwasher and lined them up along the bar.

"Where do you teach at?" he asked Gretchen.

"Lancastle Middle."

Fuck.

I tilted my head and asked, "What do you teach?"

"Seventh grade English."

"My worst subject," Derrick said with a laugh. "Isn't it ironic that I did better in Spanish than my own native language?"

As she explained why that was normal for a lot of people, I subtly pulled my phone from my pocket and fired off a text to Brayden.

Me: Who's your English teacher?

Brayden: Mr. Wetherbee. Why?

Me: I was just curious. I met Ms. Wainwright and thought maybe she had you in class.

Brayden: I wish! Maybe my grade would be higher if I were in her class. She's so nice.

Not to mention hot.

But you probably had to be older than thirteen to appreciate her sex appeal. That was undoubtedly a good thing, considering some of the stories in the papers these days.

Me: She's pretty, too.

Brayden: Yeah, I guess for an older lady.

I pressed my lips together to keep from smiling at my dumbass child's text. Gretchen Wainwright was not "an older lady". But I'd bet my son thought anyone over eighteen was old.

I remember feeling like that once. Now I found myself using phrases like, "when I was your age," or, "back in the day".

Brayden: I guess she just got divorced. Are you going to ask her out?

Me: What?! No! Of course not.

Brayden: Oh. Well, if you did, I'd be okay with it.

Me: Not sure Britt would feel the same way.

Brayden: She would. We talked at Christmas and decided you should get married again. We don't like you being alone.

Me: You guys don't have to worry about me. In addition to you two, I've got Grandma and Grandpa and your uncles to keep me company.

Brayden: Yeah, but it's not the same. We just want you to be happy.

I wondered where this was coming from and questioned if things were getting more serious between Becky and her latest boyfriend. Hopefully he was content not having his own biological kids.

Me: I am happy. I've got terrific kids, a great family, and a business I love. I couldn't ask for anything more.

Brayden: Except a girlfriend.

I needed to end this conversation.

Me: Great game today! Uncle Derrick says hi and congrats on the goal. I'll pick you up on Wednesday after practice. Love you, buddy.

Brayden: Tell him I said hi back and thank you. He should come to my next game. I'll see you Wednesday. Love you too, Dad.

Derrick cocked his head and nodded toward my phone. "Everything okay?"

"Yeah. Just texting with Brayden. He says you should come to his next game."

"When is it?"

"Tomorrow at three. His school is hosting a tournament this weekend."

"I'll try to make it."

"I know he'd love that."

Gretchen set her glass on the bar and asked, "Is Brayden your son?"

"He is." I hesitated to expound, in case she knew of my son and put together the name. Still, in the interest of not being a liar... "He goes to Lancastle Middle, too. But his English teacher is Mr. Wetherbee."

"Wayne is a good teacher."

"That's good to know. I guess his grade isn't so great."

"He should take advantage of the after-school tutoring. It's free."

"Isn't that what you do on Tuesdays?" Laura asked her.

"Yeah." Gretchen turned her attention back toward me. "But it's offered every day, Monday through Thursday. All he has to do is show up at the library after school."

I shook my head. "He has lacrosse practice after school."

"Well, his grades must be good enough if he's still eligible to play."

"Good point. His mom hasn't said anything, so they must not be too bad."

I'm sure if it was, Becky would find a way to blame me for my son's failing grades. She'd probably try to argue that coming to my house on Wednesday evenings for a few hours was the root cause. She already bitched that being at my house in the middle of the week "disrupted their schedule too much," so I'd agreed to take them home instead of having them sleep at my house.

"Are you a teacher, too?" Derrick asked Laura as he set another drink in front of her.

"Hell no. I like money, thanks." She took a sip then continued, "Besides, I'd probably last one week before telling an enabling parent to stop making excuses for their snot-nosed kid's bad behavior and do something about it."

I felt my eyebrows go up, and I looked at Gretchen.

"Are parents really that bad?"

Laura answered on her friend's behalf. "She has horror stories."

"They're not *horror* stories."

Laura scoffed. "Remember Rob Bennett?" She directed her next words at me. "The guy emailed her *three* times a day the entire semester, making excuse after excuse about why his kid couldn't do any work—in class or at home. *Then* he tried to get Gretchen in trouble for trying to hold his kid accountable."

I shook my head. "What a dick. I couldn't do what you do."

"That was at my old school. Fortunately, the administration at Lancastle is better about protecting the teachers. They would never allow a parent to treat me that way."

I was glad to learn that. I didn't like the idea of entitled parents abusing her while the powers that be did nothing about it.

"We want our kids accountable for their choices, so it's good to know Lancastle Schools shares that philosophy."

"They do. Your children are in good hands." She traced her finger around the base of her martini glass. "You said kids. You have more than your son?"

"My daughter is in fifth grade."

"A boy and a girl. You're lucky. I want two, but my cheating prick of a husband bailed before…"

Her eyes grew wide, and a small hiccup escaped her. I knew she'd been far more forthcoming than she normally would be without the alcohol coursing through her tiny body.

"I can't believe I just said that. I swear I'm not really a bitter divorcée."

I chuckled softly. "No one would blame you if you were, darlin'."

You're entitled when you catch your husband fucking his secretary.

Of course, I kept that bit of knowledge to myself, since she hadn't shared it with me tonight.

"It's just my clock is ticking, ya know? And I wasted so much time with him."

A part of me was jealous of the man who got to put a baby in her.

I leaned closer to whisper in her ear, "Your ex was a fool to ever let you go."

Chapter Eight

Gretchen

Gabriel's lips touched the outer shell of my ear, causing my body to break out in goosebumps. A tiny shudder ran down my spine as my nipples became hard points.

Laura was right. Toys were no substitute for the real thing, because if this man just whispering in my ear affected me like this, I could only imagine how my body would react if I were naked underneath him.

And telling me Troy was a fool to let me go? That felt like balm to my bruised ego.

"What makes you say that?"

"No man in his right mind would."

Still, I wasn't a believer, and I brushed off the compliment with a flippant, "You're very sweet."

I was hyperaware of his arm along the back of my chair and his masculine, woodsy scent, when he chuckled, "Darlin', I'm a lot of things, but sweet ain't one of 'em."

I stared up at his handsome face. The scruff along his cheeks was probably four or five days old and had hints of grey mixed in with the black stubble. I found myself wanting to lean against his frame and run my fingertips along his jawline as I softly kissed his neck.

"I find that hard to believe. You just came from your son's lacrosse game, so you're obviously a caring father. You haven't bad-mouthed your ex once, so that tells me that you're a decent guy. And Derrick looks at you like you're the best big brother in the world. If that's not sweet, then I don't know what is."

That made him laugh out loud.

"I'll give you I'm a pretty great dad."

His admission made my heart ache for my son who would never have that. At least he had my dad and my brother for male role models.

Gabriel continued, "The worst part about being divorced is not being with my kids every night."

Okay, I might have swooned a little while he continued, "Bad mouthing my ex would mean I'd have to spend energy thinking about her, and I try not to do that. And as far as the best big brother award, that would have to go to our oldest brother, Pete—also known as Maverick. He's a silent investor in all of the brothers' businesses, and he's as wise as he is rich. For the most part."

That made me cock my head. "For the most part?"

"Well, after his oldest two boys were all grown up and moved out, he had a baby with his now-second wife."

I felt my mouth turn down at what he was implying.

"So having a baby with his new wife makes him unwise?"

"Starting over at his age does, yeah. I couldn't even imagine having a baby at thirty-nine let alone forty-two. It'd be lunacy."

Disappointment zinged through me.

Gabriel's response immediately moved him into the "not gonna happen" column. I was surprised at how let down I felt about that. Not that I'd had a chance to begin with. But even if he really was interested, I wouldn't date him now.

"But I've never seen Mav happier," Derrick chimed in as he wiped down the bar in front of me.

"That's true," Gabriel replied with his arm still thrown along the back of my chair.

I liked the feeling of his possessiveness, and Laura's one-night stand suggestion sounded better and better. Maybe there wasn't a future beyond tonight with this man, but maybe tonight was all I needed.

Besides, my confidence could use a boost.

I can't go home with a stranger, my conscience reminded me.

The drunk devil on my shoulder chimed in. *Get to know him better so he's not a stranger.*

I leaned into Gabriel's body and asked, "So, what's your business?"

He narrowed his eyes, like my question confused him, so I clarified.

"You said Maverick is a silent investor in all the brothers' businesses. I know Derrick's is the bar, what's yours?"

"Oh, I—"

"Sorry this took so long," Derrick announced as he set a hamburger and fries in front of me, sliders and fries in front of Laura, and then a burger and fries in front of Gabriel.

Gabriel looked up at his brother. "I didn't order this."

Derrick shrugged as he set silverware rolled in napkins in front of us. "I figured you were hungry."

Gabriel smiled as he placed his napkin in his lap. "Thanks, bro. I am."

"I got your back, big brother."

I bit a fry and groaned out loud.

"You weren't lying," I told Laura. "These fries are amazing."

"It's the beer batter," Gabriel interjected.

"That's what Derrick said." I picked up another fry, but before putting it in my mouth, said, "So, you were telling me about your business."

Before Gabriel could answer, Derrick asked, "Do you want ketchup or mustard?"

"Can I have Ranch dressing?" Laura asked.

"Oh, yes, can I have some, too? And ketchup?"

Derrick's eyebrows went into his hairline. "Ranch dressing?"

"For the fries."

"I can't decide if I should be offended," he grumbled. "Please tell me you don't put steak sauce on your steaks."

"Of course not," Laura answered.

Derrick turned his attention toward me, waiting for me to answer, as well.

"I would never," I told him, then muttered "in front of you."

That made Gabriel bark out a laugh, which he quickly tried to disguise by covering his mouth with his napkin then pointed at his almost empty beer mug and told Derrick, "I'll take one more when you get a chance."

The lines around his cobalt blue eyes crinkled, and it made him even hotter, if that was possible.

"So, what were we talking about?" I asked. The three Cosmos I'd already had were taking their toll.

Gabriel gestured to one of the many TVs stationed around the bar where the basketball game was on. "I think we were talking about if the Celtics are going to make the playoffs this year."

No, that wasn't it.

But then Jayson Tatum dunked over his Lakers opponent, and the bar went wild. Gabriel's gorgeous face lit up with the sexiest smile, and I forgot what I was trying to ask.

****

Gabe

The tipsy little teacher sitting next to me was really making it hard to do the right thing and *not* kiss her.

Because it was obvious the way she kept brushing her tits against my biceps and looking up at me with her big blue eyes, she'd be on board if I dropped my lips to hers and explored her mouth with my tongue.

My dick thought that sounded like a great idea. The longer I sat next to her basking in her scent and listening to her giggles while her petite hands occasionally stroked my arm, the harder it became for me to disagree with him.

Gretchen wasn't to the point where she couldn't give consent. But there's no way she'd agree to go home with me if she knew who I was. And I'd have to come clean about that if I even *considered* making a move.

But, I conceded, I didn't want to come clean. I really was having a good time just hanging out with her. Admittedly, the flirting was a nice bonus, and my dick had jumped more times than I could count, but I found I *liked* her. Fucking Derrick was right.

The basketball game was over, and the crowd started to thin. Laura and my brother were engaging in what could only be described as foreplay. The smoldering looks and innuendos left no doubt how their night was going to end.

Gretchen turned to me and demanded, "So, Gabriel. Are you ever going to tell me what your business is? Or should I just assume you're a spy?"

I couldn't help but laugh.

"Not a spy, sweetheart. No, I'm far more boring. I make custom furniture."

"What kind of furniture?"

This is where I should have led with cabinets—since that was a large percentage of what I did and what I'd done for her, but instead I found myself saying, "Oh, you know, tables, bedroom furniture, chests with pop-up TV lifts, cabinets, that kind of thing."

She narrowed her eyes at me as she twirled a strand of her hair, and I thought she'd put the pieces together. Instead, she pointed a finger at me, her words slurring slightly when she said, "So, let me ask you this. If you made a piece of furniture for someone, and they wanted to cancel the order, would you sue them?"

"Well, normally I try to get paid up front, so I wouldn't have to. But in the event that I only got a deposit..."

Gretchen gnawed on her bottom lip as she waited for my answer.

"I would have to."

I could tell by her frown that she didn't like that response, so I decided to try to reason with her. Probably not my smartest move, considering she was at least four Cosmopolitans in, but I figured I'd give it a shot.

"You wouldn't teach for free, would you? Even though you love it, you still have bills to pay. It's the same with me. If I spend time working on a piece, I have to get paid. I have staff who depend on me, a building with a mortgage, utilities, materials, not to mention, I have my own personal bills."

She slumped against the back of her barstool.

"I guess that makes sense."

Because I wasn't ready to give up the ruse of not knowing who she was, I continued. "Why do you ask?"

"I was just curious."

Part of me was relieved at her response, because if she had explained her situation, I would have had no choice but to confess.

She'd left me with plausible deniability, and I appreciated that. I was having too good a time for it to end just yet.

Chapter Nine

Gretchen

"Okay, kids. You don't have to go home, but you can't stay here," Dan the bartender said with a smile when he removed the empty glasses in front of us as the lights came up.

Derrick appeared from behind the bar, wearing a brown leather bomber jacket. With his hands in his pockets, he held out his arm for Laura, which she took with a giggle.

I wasn't surprised the two were leaving together; they'd been flirting and eye-fucking each other all night. But I was surprised Derrick wasn't staying later than we were.

"You don't have to stay and close?"

"Nope. Not my turn."

Although the way my friend looked at the handsome bar owner, I suspected if it had been his turn, she would have waited with him and the two of them would have gone at it in one of the booths. I'd be impressed if they made it out of the parking lot with their clothes on.

Laura looked at Gabriel.

"Can you stay with her until her Uber gets here?"

"No problem," he said, and with a wave, the horny couple practically ran to the parking lot. Gabriel directed his attention toward me. "Why don't I just drive you home?"

"Oh, I don't want you to go out of your way."

"It's no problem, sweetheart. Besides, I'd feel better knowing you made it home safe and sound."

"I could just text you when I got home."

"No..." The corner of his mouth turned up. "You'd forget, then I'd have to call Derrick to ask Laura for your number. But he wouldn't answer, so then I'd have to go to his house and pound on the door. Except they would be at Laura's, so then I'd have to drive around all night looking for his car, and I wouldn't get any sleep." He shook his head. "It'd just be easier if I drove you home."

I wasn't going to point out I could just give him my number right then. I liked the idea of him driving me home.

"Well, I wouldn't want you to have to drive around all night and not get any sleep..."

He reached for my hand.

"My truck's this way."

****

Gabe

Gretchen's hand felt soft and tiny in my calloused one, and I had to fight the urge to stop in the middle of the parking lot and pull her into my arms. Or keep my hands off her ass when I helped her into the passenger seat of my truck.

Not for the first time tonight, I wished our circumstances were different. Because this night would end very differently otherwise. Like, with her waking up in my bed, instead of me driving her home and politely making sure she got inside before driving away alone.

I slid behind the wheel and took my phone out of my pocket.

"Where to, sweetheart?"

"1215 Evergreen Road."

I plugged her address into my navigation app and was disappointed to find it was only seven minutes away.

The smell of her perfume filled the truck's cab, and for the first time in my life, I cursed there wasn't any traffic in our small town. I didn't want this night to end. I gave zero fucks that my ass was going to be dragging in the morning.

"Oh, I didn't realize it was a full moon tonight," she observed as we drove along the quiet streets of Lancastle. Her voice dropped to a whisper. "That explains it."

My glance briefly left the road to look at her. "Explains what?"

With wide eyes she turned toward me. "You heard that?"

I couldn't help but chuckle when a small hiccup escaped her. "I don't think you were as quiet as you think you were, darlin'." I asked again, "Explains what?"

"Me going home with someone I just met."

The way she phrased it made me think she had more in mind than a car ride home, and my cock jumped up and took notice. He was on board with the idea, one hundred percent.

Hell, *I* was on board with the idea. The thought of her soft body underneath mine, kissing her perfect bow lips while my hands roved along her curves… fuck yes.

Except for that one small detail. She thought I was the "infuriating Jerk of the Year". She just didn't know we were one in the same. No, she wasn't looking at me now like she thought I was a jerk. There was no mistaking the lust in her eyes.

When my GPS announced her house on the right was in one hundred feet, I slowed my truck. All the colonial brick houses in her upscale subdivision looked similar, so I wanted clarification which was hers before pulling into a driveway.

Gretchen pulled her phone from her purse and clicked some buttons. A second later, a garage door opened.

She gestured to the lit-up garage. "It's that one. You can just pull in."

I knew if I pulled my Ford into that stall, I wouldn't be leaving until morning.

I had an ethical decision to make.

Chapter Ten

Gabe

I'm just making sure she gets inside safely, I told myself as I drove my truck into one of the three empty stalls in her garage like I owned the place.

"Wow. Your garage is huge."

"Yeah, when my ex cleaned out his stuff, it freed up a lot of space."

"You've got so much room for storage." *For things like kitchen cabinets.*

The thought was a somber reminder of the notice our attorney had sent her earlier today.

Gretchen looked around, as if just noticing how much room there was.

"Yeah. Maybe I can start an online store or something."

"An online store? Doing what?"

She shrugged. "I don't know. I'm going to need to do something though."

She opened her door and hesitated before getting out. I didn't know if she was reluctant to end the night or because she wasn't able to get out on her own.

"Hold on, let me help you," I told her and quickly got out of the truck to go around to the passenger side to help her. My F150 had running boards, but I wasn't sure how steady she was on her feet. But that didn't explain why after she was on the ground, one of my hands lingered on her hip while the other was still holding her hand.

She was a magnet that I was drawn to touch.

I knew I wasn't the only one who felt the connection. Her wide eyes staring up at me told me she felt it, too, without her having to say a word.

"Do you want to come in?" she whispered breathlessly. "I don't have any beer, but I have wine, and maybe a bottle of whiskey or rum. Or some coffee?"

My thumb caressed her hip bone, and I gave her a sad smile.

"More than you know, darlin."

"But...?"

"But you've had too much to drink. It wouldn't be right to take advantage of you."

So, my reason was only half-true. I decided the fact that I was still doing the right thing gave me a pass for not coming clean about who I was.

She closed the distance between us, so her chest was pressed against mine as she looked up at me with her beautiful cornflower-blue eyes.

"What if I *want* to be taken advantage of?"

I felt my Adam's apple bob as I swallowed hard. No matter what I did in this situation, I was going to lose. You'd think after being married to Becky for ten years, I'd be used to it by now, but I didn't like my predicament one bit.

Gretchen was going to think I was rejecting her, and unless I owned up to being the "Jerk of the Year," she was going to take it personally.

"Sweetheart..."

She lifted on her toes and silenced whatever I was going to say next by planting a kiss on my mouth. I wanted to pull away—honest, but her lips were soft, and she let out a little moan, and my willpower went out the window. My fantasy girl had just kissed me. I was a good guy, but I wasn't a saint.

So instead of pushing her away, one arm instinctively wrapped around her waist to pull her closer while my fingers wove into her silky blonde hair as I angled my mouth to deepen the kiss.

****

Gretchen

I couldn't remember the last time I'd been kissed like this.

Probably because it'd never happened.

Troy had never made me feel like he needed me like he needed oxygen, but that's exactly how Gabriel made me feel.

I had to admit—I loved it. I felt wanted.

Needed, even.

And I hadn't felt needed—at least, sexually—in a really, really long time.

I probably should have felt apprehensive about throwing myself at a man I'd just met, but every cell in my being told me Gabriel was trustworthy.

Not to mention he knew how to kiss.

Damn, did he know how to kiss.

I ground against his erection like a cat in heat. I wasn't proud of it, but I hadn't had sex in almost a year, and a strong, handsome, sexy man was kissing me like I was the most beautiful woman in the world. A girl could only take so much.

I knew my panties were soaked.

He burrowed his face in my neck to trail kisses down my throat, and I realized I was making out with a man in my garage with the door open and the lights on for all my neighbors to watch.

"Gabriel, let's go inside."

It was like my words broke whatever spell he'd been under, because he lifted his head to look at me, then closed his eyes tight and took a step back.

"Fuck, Gretchen. I'm so sorry. I shouldn't have—"

I felt my spine stiffen when I realized what was happening.

"I'm not drunk," I grumbled defensively.

"That's not it."

No, I wasn't drunk, but I was still a little tipsy, so I couldn't make sense of what the problem could possibly be.

Suddenly, I gasped, "Oh my god, you're in a relationship! I'm so sorry! Derrick said you were single, and I just thought... we were flirting at the bar, then you offered to take me home... I'm so embarrassed!"

"No! I'm not in a relationship. That's not it."

I cocked my head. "Then I don't understand."

"Sweetheart, I'm not who you think I am."

Chapter Eleven

Gabe

I could see the panic on her face at my declaration and she flinched when I reached out to touch her arm.

Dammit!

"That came out wrong. I'm not dangerous or anything like that. I am single, and I am Derrick's brother, but you need to know—"

"Do you have an STD or something?"

Jesus Christ, this was going from bad to worse.

"God, no! Nothing like that. I just—"

Fuck, fuck, fuck. How was I going to say this?

I took a deep breath and looked into her mesmerizing blue eyes, willing my brain to find the right words so that I could still salvage this. Although, I didn't see how that was possible.

Man the fuck up, Gabe!

"My name is Gabriel, but I go by Gabe. Gabe Mitchell."

It took a second for her brain to process my name, then her eyes went wide.

With a wry smile, I supplied, "Also known as the infuriating Jerk of the Year."

I steeled myself to duck in case she tried to throw a punch or deliver a slap across my face.

Instead, she stared at me for a beat before pulling her shoulders back and standing up straighter. She gave me a devious smile and asked, "So, if I ride your cock, you'll cancel my contract?"

****

Gretchen

The alcohol made me ask.

That's my story, and I'm sticking to it.

Or maybe the sexy-as-sin man had turned my brain to mush when he'd kissed me.

Maybe it was a combination of the two.

Then again, it could be the fact that I hadn't been touched by a man in almost a year.

I'd heard lack of sex can cause a person to make poor decisions.

Whatever the reason, I decided the consequences were a problem for tomorrow's Gretchen. Tonight's Gretchen was going to be bold and do what she wanted. If I got the contract for the cabinets I couldn't afford canceled *and* rode a hot Zaddy's cock in the process, I'd chalk it up as a win-win.

He chuckled when he replied, "I wish I could sweetheart, but my brother would probably run me out of business if I did."

I studied him a little longer, and he shifted his feet under my scrutiny, like he was nervous about my response.

"Hmm... so if we have sex tonight, the only thing in it for me is an orgasm?"

"Orgasmsss..." He drew the "S" out. "Plural."

I could work with that.

"And it'd just be for tonight? You're not looking for someone to date."

Because obviously if he was, it wouldn't be with someone like me. I had a two-year old son and desperately wanted to try for a daughter. He'd told me point-blank he didn't want to start over and thought his older brother was a fool for doing so.

He hesitated, like he wasn't sure what answer I was looking for, but finally replied, "I'm not interested in a relationship."

"Good."

Reaching for his hand, I pulled him toward the door leading to the house and hit the garage door button as we walked inside.

Chapter Twelve

Gabe

The second the door to her house closed, I pressed her against it and crashed my mouth down on hers.

She whimpered as she clung to my back while our tongues tangled.

How was this possible? She'd called me an infuriating Jerk of the Year not eight hours earlier, and now I had her pushed against a door while my hands roved down her sides in her mud room.

This can't be happening. She must have misunderstood me.

I pulled away, panting.

"You understand I'm the guy who built your kitchen cabinets? The same one whose lawyer served you with an intent to sue letter today."

She pulled her shirt over her head. "I know," then reached for my hand to lead me further into the house.

I paused to survey her kitchen.

Yeah, the cabinets are going to look amazing in here.

With a tug, she led me up the stairs, down a hallway, and into her bedroom.

My gaze turned to her heavy breasts spilling out of her lacy bra, and I swallowed hard. Still, I hesitated.

"I really can't cancel your contract, even if we have sex."

Gretchen seemed undeterred when she reached behind her back to unclasp her bra. She let the straps fall down her arms and onto the floor, so she was standing topless in front of me. She was more fucking gorgeous than I'd even imagined.

"I understand."

Her stiff, rosy nipples begged for attention. Attention I was dying to give with my mouth and hands. Her tits looked like they would fit perfectly in my palms.

I felt the need to reiterate, "I'm not looking for a relationship."

It was like I was trying to talk her out of fucking me. What the hell was I doing?

"You said that already. I'm not either."

All I could do was stare at her bare tits. My fingers itched to touch them. My mouth watered when I thought about suckling on her stiff, pink nipples. My gaze slowly traveled back to her face.

"You are so beautiful."

Yet, I remained frozen, wanting to give her an out in case she came to her senses.

Instead, she reached for the hem of my Henley and lifted, but her arms couldn't reach over my head, so I took over taking off my shirt.

"Good grief," she muttered as she looked at my bare chest. "You're..." Taking a step forward, her hands traveled along my abs and skimmed the waistband of my pants. I willed her to unfasten my belt, but her touch moved back to my abs, like she'd never seen someone with a sixpack. Her gaze caught mine and she uttered, "You're perfect. Do you work out like, every day?"

My lips twitched as I fought a smile. "My job can be pretty strenuous at times, so I don't really need to hit the gym more than a few times a week."

Gretchen glanced down at herself, and her arms wrapped around her middle. I immediately grabbed her hands and pulled her arms over her head as my gaze raked down her curves.

"Uh uh. You don't cover your body up in front of me. You are a fucking goddess."

She snorted. "Yeah, maybe from a Rubens painting."

I finally let my hands touch her tits like I'd been aching to do. Thumbing her nipples with both hands, I leaned down so my mouth was inches from hers when I reiterated, "A. Fucking. Goddess. From the first time I laid eyes on you."

I wasn't willing to admit that she was my soulmate, but there was no doubt in my mind she was my dream girl come to life.

And now I was about to have a night in heaven with my own Aphrodite. I just hoped one night would be enough.

****

Gretchen

This man with his silver tongue, ripped abs, and gorgeous face...

I really should hate him. Because of him, I might have to sell my beloved house. But it was hard to hate him when all I wanted was to feel his hands all over my body. And yes, ride his cock.

Lack of sex was obviously messing with my brain.

I reasoned with myself, *it's Troy's fault, not Gabe's, that I might have to sell the house.*

Troy was the one I should be mad at—he's the one who ruined our family, not the Greek god who was currently running his tongue around my nipple.

Gabe lifted his head to look at my face. "Where'd you go, sweetheart? Stay with me."

I couldn't believe he'd been that in-tune with me to notice my mind had flitted elsewhere, so I swallowed hard and whispered, "I'm sorry."

"Don't be sorry, baby." His lips grazed my neck before he murmured in my ear, "The only thing I want you thinking about is what I'm doing to you and how it makes you feel." He nipped at my earlobe, then growled, "Can you do that for me, darlin'?"

Fuck yeah, I could.

I nodded in response.

"Good girl."

His fingers kneaded my right boob while he dipped his head and resumed his oral attention to my left nipple. The scruff of his face was rough against my skin, reminding me he was *all* man. I wondered how the stubble would feel along my inner thighs.

As if reading my mind, he ran his index finger along the waistband of my painted-on jeans.

"What do you say we take these off?"

"I will if you will."

With a smirk, he took a step back and unbuckled his belt, then popped the button open on his cargo pants, and smoothly slid them down his muscular thighs—his eyes on me the entire time he undressed.

Me? I was a little less graceful as I kicked off my heels, shimmied my jeans over my hips, then tugged them down past my knees, and almost fell over as I awkwardly pulled them over my ankles. All while he stood watching me with his cock tenting his grey boxer-briefs.

And what a spectacular tent it was. It almost made me forget to be embarrassed at the spectacle I was making of myself as I tried to get down to my underwear.

And I thought I'd done such a good job of projecting "sexy" when I took off my top and bra...

So much for being a temptress.

I was noticeably shorter without my heels when I stood before him in my black satin panties.

His nostrils flared as his gaze traveled down my body and back up again, but instead of reaching for me, he asked, "You're sure about this?"

Good grief, what did a girl need to do to get laid around here?

Cupping his cock over the fabric of his underwear while pressing my naked tits against his bare chest, I looked up at him and breathed, "Positive."

The skin-on-skin contact was electric, and my body broke out in goosebumps. Something he noticed because he chuckled as he lightly traced the raised hairs along my back.

"I like having this effect on you."

My hand slid under his waistband, and I palmed his warm, smooth cock in my hand.

"And I like having this effect on you."

"You have no idea how much, baby."

Slowly stroking his shaft, I whispered, "Actually I think I do."

He grinned as he ran his hands along the satin covering my ass, then worked his fingers around the lace waistband to trace the seam of my pussy. I knew the fabric was drenched.

"Your panties are wet, sweetheart."

"I wonder why," I replied cheekily as I smeared his precum around the tip of his cock with my thumb.

"Do you need to be fucked?"

I arched my boobs against him. "Mmm, god yes."

Gabe grabbed a handful of my hair and tugged my head back, so I had no choice but to look at him.

"Beg me."

Ho-lee fuck.

I had not been expecting that, but it had to be the hottest thing ever.

I think my juices are running down my leg.

"Please fuck my pussy," I whispered breathlessly. "Please. I need your cock so badly."

Not letting go of my hair, with his other hand, he reached between my legs, moved my panties to the side, and ran a finger down my center. The corner of his mouth hitched.

"You're fucking soaked."

Uh… yeah. You just told me to beg you while you pulled my hair.

I decided to try again.

"Please, Gabe."

Tugging a little harder on my hair so my head tilted farther back, he stared into my eyes and growled, "No," before releasing his hold on my tresses.

I'm sorry—what?

Chapter Thirteen

Gabe

Gretchen's eyes flashed, and I knew I better not keep her waiting for an explanation or I'd be risking a knee to the balls.

"I need to taste you first, sweetheart." Not pausing for her response, I instructed, "Get on the bed, spread your legs, and get comfortable. I'm going to be a while."

Her pretty little bow-shaped lips formed an "O" before she scrambled to pull the covers back to do as I ordered; quickly dispatching her underwear in one fluid movement before widening her legs. Her glistening folds on full display made me groan.

My goddess lay spread out before me like a buffet, and I couldn't wait to dive in.

Crawling up the bed between her thighs, my mouth watered at the scent of her musk.

"Your pussy smells so sweet, baby. I'm going to eat you like a peach."

"Oh fuck!"

I grinned as I looked up at her. "We'll get to that. I believe I promised you multiple orgasms tonight, and I'm a man of my word."

Without further preamble, I swiped my tongue down her slit, and her back bowed off the mattress as she let out a small gasp.

"Oh my god, Gabriel!"

I smiled against her skin.

"Just Gabe, baby."

Circling her clit with my tongue, I pressed one finger inside her channel.

"Damn, sweetheart. You're tight."

"It's been almost a year."

A year?

I knew her dipshit ex-husband had been neglecting her. What a fucking moron. Her body was made for worshipping, and I was going to do just that—all night.

"I'll take care of you, darlin'. And I won't even make you beg me. You taste so fucking good."

"I liked begging you."

Just when I didn't think my dick could get any harder, she goes and says something like that.

With my mouth hovering against her center, I looked up at her and growled, "Good. Then beg me to eat your cunt."

Ker-splash!

There was no denying how much she liked that.

Her hands cupped her tits, and she arched her back while moaning, "Oh. My. God."

My mouth hitched, and my ego swelled.

"That's not begging, baby."

"Gabe, please..."

I watched in awe as my finger slowly moved in and out of her slick heat. I was dying to fuck her.

But first things first.

"Please what?"

"Please..." She hesitated. I could tell she wasn't used to talking dirty, but it was obviously a big turn-on for her.

Slowing my movement, I asked again. "Please what?"

Her hands wove into my hair, and she pulled my face toward her center when she whispered, "Please eat my cunt."

I grinned in satisfaction. I knew she was scandalized but her body told me another story.

"Of course. It'd be my pleasure to eat your cunt."

I took my time swirling my tongue around her clit before exploring her folds while pressing another digit inside her. I had every intention of savoring her, but she had other plans.

"Faster, please."

"So impatient," I tsked as I pulled the hood of her clit back and admired the pearl I found beneath.

"Gabe, I need you to make me come. Please."

How could I say no?

My tongue flicked her clit while I increased the tempo as I finger fucked her.

"Oh my god, that feels so good."

I glanced up to find her eyes closed and mouth open, with her blonde hair fanned out on the pillow.

The sight was hot as fuck.

Her hands clutched her tits as she lifted her hips slightly to press against my mouth.

I took the invitation and sucked on her little engorged jewel while my digits quickly moved in and out of her.

Her body tensed, and I could tell she was close, so I wiggled my tongue as I sucked her clit. Adding an aggressive head shake and moan for good measure while pumping my hand harder.

"Don't stop," she begged with her eyes shut tight. "Please, Gabe. Don't stop."

Deciding actions spoke louder than words, I didn't even pause to tell her I had no plans of stopping until her soft body was writhing around my face.

****

Gretchen

"Oh. My. God. What did you just do to me?" I whelped between pants as I lay on my bed with my hand across my stomach. He grinned when I looked down at him still between my legs; then he kissed his way up my body.

His arms came possessively around my sides when his lips grazed my neck, and he murmured, "There's one."

I'm pretty sure he'd just ruined me for any other man with just that one orgasm. How would I survive more?

Still, I was willing to risk it.

I was a trooper like that.

My hand came around his head, and I pulled his face toward mine for a kiss. His cock, still confined in his underwear, jumped against my thigh when his lips touched mine. I think the thought of me tasting myself turned him on.

It kind of did me, too.

Troy had never been a fan of going down on me, and the few times he did, just as I'd get close, he'd stop and immediately jump up to go brush his teeth—often leaving me in the lurch, sans climax.

The taste of myself on Gabe's lips represented a job well done on the Greek god's part. All while making me feel sexy.

Gabe pressed his erection harder against me.

"I want you, sweetheart."

I was feeling pretty cocky, so with a smirk, I replied, "Beg me."

His hand kneaded my boob, and I bit back a groan when he murmured in my ear, "I don't beg, baby. But you will, again. I guarantee it."

Arrogant ass.

Had this not been the most action I knew I was going to get in a while, and had he not been so damn good, I might have been tempted to stubbornly refuse to do any such thing.

But who knew when the next time I was going to have sex? Not to mention I doubted my next partner would have Gabe's skillset. And I hadn't been lying when I'd told him I'd liked begging him; his dominance was hot. So, really, refusing to beg him would only be hurting myself; making me inclined not to disagree with him.

I decided to try and turn the tables, instead.

Dragging my nails down his bare back, I arched my breasts against his chest and breathed, "Please fuck me, Gabe. I need to feel your thick cock inside my wet pussy."

His mouth turned up in smile, and he smugly replied, "Of course. All you had to do is ask, darlin'," before he skimmed his boxer-briefs down his thighs.

My eyes widened when his cock bounced free.

Dayum.

After he used his teeth to rip open a purple square package I hadn't noticed before, I watched in fascination as he sheathed his impressive shaft.

"Um, I'm not sure that thing is going to fit," I said with a laugh to imply I was joking, although part of me was a little worried.

He didn't seem deterred as he lined the tip up with my entrance.

"It'll fit; I promise. Not only will it fit, but you'll love it."

That's kind of what I was afraid of. Like I said, he'd already wrecked me for future partners just going down on me. If his dick was magical, too, it was only going to compound my problem.

We both moaned in unison when he pressed inside.

"Fuuuuck, sweetheart," Gabe shuddered. "Your pussy is so tight." He moved slowly, then paused and closed his eyes tight and groaned, "You feel so fucking good!" almost like it was a bad thing.

His words made me feel desirable. I had been worried that maybe having Jake had ruined my vagina, and that's why Troy had turned to someone else. Or maybe it'd been the extra baby weight I hadn't been able to lose.

The way Gabe looked at me, I realized it wasn't about my imperfections; my husband was just an asshole.

And that was empowering.

"Fuck me, Gabe," I said boldly as I spread my legs wider and tilted my hips to take him deeper. "Fuck my pussy. Hard. I want to feel your balls slapping my ass."

Whoa, hussy. Where did that come from?

Gabe's hand circled my neck, and he snarled, "You dirty girl. You make my cock so damn hard."

My inner slut gave me a high five. I'd never let her come out to play before, and she was ready for whatever was going to happen next.

Chapter Fourteen

Gabe

The sexy teacher had just knocked me on my ass—metaphorically speaking.

I hadn't expected her to become so brazen. It was hot as fuck.

But she still needed to know who was in charge.

Spoiler alert: it wasn't her.

So, I wrapped my hand around her neck and softly squeezed. Not enough to hurt her, just enough to let her know I wasn't relinquishing control.

"You dirty girl. You make my cock so damn hard," I snarled as I slammed into her warm heat.

"The better to fuck me with," she quipped as she stared me in the eyes. I think it was her own way of challenging me.

"You like it when I fuck you, sweetheart?"

"God, yes."

My free hand bit into her hip as I pulled almost all the way out only to ram back, balls deep.

Over and over.

My balls did, in fact, slap her ass as she requested.

After all, I did aim to please.

"Do you like being at my mercy, baby? Being pinned in place while I fuck the shit out of you?"

A low mewl escaped her lips, so soft, I almost didn't hear it.

"I love it."

I released my hold on her neck and chuckled as I rubbed her clit.

"I know you do, you dirty girl."

Her eyes dropped shut and she panted, "So dirty," as she arched her back off the bed and pulled on her nipples.

"Are you my little slut tonight?"

"Yessss."

I felt her body tighten and her pussy clench my cock, so I knew she was close again. Which was a good thing because I was, too.

I rubbed her clit faster and murmured, "Come on my cock, baby."

She fell over the edge chanting my name. Her body spasmed underneath me, and when her pussy quivered around my dick, it pushed me over the edge right behind her.

I held her close as I buried my cock deep and roared my release with my eyes shut tight.

When I'd spent my entire load, I dropped down on top of her, conscious not to crush her, and felt her arms instantly come around me.

"Wow," she whispered as her finger traced up and down my spine.

Wow indeed.

I pulled out before my cock softened and disappeared into her en suite bathroom to dispatch the condom and clean up. Then I pulled the towel off her rack and brought it back to the bedroom with me.

Her smile was shy as I tended to her. The brazen vixen was gone, and I wasn't sure if it was regret I saw in her expression or embarrassment. Or something else.

****

Gretchen

Okay, now what?

I didn't really know the proper etiquette for a one-night stand. Was he going to get dressed and leave now, or would he crawl back in bed next to me and fuck me until morning? I wasn't sure my poor pussy could take being fucked until morning.

Gabe must have felt my uneasiness as he sat on the edge of the bed, because he tucked my hair behind my ear. I could make out his soft smile in the moonlight.

"I can leave now, if you want." I didn't respond, so he added, "Or I can stay and hold you in my arms all night."

Okay, being held all night could work.

But did I want him to stay?

I thought so. If for no other reason than I would feel cheap if he left now.

Don't get me wrong; I'd loved being filthy with him when we were in the throes of passion. But now that our horniness had subsided, I found myself wondering how I could have been so uninhibited. That was not like me.

At least if he held me in his arms tonight it wouldn't seem so, "wham, bam, thank you ma'am"-ish.

But then again, things were probably going to be awkward as fuck in the light of day. Maybe it'd be better if he just left now.

And this is why I don't do one-night stands.

"Um, what do you want to do?"

He answered without hesitation, "I'd like to take you to breakfast in the morning."

Breakfast? Really?

"Is that what you normally do?"

He tilted his head, like he was confused.

"Don't you eat breakfast in the morning?"

"No, I mean, after you… you know." I gestured to his naked cock between his legs. "Go home with someone for the night."

He studied my face for a minute without replying, and I blurted out, "I'm sorry, I shouldn't have asked that. I'm just kind of new to this no-strings sex thing."

"Well, if I'm being honest, no. I don't usually stay until morning. But…" he trailed off.

"But?" I prompted.

His gaze was tender as he stared down at me. "But I don't want to go yet."

I pressed my lips together to keep from smiling.

"Oh. Well, in that case"—I scooted over to make room for him and patted the mattress next to me—"let's snuggle."

His face broke out in a grin as he got in beside me and pulled up the covers around us. He turned to his side to face me and murmured, "I get to be the big spoon," before pulling my body next to his so my ass nestled against his cock.

His dick jumped against my backside, and his hand skimmed up my stomach to cup my breast.

As if my body had a mind of its own, I subtly ground my ass against him and secretly loved it when I felt things grow harder. It made me feel powerful, being able to turn him on just by wiggling my butt against him.

His grasp on my boob tightened, and he grumbled in my ear, "If you don't hold still, you're going to find yourself getting fucked again."

I couldn't help but grin when I sassily replied, "Promise?"

"Guaranteed, sweetheart."

A yelp escaped my body when he flipped me onto my stomach, and his hand came down to swat my backside. It didn't hurt, but the sound reverberating off the bedroom walls suggested it should.

Score one for extra padding.

Chapter Fifteen

Gabe

Something felt off when I opened my eyes in the pre-dawn, and I blinked to adjust to the dim light in the room.

The cream-colored walls and dusty-pink accent pieces were foreign. And the white fluffy comforter covering my body didn't smell familiar.

I rolled to my side and found blonde hair spread across the pillow next to me, along with a naked back. I couldn't help but smile as the events of the night before came flooding back to me.

How I'd made the little minx lying naked next to me scream my name two more times before I finally came all over her tits.

Like she'd begged me to.

It'd been so fucking hot, I'd seen stars when the last rope of cum blasted onto her porcelain skin.

The memory had my morning wood getting even harder.

Ms. Gretchen Wainwright had been hiding a naughty side, and, being the debauched bastard that I am, I'd been more than happy to help bring it out.

I remembered falling asleep with her nuzzled against my side with her head on my chest, feeling more content than I had in a long while.

Judging by the grey light peeking through the curtains, I guessed it was around six in the morning, my usual time to wake up. But unlike my work days, I didn't have anywhere to be until that afternoon.

I looked at the sexy woman lying next to me and was glad I didn't have to get out of bed yet. She might be too sore for another round this morning; I'd pounded her pussy thoroughly last night, but I needed to feel her warm body against mine.

Sliding next to her, I wrapped my arm around her stomach, breathed in the now-familiar floral scent of her shampoo, and nestled my erection between the cleft of her ass. She let out a soft, "mmm," but otherwise didn't stir. I found myself easily falling back asleep, amazed at how relaxed I felt with her in my arms.

Not to mention the cozy, soft, pink sheets felt fucking fantastic.

~~

I'd dozed back off but woke up when I felt her slip out of my embrace and the mattress lift when she got out of bed. The bathroom door closed with a soft click, so it was apparent she was trying to be quiet and not wake me.

I appreciated her being considerate, but the question was, would she climb back into bed when she was done in the bathroom? I hoped so.

Hearing the door open, I closed my eyes and pretended to be asleep. But it was hard to keep up the ruse because I could feel her gaze on me, and then she murmured something with a sigh that sounded an awful lot like, "So handsome."

My eyes flew open at that, and I found her wearing a white fuzzy robe as she hastily stepped away from my side of the bed. Her expression was guilty, like I'd just caught her with her hand in the cookie jar, and she turned on her heel and headed toward her closet door.

"Good morning," I called with a soft smile.

Her smile seemed forced when she stopped and looked back at me. "Good morning. How did you sleep?"

"Like a baby. Must have been the company. How about you?"

"Great!" I think she realized her words were far too peppy for the situation, and so she toned it down when she reiterated, "I slept great. I have an amazing mattress. My ex and I actually fought for custody over it, but my lawyer was better than his. What kind of mattress do you have?"

Now she was just rambling.

"I have a memory foam, too."

"Aren't they just the best?"

I couldn't help but smile at how awkward she was being.

"Yeah. NASA technology is pretty great."

She was obviously uneasy as she pulled her robe tighter around her chest and glanced around the room, like she was searching for something else to say.

Finally, her gaze returned to me, and we stared at each other for a quiet beat until she cleared her throat and gestured to the bathroom door.

"Um, feel free to use my shower if you want. I set a spare toothbrush on the counter for you. I'm going to get dressed and make some coffee."

"Thanks."

I threw back the covers and stood, my dick swinging between my legs as I did. Gretchen quickly glanced away, like there was a spot on the floor that fascinated her, but I could see the blush creeping up her cheeks. It was so adorable, I couldn't help but chuckle.

"No need to act shy now, sweetheart."

"I'm not," she said defensively, and I raised my eyebrows as I stalked closer to her.

"You're not?"

She lifted her chin defiantly to meet my gaze and affirmed with gusto, "No, I'm not," but I noticed she was careful not to look down.

"That's good." The smirk on my face was apparent as I untied her robe and pulled it open to blatantly appraise her naked body from head to toe.

I liked that she didn't shrink from my perusal. If her pointed nipples and goosebump-covered skin were any indicators, I'd even venture to say she liked it.

"Gretchen Wainwright—you are fucking stunning."

"Kelly," she uttered.

I cocked my head in confusion, so she clarified, "I'm legally Gretchen Kelly now."

Good, she got rid of that fucker's last name.

I found I liked that more than I probably should.

"Gretchen Kelly," I said softly, trying out how her name sounded on my tongue while I stroked my fingers up and down her bare sides. "It suits you."

A smile escaped her lips. "Thanks. I think so, too."

"So, Gretchen Kelly. What do you say you join me in the shower?"

****

Gretchen

I really wanted to take him up on his offer. Last night had been the best sex of my life, hands down, and I wouldn't have minded "one for the road," but...

"I'm kind of sore," I confessed.

You didn't go a whole year having sex with only toys every few months to getting pounded into the mattress by a thick eight-inch cock all night without repercussions.

He stopped caressing my side and slid his hand around my waist to pull me closer.

"Oh, darlin', I'm so sorry."

I felt the corners of my mouth curve up when I looked up at him. His close proximity had lifted the awkward feeling I'd felt when I woke up with an unfamiliar arm possessively wrapped around me.

"I'm not. Last night was amazing. Thanks for popping my one-night stand cherry."

"The pleasure was all mine."

His blue eyes darkened and the mirth that had been dancing in them just seconds before disappeared.

"You're not going to do it again, though, are you?"

I furrowed my brows. "What do you mean?"

Does he think I'm never going to have sex again?

"Have another one-night stand, now that your cherry has been popped."

"I mean... maybe?"

His jaw ticked like he was clenching it and his grip on my waist tightened.

What is that about?

I cocked my head and asked, "Why?"

Finally, he unclenched his jaw and replied, "It's not safe."

I snorted—actually snorted.

"You recognize the hypocrisy in what you just said, right?"

"I do." His mouth hovered inches from mine. "And I don't care."

Before I could offer an indignant retort, his lips captured mine. I couldn't even pretend I didn't want his kiss. With a moan, I wrapped my arms around his neck and pressed my body against his, feeling his cock stiffen against my tummy.

Maybe I wasn't too sore after all.

Chapter Sixteen

Gabe

There's just something about shower sex to start your day out right.

We put Gretchen's shower bench to good use. Knowing she was sore, I let her straddle me and control the tempo and how deep she took my cock.

And the view as her tits bounced while she rode me was definitely a plus.

I strummed her clit with my fingers and had her coming on my dick in no time. I loved how responsive her body was to my touch and how good she felt when she collapsed against my chest to catch her breath.

That's when I realized—

Fuck.

Instead of bending her over the bench and finishing like I was dying to do, I lifted her ass with both hands and pulled her off my lap.

She looked down at me with puppy dog eyes.

"What's wrong?"

"I—I'm not wearing a condom." I felt like a jerk. One more check in her "con" column. "I'm sorry, I'm never this reckless. I'm clean, I promise."

"Oh... Um, well, it's not like I didn't notice. I'm on birth control. I guess I should have said something, so I'm the one who's sorry."

Even if a chick tells me she's on birth control, I don't risk it. I didn't need an STD or another kid.

Not that I didn't trust that Gretchen was clean or thought she'd try to trap me with a baby, it was just...

"Old habits die hard," I said with a smile, thinking that was the end of our shower tryst.

I thought wrong.

Her petite fingers circled my shaft, and she slowly moved her hand up and down.

"I guess we'll have to think of something else."

I leaned my head and shoulders against the shower tiles and watched her stroke me.

"I like how you're thinking so far."

She dipped her head into my groin.

"What about this?" she asked before her flat tongue circled the circumference of my crown.

Fuck that feels good.

I pulled the curtain of her wet hair back so I could watch what she was doing.

"Your ideas are just getting better and better."

"What about this?"

She pulled my length into her mouth. All the way in, until my tip bobbed against her throat.

Fuck yes.

I bit out a low moan and wrapped her hair around my fist to guide her mouth up and down my shaft.

"You're bordering on genius, baby."

"Mmm, good," she murmured with a mouthful of my cock.

Gripping me at the base, she stroked her hand up while moving her mouth down, to meet in the middle. All while letting me use her hair for a handle to set the rhythm.

It was fucking hot as hell to watch her blow me, then she looked up and held my gaze as she deepthroated my cock. Her eyes watered, and I about blew my load right then.

"Fuuuuck, sweetheart. You are a dirty girl."

A grin escaped her as she released my dick and took a big breath.

A string of her spit connected her lips to my tip, and I groaned out loud at the sexy sight.

Then my little vixen quickly resumed her oral and manual attention to my cock with a long moan.

The base of my spine tingled, and I thrust my hips up while pressing her mouth down.

"That's it, dirty girl. Take that cock."

I felt my balls draw up, and I grunted as my grip on her hair tightened while I directed her head up and down until I knew I was past the point of no return.

"I'm going to come, baby."

I loosened my hold on her hair in the event she was a spitter and not a swallower.

Gretchen didn't let up, and loudly slurped my shaft as she simultaneously jerked me off.

"Oh fuck. Oh fuck. Are you ready for it, dirty girl?" I thrust up harder. "Here it comes. Take it."

I let out a long grunt before exploding in her mouth, roaring, "Fuuuuck yes," as I emptied myself into her throat. I knew there wasn't a lot, since I'd drained my balls three times last night and there hadn't been enough time to refill my tank, so to speak.

But still, the sexy teacher let a little dribble out the side of her mouth and down her chin to drip onto her luscious tits. That sight was going into my spank bank.

I reluctantly closed my eyes and tipped my head against the slate tiles as I tried to find my breath.

When my breathing finally slowed, I looked back down at her. She hadn't rinsed my cum off her, and I swiped my thumb along the side of her mouth, whispering, "A fucking goddess."

She turned her face into my hand with a contented smile, and in that moment, I knew there was no way I was going to be satisfied with just one night with her.

Now I just needed to convince her to see me again.

That might be hard to do, considering my company was probably going to sue her.

Chapter Seventeen

Gretchen

"Should we go out for breakfast?" Gabe asked as we toweled off in the bathroom.

I blinked at him. "You want to go to breakfast?"

I was surprised he wasn't ready to part ways with me by now. I wasn't well-versed on one-night stand etiquette, but I'd kind of envisioned him getting dressed and being in a hurry to leave now that we'd had our morning fun.

"I told you that last night, sweetheart."

That's true, he had.

"I guess I just thought..."

His eyebrows shot to his hairline. "That I was handing you a line?"

With a shrug, I admitted, "I mean, kind of?"

He tucked his towel around his waist and reached for me. I willingly leaned against his damp chest when he put his arms around me.

"Not a line. I really want to have pancakes with you."

That made me burst out laughing, and I pulled back to examine his handsome face.

"You strike me more as a bacon and eggs kind of guy."

"Who says it can't it be both?"

"No one, I guess. But don't you have Brayden's lacrosse tournament?"

"That's not until this afternoon. I'm all yours this morning." He paused before sputtering, "I mean, if you're available. I guess I'm being rather presumptuous that you don't have plans."

"No plans. I mean, I need to grade some papers, but that can wait until this afternoon."

I wasn't picking Jake up until lunchtime tomorrow, so my day was flexible. I knew our time together had to come to an end, but I liked the idea of it lasting just a little bit longer.

Gabe tapped my butt.

"Good. Go get dressed. I'm starving."

Pancakes never sounded better.

****

Gabe

What the fuck was I doing?

I'd never gone to breakfast with one of my hookups. Then again, I'd never woken up with one either.

Still, I didn't regret it. In fact, it'd been nice to wake up and find her lying next to me.

A first time for everything, I guess.

Gretchen ushered me toward the garage when I tried to pause and take in her kitchen in the light of day.

"Your new cabinets are going to look great in here," I said with a cocky grin because... they really were fucking awesome.

"Hmph," she said with pursed lips. "I guess we'll let the courts decide about that."

"Sweetheart," I said in a gentle tone as we walked out the door. "You don't want to go to court. You're not going to win."

She hit a button on the wall next to the doorjamb, and the garage door made a whirring noise as it came up. "I can't afford them, Gabe."

Pausing before I opened the truck door for her, I made a show of looking around the two empty garage stalls.

"Let me at least deliver them so I don't have to tack on storage fees to your total. You've got plenty of space in here."

Her eyes were narrow slits of blue when she stared up at me. "Won't you expect payment on delivery?"

I pulled on the handle and put my hand on the small of her back as she stepped on the running boards.

"I'm not worried about that right now. But I really need them out of my shop by Tuesday. I have a lumber shipment coming in and your cabinets are taking up too much space."

She settled into her seat and let out a defeated sigh.

"I guess you could store them here until we get things figured out."

And by "get things figured out," I hoped she'd realize that meant having them installed.

****

Gretchen

It really was a shame that I wouldn't be seeing Gabe again. He seemed like the kind of guy I was looking for. Handsome, funny, down-to-earth, and trustworthy. The kind of man who would be a good role model for Jake.

Of course, my trustworthy meter might be broken because I had once put all my trust into Troy, who turned out to be a cheating asshole who ditched his family for a barely legal woman who fawned all over him.

I had once fawned all over him, back when we were in college, and I was the geeky, shy girl who had caught the eye of the handsome frat guy. He'd made me feel special. All the girls had wanted to be with him, and he'd chosen me. But I grew up, started a career, became a mom, had a household to worry about.... I had other things besides my husband's ego to attend to. I guess that was why things deteriorated in my marriage. Maybe I should have tried harder to put him first, but then again, he should have made his family a priority.

I see now that it was for the best. When I found myself legally alone, I realized that my life hadn't changed that much, other than I had to more closely watch how much I spent at the grocery store and give up a few luxuries. I had essentially been a single parent all along. That had been a sad realization, but it'd made me stronger.

The next man I ended up with would be my partner, in every sense of the word.

I glanced at Gabe's profile as he maneuvered his black F150 through Lancastle. I could see him being a good partner. The things I'd said last night were true—he seemed to be a caring dad, he hadn't bad-mouthed his ex, and his brother thought he was great. I wondered what happened with his marriage.

Giving myself an internal shake, I chided myself.

It doesn't matter. It's none of my business.

"Did you cheat on your wife?"

What the hell, Gretchen?

I couldn't believe I'd just blurted that out.

Gabe took his attention off the road to look over at me with raised eyebrows.

"That's not my style."

"Did she cheat on you, then?"

He shook his head with a chuckle. "There was no cheating involved. Why?"

I shrugged even though he was looking at traffic again and couldn't see me.

"I'm just trying to figure out why someone would divorce you. You seem like a real catch."

He seemed to be fighting a smile when he replied, "You mean, aside from being the infuriating Jerk of the Year."

"I've managed to compartmentalize that part of your personality. You've graduated to just Mr. Infuriating." I returned his grin. "The orgasms helped."

He barked out a laugh.

"I told you I'd deliver."

"Oh, you delivered. In spades."

We were quiet as he turned the steering wheel. When the truck was headed straight again, he quietly observed, "You were pretty amazing yourself. You are definitely a catch. I don't know what your ex was thinking."

I glanced out the window at the stores as we passed and quietly uttered, "I couldn't compete with someone ten years younger who fed his ego all day, every day."

"He's an insecure idiot."

"I can't argue there. But what about you? If there was no cheating, why are you divorced?"

His expression grew grim. "We just grew apart and wanted different things. Resentments festered that eventually grew into what the courts call 'irreconcilable differences'."

"I'm sorry," I offered, unsure what else to say.

"I appreciate that, but don't be. I don't miss being married to her, but I do miss being with my kids."

I wish Troy would at least miss being with Jake.

"Your kids are lucky to have such a good dad."

His grin returned.

"I am pretty great."

I once again found myself wishing there could be more between us.

But Gabe was my first venture into being with the opposite sex since Troy. Surely, there had to be more men like Gabe, only who'd want kids.

Somehow, I couldn't help feeling like that was wishful thinking. I wasn't going to find a man who'd be interested in raising another man's child.

That was okay. I was prepared to do this alone.

I just didn't want to have to move out of my house while doing it.

Chapter Eighteen

Gabe

Our breakfasts had just been served and as Gretchen buttered her pancakes, out of the blue she asked, "Is there any way you'd consider a payment plan for the cabinets?"

I took a long swig of coffee to buy myself some time before answering. I didn't want to upset her, but I knew I needed to be honest.

Setting my mug back on the peeling brown laminate table, I remarked, "We never have."

"But there's a first time for everything right?"

She sounded so hopeful, but I could hear Maverick now.

We're not a financing company, Gabe. Payment on installation. We don't need that hassle of chasing people down for our money.

Normally, I'd agree with him. But Gretchen wasn't just any client. Maybe we could make an exception. While my brother was technically the "silent" partner, we made decisions together. I wouldn't make this decision arbitrarily. I'd want his buy-in.

Still, I didn't want to get her hopes up.

"I'm not sure how that would work. My brother would insist on a lot of stipulations. It'd probably be more cost effective to just go through your credit card or bank."

"Don't you think if you offered financing, you'd increase business?"

The clientele we usually dealt with didn't need financing, but she had a point. That was another market we could tap into, if I had the space and manpower to accommodate it. I know Maverick would be concerned about cheapening the brand if it was more easily accessible. But it could be a new revenue stream. Maybe we could do an offshoot label.

"I'll talk to him."

"How much would it knock off my bill if I installed them myself?"

I tried to school my expression. I couldn't decide if I should be insulted. Like she was saying cabinet installation wasn't a skill, and anyone could do it with no training. I knew she was just trying to find a way to save money, so my ego settled down.

"You know how to install cabinets?"

She sheepishly glanced down at her breakfast plate.

"Well, no. But you can learn a lot from YouTube."

"I don't think you want to be experimenting a DIY project with custom kitchen cabinets."

She persisted and cut into her hot cakes with gusto.

"But let's say I did. How much would that reduce what I owe?"

"I'm not exactly sure what your quote was, but normally installation is about twenty-five percent of the cost."

I could see her doing the math in her head.

"I promise you, it's not worth whatever you'd save to have your cabinets installed incorrectly. Your beautiful, custom cabinets would lose their value if they're not put in right."

"At least I'd get to keep my house."

I drew my neck back. *Keep her house?*

"What do you mean?"

"I probably shouldn't tell you this, since I'm essentially giving my secrets to the enemy, but my lawyer told me I wouldn't win in court. He advised me to let the cabinets be installed and have you put a contractor's lien on the house which means—"

"You'd have to sell your house," I finished for her.

"Yeah." Tears filled her eyes when she looked across the table at me. "I don't want to have to leave Lancastle. So, if it means living with crooked cabinets, or even cabinets just taking up space in my garage, I'll do it."

Aw hell.

Tears were worse than having her pissed off at me. I could take her ire and calling me the Jerk of the Year, her crying on the other hand...

"Let me deliver the cabinets this weekend, so at least you won't have the storage fees tacked on, and I'll talk to Mav about what we can do about a payment plan."

A big sigh of relief left her body as she gushed, "Thank you."

"Don't thank me yet. I can't promise anything."

"But you're willing to try, and I appreciate that more than you can know."

I liked the idea of being the guy who saved the day for her. The idea of having to face Mav, not so much.

But the way she was smiling at me from across the table, I'd be willing to take my brother's wrath.

"I can bring a load over tonight after Brayden's game, then maybe we could grab a bite to eat?"

Gretchen cocked her head at me. "Like a date?"

"I mean, if you want to label it, yeah, like a date."

Her eyes narrowed, and I got an uneasy feeling I wasn't going to like her response.

"I don't think that's a good idea."

Before I could ask her why not, she continued, "We agreed last night was a one-time thing. You said so yourself you're not looking for a relationship. I feel like if we went on a date, my heart might get the wrong idea."

Yeah, mine too.

Yet, I still wanted to see her again. Consequences be damned.

"How about this? Instead of looking at it as a date, we just consider it a continuation of last night. Instead of one night, it's one weekend?"

She took a bite of her pancake stack and chewed slowly as she contemplated my offer.

When she swallowed, I braced myself for her reply. But instead of answering me, she took a swig of her orange juice.

You're killing me, woman!

Finally, she said, "Okay, but how about I make dinner instead of us going out?"

"Deal," I blurted out, not wanting to give her an opportunity to change her mind. "I'll be at your house about six."

"I can have dinner ready by six-thirty. Will that give you enough time to unload the cabinets, or should I plan on seven?"

"Six-thirty is perfect."

For the first time in a long time, I had something to look forward to other than spending time with my kids or going to work.

****

Gretchen

It felt like if Gabe and I went somewhere for dinner, it'd be a date—no matter what he wanted to call it.

Even though we were staying in, and I was cooking, I still styled my hair and "made myself pretty," as Laura liked to call it. But the evening would be casual, less date-like.

I can keep it superficial.

I knew I was full of shit.

That wasn't how I operated. I liked the guy. I wouldn't have taken him home if I hadn't. But I also knew there was zero chance of anything coming of it.

I should have taken him up on his offer last night to leave once we'd done the deed. But even as I thought it, I had to admit that I was glad I hadn't. It'd been nice to wake up next to him.

Now, I just needed to keep reminding myself that it wasn't going anywhere. I was living in fantasyland this weekend, but come Sunday, I'd be back to my real life. Juggling work, being a mom, and making ends meet.

Maybe meeting Gabe and not knowing who he was at first had been fortuitous. I never would have gone home with him if I'd known he was the guy I'd reamed out via text message earlier yesterday. And I doubt very much he would even have considered letting me make payments had I not actually ridden his dick.

And even though that wasn't why I'd done it, I guess some people would still think that it made me cheap.

Of course, to those people, going home with a man I'd just met would confirm it.

Hell, *I* was one of those people. I didn't do one-night stands.

And yet, I had.

I couldn't find it in me to regret it, though. I'd had the best sex of my life, and it just so happened that I might be able to figure out a way to keep my house in the process.

Win-win.

And I was going to continue telling myself that.

Chapter Nineteen

Gabe

Only two cars were in Flannigan's parking lot when I pulled in, a far cry from how crowded it'd been the night before.

I drove up next to a late-model silver Accord and put the truck in park before turning to face her, only to find her sporting an amused smile.

"What makes you think the Porsche isn't mine?"

It was my turn to smirk.

"Because it's my brother's."

"Oh! You don't think he's still out with Laura, do you?"

"The only reason his car would be here is if he's inside. He'd never leave his car unattended overnight. Not to mention, he doesn't do sleepovers."

Then again, neither did I. But here we were.

Gretchen nodded slowly, her mouth turned down like she disapproved. That made me tilt my head.

"I was kind of under the impression your friend was on the same page? She didn't think it'd be more, did she?"

"No, I think they had the same thing in mind. A good time, one night. Nothing more." Her smile was forced when she glanced over at me. "That's the unspoken agreement when you leave a bar with someone you just met, right? Or, in our case, we actually said it out loud."

And yet, I was having dinner with her later.

That was either going to turn out to be a very good idea, or a very, very bad one.

****

Gretchen

Gabe reached across the console for my hand and drew my fingertips to his lips.

"I'll see you tonight. I'll bring the dessert and wine. When you figure out what we're having, let me know so I know whether to bring red or white."

"I thought I'd make lasagna with meat sauce, if that's okay?"

I'd decided to revisit my lasagna recipe. I hadn't made it since I'd dropped it on Troy's office floor while he was balls deep in his assistant. Tonight seemed like a good time to try to pair new emotions with what used to be a favorite dish of mine to make.

"My mother's maiden name was Pomponio. I love lasagna—it was a Sunday night staple growing up."

So much for that.

Okay, maybe tonight wasn't the time to bring the lasagna back.

"An Italian mother's cooking? That's a lot of pressure to live up to. Maybe we should grill steaks or something."

"You can't dangle lasagna in front of me, then snatch it back. That's just mean."

That made me laugh out loud.

"Okay. Lasagna it is. I'll make garlic bread, too."

"My mouth is watering just thinking about dinner." He squeezed my hand before releasing it with a wink. "Among other things."

I bit my lower lip to suppress my smile as I reached for the door handle. He'd had his way with me more than a few times last night and this morning, and he still wanted more. How had I allowed myself to spend so much of my marriage feeling like chopped liver?

In Troy's defense, after Jake was born, I wasn't exactly the picture of sexy when he walked in the door at night. More often than not, I was exhausted and either in pajamas or yoga pants and an oversized t-shirt that probably had baby food, or worse, on it.

Of course, he didn't do anything to try and alleviate my exhaustion. I guess it was easier to just find a younger, peppier woman than man up to his responsibilities.

Water under the bridge, I reminded myself. I refused to give my ex any more of my energy, and that included my thoughts. My attention was on the sexy man who'd given me orgasms—plural, just like he'd promised.

"I'll see you tonight. Let me know if you need to change the time."

"I won't need to. I'll be there at six."

As I pulled on the handle, he said, "Hang on," and hopped out the driver's door to come around to the passenger side.

"Are you always this chivalrous?" I quipped as I took his hand and stepped down.

He pulled me closer and leaned down to utter in my ear, "I think I proved last night I can be far from chivalrous."

Boy, did he.

I whispered back, "For the record, I'm not complaining, either way."

I felt his chest vibrate with a chuckle.

"That's good to know, sweetheart."

Gabe's arms came around me, and I closed my eyes as I melted against him and returned the hug, allowing myself to relish how good it felt being held by him.

He planted a kiss to my temple before murmuring, "I'll see you tonight," then he released his hold on me.

Immediately, I missed his warmth, but only nodded my agreement while unzipping my purse to dig for the key fob in the side pocket.

When the door unlocked with a chirp, Gabe opened the driver's door and waited for me to get inside before gently closing it.

I pushed the start button, fastened my seatbelt, and gave him a small wave as I put the car in drive and pulled away.

Next stop: the grocery store to buy all the ingredients for my non-date dinner tonight.

****

Gabe

I watched her Honda until it disappeared, then fired off a text to Derrick before getting back in my truck.

Me: You at work?

He answered right away.

Derrick: Yeah, what's up?

Me: I just dropped Gretchen off in the parking lot so she could get her car, and I saw your Porsche.

Derrick: Come in, I'll make you lunch.

Me: We just finished with breakfast, but I'll come in for a minute.

Before I even reached the edge of the parking lot, he opened the front door and waited while I covered the distance to the entrance.

When I was a foot away, his face lit up with a shit-eating grin.

"I take it since you took her to breakfast, things went well last night between the two of you?"

"Very well."

"And I'm guessing she still doesn't know who you really are?"

I shot him a look as I walked past him into the bar. The place looked different with all the lights on.

"Come on, D. I know I can be an asshole, but you can't possibly think I'd be that shitty."

"Wait," he pulled the door shut and turned the lock. "So, she knows? Was this before or after you were naked?"

Walking toward the bar, I snarled, "*Before*, dickhead."

"And she still slept with you?"

"We reached an understanding."

"Which was?"

"Probably the same one you had with Laura."

He snickered. "Laura and I didn't do much talking."

I let out an exasperated breath as I sat down on a barstool.

"That neither of us are looking for a relationship. No expectations."

"But... what about your lawyer sending her an intent to sue?"

"We kind of set that aside for the night."

He looked at me incredulously. "You must be smoother than I give you credit for. I thought for sure she'd deck you if she found out."

"You and me both."

"So, you stayed the night? The *whole* night? *And* went to breakfast?"

"And I'm having dinner with her tonight after I deliver her cabinets."

A knowing grin spread across his face.

"Ahh, I get it. You decided to hypnotize her with your dick, so she'd agree to install her cabinets." He pointed to his temple as he went around the other side of the bar. "Smart."

"It's not like that."

Derrick pulled a frosty mug from a metal cabinet and placed it under the tap of my favorite beer.

"You sure about that? Because just last night you told me you were going to sue her since she refused to take delivery." He set the beer down in front of me, then continued, "And now after dicking her down, she suddenly agreed to have her cabinets delivered."

"Fuck off," I grumbled before taking a swig. "That's not why I slept with her."

He threw up his hands in front of his chest.

"No judgment, man. It sounds like a win-win. But be careful if you're going back for Round Two. You might give her the wrong idea. And whatever you do, do *not* spend the night again."

That's exactly what I was planning on doing. It had been nice waking up next to her. I hadn't had that in a really long time.

"Yeah, we'll see."

"Trust me on this, Gabe. I know what I'm talking about." He paused and cocked his head as he studied me. "Unless you don't really want *an understanding*."

He used finger quotes when he said, "an understanding."

"It's complicated. She's a client, and I slept with her. I can't just not call her or see her again. That doesn't scream "good business," ya know?" I took another drink before setting my mug down aggressively, causing some of the contents to spill onto the wooden surface. "Maverick would lose his shit if he found out."

"No, he wouldn't. He knows I sleep with customers all the time, and he never says a word."

"It's not the same, and you know it. A forty thousand cabinet installation is a lot different than losing a bar customer, who probably doesn't even pay for her drinks anyway, just because you ghosted her."

My little brother lifted my glass and wiped the bar before putting it back down.

"Well, for what it's worth. I thought Gretchen was your soulmate the first time I met her. And seeing you two together last night only solidified it. The fact you went home with her tells me you felt something, too."

"Yeah, horny."

"You sure that's all it was?"

No, I'm not sure.

"I like her, but neither of us are interested in anything more than a good time."

He shrugged. "If you say so."

"I do. Hell, her divorce was just finalized what, a month ago?"

"Yeah, but they separated way before that. The divorce being finalized was just a formality to the marriage ending."

"She wants kids."

"Once upon a time, you wanted more, too."

"And then I made peace with that not happening. Britt's eleven now. Starting over would be stupid."

"Why? You agreed that Mav's never been happier."

"Maverick doesn't have to go to work every day, either."

"What's that got to do with it?"

I don't know. It sounded like a good reason in my head.

"Just drop it, okay?" I needed to change the subject. "You still coming to Brayden's lacrosse game this afternoon?"

Thankfully Derrick let it go and responded with, "Hell yeah!"

I slid off my barstool. "Make sure you bring a camping chair or you're going to be sitting on the ground."

"They don't have bleachers?"

"No."

My brother's mouth turned down, prompting me to ask, "You don't have a camping chair?"

"I mean, I'm sure I do. Somewhere."

I rolled my eyes. Derrick was the quintessential baby of the family. Everyone always took care of him.

"I'll bring an extra one."

His face lit up with a smile, revealing his dimples, and I understood how he got laid all the damn time.

"Thanks, man. I appreciate it."

"Yeah, yeah." I headed toward the door, then stopped and turned around. "Game starts at three. Get there early or you'll be parking in the far lot and hoofing it to the field."

"Eh, a little walk wouldn't kill me."

Meaning he was going to be late.

"They're only twelve-minute quarters," I warned.

"I'll be there. I wouldn't let Brayden down."

When he said that, I knew I didn't have anything to worry about. The Mitchell men were known for being true to their word.

~~

As I set up the second camping chair, not far from Becky and Britt this time, I heard my daughter shriek, "Uncle Derrick!"

A small smile escaped my lips. The fucker was even early.

I turned to watch him swing Brittany around before setting her on the ground and pulling her in for a giant hug. The joy on her face brought joy to my heart.

Although we'd fought like wildcats growing up, I knew my brothers always had my back, and by default, my kids' backs. Even though Britt probably couldn't express it, I think she instinctively knew it, too.

When he released her from his embrace, she grabbed his hand and led him to where I was setting up the chairs, not letting him get a word in edgewise as she peppered him with questions.

"How have you been? Do you have a girlfriend yet? How's the new bar? Dad said he'd take me to see it, but only during lunch."

Derrick chuckled at her enthusiasm, and when she finally paused to take a breath, he responded.

"I've been great—really busy. I don't have time for a girlfriend. Technically, Flannigan's is a bar—slash—restaurant, but lunch would be the best time for you to come. It can get rowdy at night."

"But Dad said the nighttime is when you shine."

He looked over at me with a raised brow, and I shrugged unapologetically.

"It's not a lie."

"He's right," he conceded, then his mouth turned up in a wicked grin. "I do some of my best work as the night goes on."

Britt cocked her head as she looked up at him. "What do you mean?"

I openly smirked at him. "Yeah, Uncle Derrick. What do you mean?"

My brother didn't miss a beat.

"I gotta be on my toes because people like to fight once they've been drinking. I have to be sure anyone who's getting behind the wheel hasn't been overserved. By the end of the night, most of my staff are tired and they can start to drag, so sometimes I gotta pick up their slack. I have to do all that while making sure my customers are happy and want to come back."

Brittany's eyes grew big. "Wow, you are busy."

"You have no idea, kiddo. And now I have two locations that I have to keep running smoothly."

"Maybe when I'm in college, I can come work for you and help you out."

"Your job will be waiting."

Becky approached and scrunched up her nose disapprovingly. She'd obviously caught the last of their conversation and didn't like it.

"What job?"

"I'm going to help Uncle Derrick at Flannigan's when I go to college."

My ex-wife pursed her lips, and I silently willed her to let it go. It was seven years away, for fuck's sake.

But of course, she wouldn't.

"I don't think that's a good idea, baby."

Britt's voice got small as she asked, "Why not?"

Derrick's, on the other hand, got louder while he crossed his arms menacingly across his chest.

"Yeah, why not? My waitresses make damn good money, and their schedules are flexible around their class schedules. Plus, she'll be working for me, so she'll basically be able to do whatever she wants." He gave my ex a "fuck you" smile and continued. "I'm a big believer in nepotism."

Becky returned the "fuck you" smile.

"Well, that doesn't surprise me, considering..."

Both Derrick's and my eyebrows shot up, and she wisely didn't continue her thought.

This is where I would have dropped it and gone about ignoring her.

But not my baby brother.

"Considering what, Becky?"

She glanced at Brittany, who seemed enthralled watching the whole exchange.

"Nothing."

Now I was silently willing *Derrick* to drop it.

Alas...

"It's not nothing. You started to say something; please continue."

Becky had never been one not to take the bait. Things hadn't changed.

She planted her hand on her hip and jutted her jaw toward us.

"I was going to say I'm not surprised you're a big fan of nepotism, considering how you were able to afford the bar in the first place. You never would have gotten it off the ground without Maverick's help." She cast a glance in my direction, but since I hadn't said a word, it seemed she decided to spare me from her wrath.

At the moment.

Derrick shrugged, like he had no fucks to give on Becky's behalf. I knew I was going to be the one paying for that later, one way or another.

"What can I say, our family's awesome." He dropped his arms to his side and winked at Britt. "You're lucky you're a Mitchell. Don't ever forget that."

Becky's face grew even more sour while my daughter beamed up at my baby brother like he was a rockstar.

"I won't."

No sooner had they gone back to their chairs, when we heard, "Uncle D!" Brayden looked at us from the sidelines with a big smile. "You made it!"

Derrick raised his fist.

"Heck yeah! I wouldn't have missed it! Score a goal!"

"I'll try!"

My brother dropped into the chair I'd brought for him and cast me a sideways glance as he buffed his nails on his shirt.

"What can I say? They love their Uncle Derrick."

"Much as I wish I could, I can't even argue."

"I mean, what's not to love, right?"

"Yeah, sure."

His face fell and he leaned further back in his chair, taking obvious offense.

"What's that supposed to mean?"

"I'm sure there are plenty of women who could think of a few things."

He pawed at the air, as if dismissing my words.

"I never lie to anyone. They all know the score. It's not my fault if they choose to think they're going to be the exception. You know as well as I do that there are—"

"No exceptions," I supplied for him.

It was a matter in which we usually agreed.

Only, I found myself considering making a business exception for a hot seventh-grade English teacher.

And I couldn't help but think it wasn't just about business that I wanted to bend my rules.

"Hey, speaking of being lucky to have you for my brother..."

He narrowed his eyes at me. "I never said those words, exactly."

"Well, do you think you could help me load some cabinets into my truck after the game?"

Chapter Twenty

Gretchen

At five forty-five, I received a text from Gabe that he was on his way.

It was a small gesture, but I appreciated it. Troy had done that in the beginning of our marriage, but slowly got worse about it until he'd just stopped.

At the time, I'd chalked it up to him being so busy at work that he didn't even have time to break away to call me.

I couldn't count how many dinners I'd prepared that I'd ended up eating alone. By the time Jake was born, I didn't even count on Troy to be home for dinner and would be surprised the few times he did show up.

And I'd actually felt bad for him, taking care to reheat his plate for him when he finally arrived home. Even if I were already in bed, I'd get up to ensure he had a warm meal.

I'd been so stupid.

Troy had shown me all along who he was, but I hadn't wanted to believe it. I'd been so desperate for him to be the husband and father I'd made him out to be in my head that I ignored all the warning signs: late nights, showering the second he got home, moving his phone so I couldn't see who he was texting, constantly picking fights. I'd even chalked our lack of intimacy up as a byproduct of how much he was working to provide for his family. He did, however, find time to work out on a regular basis. I convinced myself it was so he'd be a healthy dad.

Even when my attorney told me that Troy wanted to relinquish custody, I'd made excuses for him, wanting—needing—for them to be true. How could he not want at least partial custody of our son? He fought me more for the mattress than he had our child.

I'd been so devastated when I realized he really didn't care about Jake that I would have let him walk away without having to pay child support. Fortunately, my attorney quickly put the kibosh on that.

In exchange for no alimony, I got the house—and the mortgage. Granted, it was at an enviable interest rate in today's market, and I had good equity, but making the monthly payment on my salary stretched me thin.

I was awarded child support, although it was the lowest amount Troy could get away with since I had sole custody of Jake. When my ex relinquished his parental rights, my heart hurt for my son that his dad wouldn't be in his life. But as time passed, I came to see it as a blessing. Troy was the last person my son should look to as an example on how to be a good man.

When it came time to sign divorce papers, I'd finally come to see my ex for what he really was.

I vowed the next time a man showed me his true colors, I wouldn't try to put a rosy spin on it. Which was why things between Gabe and I had to end tomorrow morning, after one more night of amazing sex. I'd tuck away the memories of our weekend together and bring them out for future use with my battery-operated boyfriend.

Gabe had flat-out told me he wasn't interested in more kids. Jake and I were a package deal, not to mention I wanted more kids. I had no grand illusions that Gabe would change his mind.

But hopefully he'd find a way to work with me about making payments on the cabinets.

A thought popped in my head.

What if he wanted the occasional hookup in exchange for making a deal?

The idea didn't repulse me like the little voice in my head—the one that sounded an awful lot like my mother's—said it should. In fact, thinking about it kind of turned me on.

What did that say about me?

That raising Jake in Lancastle is important, and I'll do what it takes to make that happen.

It was a weak justification for a kink that I hadn't been aware I had until last night.

And why should I have to justify it? I'm a modern, single woman. He's a virile, single man. We're consenting adults...

That annoying voice whispered, *I'm also a mom and teacher who's supposed to be a role model.*

Would something like that violate the morality clause in my contract?

Yeah, probably.

So much for that idea.

*****

Gabe

It did something to my solar plexus when I pulled up to her house and found her waiting outside with the garage doors open. She was dressed in those sexy black yoga pants that first caught my attention all those months ago, a teal-green hooded pullover that made her blonde hair stand out, and a bright smile.

It felt nice to have a woman happy to see me. At the end of our marriage, Becky hadn't even bothered to look up from her phone when I walked in the door. Gretchen had actually looked forward to seeing me.

Derrick and I had only been able to fit a little more than a third of her order in my truck bed, which I was okay with. It gave me a reason to have to come back at least two more times.

Rick had already wrapped the cabinets on Friday for transport because I'd told him one way or another, they needed to be gone by Tuesday. He was going to be beside himself when he found out he wouldn't have to deal with that.

I was more than happy to take over all communications from now on with the former Mrs. Wainwright.

After backing into her drive, I grabbed the work gloves off the front passenger seat and hopped out.

"Hi!" she said warmly.

I knew I was grinning like a fool when I invaded her space and uttered, "Hi yourself."

We stared at each other for a beat before she finally glanced at the back of my truck.

"Do you need any help?"

"Nah, Derrick should be here any sec. He's going to help me."

"That's sweet of him. Should we invite him to have dinner with us? There's plenty."

I glided an arm around her middle and slipped my hand under her shirt. Skimming my fingers along her bare back. I whispered in her ear, "Not a chance. I want you all to myself tonight."

I had to admit, the goosebumps on her skin and the way her body shuddered, made me feel like beating my chest. Fortunately, before my inner caveman could come out, I heard the exhaust from my brother's Porsche as he drove through the neighborhood.

"Here he comes now."

A few seconds later, Derrick pulled his Agate Grey Metallic Cayman into her driveway and got out.

"Hey, Gretch, long time, no see!"

She gave him a small wave. "Hi, Derrick. Good to see you."

"How's Laura feeling today?"

I shot him a look.

When I'd asked him to help me with Gretchen's cabinets, he'd whined that she was probably going to ask him about her friend and try to feel him out about seeing her again.

"It'll be so awkward!"

I'd assured him I'd run interference if that happened, yet here he was, two seconds out of his car, and already asking about her.

"Honestly, other than a text to make sure we each got home okay, I haven't really talked to her. She has a big project that she's working on for her boss, so she wasn't available to chat." The corner of her mouth lifted. "Why? How should she be feeling?"

The arrogant little shit puffed out his chest. "She was smiling when I left."

Gretchen giggled. "That's always a good sign. Better than scowling."

"Or worse, crying."

Been there, done that.

That had been the worst hookup in the history of hookups. But it had been a good lesson. Expectations up front.

Exactly like Gretchen and I had done last night. It wouldn't hurt to go over them again tonight at dinner.

More for myself than anything.

"I don't think you have to worry about that with Laura. The only reason she'd be crying is if your performance was lacking."

Derrick barked out a cocky laugh as he told her, "No problems there."

"That's what they all say."

Gretchen's sassiness surprised me, in a good way.

My brother gave her a chin lift and said, "Ask her if you don't believe me."

Her lips curled into an amused grin, like she knew she was getting under his skin and enjoyed it. "Don't worry, I will."

I could tell Derrick wanted her to do it right then, like his ego needed the reassurance. When she didn't move to retrieve her phone from her back pocket, he subtly rubbed the fingers together on his left hand while chewing the inside of his cheek—one of his tells that he didn't like something. He'd had it since he was a kid.

Derrick had to know I'd give him shit for acting like a little bitch if he pressed Gretchen to call her friend. I didn't think he wanted to know because he liked Laura any more than his other "special customers". I knew it was all about his pride.

Since he was doing me a solid by helping me unload the cabinets, I took pity on him and changed the subject.

"Let's get these in the garage. I know you need to get to Flannigan's."

****

Gretchen

After watching Gabe and Derrick unload the cabinets, I was convinced there was nothing hotter than a guy doing manual labor.

The way the Mitchell men's muscles moved under their Henleys as they lifted the cabinets off the truck bed made my heart race.

I wasn't attracted to Derrick, but I had to admit, he was hot. I could understand why Laura had wanted to take him home.

But that was nothing compared to what watching Gabe was doing to my lady parts. I was glad I'd already given myself permission to enjoy his company—and talents—one more night. Because even if I'd told myself it wasn't happening, once I watched him break a sweat, I would have caved in a heartbeat, provided he was interested. But after what he'd whispered in my ear when he got here, I knew we were on the same page: dinner, followed by a repeat of last night, then maybe breakfast.

After that, it was back to reality. I'd told my parents I'd pick up Jake by noon tomorrow.

Which meant I had one more night with the sexy man in my garage whose shirt was clinging to his muscles and making my mouth water.

The same man who held the fate of my future in my house in his hands.

I just wished he wasn't so dang *likeable*.

Chapter Twenty-One

Gabe

After the last cabinet was lined up neatly next to the others along her garage wall, Derrick took off his gloves and tapped them to my chest.

"Here you go. What time do you want to bring the rest over tomorrow?"

I took the gloves and glanced at Gretchen.

"Is ten too early to bring the next load?"

Her eyebrows shot up. "There's more?"

I couldn't help but laugh. "Yeah, sweetheart. Two more truckloads worth."

"Oh, wow." She studied the number of cabinets sitting in her garage before nodding her head. "Yeah, that makes sense."

Squeezing Derrick's shoulder, I told him, "Thanks for your help, little brother."

"That's what family's for. I'm sure I owe you."

I shook my head as we walked toward his car. "I'm not keeping score."

He grinned when he opened up the driver's door. "That's probably a good thing, since I'm sure you'd be winning."

Gretchen stood at my side, and I almost—*almost*—wrapped my arm around her, like we were a couple.

She'd silently watched us as we moved her cabinets, and I'd wished they weren't wrapped so she could see how beautiful they were. And maybe she'd envision them in her kitchen.

A reminder that I needed to talk to Maverick about a payment plan for her.

She called to Derrick, "Thank you. Do you want some water for the road?"

"I've got my water bottle in the car but thank you." He flashed a knowing grin at the two of us before sliding in the driver's seat. "You kids have a good night. I'll see you tomorrow at your shop at nine-thirty." He reached for the door handle, then paused before closing it. "Don't be late."

His door shut before I could respond I was never late.

Then again, he knew that.

We stood in the driveway and waved as Derrick drove away, then I reached for her hand.

"Come on, I want to show you how great your cabinets turned out."

****

Gretchen

I want you to show me how great you look naked.

I'm pretty sure I'd started ovulating as I watched Gabe move the cabinets from his truck bed to my garage floor and couldn't wait until we were alone.

It would probably be bad form to jump him right there with all the neighbors to see. I'd given them enough of an eyeful last night.

But I don't know how anyone could even fault me... the guy was freaking hot.

And as he removed the roll of foam wrapped around one of the cabinets, I could add "talented" to the list of all the things I liked about him.

I ran my hand along the top of one of the doors, and whispered, "Wow."

When I looked over at him, he was grinning from ear to ear.

"I told you they were beautiful." He stared down at the woodwork before adding wistfully, "I put a lot of blood, sweat, and tears into these babies."

"I can't believe you made these—by hand."

Gabe's laughter echoed off the garage walls.

"What did you think you were paying for, sweetheart?"

I shrugged.

"Honestly, I hadn't really thought about it. Troy wanted to update the kitchen—which you saw is perfectly fine. I thought he just wanted to have something to brag about. But gosh," I stepped back to admire Gabe's craftsmanship in full, "these are amazing. You're so talented."

I could tell he was uncomfortable with the compliment when he pretended to play coy by sticking his hands in his pockets and rocking back on his heels. "Aw, shucks. You flatter me."

I stared him in the eye when I replied, "I'd like to do a lot more than flatter you."

His eyebrows lifted and a slow smile spread across his face.

"Oh, yeah? Such as...?"

What was it about this man that made me feel so emboldened? Was it because I knew this was just temporary? Or was it the way he looked at me, like I was a goddess?

Maybe it was because this wasn't the real me. I wasn't a woman who had one-night stands or fantasized about striking a deal where I used my body as a means to get what I wanted.

No, I was a seventh-grade English teacher and a single mom to a two-year-old boy. In addition to a laundry list of responsibilities a mile long, I had stretch marks, cellulite, and was still carrying an extra ten pounds of baby weight that I hadn't been able to lose since Jake was born. I wasn't sexy. Far from it.

But damn, I sure felt like I was whenever Gabe looked at me.

I closed the distance between us and subtly cupped his cock over his jeans.

"Well, for starters, I'd like to wrap my lips around this."

Who am I?

I had never—in the history of ever—said something like that to a man before. Not to mention, I found that I really meant it.

"Be careful, darlin'," he warned. "Or you might find yourself bent over the tailgate of my truck."

While the idea had merit, I'd already given my neighbors a show last night. Far more PDA than they ever saw between me and Troy in the five years we'd lived there together. I'm sure the text thread between the stay-at-home moms' group was burning up.

Hopefully there weren't any pictures.

I took a step back while murmuring, "Hold that thought," then went to the keypad outside the garage and punched in the code so the third stall door lowered, leaving Gabe's truck on the other side. I approached him again and ran my fingertip down his chest, past his stomach, and circled the button on the fly of his jeans.

"Where were we?"

He pulled me closer while looking down at me with a smirk.

"That closed door's not going to save you, baby. Tailgate, work bench, stool… I'm not picky about what I bend you over."

Damn!

"That might be the hottest thing anyone's ever said to me."

His eyebrows went to his hairline.

"The hottest? Really? I must have been off my game last night if that's the hottest thing anyone's ever said to you."

"You're right—last night was super-hot. Let me clarify. That's the hottest thing anyone's ever said to me with my clothes on."

"We should rectify the *with your clothes on* part." Gabe lifted the hem of my sweatshirt with a wicked grin. "ASAP."

He pulled my shirt over my head and his gaze dropped to my boobs busting out of my lacy black bra.

The sexiest one I owned. And yeah, I'd had to fish around until I found it in the back of my drawer. I hadn't worn it since before Jake was born, but it still fit. Albeit, now there was a lot more of the twins spilling out, but Gabe didn't seem to mind.

"Fuuuck," he groaned as he looked down at my chest. "You are perfect." Grazing my stiff nipples over the fabric with his thumbs, he continued, "I want to fucking devour you."

I could only form a small whimper in reply.

The corner of his mouth turned up, and he offered me a wink.

"Stick with me, sweetheart. That's just the tip of the iceberg of my dirty-talking repertoire."

If only I could stick with you. And not just for your naughty, talented mouth.

But that wasn't in the cards for us.

It didn't mean I wasn't going to enjoy the hell out of our last night together though.

****

Gabe

I really liked this woman.

Fucking Derrick was going to have a field day when he found out he was right. She was perfect for me.

Chapter Twenty-Two

Gretchen

I shivered as Gabe openly leered at me, but I wasn't sure if it was from my own desire or because I was chilly.

The weather in Massachusetts had started to warm up, but it hadn't reached *run around outside in your underwear* temperatures. And I was standing in the garage in my bra, with the main door wide open.

While technically no one could see me, since we were in the third stall, all it would take for a neighbor to catch us would be for him or her to come around the corner.

Something I found thrillingly erotic.

My god, what has gotten into me?

I stared into the sexy-as-sin man's cobalt-blue eyes and had to suppress a giggle when I concluded it wasn't *what*, but *who* had gotten into me.

He lowered his mouth to mine, and the only thing I could focus on was how soft his lips were, and how safe I felt when he pulled my body tight against his and wrapped me in his warmth.

As I basked in his embrace, it was all I could do to keep from sighing with contentment.

Instead, I settled for wantonly rubbing against him.

Purely to try and steal his body heat, not because I was slutty.

Although I had to admit, it was hard to argue how virtuous I was when I was half-naked from the waist up while making out in my garage with a man I met less than twenty-four hours ago.

But damn could this man kiss!

That was also on the list of the things I liked about him.

I shivered again and nestled closer to him, and this time, I knew it was from the cold. Gabe noticed because he rubbed his hands up and down my bare arms and whispered, "Let's go inside, sweetheart."

"Good idea."

He swooped down and picked up my pullover, but instead of handing it to me, he draped it over his arm.

"You can have this back when I'm done with you."

And....my toes just curled.

****

Gabe

It was déjà vu when we walked into her house, and I pressed her against the door and captured her lips with mine. And just like last night, she clung to me while making the cutest noises.

Maybe it was because before meeting Gretchen, I hadn't had sex in a while, but I could not get enough of her. Her scent, her taste, the little sounds she made... they all had me rock hard.

I wanted to feel her legs wrapped around me as I drove into her heat until her pussy clamped around my cock when she came. Then I wanted to explode inside her.

I couldn't even wait to make it to her bedroom to have her, so I pushed aside a bin of hats and scarves on the counter in her mud room and lifted her up onto it. It wasn't a workbench, and she wasn't bent over, but my dick didn't care.

When had I reverted back to a seventeen-year-old teenager?

Beep! Beep! Beep!

The blaring sound of a smoke alarm echoed off the walls, followed by Gretchen's exclamation of "Oh shit!" as she leapt to her feet and flung open the door that led to her kitchen.

Smoke billowed from her oven when she opened the door, pulled a casserole dish out, and promptly took it out the slider off the family room while I quieted the smoke alarm.

The scene was a funny reminder that I was, indeed, not seventeen anymore.

Burnt dinner aside, she looked like a domestic goddess wearing nothing but her bra and yoga pants while donning two oven mitts on her hands.

She came back inside with her head hung low and her shoulders sagged in defeat.

"My lasagna is jinxed."

I pulled her into an embrace and kissed her hair.

"Aw, it's okay, sweetheart. We'll go out to eat. And I still have dessert and wine in my truck."

She pulled back to look me in the eye.

"No, you don't understand. My lasagna is cursed. I'm never going to be able to make it again, and I really liked making it."

"*Never?*"

That seemed a little extreme; definitely dramatic. I'd divorced drama and had no interest in ever being involved with it again. Maybe our weekend-only deal was a good thing after all.

I studied her face, hoping to find a grin or something to tell me she was kidding, but I could tell by her expression that she was serious.

"Because you burned it?"

"No. Well, sort of. Burning it tonight only confirmed it. I'd also taken it to my ex's office to surprise him with dinner when I found him…" Her voice got softer. "You know."

Okay, her reaction made a little more sense now.

"Well, technically this time, it's my fault. I distracted you. So, I think you should try it one more time before deciding it's cursed."

And you should invite me over when you do.

Of course, I kept that to myself, but I couldn't help but think we were on the same wavelength when she offered me a weak smile, and replied, "Yeah, maybe."

****

Gretchen

I was suddenly very aware of my state of undress and realized I'd gone out in my backyard in my skimpy, see-through bra when I put the smelly, burnt lasagna on the pony wall of the patio.

My neighbors had to be beside themselves.

Yet, I didn't have it in me to give a damn. It wasn't like this was going to be a regular occurrence. The neighborhood gossip would blow over soon enough when there were no new developments.

Gabe handed me my hooded shirt.

"Come on, let's go have dinner."

I took the offered pullover but didn't move to put it on.

"I probably should go change if we're going to go out."

While I'd been careful to curl my hair and make sure my makeup was on point, I'd purposefully worn yoga pants and a hoodie to give the impression this wasn't a date. But if he wanted to go out in public, I needed to at least put on a pair of jeans and a sweater.

He shook his head.

"You look beautiful in what you have on. Besides, I'm not exactly dressed to go anywhere fancy. How about if we grab a pizza at Caruso's?"

Caruso's was pretty low-key. Plus, they served alcohol, and I could use a drink at the moment.

"That sounds perfect."

Chapter Twenty-Three

Gabe

"Mrs. Wainwright!" the teenage boy behind the counter at Caruso's called when we walked in.

I fucking hated hearing her called that.

It took her a second, but Gretchen replied, "Landon?" with a bright smile.

He came around to give her a big hug, and she laughed when she looked up at him.

"You've gotten so tall!"

"I hit my growth spurt the summer before my freshman year like you said I would."

"I told you that you just needed to be patient."

He gave her a sheepish grin. "It's hard to be patient when your friends are all towering over you."

"Well, look at you now."

"Yep. I'm even the captain of my baseball team. You should come watch us play sometime."

"I would love to."

"Great! Our schedule is online." He looked over at me and stuck out his hand. "You must be Mr. Wainwright."

Oh hell no.

I took his offered hand, but before I could even correct him, Gretchen intervened.

"No. This is Mr. Mitchell. Um, I'm divorced now."

He looked between the two of us with wide eyes. "Oh, gosh. I'm sorry."

I didn't know if he was saying he was sorry because she was divorced or because he got it wrong.

"Gabe Mitchell, nice to meet you."

"Nice to meet you, too, sir." He cast a sideways glance at Gretchen. "You're a lucky man. Mrs. Wain— er, *Ms.* Wainwright is the best." He stole another look at his former teacher, and I recognized there was more than admiration on the young man's face.

And I didn't like it one bit.

Possessively putting my arm around her with a grin, I replied, "She is indeed."

****

Gretchen

Gabe and I ordered, then sat in a corner booth as we waited for our pizza and beer.

The pitcher of Modelo arrived first, and after Gabe poured us each a glass, he held his drink up and offered a toast.

"To unexpected surprises. When I woke up yesterday, I would have never imagined I'd be spending my weekend with such an amazing, beautiful woman."

"To unexpected surprises," I murmured and clinked my mug against his.

I took a sip of the ice-cold beer, then set it on the scratched, wooden table.

"When I got your lawyer's letter yesterday, I never in a million years would have thought I'd spend the weekend with *you.*"

He let out a low chuckle. "You didn't imagine you'd be getting naked with the 'infuriating Jerk of the Year'?"

"After getting that letter? No, I had a few ideas what I wanted to do to you and getting naked was nowhere on the list."

"I'm sorry about that. I needed to get your attention, since you wouldn't respond to Rick."

I was still harboring a little resentment with how aggressive the letter had been.

"There are other ways you could have gone about it, you know."

"True, but to be fair, you wouldn't return Rick's calls, and I needed the cabinets out of the shop to make room for a lumber shipment I have coming on Tuesday."

"And they're almost out. No lawsuit necessary."

He seemed unfazed by my sassy response and raised his glass again.

"Like I said, to unexpected surprises."

"Hopefully, that will also include a payment plan I can afford."

Gabe set his glass on the table without taking a pull.

"I'll talk to Maverick on Monday, I promise. But for tonight, let's forget about the cabinets and enjoy our time together."

"You're right. Tomorrow will be here before we know it, and it'll be back to reality."

His voice was soft when he replied, "Yeah."

A tiny part of me wanted him to ask for more than the weekend with me.

I knew that was my pride rearing its ugly head. We were at two different stages in life, and he'd already told me he didn't want more kids. But my ego didn't care. I wanted him to want me for longer than the weekend.

The sex had been incredible, but it had seemed like it was deeper than that. I mean, we were out to dinner and not naked in bed together. Granted, it was the local pizza place, but still. It felt like Gabe was interested in more than just getting between my legs.

It doesn't matter!

I'd purposefully not mentioned Jake and had even put his high chair in the pantry when I got home from breakfast. It'd been tucked in the corner and the second I noticed it as we were leaving, I'd ushered him out the door. Not because I was ashamed of my son, but I didn't see the point of bringing him up when I knew my fling with Gabe had an expiration date of tomorrow morning. What would be the point of putting a damper on things tonight?

He casually put his arm along the back of his chair.

"So, tell me more about you. Did you grow up in Lancastle?"

****

Gabe

We finished the pizza and beer, then even shared a slice of cheesecake, laughing and talking the entire time, then opted for a pitcher of soda as we continued getting to know each other better.

Which may have been a mistake because I found I liked her even more than I had last night. She was witty, insightful, and just a tad nerdy.

And hot as fuck without even trying to be.

The next thing I knew, the staff were putting the chairs on the tables, and I looked around to realize we were the only customers left in the place.

Gretchen seemed equally surprised because she looked at her watch and gasped, "Oh my gosh! How did it get so late?"

With a wink, I replied, "We were having so much fun, we lost track of time." I lowered my voice as I glanced around again. "We should probably go before they throw us out."

She let out a small giggle. "Good idea."

I stood and offered her my hand to help her out of the booth and didn't let go once she was on her feet.

It just felt *right* to hold her hand as we walked to my truck.

I knew one thing for certain. I didn't give a damn what my brother had said about not spending another night with her. The only thing that could keep me out of her bed tonight was if she told me I wasn't welcome.

But the way she wrapped her other hand around my arm and leaned her head on my shoulder, I wasn't worried.

Chapter Twenty-Four

Gabe

"Tonight was a lot of fun."

I glanced over at Gretchen in the passenger seat and nodded my head.

"I can't remember when I had a better time."

I was just about to suggest we do it again, when she murmured, "It's probably because there wasn't any pressure, since we know this isn't going anywhere after tomorrow."

Self-preservation told me to agree and drop it, but I didn't mind feeling vulnerable with this woman.

"What if it did go somewhere after tomorrow?"

She pulled her neck back like my question took her off guard.

"What do you mean?"

Her suspicious tone was not what I expected, but I pushed forward, albeit a little more cautiously than I would have had her reaction been more welcoming.

I shrugged like I wasn't vested in her reply.

"I don't know. Maybe we could do this again, on a regular basis."

"Like, date? *Each other*?"

Yeah, each other. Who the fuck else would I be talking about?

Before I could find a polite way to phrase that so I could say it out loud, she continued, shaking her head as she did.

"We agreed this was just for the weekend. You're not looking for a relationship. You said so yourself."

"That was before I—"

She cut me off.

"I don't think it's a good idea."

I hated sounding needy, but I had to ask.

"Why not?"

"We just—we want different things, and I know I'd end up heartbroken in the end. I have this big house that I love, and I want to fill it with kids. You think your brother's a fool for having a baby at his age and said it'd be lunacy to start over now. Neither of us is wrong, but we're obviously not compatible."

Fuck.

Of course she wanted kids. She was a teacher for chrissakes. Like her friend, Laura pointed out, it wasn't exactly like she was raking in the money. She had to be doing it because she loved children. It made sense she'd want her own.

I pulled into her drive and put the truck in park before turning to face her.

"You're right. I've just had such a great time with you that I didn't want it to end."

Since she hadn't opened her garage for me tonight, I was guessing that our time together was ending sooner rather than I'd hoped.

Gretchen reached across the console and stroked my arm with a seductive smile.

Her touch made my cock jump, and not for the first time tonight. I'd had a semi the entire time we'd been at the restaurant. Every time she threw her head back and laughed, my dick would move. Or when she said something that made me laugh. Or when she'd smile warmly at the staff.

It was like I was addicted to her, and sadly, I was going to have to break that addiction.

Her sultry voice purred, "Maybe you should follow your own advice. Let's forget about everything else and enjoy our time together tonight."

It took me less than a nanosecond to decide, I'd worry about going cold turkey tomorrow.

****

Gretchen

My mother was right; be careful what you wish for.

I'd thought I'd wanted him to ask for more than the weekend with me. But then he did, and I completely panicked.

Not because I didn't want to see him again, but because I *did*, and now I had to make a decision. Stick to our original agreement or keep seeing him and end up heartbroken. I knew if we continued dating, I could easily fall in love with him, and that would not end well for me; either because we'd eventually break up, or because I'd stay with him and give up my dream of having more kids.

Knowing he wanted more from me complicated everything.

I needed to stick to this being a weekend-only fling. Emphasis on *weekend*—which technically meant I had until tomorrow.

I needed to lighten the mood, so I softly ran my fingertips along his arm.

"Maybe you should follow your own advice. Let's forget about everything else and enjoy our time together tonight."

He stared at me for a beat before he traced the backs of his fingers along my jawline and whispered, "Yeah, let's do that," then lowered his mouth and captured my lips with his.

I tried to memorize everything about that moment. How soft his lips felt, the piney fragrance of his cologne, the possessive way his fingers tangled in my hair to pull me closer... I wanted to climb into his lap and fuck him right there in the front seat of his truck.

Then I remembered where we were—in my driveway, for all the neighborhood to see.

It was as if he read my mind when he murmured, "Let's go inside so I can do all the dirty things to you that I'm fantasizing about without your neighbors watching."

"Good idea."

Chapter Twenty-Five

Gabe

I was disappointed she wasn't on board with us continuing to see each other, but when she pulled my cock between her lips and took me deep in her mouth, I decided that was a good consolation prize.

"Fuuuck, sweetheart, that feels so good," I moaned as I reached for her hair to slow her pace, otherwise I was going to be spurting down her throat in thirty seconds.

She looked up at me when she pulled her mouth off my dick and replaced it with her hand so she could sass, "That's kind of what I was going for."

Using her hair as a handle, I steered her face back to my shaft until the tip touched her lips.

"No need to stop, baby."

Her grin was wicked.

"Good."

Then, without warning, she engulfed my cock until the tip bobbed against the back of her throat.

My hips jerked, and my hold on her hair tightened.

"You're not playing fair, sweetheart."

She slurped off my shaft long enough to mutter, "So?" before resuming her oral attention.

I had no reply, so I just watched, mesmerized, as she moved her mouth up and down on my cock.

Big mistake.

She looked like a siren with my dick in her mouth, and my balls drew up as my spine started to tingle.

With a groan, I pressed on her shoulder and pulled out.

Her eyes were wide when she looked up at me.

"Did I hurt you?"

"Fuck no." I tugged on her arm to haul her against me. "Just the opposite, darlin', and there's no way I'm coming before you do."

A small smile escaped her lips.

"Yes, that would be tragic."

"It would be." My hands skimmed up her sides until I cupped her tits in both palms. "Humor me and my fragile male ego."

I wasn't sure she was aware she subtly pressed against my touch.

"I mean, if there's an orgasm in it for me, who am I to complain?"

Tweaking her right nipple, I corrected her. "We've had this discussion before, darlin'. Orgasmssss, plural."

****

Gretchen

I'd had more orgasms in the last thirty-six hours than I'd probably had in the last three years of my marriage. Well, at least with a partner.

And I was not complaining.

Whoever ended up with Gabe was going to be a lucky woman.

I wondered what she would be like, and I felt a pang of jealousy toward this fictitious woman.

Would he be opposed to a woman who already had kids who were older than his kids, or at least their age?

It was on the tip of my tongue to ask as we lay snuggled together in the dark, but then I realized, what did it matter? So, I opted to wiggle closer to his side instead.

I fell asleep wishing things could be different between us, even though I knew that was impossible.

****

Gabe

While I listened to Gretchen's breathing even out, I kissed her hair and pulled her closer to bask in our post-coital glow.

But as I lay there in the dark, a sudden sadness washed over me.

I was holding the most beautiful, fascinating woman I'd probably ever met, and I wouldn't be seeing her again after tomorrow morning. At least not in the capacity that I wanted.

She was right; we weren't compatible.

And that sucked.

Chapter Twenty-Six

Gretchen

I woke up in the morning to Gabe's arm still around my waist and his bare chest nestled against my back. It was like I was safe and cozy in a little Gabe cocoon.

I found myself wondering what it would have been like if I'd married Gabe instead of Troy. My kids would have an involved dad, and I would have had an attentive partner—how wonderful would that be?

While I had no doubt I wouldn't be divorced had that happened, I wouldn't have had Jake either, and I wouldn't trade that little guy for anything. The shitty marriage to Troy had been worth it because I'd gotten my son out of it.

Thoughts of Jake filled my mind, and I realized that as much as I'd enjoyed living the life of a single bachelorette this weekend, I missed my munchkin. Sticky fingers, potty training battles, and all.

I was sad my time with Gabe was coming to an end, but it was time to get back to the real world and all the responsibilities that came with that.

When I tried to move Gabe's hand and slip out of bed, he tightened his embrace while murmuring in my ear, "Let me hold you just a little while longer."

I mean, who was I to argue?

Rolling over, I burrowed my face into his chest and took a deep breath, filling my olfactory senses with his masculine scent. I hoped two days in my bed would be enough time for it to linger. If I couldn't have him, at least I could hug a pillow at night that smelled like him. Maybe I'd ask him what cologne he used and spritz the pillowcase when it started to wear off.

How lame was that?

And... this is why I'm probably going to be alone for the rest of my life.

I wiggled closer to him and let out a sigh of contentment when he hugged me tight. Listening to his heartbeat, I couldn't help but think, *I'm not alone now.*

And in the moment, that was enough.

****

Gabe

Waking up with Gretchen in my arms was the perfect way to start my day.

I could get used to this.

Then my realistic side lambasted my romantic one.

Not gonna happen, sucker. Once you get out of this bed, you're never coming back.

Which was probably why I didn't let her go when she tried to get up.

"Let me hold you just a little while longer."

To my relief, she turned over and melted into me.

Maybe we can stay in bed all day.

"What time are you meeting Derrick?"

The sound of sad trombones played in my head.

So much for that idea.

"Nine-thirty."

"You probably better get going, then."

"Why? What time is—" I glanced at my watch and exclaimed, "Oh shit!" as I sat up with a start. "I never sleep this late!"

"Well," she giggled. "We were up pretty late. *Again.* Two late nights in a row takes its toll."

My left knee creaked when I stood up and glanced around for my clothes.

"Especially on an old man like me."

She gave me a soft smile. "You're not that old. You're only eight years older than I am."

For what we each wanted in our lives, those eight years might as well have been decades. In seven years, both my kids would be adults, while if she got pregnant tomorrow, her child might be starting kindergarten or first grade.

"Things look a lot different when you're pushing forty than when you just turned thirty. You'll see."

She sat up in bed with the covers tucked under her armpits while she watched me yank my underwear and jeans on.

"My goodness, you gonna tell me about your tour in 'Nam, too, Gramps? Yell at the kids to get off your lawn? Or do you not care who walks on the grass at the retirement home?""

"Har har. You're hilarious."

After I buttoned my jeans, I couldn't help but pause and take in the sight of her makeup-free face and mussed hair from a combination of sleep and being properly fucked.

I didn't want this to be the end.

Chapter Twenty-Seven

Gabe

"And why can't you keep seeing her?" Derrick asked as we walked the first cabinet into the bed of my truck.

As we set it down, I grunted, "Because I like her."

My little brother stood up straight and rolled his eyes. "Yeah, that makes sense."

"I can't give her what she wants."

"What the fuck are you talking about?"

I needed to keep moving, like that would keep me from thinking too much, and headed back toward the shop for the next cupboard.

"She's still young. She wants babies."

"So? Are you shooting blanks or something? Did you get snipped?"

"No!"

We squatted on either side of the cabinet and lifted at the same time.

"So, I don't understand the problem."

"The problem is, I'm not Maverick. I don't want any more kids."

"Well, to be fair, I don't think Maverick *wanted* another one, either."

"That's true. But when it happened, he saw it as a blessing and a second chance. I don't know if I'd feel that way."

"Maybe you need to change your mindset. I saw you two together, Gabe. There's definitely something there. I'd hate for you not to pursue it. It wasn't that long ago that you wanted more kids, too."

"That ship sailed."

We set the cabinet next to the first one, and I started back to the shop. Derrick, however, didn't move past the tailgate.

"Is this about Bodhi?"

Hearing my dead son's name out loud felt like a blow to the stomach, and I froze in my tracks.

Without turning around, I stated flatly, "No."

"You sure about that?"

My fists clenched, and I turned to glare at my brother. His sad expression mirrored how I felt whenever I thought of Bodhi, so I consciously relaxed my fingers.

I still didn't want to talk about it, though.

"It's not about him. I just don't want more kids, okay?"

"Why not? You always wanted a big family. Bodhi's death is the only thing that makes sense about why you wouldn't want another one. Or two."

I'd never told anyone why Becky and I never had more children. It didn't take a psych degree to figure out that losing our son had put a serious strain on our marriage. The divorce two years after Bodhi's death said all that needed to be said; there was no need to discuss all the reasons behind our failed relationship.

Maybe now was a good time to be more forthcoming.

"We never had any more because Becky had her tubes tied without telling me. She let me go a whole year thinking we were still trying."

Derrick sagged against the tailgate.

"You're kidding me. Why would she do that?"

I found I needed the support of the truck's steel frame, too, and moved to stand by him.

"She said she couldn't bear the thought of losing another child, so she didn't want to risk bringing another one into the world."

"I mean, I get it. But why wouldn't she talk to you about it first?"

I shrugged.

"We were both grief-stricken and dealing with his death in our own way. In other words, not communicating, so it made grieving together impossible. Unfortunately, I didn't realize she blamed me for the accident until we were getting divorced."

"*She what*? How was it your fault? You weren't even in the car!"

"Yeah," I said softly as I thought back to that horrible night. "But I was supposed to be the one to pick him up from daycare. Since I ended up having to work late, I asked her sister to get him. Sienna had only had her license for about a year, so she wasn't an experienced driver and expressed her apprehension about taking Bodhi in the car with her."

"Still not seeing how the accident was your fault."

"I assured her it would be fine, but suggested she take the route she did. It had less traffic, so I thought it'd be safer." My voice trailed off. "Obviously, it wasn't."

I could still hear Sienna sobbing, "I'm so sorry!" when I'd rushed into the emergency room.

It hadn't even been her fault. The other driver hadn't yielded when Sienna had a green light, and he made a left hand turn into her rear passenger door. Right where Bodhi's car seat was.

My son would be nine years old today if he hadn't died in the ambulance on the way to the hospital seven years ago.

Unbeknownst to me, my ex-wife had her tubes tied five months later, all while taking a pregnancy test every month for a year and pretending to be disappointed when it came back negative.

That's not exactly something a relationship bounces back from, even if we hadn't buried our youngest.

"Fuck, Gabe. I had no idea. I'm so sorry."

"The sadder thing is, after lots of therapy, I understand why Becky did what she did. She was probably right. How could we have another child after losing our son? I just wish she would have gone about it differently, ya know? It took a while to make peace with not having more kids, but it turned out to be the right decision. I don't think I could alter course again; it'd be too hard."

"I still think Gretchen's your soulmate."

I barked out a laugh.

"Isn't that something *I'm* supposed to know, not you?"

"I can't explain it... from the moment I met her, I thought she was perfect for you."

Yeah, me too.

"Maybe we'll run into each other again in the future when our timing is right."

"Are you sure the timing isn't right now?"

A picture of her this morning as she laid in bed watching me get dressed popped in my head.

"I'm not sure about anything, anymore, D."

Chapter Twenty-Eight

Gretchen

I'd just gotten dressed and was in the middle of brushing my wet hair when my phone rang.

My face broke into a big smile, because I knew exactly who it was: Jake.

Well, it'd be my mom first, then she'd hand the phone to my little man.

I glanced at the caller ID to confirm my suspicions were correct, then answered with a cheerful, "Hey, Mom!"

"Hi, sweetie. How was your night? I hope you were able to relax a little."

Looking at my bed that still needed to be made and thinking about how tangled Gabe and I made the sheets last night, I suppressed a giggle.

"I did, thanks. How was Jake?"

I'd talked to him yesterday. Well, as much as one could talk to a two-year-old over the phone, and he seemed happy. He loved going to my parents' house because he usually had at least three or four people doting on him, depending on which of my siblings were visiting.

"He slept well but he was a little fussy this morning. I think he misses his mama."

"You're just saying that to make me feel better. We both know he won't want to leave when I pick him up later."

"No, he really was grumpy when he got up this morning. Your dad and I are going to run some errands, so we can just bring him by later. Save you a trip."

Maybe he really had been grumpy.

"Thanks, Mom. I appreciate that."

"Of course, honey. Do you want to talk to Jake?"

"Sure."

"Let me see if I can wrangle him. He's helping his *daideó* in the garage."

"Oh, don't bother him. I'm sure he's having fun. I'll see him soon enough."

"Okay, we'll see you later."

"Bye!"

As soon as I disconnected the call, the mom guilt took over.

I'd been so wrapped up in Gabe—a man I wasn't even dating—I hadn't done any housework this weekend, not even laundry, and I hadn't graded my students' essays that I'd brought home. That meant I'd be doing all that tonight when I should be spending time with my son.

Throwing my still-damp hair into a ponytail, I dashed into Jake's room, grabbed the laundry hamper in his closet to start a load of his clothes, then made quick work of cleaning the kitchen before starting the robot vacuum. If I restricted the area it stayed in, I could mop before my kiddo arrived home.

I paused before pulling his high chair from the pantry.

Should I have told Gabe about Jake?

As seemed to be the norm lately, I found myself second-guessing my decision.

Since we aren't seeing each other again after today, it doesn't matter.

My stomach still twinged, like my gut wasn't on board with my decision.

I knew Gabe was coming back with more cabinets, and I wasn't sure if he'd come back inside, so I decided to leave the chair where it was. I reasoned it'd be easier to mop if it was out of the way.

Yep. That's why I was leaving it in the pantry. Easier mopping.

****

Gabe

Gretchen left the third stall garage door open, but she wasn't outside when I pulled up with another load of her cabinets. It was chillier today than it had been yesterday, so I understood why she'd still be inside.

I paused at the door leading to her house. Should I knock or walk in and announce myself?

The woman sat on my face less than twelve hours ago, we're way past knocking on her door.

At least, when she's expecting me.

Besides, if she were still upstairs, she probably wouldn't hear me knocking anyway.

I rapped on the wood as I opened the door and loudly called out, "Knock knock!"

She poked her head around the corner, and I noticed a bucket on the floor.

"Hey! You're back! I'll be out in a sec, I'm just finishing mopping the kitchen."

"Take your time. I just wanted to let you know I was here. Derrick should be here any minute; he was going to stop and get a cup of coffee first."

When Derrick had told me he was swinging by Starbucks on his way to Gretchen's, I'd groaned, "God, I'm an asshole. You're doing me a favor; I should have thought to bring you one."

"Eh, how could you know I hadn't already stopped?"

"I'll buy you lunch."

He shook his head as he sat in the driver's seat of his Cayman. "I gotta get to work after this. We've got a delivery coming."

"Raincheck?"

"You know it."

But that meant we wouldn't get all the cabinets delivered today. Which I wasn't exactly mad about.

Seeing Gretchen doing something as mundane as mopping the floor made me smile. I hoped to catch more of those moments.

I paused with my hand on the doorknob leading to her garage.

"So, I'm going to have to bring the final delivery over tomorrow, if that's okay? Derrick has to get to work after we get these unloaded."

"Oh, um, sure? I can give you the garage code."

No, that's not going to work.

"Or I could just come by after work. Maybe we could grab dinner?"

She offered me a sad smile.

"Gabe... we talked about this."

"It's just dinner. You gotta eat, right?"

She stared at me for a beat then her shoulders dropped as she let out a sigh.

"There's something I haven't told you..."

That sounded ominous, and I held my breath as I waited for her to continue.

I was startled by a loud knock at the door behind me.

When I opened the door, Derrick was wearing a big grin, with a tray of coffees in his hand, and he gleefully proclaimed, "Caffeine delivery!"

He offered a cup to Gretchen, spurring her to come into the mud room.

"Oh my god, thank you!" She closed her eyes as she took a long sip. "So good."

Her eyes flew open, and she continued, "I probably should be the one buying *you* coffee."

Derrick grinned at me. "I'm racking up coffee IOUs today."

"And don't worry," I told her. "He *will* collect."

"I will gladly pay up."

My little brother's dimple was on full display when he replied, "It's a date."

Before I could correct him that, no, it wasn't a date; there would be no date between him and Gretchen—ever, the little shit brought the lid to his mouth, and walked out the door, still wearing a grin.

I made a point of looking at the garage where Derrick had disappeared to, before murmuring, "Can we talk more once he leaves?"

"Yeah, of course."

But as I joined my brother outside, I couldn't help but wonder, what hadn't Gretchen told me?

"Everything okay?" Derrick asked when I met him at the back of the truck and put the tailgate down.

"Yeah, she just said something cryptic, and I'm trying to figure out what it meant."

"What'd she say?"

"That there was something she hadn't told me."

"Uh oh. You don't think she's still married, do you?"

"No," I blurted out, then paused. "I mean, I don't think so. That's been the whole premise behind why she didn't want the cupboards—she got divorced and can't afford them. Plus, her ex wanted them, not her."

"Yeah, and even Laura said she was divorced."

We lifted the first cabinet, and my little brother asked, "What do you think it is?"

"For the life of me, I don't have any idea."

Chapter Twenty-Nine

Gretchen

I felt a little better about my parenting skills when I finished mopping the kitchen, put Jake's clothes in the dryer, and after emptying the robot vacuum, let it go through the rest of the house.

At least the floors would be clean when my toddler half-crawled, half-walked around on them this week, and he'd have clean clothes to wear to daycare.

I could work on grading essays after I put him to bed.

Now that my mom guilt was somewhat assuaged, I only had the Gabe guilt.

I don't have anything to feel guilty about, I reminded myself for the fiftieth time. *I don't owe him anything.*

Yet, I couldn't help but feel after what we shared this weekend, I kind of did. Even though we weren't going to be dating anymore, I at least owed him honesty.

Not that I'd been dishonest.

I mean, you kind of were, my conscience whispered. *Omitting the truth is no better than lying.*

"There's a lot of things I didn't tell him. It doesn't mean I was hiding it from him," I grumbled out loud. "There was no need to tell him about Jake before now."

Once Derrick left, I'd tell Gabe I had a son, and he'd agree we shouldn't see each other.

Easy peasy.

Except, why did that sound so unappealing?

****

Gabe

We only had one more cabinet to unload when Gretchen stepped into the garage wearing a pair of leggings she'd tucked into a pair of fuzzy pull-on boots and a sweatshirt with the same logo as the one I'd bought Britt a few weeks ago. Her hair was still in a ponytail, and she didn't have a stitch of makeup on. And when she smiled at me, I thought she was the most beautiful woman I'd ever seen.

"Oh, you've got it bad," Derrick murmured as we hoisted a cupboard and walked it toward the growing collection of wrapped cabinets in her third stall.

My back was to her, so I mumbled softly so she couldn't hear as she walked toward us, "It doesn't matter. Our timing isn't right."

My asshole brother chuckled. "Yeah, keep telling yourself that, big guy."

Her phone rang so I was able to grumble through gritted teeth, "Fuck off," while she was preoccupied answering the call.

We set the cabinet down as her voice echoed off the cement floors, "*Right now?*"

I glanced at Derrick with furrowed brows. He was obviously as concerned as I was, because he made no move toward his car.

"No, no. I'm here. Um, just the men are here delivering my kitchen cabinets."

Gretchen nervously looked over at us before continuing. "I'll explain when you get here."

Another pause.

"It's fine. I'll see you in a minute."

She ended the call, put the phone in the front pocket of her hoodie, and took a deep breath before turning to face me directly.

"Um, remember that thing we were talking about earlier that I needed to tell you about?"

I cocked my head. "Yeah?"

"Well, he's going to be here in about thirty seconds."

I felt my stomach drop to my feet.

He?!

Before I could question her further, a blue Toyota Highlander pulled into the drive and parked behind her Honda.

I noticed an older gentleman behind the wheel, and my mind raced to make sense of things.

Did she have a sugar daddy or something?

Then I noticed a woman around the man's age in the passenger seat.

I was so fucking confused.

The woman waved and smiled brightly when she got out and opened the back passenger door. At the same time, the man got out and called, "Hey, Gigi," before going around and opening the rear hatch.

Seconds later, I heard a tiny voice squeal, "Mama!" and a little boy toddled toward Gretchen with his arms spread wide.

He was wobbly on his feet as he made his way to where she was now squatting with her arms open and a big smile on her face. He appeared to be about two years old, based on how short he was and how unsteady his gait was.

The same way Bodhi's used to be.

I felt like I couldn't breathe.

Part of me wanted to grab the little guy and hug him tight, and part of me just wanted to get as far away as possible.

I opted for the latter.

****

Gretchen

I scooped Jake up and gave him a big hug, then looked over at Gabe's stunned face with a sheepish smile.

"This is my son, Jake. And, my parents, Warren and Molly." I nodded in the Mitchell men's direction. "This is Gabe and Derrick Mitchell. Gabe owns Mitchell Woodworking. He custom-made my kitchen cabinets, and Derrick owns Flannigan's, the new bar in town."

My mom smiled warmly, and my dad offered a cordial, "Hello," as he came around to the front of the car holding Jake's racecar-themed suitcase.

My mother turned to me. "I didn't know you were getting your kitchen redone."

"It's a long story, but suffice it to say, it was originally Troy's idea."

At the mention of my ex's name, my father scowled.

Gabe still seemed disoriented, and in that moment, I knew I'd been right not to mention Jake sooner. Although I knew

Gabe's stance on little kids up front, his reaction still hurt my feelings.

He glanced at my parents and forced a smile.

"It's nice to meet you." He moved toward his F150, barely looking my way when he called, "I, uh, have to get going. I'll be in touch about when we can deliver the last of the cabinets."

Without another word, he got in his truck and drove away, leaving me dumbfounded.

I mean, I knew he wouldn't want to see me again once he found out I had a young child, but this felt a little extreme.

Derrick's creased brow seemed to indicate he was also confused about his brother's reaction, but he offered a weak wave before opening his car door.

"It was nice meeting you all." He then directed his attention to where I still stood holding Jake in the garage. "Gretch, it was a pleasure. I hope you decide to keep the cabinets."

The jury was still out about that, so I simply replied, "Thank you for the coffee."

He offered the smile that showcased his dimples. The one that I was sure got him laid a lot.

"Anytime. Don't be a stranger. Be sure to come see me at Flannigan's again soon."

Based on his brother's reaction, I doubted I'd be going near Flannigan's anytime in the near future, but I nodded and said, "I will."

I waved as he backed out the drive, and I noticed Jake did the same, even though he didn't know the man.

Derrick responded by rolling down the window, sticking his hand out, and calling, "Bye, Jake!" to my son's delight.

"You're such a sweetie," I murmured as I brushed my lips against Jake's soft hair.

"These are really beautiful, Gigi. They're going to look great in your kitchen."

I turned to find my dad had peeled back the protective foam on one of the cabinets.

"If I decide to install them."

"What do you mean?"

I shrugged.

"Honestly, they're more than I can afford. Troy and I were still married when we ordered them, and with the divorce and everything, I kind of forgot that we had. I'm still trying to figure out my options."

I had a sinking feeling a payment plan was no longer an option, and judging by the ashen look on Gabe's face, I definitely wasn't going to be paying with sex.

I mean, not that I really ever thought that was a possibility. It'd been a sexy fantasy, though.

But now I doubted I'd ever even hear from him again.

It was just as well. Jake already had a dad who'd rejected him, I'd be damned if I'd ever let another man do the same.

Chapter Thirty

Gabe

My hands shook the entire drive home, and I tried to figure out why seeing her son had such an effect on me.

Obviously, I'd seen toddlers in the seven years since Bodhi died; what was it about Gretchen's little boy that had me so rattled?

Maybe it was because I wasn't expecting her to have a kid.

Or maybe I'd let myself have a tiny sliver of hope that I could be the man she was looking for. The reality of what that looked like had smacked me upside the head.

So much for that little daydream.

I'd been right—having another kid wasn't for me. I'd leave that to my gazillionaire brother.

After pulling into the garage and shutting my truck off, I heard the roar of Derrick's car exhaust as he pulled up behind me.

My little brother hopped out as soon as he shut the car off and approached where I stood in the garage.

"What are you doing? I thought you had to get to Flannigan's?"

He shook his head with a solemn expression.

"Flannigan's can wait. I needed to check on you first. Are you okay?"

I blew out a long breath. I knew I'd behaved poorly at Gretchen's, but I'd had to get out of there.

"No, not really."

Derrick gripped my shoulder and directed me toward the door leading to the house.

"Come on, let's talk."

"There's nothing to talk about," I grumbled even as I let him steer me inside.

"Sure there is," he said as we walked through the threshold and into the kitchen. "We can discuss the weather, politics, the Celtics, the Red Sox, or the Bruins. We can even talk shit about your ex-wife, if you want." He plopped onto a stool at the kitchen island and motioned for me to do the same. When I was seated, he swiveled so he faced me. "Or we can just sit and stare at each other; it doesn't matter to me. But I don't think you should be alone right now."

I snorted. "I'm fine."

"You looked like you'd seen a ghost when Gretchen's little boy showed up."

My gaze fell to the black flecks in the granite countertop, and I uttered, "Because it felt like I had."

"It probably didn't help that we'd just been talking about Bodhi this morning."

"No, probably not."

"Are you still seeing Dr. Frank?"

I shook my head. "Not in a few years."

He nodded slowly. "I guess you'll have to make do with some Mitchell therapy then."

I had an ominous feeling about this, but I still asked, "What are you talking about?"

My answer came in the form of my brother Beau's voice echoing off the kitchen walls.

"What up, suckas?"

I glared at Derrick. "You called Beau?"

The asshole didn't even have the decency to act contrite. He just grinned when he replied, "And Mav."

Beau opened the fridge and pulled out three beers before sitting down opposite us at the island and sliding two of them across the counter to me and Derrick.

"And Mav will probably call Nick."

Derrick took a bottle opener from his pocket—a byproduct of being a bar owner, I was sure, and opened his bottle, then offered it to me.

I pushed the beer away and shook my head.

Unbothered, he held it out to Beau, who took it.

"Look," I said as they both took a pull. "I appreciate that you guys are worried about me. I'll admit, I didn't handle things as well as I could have at Gretchen's. It just took me by surprise, that's all."

Beau asked, "What did?" and I scowled at Derrick.

"You didn't tell him?"

"It wasn't my place."

"But it was your place to invite everyone over?"

He lifted his pinky finger as he brought the bottle to his lips with a grin.

"Yup."

I muttered under my breath, "Asshole," even though I couldn't really be mad at him for caring about me.

"What took you by surprise?" Beau reiterated. "Why am I here?"

"Let's just wait for Maverick to get here so I don't have to repeat myself."

Chapter Thirty-One

Gretchen

Monday at lunch, I turned my phone on to check my messages.

Not surprisingly, there was nothing from Gabe. Same as last night.

I'd predicted his response, although I wasn't necessarily happy about being right.

I tried to offer myself some consolation.

I still had amazing sex over the weekend.

But the memory was tainted now.

I hadn't expected him to greet my son with open arms; in fact, I'd never planned on them ever meeting. But the fact that they had, and he'd practically shunned my kid, spoke volumes.

I jumped in my seat when my phone rang in my hand.

The caller ID read *Mitchell Cabinets,* and my heart skipped a beat.

I wasn't sure I even wanted to talk to him, but a part of me was glad that at least he hadn't ghosted me completely—even if he was probably just calling to schedule a time to bring the last of the cabinets.

I had to have a little bit of masochist in me, because I decided to answer.

"Hello?"

A deep voice I recognized but wasn't expecting said, "Is this Gretchen?"

"It is."

"Hey, it's Rick from Mitchell Cabinets and Woodworking. How are you today?"

That son of a bitch couldn't even call me himself?!

I responded with a clipped, "I'm fine, thank you."

"That's great. Well, the reason I'm calling is to see if I can bring the rest of your cabinets by on my way home from work tonight. Say, five-thirty?"

"You're going to bring them? By yourself?"

"Yeah, I'll have the company truck, so they'll be easy to offload with a dolly."

"Oh, I see."

Why hadn't Gabe done that to begin with? He probably could have delivered them all in one load.

Then he wouldn't have had an excuse to come back.

And now he didn't want to come back, so he left it to Rick, a dolly, and the company truck.

I wavered between being hurt and pissed—something I hadn't experienced since my divorce proceedings, and I didn't like it one bit.

"Yeah, that's fine, Rick. I should be home by then."

Before I hung up, I wanted to add, *And tell your boss to fuck off,* but I was at school and didn't want to risk being overheard.

But I hoped my snippy tone conveyed the sentiment.

****

Gabe

I felt a twinge in my gut on Tuesday morning when I flipped on the light in the shop and noticed the empty space where her cabinets used to be.

I was a chicken shit, plain and simple.

Or an asshole.

Maybe both.

I'd had Rick call her to schedule a drop off time yesterday, and I didn't even have the decency to be the one to deliver them.

The Mitchell Men Therapy Session had yielded mixed results, at best.

We'd had a good sob session about Bodhi, where my brothers all talked about their memories of my little man. It had been painful, yet cathartic

I still didn't understand God's plan or whatever bullshit people spew when a tragedy strikes, but I did accept it was out of my control, and it wasn't my fault.

Something I thought I'd worked through but the more I talked with my brothers and nephew, I realized the wound had still been there, festering.

So, in that regard, my brothers' visit had been helpful. But when it came to Gretchen, I ended up feeling worse. Maybe, in part, because I hadn't been completely honest with how I felt about her.

But by the end of the afternoon, I came to the conclusion that she and I had been a fling, nothing more. And it was in both our best interests to steer clear of each other.

Hence, the reason I made Rick deal with her.

That didn't mean I didn't pounce on Rick the second he walked through the door Tuesday morning.

"How'd it go with Gretchen Wainwright?"

I hadn't divulged how exactly I'd convinced her to take possession of the majority of the cabinets over the weekend, so I couldn't act like she and I were on a first-name basis.

"Fine."

Fine? What the fuck does "fine" mean?

"Did she say anything to you?"

"I didn't even see her. When I pulled up to the house, the garage door started to go up, but she wasn't anywhere in sight. I saw where you'd put the other cabinets, so I just put the ones I had next to them. I noticed the door go down as I drove away."

"And she didn't come out to talk to you?"

He cocked his head and looked at me like I was stupid.

"I literally just said I didn't see her."

"Right. Right. I just wanted to make sure there weren't any problems."

"Did something happen this weekend that would have led you to believe there would be?"

I replied quickly, "No. No. There were no problems. It was fine. Everything was fine. No problems."

He narrowed his eyes at me.

"You okay, boss?"

I took a deep breath through my nose.

No, I'm not okay. I've slept like shit the last two nights, and when I am awake, all I can think about is her.

I offered my foreman a weak smile. I knew I sounded like a crazy man. Probably because that's how I felt.

"All good. The lumber shipment should be here at two, so make sure you're around to doublecheck the quality when they offload it."

I didn't wait for his reply, just slid my safety glasses down from where they'd been on top of my head, turned the miter saw back on, and prayed I was able to focus enough to keep from losing a finger.

Chapter Thirty-Two

Gretchen

Once my students left for the day on Friday, I congratulated myself for making it through the week without breaking down at school.

The nights, on the other hand... those had been tough.

Things were the worst after I'd put Jake to bed and would have time to sit and think about my time with Gabe.

Eventually "thinking" gave way to "stewing".

I preferred stewing. My righteous anger kept me from crying, and I'd done enough of that in the beginning of the week when I lay in bed and hugged the pillow he'd used.

Not my proudest moment.

But tonight, I was doing laundry and washing away any trace of Gabe Mitchell.

That was the plan anyway.

But when I got home, after I put Jake to bed, I found myself coming up with other things that "needed" to get done first.

Like organize my sock drawer.

My phone rang as I sorted my knee-high from my anklets, and I glanced at the screen.

Laura.

I answered with a cheery, "Hey, gorgeous, what's up?"

"My beautiful friend! What are you doing?"

"Just some stuff around the house; what about you?"

"You should get a sitter and come out with me!"

"Um, it's eight-thirty on a Friday night. I don't think you understand how getting a sitter works."

"I know, I forget you can't be spontaneous when you're a mom."

"My days of spontaneity are behind me. At least until Jake doesn't need a babysitter. And that's probably when you'll be having kids, so I think our Thelma and Louise era will have to wait until our sixties."

"Come on, I'm not waiting until Jake's old enough to not need a babysitter before I have kids. I'm two—three years tops, away from procreating."

"Don't you need a partner to do that?"

"Eh, I've got a little bit more time to have fun before I have to think about settling down. Which is why I was calling you! I thought we could go see what's shaking at Flannigan's tonight. Maybe we could get you an encore with Gabe."

"Yeaaaah, that's not going to happen."

"What? Why not? Was he a bad lay?"

"No, just the opposite, actually. Hands down the best sex I've ever had. He spent the night, and we ended up spending Saturday night together, too."

"Oh, wow! Quite the contrast from his brother. Derrick gave me five minutes of pillow talk before he put on his pants and was out the door."

"You're kidding. Ugh, I'm sorry."

"Oh, don't be. I was glad I didn't have to kick him out."

I shook my head even though she couldn't see me. That sounded awful.

"I am so not cut out for dating in today's world."

"You just need practice compartmentalizing. Sex can just be about the physical act. Feelings don't have to be involved.

But if you and Gabe spent the weekend together, it sounds like that wasn't the problem, so why won't there be an encore?"

"Well, for starters, he doesn't want more kids."

"Okay, so he's not Mr. Right. Why not let him be Mr. Right Now? Keep enjoying the great sex until Mr. Right does come along."

"I'm not wired that way. There will always be feelings involved for me when it comes to having sex."

"Maybe he'll change his mind about kids?"

"That's not gonna happen. My parents brought Jake home while he and Derrick were here delivering the kitchen cabinets, and he took one look at him and practically ran to his truck. I haven't heard from him since."

"Ouch." There was a brief pause before she said, "Wait. Derrick was at your house? Delivering cabinets? The cabinets you weren't going to get?"

"Gabe said he was going to talk to his brother, Maverick, about letting me make payments. I'm guessing since he had someone else deliver the last of the cabinets on Monday, that's probably off the table."

"And Derrick was there?"

"Yeah, on Sunday—and Saturday. He helped Gabe unload them."

"Did he ask about me?"

"He asked how you were doing."

"Aw, that was nice of him."

"Do you think there's something there between you two?"

"No. But he was good in bed, so I wouldn't mind the occasional hookup. But not anytime soon. That sets a bad precedent."

"I'm so not equipped to date," I reiterated under my breath.

"Anyway, back to you and Gabe."

"There is no Gabe and me."

Saying it out loud made my chest hurt.

Why was that?

Maybe it was because he'd rejected me, and my pride was hurt.

But it felt like more than pride that kept me from getting rid of the last remnants of my weekend with him.

I continued, "It was only for the weekend. We were upfront about that from the start, so even if he hadn't freaked out and ghosted me, I knew where we stood."

"We need a girls' night in," Laura declared. "I'll be over in thirty minutes with wine, snacks, and ice cream."

I haphazardly tossed the socks I was supposed to be organizing back into the drawer.

"See you then."

I knew if we were drinking wine, my BFF would spend the night, and since I didn't have a guest room set up—I'd given Troy the guest room furniture—I knew she'd be sleeping with me.

And that was the catalyst I needed to change the sheets.

I may have tucked the pillowcase Gabe used in a drawer, though.

Obviously, I had issues. Or I really was a masochist.

****

Gabe

"You want to tell me what is going on with you?" my oldest brother asked when he came by the shop two weeks after the "therapy session" with my brothers.

I didn't look up from where I was sanding the wood for an entertainment center.

"Not a damn thing."

"Bullshit. In the four years since we've been in business, there's never been one complaint about your work. Not one. But in the last ten days, we've had two pieces sent back for repairs because they weren't up to the quality we promise—and charge for."

One of those returned pieces was the entertainment center I was currently working on.

I didn't say anything, so Maverick continued, "And your staff is so worried you're going to bite their heads off, they're calling me for direction on how to handle bringing the furniture back to get fixed." He paused a beat then said quietly, "This is about that woman, Gretchen, isn't it? The one with the kid."

I stood up straight and threw the sandpaper to the ground in disgust.

"What the hell are you talking about?"

"You're not on your A-game, Gabe, and that's not like you. Considering the timing, the only thing that makes sense is you're still upset about how you fucked things up with her."

"What is that supposed to mean? You assholes were the ones who said to stay clear of her."

"Because you fucked things up."

I scoffed, "Whatever."

My older brother didn't let me off the hook.

"I'm sorry, how would you describe getting in your truck and driving away with hardly a word once her kid showed up? And never calling her again?"

I let out a long breath as I ran my fingers through my hair.

"You're right, I didn't handle it well, and I regret that. But that has nothing to do with my work."

That was such a lie, I half-expected my nose to start growing or my pants to catch on fire.

The whole way I'd left things with Gretchen had been eating at me, to the point I was hardly sleeping and was ready to bite anyone's head off who spoke to me.

"Gabe, you need to fix things with her."

"I don't think that's possible."

"Then you need to find someone else and get over her already."

"Yeah, you know, 'cuz it's that easy. I'm sure if Olivia left you, you'd just need to find someone new to get over her."

Mav cocked his head.

"Are you comparing how you feel about Gretchen to how I feel about my wife?"

"No! Don't be silly. I was just trying to make a point."

"I think the point you made was you care about her."

"I'll admit, I owe her an apology. But I think I've let too much time go by."

My brother shrugged. "Only one way to find out."

"You make it sound so easy. Sure, I could apologize, and then what? It's not like we have any possibility of a future together."

"It might make you feel better anyway."

Yeah, there was that. Or I could just try taking sleeping pills at night and not being an asshole at the shop during the day.

It was worth a shot.

Chapter Thirty-Three

Gabe

I didn't stop at the pharmacy for sleeping pills, but I did make an effort to be nicer to the staff.

Well, at least to Shelly.

I may be the guy who made the furniture, but she was the one who really ran things, and we'd be lost without her. I was under no illusion to the contrary.

So, when she came into the shop holding a file folder, I shut down the saw and offered a smile.

"Hey, what brings you back here?"

"Well, I have a question about what you want to do about the Wainwright account." She opened the file and leafed through some papers. "The cabinets were delivered over two weeks ago, and I'm getting ready to send her an invoice. But I'm not seeing where they were installed."

"That's because they haven't been yet."

"Oookay. Are we planning on installing them?"

"Yeah, we just need to get something scheduled. But as far as the invoice, we're going to setup a payment plan for her."

"A payment plan?"

"Yeah."

"Do we have a contract for that?"

"Not yet. Maybe you could look into drawing something up?"

"I'm sure I could. What kind of terms?"

I did some quick math in my head and threw out some numbers.

"Three years, no interest, with equal monthly payments."

I hadn't talked to Mav about any of that, but I was making an ownership decision. He could be pissed at me; I was willing to take the heat.

"And what about the install?"

"I don't know. Let me talk to Rick about scheduling something, and I'll get back to you with a figure."

****

Gretchen

I called around to a few handymen about getting a quote to install the cabinets. But the one guy who actually showed up gave me an estimate that made me choke.

Although Gabe had never told me an exact number, I was certain it'd be cheaper to just have his company do it.

"We could do it," Laura suggested one night when she came over for dinner.

That was an idea. I'd taught myself to do a lot of things, thanks to YouTube.

But after watching a few videos, it didn't take long for me to realize we were not equipped to handle a job that big. Not just physically, but I didn't have the tools necessary.

Laura observed, "I mean, don't we just need a sledgehammer to do the demo work?"

"Okay, so we rip out all the existing cabinets, then what? I don't want to destroy my kitchen only to then realize I have no idea how to put it back together."

"Good point. So, what... you're just to pay for a garage full of cabinets you never install?"

I let out a heavy sigh. I'd gotten my first invoice from Mitchell Cabinets in the mail yesterday.

"I think I'm going to have to move."

"What? No! You love it here! And we already talked about this—anything you buy now is going to cost as much as your current mortgage payment, so what would be the point?"

"I'll just have to move to Parkview."

"*Parkview*?"

"It's not that far, so I can always commute to Lancastle if I can't find a position in their district."

"But, it's *Parkview*. You really want Jake to grow up in Parkview?"

Hell no, I didn't want Jake to grow up in Parkview, but my hands were tied.

"Stop being such a snob."

"There's got to be something you can do. Can you take Troy back to court for more child support? Surely, it's in his son's best interest to stay in his house."

"Andrew said if I want to let Gabe sue me, then he would name Troy as a co-defendant since his name's on the contract, but it has nothing to do with the divorce decree."

"I guess that's an idea?"

"No, it's not. Troy already said he wouldn't pay, and Andy said I'd lose. Then I'd be responsible for Gabe's attorney's fees, which would probably be more than the cabinets themselves."

"Ugh, I hate this for you. Did you talk to Gabe about making payments?"

"Yeah, well, not *Gabe,* but his office manager called. They agreed to let me make payments with no interest."

"That's great! So, I don't understand the problem?"

"The problem is, I still have to come up with over eight hundred dollars a month."

Laura drew in a quick breath. "Ohhhh."

"And that's *without* installation."

"*Ohhhh!*"

"I don't have that kind of money."

"That is a pretty big chunk of your salary. Maybe you could talk to Gabe about extending the term?"

"I would rather smash my hand with a sledgehammer than ask that man for anything else."

"Would you rather move to Parkview?"

I placed my arms on the table and dropped my forehead onto them as I mock sobbed, "I don't know!"

After my dramatic moment passed, I raised my head.

"I feel like they're already doing me a favor. They've never let someone make payments before—something their office manager reminded me of several times. And I'm not going to grovel to Gabe, because fuck him. So, yes, I guess I would rather live in Parkview than beg him or anyone, for that matter, for charity."

Laura scoffed. "It's not charity. It's not like you're asking for them for free. You're still paying them."

"Maybe so, but it feels like it."

"Well, hopefully you've got some time to figure things out before you have to make a decision."

"I don't know what there is to figure out. Short of a miracle, there's not much I can do."

"Start praying for that miracle, then, girl. Light some candles, throw a few coins in a wishing well, start looking for shooting stars..."

"As solid a plan as that sounds, I think my time would be better spent looking at real estate in Parkview and filling out a job application with their district."

"No! I refuse to give up that easily! There's got to be something you can do."

I wrapped an arm around her shoulder and threw out a quote from *Dodgeball*, one of our favorite classic movies from college.

"I know how we can raise the money... carwash!"

~~

Even though I'd been glib with Laura, my soul hurt thinking about having to move.

When my phone rang after school a week later, my stomach dropped as the words *Mitchell Cabinets* flashed on the screen.

And so it begins...

I thought about ignoring the call, but then I remembered the Intent to Sue letter and decided I needed to address the situation head on.

"Hello?"

A deep voice asked, "Is this Gretchen?"

"It is."

"Hi, it's Rick from Mitchell Cabinets. How are you today?"

Of course it was Rick calling.

I hadn't heard from Gabe since he practically tore out of my driveway almost a month ago.

Asshole.

My voice was flat when I responded, "I'm fine, Rick."

"The reason I'm calling is I'd like to know if you want to schedule your cabinets to be installed."

Chapter Thirty-Four

Gabe

"Hey, boss!" Rick called out as he walked into the shop.

I looked up from marking lines for the design I was putting on a TV lift cabinet.

"What's up?"

"So, I called Gretchen Wainwright about scheduling the cabinet installation, like you asked," he motioned to the phone in his hand, and I eyed it with suspicion.

Something Rick noticed because he quipped, "She's on hold—I triple checked. But she's wondering about a contractor's lien."

What the hell?

"Why would she want a contractor's lien? We came up with a payment plan for her."

Rick's brows went to his hairline. "We did?"

Fuck, I hadn't meant to let that slip out. I didn't want this to become a habit, and thought it was best if my employees didn't know it was an option, lest they mention it to future customers.

"Yeah. It was a one-time exception."

My foreman lifted his shoulders to his ears.

"I don't know. All I know is I asked if we could schedule an installation, and she came back with a date in June after she gets out of school. Then she mentioned the lien. I told her I'd have to check with you about how that works."

I knew she was pissed at me, and she had every right to be. But I really hoped she wasn't cutting her nose off to spite her face.

I needed a few minutes to think about things.

"Tell her I'm not here, and you'll call her back."

Rick pushed a button, then put the phone to his ear and said in a friendly voice, "Hey, Gretchen?"

I was taken aback by how jealous I felt that he got to talk to her.

"Yeah, I can't find Gabe anywhere. He might have run to the hardware store; his truck's gone."

Oh, nice touch.

I gave him the thumbs up sign, and he grinned at me while listening to what she had to say.

"I'll call you back as soon as I'm able to talk to him."

There was another pause, then he continued, "Yeah, in the meantime, I'll get you on the books for mid-June."

Pause.

She must not have trusted Rick was going to talk to me because he told her, "I promise I will talk to him and get back to you no later than tomorrow."

Another long pause.

"That won't be a problem; there's no need for that. Talk to you soon."

He ended the call and turned to me with narrowed eyes.

"What's going on with you two?"

"Nothing! Why?"

"She just said…" He trailed off, and I waited with bated breath for him to finish his thought, but he didn't.

Finally, I burst out, "She just said *what*?"

"She said to tell you not to worry, she'd make sure she and her son were out of the house while we were doing the work." He cocked his head and crossed his arms across his chest. "Now, why would she say that?"

I hung my head and let out a long sigh as it dawned on me how epically I had fucked this situation up.

"I think I gave her the wrong idea when I met her son. But I think I at least know how to fix the issue with the contractor's lien."

Chapter Thirty-Five

Gretchen

I got Jake out of his car seat when we arrived home at the end of the day.

Once inside, I plopped him on the counter and asked, "What should we have for dinner?" like he'd respond, although I knew better.

I'd love to say I offered him a host of selections that were all healthy and nutritious, but being single, exhausted, and struggling to make ends meet made it hard to be the mother I wanted to be.

"How about fish sticks and tater tots?"

He clapped his hands and enthused, "Shticks!" which I took as a yes and set him on the ground to let him play on my tablet so I could get dinner started.

At least the tots were sweet potatoes, and I could add some red and yellow bell peppers to his plate to add some color. I gave myself credit for introducing him to vegetables while he was teething, so he was already accustomed to having them with every meal.

"Yes, I'm just a regular June Cleaver," I mused out loud as I shut the oven door after placing the pan of tater tots and fish sticks inside.

Leaning my butt against the warm appliance, I looked at my son in the adjoining family room playing on my iPad and couldn't help but feel like I was failing at this mom thing.

I rarely made homemade meals for my kid, and I wasn't home during the day to make sure he was doing all the enrichment activities his little developing brain needed. I let him have too much screen time. Sometimes he got wiped down with a washcloth at night instead of getting a full bath. I wasn't consistent enough with potty training and at the rate we were going, Jake was going to be wearing training pants to middle school.

In Parkview.

That felt like my biggest failure. We were going to have to move. He wasn't going to attend Lancastle schools, and I knew I'd have to be extra vigilant that he didn't have any educational gaps.

I watched him study the game he was playing, and he let out a little cheer as his face lit up with a smile while he raised his arms in victory.

My son was happy and healthy and knew he was loved, so at least I had that going for me.

The doorbell rang, and Jake's eyes got big before he jumped off the couch and darted toward the door.

"Not so fast, mister!" I exclaimed as I scooped him up. "Kids don't answer the door."

Parking him on my hip, I swung the door open and immediately moved the wooden barrier, so Jake was obstructed from Gabe Mitchell, who was standing on my welcome mat, looking sexy as fuck in his work boots and messy hair.

Somehow him looking that damn good only made me madder.

Trying to keep the anger out of my voice, I cautiously said, "Hi?"

He offered a contrite smile and replied, "Hey. I was hoping I could talk to you."

When I didn't move to invite him in, he clarified, "About your cabinets. And the lien you asked Rick about..."

I eyed him up and down and noticed he had a Caruso's bag in one hand and a toy toolbox in the other.

He saw where my gaze landed, and he lifted the items higher.

"I brought you cheesecake, and I brought your boy a carpenter set."

My eyes narrowed, and I blurted out, "Why?"

"Well, I remember how much you liked Caruso's cheesecake, and I know how much my kids loved their toolsets, so I thought Jake might enjoy one, too. I kept the receipt, so you can take it back if he already has one."

I hadn't heard from him in over a month, and now he shows up at my house with gifts like nothing happened?

"No, I mean, why did you bring us anything at all? Why are you here?"

He glanced at the ground, then looked me in the eye.

"I think I gave you the wrong impression the other day and was hoping these would help you accept my apology."

I hadn't expected that.

"Your apology?"

"That day I brought your cabinets... the way I left. I owe you an explanation, along with the apology."

I didn't want him to think that he had any power over me, like I hadn't spent the last month wavering between hurt and confused to angry and indignant, so I shrugged like I didn't care.

"You don't owe me anything. We agreed our time together was only for the weekend, and the weekend was over."

"I still shouldn't have left like that. I'm sorry."

I wanted to tell him to suck it, but I realized that would be like admitting I'd been affected and holding a grudge.

"Apology accepted."

"I also wanted to talk about a proposition I have for you, regarding your cabinets."

My heartrate sped up as thoughts of the dirty fantasy I'd had about him wanting sex as payment raced through my mind.

I swallowed hard before squeaking out, "What kind of proposition?"

Gabe gestured behind me.

"Can I come in?"

****

Gabe

Gretchen let me in her front door. That was a start.

I smiled at the small towheaded boy staring at me with big blue eyes while his mom held him, then I glanced cautiously at her.

"Is it okay if I give this to him?"

She nodded once, then set him on his feet, and I immediately knelt to offer him the toolbox.

"Here, buddy. This is for you."

He clung to Gretchen's leg with one hand while staring at the carpenter set full of oversized, colorful plastic tools.

I set the bag with the cheesecake on the ground so I could take the toy hammer out and demonstrate how it worked on a make-believe nail on the floor.

He let go of his mom's leg to take it when I extended it to him. I then pulled out two more tools from the set to show him.

The little man had obviously been around someone who used tools, because he immediately knew what the screwdriver was for and practiced on the closest piece of furniture—exactly how Bodhi used to.

My heart felt like it had a stranglehold on it, but I took a deep breath and remembered what Dr. Frank had recommended: focus on the child in front of me.

Gretchen beamed down at her son. "Just like *daideó's,* huh, baby? We'll have to take those over next time we visit him and *mamó* so you can help him."

Wearing a big grin, the little boy replied, "Help DoDo!" and continued his attempt to unscrew the nailhead trim on her brown faux-leather couch, chewing his tongue as he concentrated on the task.

"What do you say to Mr. Mitchell?"

"Tank you," and then I think he attempted to say, "Mr. Mitchell," but it came out sounding like mashed up consonants that started with an M and ended with an L.

"You're welcome, buddy."

A beeping sound came from the kitchen that I recognized as the oven timer, and I couldn't help but smile at the memory of the last time I was here when it went off, along with the smoke detector.

Jake's mouth formed an "O" when he looked at her with wide eyes. She played along and made a dramatic gasp when she exclaimed, "Dinner's ready!"

The tools were quickly abandoned, except the screwdriver, which he took with him as he scrambled to the kitchen.

I put the rest of the tools back in the box, and Gretchen snatched up the bag with the cheesecake before following her son.

I took her accepting my peace offering as a good sign and trailed behind them.

Chapter Thirty-Six

Gabe

I watched Gretchen as she prepared Jake's dinner and was struck at how beautiful this side of her I hadn't seen before was. I was willing to bet she was an amazing teacher, too.

Which I was banking on, if my plan was going to work.

Once she set Jake's plate on the tray of his high chair, I cleared my throat and said, "So, about this proposition I have."

Gretchen shot a look in her son's direction before quietly murmuring, "I don't think we should talk about that right now." She motioned her head at the little man happily munching away on his fish sticks in one hand and tater tots in the other. "Not in front of ..."

That confused me, but I stammered out, "Oh, okay."

She pulled a pot out of the cupboard, set it on the stovetop, and asked, "Are you hungry?"

"I am."

It wouldn't have mattered if I'd just come from stuffing myself at an all-you-can-eat buffet, it sounded like she was offering me dinner and there was zero chance I'd turn that down.

Fortunately, I hadn't eaten since lunch.

She pulled a container from the refrigerator, poured its contents into the pot, and turned the burner on medium.

"I'm just having cream of potato soup, but I can make you a grilled cheese or hamburger to go with it."

"Are you having anything besides soup?"

"Well, no, but it's not a problem to make you something."

"So, let me get this straight... I was a jerk to you, and you're still offering to make me something special for dinner?"

"I wouldn't call it special." She smirked as she stirred the soup with a wooden spoon. "But since I'm not sharing the cheesecake, I thought it'd be the polite thing to do."

I gave her a sly smile. "I brought two slices."

Without missing a beat, she replied, "And I'll appreciate that second slice tomorrow at lunch."

My mouth dropped open in fake outrage, and I waited for her to tell me she was just teasing. But she didn't. Instead, she continued, "So, do you want a grilled cheese or a hamburger or something else?"

"Um... I'll just have the soup with you."

Finally, she burst out laughing.

"Okay, fine, I'll split the cheesecake. But I know the soup and cheesecake aren't going to fill you up, so pick something to go with it, or I will."

I wanted nothing more than to kiss that feisty mouth of hers into submission, but considering our circumstances, that might lead to a knee to my groin.

Still, I couldn't resist raking my gaze up and down her body as I replied, "I've got something else in mind."

Our eyes locked and her mouth parted. We'd spent a weekend flirting with each other; I knew she understood the innuendo.

But after a beat, she looked away and said, "Oh, do you want a sandwich or something instead?"

I wasn't going to let it go that easily.

"Or something."

This time when our gazes met, she lifted one eyebrow and defiantly put her hand on her hip.

"Such as?"

I knew then that I'd overplayed my hand.

Hell, I wasn't even sure why I was playing any hand at all. I'd come to her house to offer her a deal—a way for her to keep her house, while my kid could improve his grades. And in the process, assuage my conscience for how big a dick I'd been after we'd spent an amazing weekend together.

When I arrived here, there hadn't been any expectation of continuing things between us.

But the second I saw her, all I could think about was feeling her underneath me again.

Judging by her reaction to my flirting attempt, the feeling was one-sided.

I dropped down onto a stool at her kitchen island. "Actually, a grilled cheese sounds perfect."

She nodded and gathered the contents for the sandwich on the counter, then took a frying pan from a cupboard and set it on the stove.

"Mama, I done!"

She glanced at Jake and shook her head.

"Five more bites." Then she clarified, like they'd played this game before. "*Big boy* bites."

He bit half a red pepper strip, and Gretchen declared, "One," as she opened the bread bag and pulled out two slices of bread.

Jake took a bite of fish sticks this time and she said, "Two..." while slathering butter on the bread. She placed one piece on the frying pan. It let out a little sizzle and she set two slices of cheese on it, before topping it with the second piece.

"Three."

I watched in awe as she stirred the soup, then reached inside a cupboard for two bowls, grabbed two spoons from the drawer, and followed it with effortlessly flipping the sandwich in the pan. All while keeping track of her son's eating habits.

"Four." She stopped what she was doing. "That's not a big boy bite. It has to be a big boy bite for it to count."

Jake took a dramatic chomp of a red pepper strip, and she praised him with, "That's better."

She ladled a bowl of soup, set it in front of me, then plated the sandwich—making sure to cut it in half before sliding it next to the soup.

"Thank you, this looks amazing."

"I didn't try to burn down the kitchen this time," she said with the soft smile I hadn't realized how much I'd missed until right at that moment.

She looked at Jake and beamed before proclaiming, "Five! Good job, sweetie."

With his mouth still full, he exclaimed, "Poo-ding, mama!"

"You want pudding?"

He nodded vigorously as he chewed.

"Okay, but you have to give me two more big boy bites first."

Jake took another bite of fish sticks, and Gretchen opened the pantry and pulled out a chocolate pudding cup in one hand and a vanilla in the other.

"Chocolate or vanilla?"

"Banilla!"

She looked over at me with raised brows, and repeated, "Chocolate or vanilla?"

I grinned broadly as I finished half of my sandwich. I couldn't remember the last time I'd had pudding.

"Oh, chocolate, definitely."

She returned my smile and put the chocolate flavor in front of my plate, then told Jake, "One more bite, baby," as she peeled the lid off the vanilla cup.

He did as his mom asked, and she set the pudding on the little boy's tray, much to his delight.

Gretchen cleared his dinner plate, rinsed it, and put it in the dishwasher.

She still hadn't served herself any soup.

"Are you going to eat?"

"Oh," she glanced at the stove where the pot of soup still sat. I noticed the burner was off. "I will."

"When, darlin'?"

"Probably after I put him to bed," she sheepishly admitted.

Glancing down at my now-empty sandwich plate, I felt a wave of guilt for having eaten my grilled cheese without her.

I stood and ushered her to the barstool next to mine. Once she was settled, I grabbed her bowl and went to where the pot of potato soup sat on the stove and ladled her a generous portion.

"Eat," I commanded as I set the bowl in front of her, then opened her pantry and pulled out a box of club crackers and deposited it next to her bowl. Next, I opened her fridge.

"What can I get you to drink?"

She jumped up from her seat.

"Oh my god! I didn't offer you anything to drink! I'm so sorry!"

"Sit your cute butt back down and eat. I'm perfectly capable of getting my own drink if I'd wanted one. Now, let's try this again. What can I get you to drink?"

Gretchen looked mildly amused when she settled back onto the stool and replied, "Just water, thanks."

Jake took the opportunity to aggressively clank his now-empty sippy cup on the high chair tray. "More miwk, pweeze!"

"No, baby. No more milk. You can have water."

Again, she stood up, and I immediately tsked, pointed to her seat, and told her, "I got it," as I grabbed Jake's cup.

I served her a glass of ice water first. Then, under her watchful eye, I rinsed the sippy cup before filling it with water from the refrigerator door.

"Does he get ice?"

She shook her head. "He doesn't like it."

After giving Jake back his cup, I sat down beside her and picked up my spoon to finish my bowl of soup.

"I can warm that up for you."

I couldn't help but smile as I took a bite.

"Thanks, it's still warm. How's yours?"

"It's good, thank you."

Out of the corner of my eye, I noticed her staring at me as she ate, so I turned and asked, "What?"

"I'm just very confused right now. I haven't heard from you since..." she trailed off as she glanced at Jake, who was happily working on his pudding. "And you show up tonight, a month later, and act like everything's fine. And worse, I'm letting you."

I knew she'd accepted my apology too easily.

"Let me explain…"

She cut me off. "No need. You don't owe me anything. I just can't figure out why you're here *now*."

"I told you; I have a proposition for you."

"Right, a proposition. Not to sound like a broken record, but why now?"

"Your phone call today made me realize how badly I owe you an apology. Plus, I thought we could help each other out."

She took a quick intake of breath, and I noticed her nipples were pointed diamonds. Which, of course, made my dick jump.

Down boy! She's not interested.

But her nipples hadn't been stiff a minute ago, and it wasn't cold in the kitchen, so I had to wonder what was up with her tits.

****

Gretchen

I swallowed hard as my mind raced to what I thought his proposition was going to be.

I couldn't decide if I was flattered, insulted, turned on, or a combination of all three.

"Like I said, I don't think we should discuss that now." I motioned my head toward Jake. "Maybe we could have lunch or something this week."

"What time does he go to bed?"

My attention went to the clock on the microwave that read 6:19.

"Around seven-thirty."

"I can wait. Or, if you'd rather me not be here that long, I can come back."

"We have play time, then he gets a bath, and then we read a story... I don't want you sitting around twiddling your thumbs."

"I don't mind. I've got my computer in the truck, so I can get some work done. I'll stay out of your way."

Of course he would. God forbid he have any more interaction with my child.

Although I did have to give him credit for how well he'd behaved around Jake tonight. A far cry from the first time they'd met, when he'd practically tripped over his feet running to his truck.

Fortunately, that interaction had been so brief, Jake had been none the wiser.

"I done!"

I took one look at my little guy and burst out laughing. His face and hair were covered in pudding.

"Oh my goodness. Did any of the pudding make it into your mouth, child?"

He just grinned at me in return.

I stood to get a rag to clean his hands and face, but Gabe put his hand on my arm.

"Finish your soup. He'll be okay until you're done."

It was such a foreign concept, finishing my food before jumping to help my kid. No one had ever encouraged me to do that before. I hadn't realized I needed permission from someone else to take care of myself, but Gabe was right—Jake was fine while I finished.

"Thank you," I said when I finally put my bowl in the sink.

He cocked his head. "For what?"

I shrugged, unsure how to put how I was feeling into words. "For telling me to eat hot soup."

It was a lame explanation, but he smiled like he understood.

"Of course."

I glanced at Jake and sighed. "I think we're going to do things out of order tonight. Bath first, then play time."

Gabe also looked at the mess that was my son and chuckled. "That's probably a good idea."

I quickly wiped Jake's hands, so he didn't get pudding all over me when I took him out of his high chair.

"We'll be back."

He gave me a soft smile. "I'll be here."

I couldn't help but wonder though, would he really?

Chapter Thirty-Seven

Gretchen

After Jake's bath, I wrapped him in his blue hooded shark towel and took him into his room to get him dressed for bed. But as I gathered his pull-up diaper and pajamas., the little stinker took off to streak through the house while screeching, "Nakey time!"

I started after him and banged my knee, which doubled me over momentarily.

"Jake William Wainwright, get back here!"

He just giggled and kept going, his little arms flapping like a bird as he ran.

Normally, naked time was not discouraged. He liked to run around the house for ten minutes with nothing but the breeze on his behind, and I was all for it, especially when he'd use the potty while doing it.

But it wasn't something I wanted him doing when we had company over. Especially around someone as little kid-averse as Gabe.

Picturing the look of horror on Gabe's face prompted me to hobble toward the kitchen, the direction Jake had run.

I heard the humor in Gabe's voice when he exclaimed, "Oh my goodness, it's a naked boy!" followed by the pitter patter of Jake's feet and his squeal of delight at being acknowledged. I suspected he thought Gabe was going to give chase like he knew I was when I called again, "Jake Wainwright!"

I limped into the kitchen—which I noticed was clean—and found Gabe sitting at the table with his computer, wearing a pair of black-rimmed glasses.

Hello Sexy Nerd.

Out of the corner of my eye, I caught sight of a naked baby butt running around the coffee table in the family room.

"No running around the table!"

Jake must have noticed the change of my tone, because he came to a halt immediately with a look of panic on his face. Which of course made me feel bad, so I softened my voice when I moved closer and told him, "You have to be careful, baby. You could fall and hurt yourself on one of the table's corners. If you got hurt, that would make Mommy so sad."

He arched his back to flop on a couch cushion like only a little kid could contort himself to do.

"Hey, I just remembered I need to take my daughter something."

I glanced over to find Gabe standing at the doorway leading to the entryway, holding his closed computer. "I'll call you tomorrow, maybe we can schedule lunch or something this weekend?"

It was painfully obvious he was lying. I wasn't sure if it was the naked boy, the way I'd scolded the naked boy, or the fact that he'd had time to reflect about what he was doing spending time at my house that triggered him. Yet I couldn't find it in me to muster feeling anything more than mild annoyance.

I knew I wasn't going to hear from him again.

"Yeah, sure."

And just like before, he was gone.

****

Gabe

"You look like shit," Derrick remarked when I sat down at Flannigan's bar.

"I feel like shit."

"Dude, when are you just going to man up and call her?"

I rubbed the back of my neck. "I actually just left her house."

"Oh." My brother's eyes got big. "Ohhh. I'm going to guess she told you to pack sand."

"No, actually, she was gracious and accepted my apology. She even made me dinner."

Derrick pulled a mug from the freezer and placed it under the draft spout.

"So, what happened?"

"I'm not sure. Her son was there, and—"

He pushed the tap to stop the flow of beer and looked over at me.

"You freaked out again."

"No, well, not at first." Derrick set the beer in front of me and I took a grateful swig before continuing. "I followed Dr. Frank's advice and concentrated on *Jake*. He's a sweet kid, and I enjoyed being around him."

"This sounds promising..."

"Then she gave him a bath because he was covered in pudding." I smiled at the memory of Jake's face and hair smeared with the dessert and how Gretchen had held him at arm's length when she carried him to the bathtub. "After his bath, he came running through the house naked, like little kids do, and I was still good, not thinking about Bodhi, just Jake.

But he started running around the coffee table, and she yelled at him. Which made him stop."

Derrick stared at me for a beat, then lifted his hands. "And?"

"Then she told him if he got hurt that would make her sad, and my mind went to what if he did get hurt? What would we do? We'd have to take him to the emergency room. Which, then of course, took me to the last time I was in the emergency room, and... I left."

My brother looked at me in disbelief.

"You left? *Again*?"

I stared at the condensation forming on my mug.

"Yeah."

"With no explanation?"

"No. I tried when I first got there, but she cut me off."

"And you just let it go?"

"She'd just let me in her house, I didn't want to rock the boat."

"So instead, you torpedoed it and left it sinking."

I didn't like the analogy but couldn't deny it.

"Pretty much."

"You need to fix this, Gabe. Now."

"I told her I'd call her tomorrow."

"Tomorrow isn't soon enough. She'll have all night to think about what a flake you are. And how you bailed on her again, just like before."

"I know you're right. But I feel like an ass."

"You *are* an ass. But you'll be an even bigger one if you don't do something about it *now*."

I took another pull of beer, set down my half-empty glass, and Derrick promptly took it away and dumped the contents in the sink.

"Go!"

I slid off the barstool, still undecided about what to do but it was obvious I was no longer welcome at Flannigan's.

I'd almost reached the door when my brother's voice rang out, "And buy her some flowers!"

Chapter Thirty-Eight

Gabe

Yes, I did stop and buy flowers. A colorful bouquet of purple lilies, yellow tulips, and pink roses that had caught my eye the minute I walked into the flower shop five minutes before they closed.

I wasn't sure why I was going back to Gretchen's. It's not like she and I were going to date.

Because I like her and don't want her to think I'm an asshole.

And I wanted her to know my bolting—twice—had nothing to do with her or Jake. It was my own hangup.

One I obviously wasn't going to get over anytime soon, in spite of going back to my therapist.

I pulled into her drive and almost backed out. What if she slammed the door in my face? I'd deserve it.

Echoing my brother's earlier sentiments, I murmured out loud, "Man the fuck up, Gabe," and put the truck in park. Before I got out though, I realized Jake was probably already in bed. I didn't want to ring the doorbell and wake him up, so I sent her a text as I walked to the door.

Me: Hey… I'm at your front door. Can we talk?

If she didn't respond, I'd leave the flowers on her doorstep and try texting again tomorrow.

The blue light on the doorbell camera lit up and her voice came over the speaker.

"What is there to talk about, Gabe?"

I shuffled my feet, uncomfortable that she was watching me, but I couldn't see her.

"Look, I need to explain why I left so abruptly. And we still need to discuss my proposition about the cabinets."

"There's nothing to expla—"

"Dammit, Gretchen, yes there is. So will you just open the door so I can tell you what's going on?"

Silence met me in response.

Fuck.

I'd been screwing up with this woman since her first phone call to the shop. Maybe it was time to admit defeat and move on.

"I'm sorry I swore. I just need to talk to you, but if you're not ready, I—"

Before I could finish my thought, the door opened and Gretchen stood before me in soft-looking pink pajama pants adorned with hearts and dogs and a matching short-sleeved shirt.

She was no longer wearing any makeup, and I was arrogant enough to wonder if it was because she'd cried it off or because she'd washed her face.

Either way, I wanted nothing more than to wrap my arms around her and hold her close.

Not gonna happen, Gabe.

We stood awkwardly staring at each other until I thrust the bouquet at her and said, "These are for you."

With furrowed brows, she extended her hand and took the flowers from me.

"You didn't have to—"

I cut her off. "I wanted to."

"They're beautiful." She brought the arrangement to her nose and inhaled. "Thank you."

"Of course."

I nodded, and when she didn't ask me inside, I put my hands in my front pockets and rocked forward on my toes.

Gretchen studied me for a minute before softly asking, "Why did you come back, Gabe?"

"I told you, I need to explain myself. And I owe you another apology."

She stared at the flowers in her hand, then finally murmured, "Okay," and stepped aside.

****

Gretchen

I think my pride needed there to be a reason why Gabe had ghosted me, and why he took off so suddenly tonight; that had to be why I let him back into the house.

"Is Jake in bed?"

"Yes. You don't have to worry about seeing him."

"I'm not worried."

I scoffed. "Could have fooled me."

He took my hand and led me to the couch in the family room.

"I need you to understand why this has been hard for me."

I didn't let him continue.

"Look, I know I should have told you about him, but since we were only a weekend thing, I didn't see the point. I never expected you to have any interaction with him. I even told Rick I'd be sure we weren't around when the cabinets are installed. What I don't understand is why you showed up at my house unannounced when you know perfectly well that I'm a single mom. Surely you had to know he'd be here?"

"Of course I did."

"Oookay, but then out of nowhere, you just up and leave? Why? Because he was naked? Little kids do that. Your kids didn't do that?"

"Of course they did. That's not why I left."

"So, what is your problem with my son?"

He shook his head. "I swear to you, I don't have a problem with Jake. I think he's a great little boy."

"So why?"

Gabe gave me a patient smile.

"If you'd stop talking, I'll tell you."

Chapter Thirty-Nine

Gabe

Gretchen was in tears within five minutes of my story, and I'm man enough to admit a little water leaked down my cheeks when I talked about the things that Jake did that reminded me of Bodhi.

She squeezed my hand when she said, "I'm so sorry, Gabe. I can't imagine how difficult that must have been—how it must still be."

"Thank you. I'm working on trying to focus on the good memories. I went back to my therapist after how shaken up I was when I first met Jake. Obviously, I hadn't dealt with it as well as I'd thought."

"I'm sure meeting Jake had to have been a shock to begin with."

"I'll admit—that was a surprise. Why didn't you tell me about him?"

She shrugged. "Why would I have? We both agreed it was a weekend-only fling. I didn't see the point. Especially after what you said about how crazy your brother was for starting over. I knew we didn't have a future."

She wasn't wrong, yet I didn't like hearing it out loud.

"I understand." I broke into a grin. "Kind of. Just so you know, it wouldn't have mattered; I still would have wanted to spend the weekend with you if you'd told me you have a son."

"You say that now..."

"I would have said it then, too."

That was true. I would have still wanted to sleep with her. The only difference if I'd known about Jake is I probably wouldn't have considered dating her.

And I wasn't even entirely sure about that.

"Well, I won't make that mistake again. I will be forthcoming next time."

It took me a second to realize she was talking about the *next* guy she slept with. I didn't like that.

At all.

Yet, I knew there wasn't a damn thing I could say about it, considering our circumstances.

She touched my hand.

"Thank you for telling me about Bodhi. I know it must not have been easy for you."

"It wasn't. But you deserved to know why I reacted the way I did. It had nothing to do with you or Jake."

"Well, I appreciate it."

We sat in awkward silence for a beat before I asked, "How about we have a glass of wine while we talk about my proposal for your cabinets?"

"Oh," she replied breathlessly. "Okay."

I noticed her nipples went stiff again under her pajama top and wondered what was up with that.

It wasn't like I was mad about it. Just the opposite, as I subtly adjusted my semi in my pants when I stood to follow her to the kitchen.

She pulled out the open bottle of Riesling I'd noticed in her refrigerator earlier, and I grabbed two wine glasses from her cupboard and set them on the counter.

There seemed to be a slight quiver in her hand as she poured the wine and handed me a glass.

"So, what did you have in mind?"

I swirled the contents of the glass as I spoke.

"I think I found a way we can help each other out."

She drew a quick breath before saying, "Oh?"

"I can install your cabinets myself after work and on the weekends in exchange for..." I took a swallow of the Riesling and noticed her pupils dilate. "You tutoring Brayden."

She narrowed her eyes and tilted her head like she was confused, and her tone was clipped when she repeated back, "You want me to tutor your son in exchange for installing my cabinets? *That's* your proposition?"

"Yeah, Brayden's grades have started to slip, so he's in jeopardy of becoming ineligible to play. I thought we could barter your specialty for my specialty."

She reiterated. "*That's* what you wanted to talk to me about? *Tutoring?*"

"Is that bad?"

"No, I, um, I just wasn't expecting that."

"What were you expecting?"

"I-I—" she stammered. "I don't know. Not that."

Gretchen didn't jump at the idea, which surprised me, so I tried to spell out what that would mean for her.

"It'd save you about ten thousand dollars."

She chewed on her bottom lip as she stared at the countertop, like she was lost in thought before murmuring, "That would help my bottom line after it closes."

"What do you mean? You wouldn't have to put a contractor's lien on your house."

Her eyes finally met mine.

"While I really appreciate you making an exception for me and letting me make payments, I still can't afford the monthly amount Shelly sent. And that didn't even include installation. It's almost a whole week of wages for me. No matter how much I cut from my budget, I can't allocate twenty-five percent of my income for the next three years on cabinets."

I felt like an ass. I hadn't thought the terms through when I'd rattled them off to Shelly. Of course, Gretchen couldn't make that kind of payment.

"How much can you afford?"

She hemmed and hawed before finally saying, "I think the most I could swing would be three hundred, so, obviously it's not going to work."

"We'll change the contract to three hundred a month."

Gretchen put her hand on her hip, like she didn't trust me.

"Just like that?"

"Yeah. I am the owner. I can do that."

"I thought you had to talk to your brother."

"He's my partner, so he's included on important decisions."

"And you think your brother would be okay with you giving me an interest-free loan for..." She paused and looked at the ceiling while she moved her lips while writing something in the air before continuing. "Over seven years?"

"Yeah."

"*And* you'd install the cabinets in exchange for tutoring your son?"

"Yeah. It's a win-win."

She scoffed. "Just how long do you want me to tutor him for?"

I shrugged. "Maybe the rest of this semester and his first semester next year."

"And how often?"

"I dunno. A couple of hours once or twice a week and maybe every other Saturday or Sunday, depending on our schedules."

Her gaze went to the sky as she did more calculations, then she shook her head. "I don't think so."

"Okay. If that's too much time for you—"

"That's not it. But it's not going to work."

"Why? You're getting a good deal."

"Exactly. I'm getting *too* good a deal. I don't want your charity."

"How do you figure you're getting too good a deal?"

"At twenty hours a month, it should take at least three years of tutoring, if not four. Not a semester and a half."

I cut her off. "Three years? Where do you get three years? Ten thousand dollars divided by sixty dollars an hour is..." I did the quick math in my head. "A little over one hundred and sixty hours. At twenty hours a month, that's only eight months. Okay, so maybe a little into his second semester of eighth grade."

She snorted. "You think I make anywhere close to sixty dollars an hour for tutoring?"

"I don't know, but you should."

"I don't disagree with you, but I don't even make half that."

"Well, for the purpose of our bartering, that's what you're charging."

Gretchen opened and closed her mouth like she wanted to argue, then finally said, "Okay, even if I did agree to that rate, there's still the matter of you giving me an interest-free loan for over seven years, when you've *never* let anyone make payments before."

"We're exploring if we want to make that an option. You're our beta test to see how it would work."

I was proud of myself for saying it with a straight face. I still hadn't told Mav we were accepting payments from her. I knew he wouldn't fight me on the deal—especially since he knew she wasn't just any client, but I doubted he'd go for us making it a regular thing with anyone else. Although, we probably could charge more if we did.

It was something to explore and at least discuss with my brother.

So, in a way, she really was our beta test. I was just discounting our services for the privilege of a payment plan instead of upselling them.

Minor detail.

Looking at her pretty face, I had zero regrets.

****

Gretchen

So, Gabe wasn't interested in sex for the cupboard installation and instead wanted me to tutor his son. Something that was totally appropriate and in my wheelhouse.

I had no idea why I'd felt a tinge of disappointment at his offer. Of course he wasn't going to suggest I sleep with him in exchange for the cabinets to be installed.

And if he'd had—there was no way I'd have agreed.

Liar! the devil on my shoulder screamed.

The angel chimed in. *We'll never know, will we?*

I swear Gabe had been trying to flirt with me earlier, but then he panicked and left again, leaving me more confused than ever.

Except now I understood why, and my heart broke for him.

While I didn't want to be a charity case, I wanted my son to grow up in Lancastle more, so I was willing to swallow my pride if it meant we didn't have to move.

"So, if we do this, when do you want to get started?"

"I can start demoing the kitchen Friday after work."

I winced at the word *demo.*

"How long will I be without a kitchen if you're going to do this in your spare time? I can't really afford to eat out every day for months on end."

"I'm hoping to have things operational in less than a month. In the meantime, I can help you move the refrigerator and microwave into your formal dining room. I know it's not ideal, but you'd at least be able to prepare a few things in a clean room."

"I'll be without a sink, too, huh?"

"Yeah, I'm sorry. I recommend paper plates."

I wasn't looking forward to that, and it must have shown on my face because he continued, "I'll try to get here as often as I can. I promise."

"Are you going to bring Brayden with you when you come this weekend?"

"I will if that works for you."

"Yeah. Just let me know what time."

"I will."

He drained his wine glass and rinsed it out in the sink before putting it in the dishwasher.

Which reminded me...

"Thank you for cleaning up tonight. I really appreciate it."

"And I appreciate you making me dinner, so it was the least I could do."

"Anytime. As long as it's not lasagna."

That made him chuckle, then he said, "You should try it one more time before abandoning it altogether."

"I think it's cursed. Besides, I won't have an oven for a while."

"When your kitchen is done, then."

"Maybe."

We stood in awkward silence until he nodded toward the direction of the front door.

"I probably should get going."

Even though I had to get up for school in the morning, I was disappointed at the idea of him leaving. I enjoyed being around him.

Still, I walked him toward the door without argument.

"Do you think you'll be here all weekend?"

"It's my weekend with the kids, but they're spending Friday night with friends, so I was thinking I'd come Friday evening, Saturday morning before Brayden's lacrosse game, and then on Sunday afternoon, I'll bring Brayden with me, if that works for you."

I thought of how I could get Jake out of the house during those times.

"That works great."

He offered me a smile when he put his hand on the doorknob.

"Thanks for letting me come back."

"Thank you for trusting me enough to tell me about Bodhi."

"I owed you that."

I shook my head. "You don't owe me anything. We're not dating."

I think I was reminding myself about that, too.

"I know we're not dating, but we were intimate. Not only that, you're a client. You deserved an explanation for why I freaked out on you twice."

I wasn't sure what being a client had to do with anything, but I replied, "I'm honored you shared that with me."

Gabe opened the door then paused before he stepped out.

"I'll have Shelly send you a revised contract with the updated terms."

"I'll look for it."

He gave a wave and left.

With my hand on the doorframe, I watched him head toward his truck. When he was about ten steps down the walk, I called out, "Gabe?"

He turned around with raised brows. "Yeah?"

"Thank you for helping me keep my house. You have no idea how much it means to me."

The corners of his mouth lifted.

"I'm glad I could help."

I closed the door feeling incredibly grateful, and yet a little sad. But I couldn't explain why.

Chapter Forty

Gabe

I told her I could be done with the cabinets in less than a month, but if I recruited my brother, Beau, for help, I think I could have everything installed in two weekends. Then I would worry about the smaller details once she had a functional kitchen again.

What was the saying? Better to under promise and over deliver.

Besides, I still needed to see if Beau was available.

I decided to swing by his auto shop the next day and take him out to lunch.

I think his employees recognized me when I walked in the garage because they didn't even question who I was or what I was doing there. Even if they hadn't known me, the resemblance between the Mitchell brothers—especially the three oldest—was obvious. We all had dark brown hair and blue eyes. Derrick looked the most like our mom with his lighter hair and hazel eyes.

"Is he around?" I called to Rob, the guy who'd worked there since Beau opened the shop ten years ago, with Maverick's backing, of course.

Rob gestured to a pair of legs sticking out from under a blue Ram truck.

I nodded my thanks, walked to where my brother lay, and squatted down so he could hear me.

"Hey, you had lunch yet?"

Beau slid out on the wheeled creeper and looked up at me with a bright smile and a smudge of grease across his forehead.

"Hey! What are you doing here? Is Freddie running okay?"

My gearhead brother named his many cars, along with the rest of the family's vehicles. He had dubbed my black truck, Freddie the Ford F150.

"He's running like a champ. I was just in the neighborhood and thought I'd see what you were doing for lunch."

Beau's brows drew together as he sat up, still holding a wrench in his hand.

"You were in the neighborhood? Doing what?"

Of course the asshole would call me out about something so trivial. I hated being caught in a lie, even if it was just a fib.

"Do you want me to take you to lunch or not?"

He put the wrench in the tool chest, pulled a rag from his back pocket, and slowly wiped his hands as he spoke.

"I dunno. It sounds like you want something."

"What if I do? Are you going to tell me no?"

His nose wrinkled in a snarl as he begrudgingly grumbled, "No, probably not."

I couldn't help but grin in return.

"Good. Let's grab something to eat, and I'll fill you in." I nodded toward his face. "And wipe your forehead."

~~

"So, let me get this straight. You're *not* dating her, but you're installing her cabinets... *for free*?"

"No, not free," I said as I dressed my cheeseburger with the condiments on the table. "She's going to tutor Brayden in exchange. His grades have started to slip, and I'm worried he's going to be ineligible."

My brother removed the bun on his burger and waited for me to pass the ketchup.

"Is Becky worried about his grades?"

I frowned at his question.

"I don't know."

"Then his grades aren't that bad. If they were, she'd be on your ass and find a way to make it your fault."

I usually loved that my brothers knew my ex-wife so well. But not today.

"I'm trying to get in front of it."

Beau held the burger with both hands and paused before taking a bite to say, "Yeah. Sure. That's what this is about."

"Fuck you," I grumbled before taking my own bite.

He swallowed before asking, "Why can't you just admit you like this woman?"

"Okay, fine. I do like her; she's a nice person. But that's not what this is about."

"Look," my brother paused and sucked a ketchup blob that had dripped onto the webbing of his hand then continued. "If you want me to give up my Friday night to help you, the least you can do is be honest with me."

I shoved fries into my mouth to buy myself a few seconds before responding.

Beau lowered his burger, like he'd had an epiphany.

"Unless you aren't even being honest with yourself."

"What does it matter? I'm not going to pursue her. We both agreed that we want different things."

Beau took another bite and studied me while he chewed slowly.

Finally, he asked, "Is she going to be there on Friday?"

"I think so. At least to let me in."

"She doesn't have to be home to do that, Boomer."

I remembered the night I took her home from Flannigan's, and she opened her garage door with her phone.

"I know!" I snarled.

"Well, find out if she's going to be there."

I looked at my brother suspiciously.

"Why?"

"Because I'm only helping you if I get to meet her."

"Why do you want to meet her?"

"Derrick said she's your soulmate. I want to see if I agree."

****

Gretchen

I pulled out my phone during lunch to play a few games of sudoku while I ate my sandwich and noticed I had a text message.

Gabe: Are we still on for tomorrow?

Me: If that still works for you. Do you know what time?

Gabe: My brother, Beau, and I can get there around six.

That didn't leave me a lot of time after school. It was a good thing I was almost finished boxing up the kitchen.

Me: Jake and I will be gone by 5:30. The garage code is 1215; you can let yourself in.

Gabe: You guys don't have to leave. I'll bring pizza from Caruso's.

Me: I don't want to be in your way.

Gabe: You won't be in my way. I actually would prefer you stay so you can show me where you want your fridge and microwave.

Me: Okay… then shouldn't I be the one buying the pizza?

Gabe: Nope. I'll see you tomorrow.

I'd thought it was best to keep Jake away from Gabe. I didn't want to upset him by reminding him of his son that he'd lost, so I'd planned on taking Jake to see the latest animated movie, even though I was worried he wouldn't be able to sit still after the first forty-five minutes. That was his max when we watched movies at home.

I decided to see if my parents or sister could watch him Friday instead and we'd shoot for a matinee on Saturday.

As luck would have it, my mom was thrilled at the prospect of babysitting her only grandchild.

"Of course. Just bring his overnight bag, and we'll keep him until Saturday."

"You don't have to do that, Mom. I should be able to pick him up no later than nine."

I couldn't imagine Gabe would want to work past then after having worked all day.

"Nonsense. There's no point waking him up when he's perfectly fine here."

"Are you sure you don't mind?"

"Honey, we love that little boy and love having him around. It's no trouble."

"Thanks, Mom."

"I'll see you tomorrow."

I hung up the phone and burst into tears, so grateful for my parents. I wasn't sure what I'd do without them.

How could Jake's grandparents want to see him more than his own father?

Chapter Forty-One

Gabe

I was going to place my pizza order with Caruso's, when I realized I wasn't sure if Jake ate anything on his. Deciding it was better to be safe than sorry, I sent Gretchen a text.

Me: What does Jake like on his pizza?

Gretchen: He usually just eats cheese, but I didn't want him to get in the way so he's staying at my parents tonight.

While my mind immediately went to cutting Beau loose as soon as possible so I could be alone with her, I didn't like the part where she wrote, "I didn't want him to get in the way".

Instead of texting back, I immediately dialed her number. She answered on the second ring.

"Hello?"

"He wouldn't be in the way."

"He's two years old. Of course he would be."

"I mean, for his safety, I wouldn't want him in the thick of things when we're ripping out your current cabinets, but I don't want you in the middle of it either. You can just keep him in the family room with you."

"I'm perfectly capable of helping you. Besides, I've already dropped him off. My parents are excited to have him."

"I mean, you're welcome to help, but that's what you're paying me for, so..."

"Technically, I'm not paying you."

"You're paying the bartered value. Jake will be with you the rest of the weekend, right?"

"I'm planning on picking him up tomorrow afternoon, and then he's going to my sister's when you bring Brayden over on Sunday."

"You don't have to do that."

"I can't tutor Brayden and keep an eye on Jake."

I didn't want her to think she had to keep her son away when I was around. That wasn't fair to her or Jake.

"What if I bring my daughter over with us? She can keep him occupied while you work with Brayden."

"Would she want to do that?"

"Oh yeah. She'd love it."

"Okay, then. I'll let my sister know."

"And you don't have to wait to get him tomorrow."

"It's just easier, Gabe. I don't want him to be in your way."

"Sweetheart, he's not going to be in my way. You shouldn't feel like you can't have your son home when I'm there."

"Are you sure?"

Now I knew for certain that she was worried about me feeling triggered.

"Positive."

I'd had another session with Dr. Frank this week. At his suggestion, I visited Bodhi's grave and had a therapeutic talk with my son's spirit where I told him about Gretchen's little boy.

A sense of peace overcame me, along with a feeling that he approved. I left confident that I could spend time with Jake and not relive the loss of my son.

"Well, maybe next weekend. My parents would be so offended if I went back and brought him home with me now."

That meant she was free tonight.

Not that it mattered.

"I should be at your place in thirty minutes. I hope you're hungry."

"I'll be there, and I'm starved."

I couldn't wait to see her. I was starving, too, and not just for food.

****

Gretchen

I drove faster than the speed limit, scolding myself the entire time for doing so.

I am not excited to see Gabe.

Then I reasoned, *So what if I'm excited. It's just because I think he's attractive, and amazing in bed. But I know it was a one-time deal. There's no way I'm going to sleep with him again.*

Okay, if I were to sleep with him again, it wouldn't mean anything—just like before.

And if it did mean something…

But that's where lying to myself stopped. There was no future with Gabe, and I knew it. Any daydream about him being my Prince Charming was just setting myself up for heartbreak.

He was, and always would be, Mr. Infuriating. I needed to remember that.

The devil on my shoulder cackled, *Mr. Infuriating with an amazingly talented dick.*

Chapter Forty-Two

Gabe

I couldn't help but smile when I pulled into Gretchen's driveway and saw her garage door open with her silver Honda inside.

Instead of parking in the middle of the stall, like I do in my garage, she'd parked to the far right, as if she was leaving room for my truck.

So, of course I pulled in like I belonged there.

Why else would she have left the garage door open?

And I didn't knock when I walked in, although I did loudly announce my presence.

"Knock, knock!"

She was nowhere to be found, so I set the pizza boxes on the island counter and stashed the bag with the cheesecake slices in the refrigerator before I went in search of her.

"Gretchen?" I called as I ventured through her house. "Sweetheart?"

I knew I had no business calling her that, but it didn't feel awkward, so I said it again as I walked down the hall toward her closed bedroom door.

I noticed Jake's room next to hers, decorated in a farm theme. She must have had the door closed when I was there before. While no doubt, I'd been laser-focused on her, I'm pretty sure I would have noticed the red toddler bed, green rug, brightly colored paint and animal decals on the wall.

The bean bags next to the bookcase full of books and easel chalkboard made me smile.

The whole room screamed, "tell me your mom's a teacher, without telling me your mom's a teacher". Jake was a lucky boy.

I heard the turning of the knob, and before I could alert her to my presence, she came out of her bedroom and ran smack dab into my chest, letting out a blood-curdling scream in the process.

Grabbing her arms so she didn't throw a right hook, I soothed, "It's me! It's me!"

She took a step back, out of my hold, put her hand on her chest, and panted, "Oh my god, Gabe! You scared the crap out of me!"

"I'm sorry! I called your name, but you must not have heard me."

"I was in my closet, changing out of my work clothes."

I took the opportunity to peruse her body. She was in a pair of black yoga pants that looked like they had some sort of design on them, almost like circular racing stripes along her thighs. Her light-blue t-shirt had red, green, blue, and yellow paint splotches on it, as if that was what she'd worn when she painted Jake's room. And she wore a pair of black tennis shoes with pink stripes and laces, and a thick pink sole.

Her hair was piled on top of her head with loose strands that framed her face; exactly like the first time she'd walked into my showroom. And same as that fateful day, I couldn't get over how beautiful she was.

I realized I was staring when she blurted out, "What?" and looked down at her outfit. "I'm not going to wear something nice to tear out cabinets."

"You're perfect."

She cocked her head and narrowed eyes at my admission, and I quickly tried to correct myself.

"What you have on; it's perfect."

She pressed her lips together, as if to keep from smiling, I suspected at how awkward I was behaving.

"Good."

I touched the paint on the hem of her t-shirt and let my fingers linger on her hip.

"I'm guessing this is what you wore when you painted Jake's room."

She seemed as affected as me by the contact because I noticed her chest rise and fall.

"Yeah. Troy and I were supposed to buy a farm house in Maine so we could spend our summers in the country. But since that's obviously not going to happen anytime soon, I thought I'd bring the farm to Jake."

She hadn't pulled away from me, so I rubbed the fabric of her shirt between my index finger and thumb, itching to slide my hand underneath and touch her soft skin.

"You're a good mom."

"How do you know? You were only around us for a few minutes."

"Long enough to notice how much you obviously love your son. And I don't think a bad mom would go to the trouble of redecorating her child's bedroom so it felt like he was at a farm."

"Laura and my sister helped."

I wondered if her fucking ex had done anything.

Even though Becky and I weren't on the best terms, I was still always available to help with any projects she was working on—especially if they directly benefited Britt or Brayden. My level of assistance usually depended on if my ex was between boyfriends or not. Fortunately, the latest one seemed handy and eager to please.

Dang, that sounded familiar.

But I wasn't Gretchen's boyfriend.

Something I needed to remind myself about.

I reluctantly released her t-shirt and cleared my throat as I took a step back.

"Let's eat while the pizza's still hot."

But fuck, did her ass look good in those yoga pants.

****

Gretchen

I pulled paper plates from a box I'd set up in the dining room while Gabe opened the pizza boxes sitting on the island.

He gestured to the two large pies—one with just pepperoni and the other loaded with toppings.

"Dig in."

"Shouldn't we wait for your brother?"

"Hell no. And he wouldn't want us to. He's probably bullshitting with one of his customers and lost track of time."

"What does he do?"

"He owns Mitchell Automotives. It was my dad's shop before he and Mav bought him out."

"I'll bet that's nice—having a mechanic in the family. I never know if I'm getting ripped off or not."

"Take your car to Beau. He'll treat you right."

Before I grabbed a slice of pepperoni, I opened the fridge to get us drinks and immediately whirled around.

"Is that...?"

"Cheesecake?" he supplied with a grin. "Yeah. And there's enough for everyone, so don't get any ideas about hogging it all."

"I would never!"

He paused filling his plate and tilted his head as he shot me a look.

"Okay, maybe. But I would never when you're doing me a favor."

"It's not a favor. It's quid pro quo."

He was full of shit. He was definitely doing me a favor, and had I not wanted Jake to grow up in Lancastle so badly, my pride would have made me turn it down.

But Jake was more important than my pride.

Still. If Gabe wanted to try and pretend this was quid pro quo...

"Then in that case, I might just hog it all."

He set his plate on the counter and came up behind me, invading my personal space as he reached past me for the bag.

His lips brushed my ear when he whispered, "Not if I eat it all first."

My mouth dropped open in surprise, and I spun around to face him.

"Give me that!"

Gabe held the bag up high, out of my reach. The lines around his eyes crinkled in amusement as I jumped to try and get it from him.

"What's it worth to you?"

His remark took me by surprise, and I stopped jumping. Was he flirting with me?

"What do you want?"

He raised his brows as he shrugged his shoulders.

"What are you offering?"

What *was* I offering?

There was no doubt we still had sexual chemistry. Could I sleep with him again, knowing there was no future in it?

Why not? You did it before, the devil on my shoulder whispered.

I looked him dead in the eye and replied, "I mean... it is really good cheesecake."

****

Gabe

My dick liked where this conversation was going. A lot.

I took a step closer, lowering the bag to my side as I did.

"The best I've ever had."

Her pupils dilated, so I knew she understood the double entendre.

I inched my face toward hers and whispered, "It's at least worth a kiss, don't you think?"

Her mouth parted slightly, and she leaned in.

Ding dong!

My brother had the worst fucking timing in the world.

Gretchen jumped back, like the spell between us had been broken.

Then the little minx snatched the bag from me and ran toward the door, giggling as she did.

Chapter Forty-Three

Gretchen

I had to blink twice when I opened the door.

There was no denying the man on my front porch was Gabe's brother. There was a resemblance with Derrick, but this guy was the younger version of Gabe.

"You must be Beau," I said with a bright smile.

He smiled back, revealing a dimple just like Derrick's, and I wondered if he was a player like his younger brother.

"I am. And you must be Gretchen. Nice to finally meet you."

I stepped to the side and told him, "Please come in," then pointed toward the kitchen after he walked inside. "Gabe's in the kitchen. He brought pizza."

Gabe yelled, "And cheesecake!"

I snickered as I gripped the bag tighter.

Of course I was going to share. Not only were these guys giving up their Friday night to help me, but I couldn't afford to eat five slices of cheesecake in one week and expect to fit into my jeans.

My empty plate was still on the counter, and I returned to the refrigerator, put the bag inside, and asked, "What can I get you guys to drink? I have Diet Coke, water, lemonade, milk, apple juice, or beer."

"Lemonade, please."

Beau nodded. "Yeah, lemonade sounds good."

We sat around the kitchen island as we ate, and Gabe laid out his plan for the evening, although he seemed to be talking more to Beau than to me.

"Let's get her refrigerator moved into the formal dining room, along with the microwave, so she at least has a clean place to make food. Then we can put up plastic in the doorways to minimize the dust to the rest of the house."

I appreciated that he was thoughtful about mitigating the mess to the rest of the house. I had already been feeling twitchy with all the boxes of my kitchen contents stacked along the walls.

"That sounds like a plan. Which cabinets did you want to start with?" Beau broke out into a grin. "I brought my own sledgehammer. It's in the truck."

"I don't want to demolish them. They're in good enough condition that they can be donated to the Habitat for Humanity's ReStore." He turned to face me. "If that's okay with you?"

"I love that idea."

Not only were we recycling, we'd be donating to a great cause.

Damn him.

We'd almost kissed earlier. I took Beau showing up when he did as the Universe's way of telling me that was a bad idea. But now Gabe had to go be thoughtful and make me wish I could kiss him.

And maybe more.

Beau wiped his mouth with his napkin and tilted his head as he looked at Gabe.

"I thought it was your weekend with the kids?"

"It is, sort of. The older they get, the more complicated it becomes. They're both at a friend's tonight, so they're only staying Saturday night with me."

"It's good they have friends though."

"I know. I'm not complaining; but it does kind of suck when they make plans with their friends during my weekend. My time with them is limited as it is."

I guess Troy not wanting time with Jake might be a blessing in the future. I kept quiet as the brothers continued their exchange.

"You still planning on coming to Brayden's game tomorrow?"

Beau's grin was devilish.

"Of course. I can't let Derrick be the favorite uncle."

I loved how close their family was and how they all seemed to support each other. It was a lot like my family. I could always count on Carrie and Andrew to have my back. I wanted that for Jake. I wanted him to have siblings he'd be close with, even when he was older.

Tears welled up in my eyes at the thought of my son growing up without siblings.

I needed to start dating. I was thirty-one; my fertility window would be closing before I knew it. I didn't have time to mess around with Gabe or any man who wasn't interested in a future with me that included children.

Was there a dating app specifically for that purpose? All the ones my girlfriends were on seemed to be more for hooking up than finding *the one*, which was why I hadn't joined.

With renewed resolve, I dabbed my eyes. And, of course, Gabe noticed.

"You okay?"

I lied. "Just feeling a little nostalgic. The kitchen was the reason I wanted this house."

"You're going to love your new one even more. I guarantee it."

"I hope so."

For the amount of money I was paying—even without installation, it'd really suck if I didn't.

****

Gabe

We made quick work of cleaning up after dinner, then Gretchen showed me where she wanted her makeshift kitchen, and Beau and I set it up.

Before long, the first cabinet came out of the wall.

"That was easier than I thought," my brother remarked as we set it a few feet from the wall it'd previously been attached to.

Gretchen seemed fascinated as she stood by and watched. I'd tasked her with removing the cupboard doors, but she was more interested in what Beau and I were doing.

I wiped my brow with the back of my gloved hand and told her, "I was thinking I'd bring the store's box truck tomorrow and leave it here until everything's out. Would your homeowner's association have a problem with it being parked in your driveway overnight?"

"I don't think so. They're not like some of the HOAs I've read about."

Beau snorted. "I dated a girl whose HOA measured how long her neighbor's grass was. I'd never been more thankful for my little five acres outside of town."

I shuddered at the thought.

"That was one of the requirements for my realtor. No HOA."

She shrugged. "Mine's not bad, and I like knowing that my neighbors can't paint their house purple."

"But you probably can't build a treehouse for Jake in your backyard either."

Her smile was sad when she replied, "Even if it were allowed, I don't see that happening. That's not exactly my skillset."

Maybe Jake's dad would build one at his house. I hoped so. Or maybe her new husband would be handy.

I didn't like the idea of that one bit and decided I was glad her HOA probably didn't allow treehouses.

Chapter Forty-Four

Gabe

We got a quarter of the cabinets removed by the time eight forty-five rolled around.

"Let's call it a night," I suggested.

"Good idea," my brother grinned. "That leaves me just enough time to go home and shower before things pick up at Flannigan's."

Gretchen was busy sweeping up drywall dust from the floor. I didn't have the heart to tell her she was wasting her time. There'd be another mess in the morning when I came back.

"Thank you for your help, Beau," she said with her sweet smile before bending over to sweep the pile into a dustpan. And yeah, my gaze lingered on her ass as she did.

"Happy to help." My brother looked at me and motioned toward the door with his chin. "Walk me out?"

Oh shit.

I wondered what I'd done that he wanted to talk to me alone.

As we walked along Gretchen's sidewalk toward his car parked behind my truck, I remarked, "Sheila sure is pretty."

Sheila being his red 1970 Chevy Chevelle SS that seemed to shimmer under the street lights.

"She should be with the amount of time and money I've put into her."

"Spend your money now, little brother, 'cuz once you get married and have kids those days will be over."

"Yeah, we'll see. Although I don't think I'll mind spending my money on a wife and kids."

"You won't." I paused, then continued. "Hey, you think you can swing by here tomorrow and give me a ride to Brayden's game?"

"You don't want my help tomorrow?"

"Yeah, I'd love the help, but are you sure you don't mind? It's a lot harder work when you're hung over."

"I don't mind. And I'm only planning on having a few beers. Hopefully, that's all the time it will take to meet someone."

Ah, to be young and single again.

"Wrap your shit up tight, dude."

Beau gave me a grin. "Always do," then he unlocked his car but didn't move to open the door. "Derrick's right, you know. Gretchen's your soulmate."

I snorted out a laugh. "How can you say that? She and I barely even talked while you've been here."

"You talked enough. I don't know. You two just seem to click, like you're on the same wavelength. The way Mav and Olivia are. And don't get me started about the way you each look at the other when you think no one's paying attention."

"I mean, I can't deny we have chemistry, but—"

"You're allowed to be happy, Gabe. It's okay to fall in love again. Why not do it with someone who's beautiful and has a nice ass?"

I raised my left eyebrow at him. "First off, you talk about her ass again at your own peril."

My brother just shrugged unaffected, and I continued. "I know I'm allowed to fall in love again, and maybe someday I'll meet someone. But it's not Gretchen. She needs someone who's going to build a treehouse for her son."

Beau gave me a wicked grin as he opened the driver's door.

"Good thing you already have one built in your backyard."

I shook my head.

"She's young. She wants more kids."

My brother looked at me like I was an idiot as he got behind the wheel.

"So, marry her and knock her up."

He said it like it was so obvious and easy.

If only...

"I'm too old for that shit."

His key was in the ignition, but he didn't turn the engine over.

"That's too bad, because she deserves someone amazing. I just hope you pull your head out of your ass and realize that could be you before someone else snatches her up."

Seconds later his V8 roared to life, and he closed the car door, then cranked down the window.

"What time tomorrow?"

"I dunno. Probably around nine, but I'll have to double check with her to make sure that's not too early to get here."

He broke out into a smug grin.

"Or you could just spend the night."

I rolled my eyes and made a shooing motion with my hand.

"Get out of here. And tell Derrick I said hi."

"Will do." With a mock salute, he backed out of the driveway.

I watched him drive away, unsure of what my next move was.

****

Gretchen

Watching Gabe work had gotten me all hot and bothered. There was nothing sexier than a man in work boots who knew what the hell he was doing. Especially when I had first-hand knowledge of how that translated into the bedroom.

My resolve when I was around the man was virtually nonexistent.

I'd be surprised if I made it through this kitchen renovation without throwing myself at him.

That didn't exactly fit into my "find a new husband and pop out some kids" plan.

Maybe I could just practice the making the kids part. So when I did find my new baby daddy, I'd be ready to rock his world, and he'd want nothing more than to put a baby in me.

God, I was lame.

Why couldn't I just admit I wanted to have sex again with the hot carpenter? I needed to channel some of Laura's energy. She'd have no trouble admitting that's what she wanted and going after it.

The problem was she could get up the next day and not think about the guy again. Meanwhile, I brought Gabe home, granted it was for the entire weekend, and was heartbroken when he ghosted me. And even more heartbroken when I learned why.

But it also confirmed there was no future with him.

I really needed Mr. Infuriating to be a little less likeable now and a lot more infuriating.

****

Gabe

Gretchen had thrown towels on her dining room chairs and was seated at the table, enjoying a slice of cheesecake right out of the container when I came back inside.

"We forgot to have dessert earlier," she said with a flirty smile.

"I think the pizza filled us up." I opened her refrigerator and pulled a slice from the bag. "Although neither of us had thought to offer any to Beau."

"We should be ashamed of ourselves. We're cheesecake hoarders."

I grabbed a plastic fork from a bag of disposable silverware that she'd neatly lined up next to the paper plates and plastic cups on the hutch she'd transformed into a microwave cart.

Following Gretchen's lead, I forwent a plate, opened the lid, and took a bite before sitting down next to her.

"Anyone who's tried Caruso's cheesecake wouldn't blame us."

A small smile escaped her, and I noticed she arched her back a little when she leaned forward.

"How should we decide who gets the last piece?"

She was definitely flirting.

I thought about what Beau had said. She did deserve someone amazing.

I wasn't that man. I brought way too much baggage to the table.

"We could just split it. Or, we could be nice and offer it to Beau tomorrow."

Her face fell and she sat back in her chair.

"Yeah, that'd probably be the polite thing to do. Since he is helping and everything."

She tossed her fork in the container next to her half-eaten slice and closed the lid.

"Besides, this piece should last me the weekend, unless Jake catches me eating it."

I laughed out loud.

"I have a mini-fridge in my bedroom closet where I hide my snacks I don't want the kids to find."

"I'm learning all the tricks. One of my coworkers hides candy in an empty oatmeal container in her pantry, and another puts it in a vegetable bag in the freezer."

"Those are brilliant ideas. I'll have to remember that this summer when the kids stay with me for weeks at a time."

"Is it hard to go from every other weekend during the school year to all the time in the summer?"

"I have them Wednesday evenings, too," I offered like that somehow made the situation better. "But, no. What's hard is going from having them all the time to them being gone again. That sucks."

"I can't even imagine," she replied wistfully.

I cocked my head. "What about you? How do you handle it when Jake goes to his dad's?"

"Oh, he doesn't. Troy relinquished his parental rights."

My blood pressure spiked when I roared, *"He did what?"*

Her shoulders went to her ears, then dropped in defeat.

"His girlfriend is like twenty-one. I don't think she's ready for kids. And this way he pays the least amount of child support the courts would allow."

"That's not how child support works."

She shook her head.

"It doesn't matter; I gladly took the deal. I'd rather do this by myself than let him have any opportunity to hurt my son."

I stared at her in awe. She was even more amazing than I'd realized. If anyone deserved the fairytale, it was her.

But I wasn't Prince Charming. Far from it. I was old and salty, and set in my ways. *Mr. Infuriating*, she'd called me.

There were probably a lot of people, especially my ex-wife, who'd agree with her.

She must have mistook the way I was staring at her to mean something else, because her flirty side resurfaced.

"I need to take a shower." She put her hand on my forearm. "Care to join me? I haven't shown you how much I appreciate the cheesecake."

My cock jumped up and down, screaming, "Hell yes!"

"Sweetheart, there's nothing I'd like more than to join you in the shower; I've revisited the memory of the last time we were together in there more than once. But..."

I'm a fucking moron.

That's the only explanation for how I continued.

"If we hooked up again, it wouldn't be fair to either of us."

She pulled her hand away and glanced down at the table.

"What do you mean?"

"I'm not what you're looking for. You'd only end up disappointed, and then I'd be left feeling bad that I hurt you."

Oh, and apparently, I'm a liar in addition to a moron.

Because I wasn't so sure she was the one who'd end up hurt in the end.

Chapter Forty-Five

Gretchen

I'd made such a fool of myself the night before, there wasn't a chance in hell I was showing my face around Gabe Saturday morning.

There was no doubt in my mind that he'd been coming on to me before Beau arrived. But while they removed cabinets and I convinced myself sleeping with him again was a good idea, he'd decided just the opposite.

Talk about proof that we never would be on the same page.

After getting up later than my normal time and eating the rest of my cheesecake for breakfast, because frankly, I deserved it, I sent him a text.

Me: I need to pick up Jake and run some errands. The garage code is 1215. I'll leave the door to the house unlocked. Please let me know what time you'll be here tomorrow.

I set my phone down and ran upstairs to quickly get dressed. I wanted to get out of the house as soon as possible in case he decided to come early.

Although since he'd seemed as uncomfortable as I was last night after he'd rejected me, I'd be surprised if that was the case.

He did, however, give me the "You're a great woman and will make some lucky man very happy someday. I hope you'll always think of me as a friend," speech, so maybe he would show up like nothing happened just to prove a point.

Yeah, fuck that.

I had enough friends.

It wasn't like I wasn't used to rejection. Hell, Troy hadn't wanted to sleep with me since before Jake was born. I'd just thought with the signals Gabe was giving me, he was interested.

Maybe Beau had asked Gabe to meet at Flannigan's when he'd walked his brother out, and he was going to find a new hookup.

Or maybe Beau had convinced him he could do better.

I mean, he wasn't wrong. I'm sure there were plenty of prettier, more successful girls than me who'd love a chance at the hot Zaddy. I'd known that from the beginning.

My phone beeped as I headed toward the garage.

Gabe: I'm sorry I'll miss you. I was hoping we could grab breakfast before I got started.

Me: Maybe another time.

Like when hell froze over.

Gabe: You should bring Jake to Brayden's game. It's at your school at noon.

Me: I don't think we'll be done with errands by then but thank you. I'll see you tomorrow.

And by that, I meant, *I'll avoid you as much as possible tomorrow.*

My pride had already taken a blow by accepting his charity with the cabinets, but I'd somehow allowed myself to think he might still be interested in hooking up with me, that's why he'd offered me the deal he had.

The reality that I was just a plain ol' charity case had really done a number on my ego. I wasn't sure how I was going to salvage my dignity around him, but I hoped having his kids there would help.

I'd worry about that tomorrow.

****

Gabe

Beau broke into a big grin when I punched in the garage code Gretchen had given me.

"You know her code, huh?"

"Yeah, she gave it to me since she's not home."

His brows furrowed.

"She's not home? Where is she?"

Hiding, I suspected, after last night's disaster.

I flipped the light switch in the kitchen and surveyed the half-demoed room.

"She had to pick up her son, then she had some errands to run."

"Did anything happen last—"

I cut him off before he even had a chance to finish the thought.

"Nope. We had some cheesecake, and I left."

"Oh, that's right. You had brought cheesecake with the pizza. And forgot to offer me any."

"Your slice is probably still in her fridge."

"I don't give a shit about the cheesecake. I wanna know why you didn't close the deal with her. The electricity between you two was palpable."

"Drop it, Beau."

We squatted at the same time to pick up the first cabinet to move to the box truck.

"Yeah, okay, I will. For now."

I needed to change the subject.

"What about you? Did you go home alone last night?"

"Pffft. Yeah right."

"Are you ever going to settle down?"

"I'm sure I will someday when I meet *the one*. But until then, I'll keep playing the field."

We maneuvered up the truck ramp and set the cupboard down at the front of the truck bed.

"How do you know you haven't already met her?"

"I haven't," he replied confidently as he wiped his hands on his jeans.

"But how do you know?"

I walked down the ramp, Beau, however, chose to hop off the back of the truck onto the ground.

"Because there's hasn't been anyone I've been willing to break, or even bend, my rules for. You know, like install an engine—or say, cabinets—for free in my spare time."

"Fuck off."

He didn't miss a beat.

"What's Mav think about this, by the way?"

"He doesn't know yet." I shot him a stern look. "And I'd prefer to be the one to tell him."

"My lips are sealed, man. But it might soften the blow if you're dating her."

"I'm not going to fucking date her!"

Beau threw his hands up in front of him as if in surrender.

"Okay, okay!" He dropped them with a grin. "But I just want to be on record as saying, I think you're a moron."

Yeah, you and me both, little brother.

Chapter Forty-Six

Gretchen

Jake was confused by the state of our kitchen when we'd gotten home. Gabe and Beau had removed almost all the cabinets except for one small section with the kitchen sink and the island.

"Where go, mama?" my son asked with his hands open as he looked around the kitchen.

"We're getting new cabinets, baby. Here, let me show you."

I took his hand, and we went out to the garage where I pulled the foam wrap off the cabinet my dad had inspected when they were first delivered.

They really were beautiful.

I swept my hand out to gesture to all the cupboards in the third stall of the garage.

"These will go in our new kitchen."

"Okay. I play Elmo now?"

There were advantages to the short attention span of a two-year-old.

Laughing, I ruffled the hair on his head.

"You can play Elmo now."

I was confident he'd be asleep in minutes since it was way past his naptime. I'd purposefully stayed away from the house until an hour after Brayden's game was supposed to start.

I knew the reprieve was going to be short-lived, since they were coming over tomorrow. But at least I had a day to lick my wounds.

And with any luck, some cheesecake to help ease my pain.

~~

I woke up the next day filled with nervous energy.

I knew who Brayden Mitchell was. Yes, I'd purposefully found out once I'd done the deed with his dad, and I observed him in the hall between classes. There was no denying he was Gabe's son. The Mitchell genes were strong.

I was a little concerned he was going to think his dad and I were dating and cop an attitude with me while I tried to tutor him. I guess I'd find out soon enough.

Wayne had filled me in about Brayden's abilities once I told him I was going to be tutoring the young man.

"He's a good kid."

That didn't surprise me. He had Gabe for a role model.

"His overall reading comprehension seems good, but he's struggling with poetry and literary devices—especially symbolism."

That wasn't unusual. Seventh grade boys were not known for their love of poetry, and, let's face it, males at any age weren't exactly known for their ability to read between the lines.

"And his essay writing is abysmal."

Okay, so at least I knew where to start.

When the doorbell rang Sunday afternoon, I was ready to face whatever lay in store for me.

****

Gabe

"And why are we going to Mrs. Wainwright's again?" Brayden asked as he took a bite of the omelet I'd made him.

He, Brittany, and I were having breakfast in the nook overlooking the backyard—the treehouse on full display in the distance.

"So she can tutor you while I work on her cabinets," I replied as I buttered my toast. "And she just got divorced, so technically, I think she's Ms. Kelly now but isn't changing her name at school until next year."

"Does that mean you two are dating?"

I was glad I wasn't in the middle of drinking my coffee because I would have spit it out before I offered a lame denial.

"No! She's just a client. We reached a bartering agreement—I'll install her cabinets in exchange for her helping you get your English grade up."

"How did you know my grade is bad?"

I hadn't exactly. Only suspected it based on some of the papers I'd seen in his backpack, but he just confirmed it.

Britt chimed in, "Mom said since you don't have the password to the parent portal, you'd never know."

And that was going to change, effective immediately.

I was a little peeved that Becky decided to keep that from me but decided to ask her about it first before I jumped her shit.

See? I'm growing.

Frankly, I was surprised she hadn't jumped mine and tried to make it my fault.

"Well, it'd be hard to hide it from me when he becomes ineligible to play lacrosse, now wouldn't it? Hopefully Ms. Kelly will help make sure that doesn't happen."

"And I really get to babysit her son?" my eleven-year-old asked with excitement in her brown eyes.

I wouldn't call it babysitting, per se, since both Gretchen and I were going to be in the house. More like keeping him occupied. But my daughter liked the idea of being responsible for Jake, so I wasn't going to rain on her parade.

"You really get to babysit, honey."

"Do I get paid?"

Brayden looked over at me with raised eyebrows.

Shit. I hadn't thought about that.

"That depends. How much do you want?"

"I'm just teasing, Dad. You buy me stuff all the time."

I decided I'd still slip her a few bucks when Brayden wasn't around.

"Think of it as an investment in your academic future. You never know, you might have Ms. Kelly for your English teacher someday. It'd be advantageous to be on her good side."

"You'll have her if you're lucky," Brayden piped in. "Will says she's really nice."

"Let's hope she's as good a tutor as she is nice."

"But you're not dating her?" my son asked again.

"Nope. She's just a client."

Unfortunately.

Chapter Forty-Seven

Gretchen

When the doorbell rang, I picked Jake up, took a deep breath, and forced myself to smile when I opened the door.

Gabe stood behind Brayden and Brittany and offered a sheepish, "Hi."

I, however, channeled my first-day school teacher energy and focused on the kids, saying brightly, "Hello! You must be Brayden and Brittany! I've heard so much about you! Please come in!"

I offered Gabe a polite smile but otherwise ignored him.

I hadn't had to worry about his kids having an attitude toward me. They were friendly and polite, and Brayden worked on his essays without grumbling. As we went through the strengths and weaknesses of his writing, he was fully vested in how he could improve.

And Brittany was too adorable as she played Jake's mother hen. Jake, of course, loved it and refused to let her attention stray for even a second from anywhere but what he was doing.

The moment he'd notice she looked away from the tablet, he'd reach for her face and steer her back to the game, while chastising, "No, *Bit-nee*. Mouse!"

After forty-five minutes, I felt bad for her so while Brayden worked on another essay, I decided to put my big girl panties on and approach Gabe. He and Beau were prying the sink loose from the cabinet in the kitchen.

I was glad Beau was there to act as a buffer and mitigate how uncomfortable things were between Gabe and me.

"I think fifteen more minutes then we'll call it a day. You can only stuff so much information into a kid's brain and expect him to retain it."

Gabe nodded.

"We should be done with this by then, and we can get out of your hair."

I chuckled. "Brittany will probably appreciate that. I think she's going to reconsider any ideas she had of babysitting in the future. Jake has been quite demanding of her time."

"I'm sure she's having a blast," Beau piped in.

"She definitely loved being a big sister," Gabe added with a sad smile. "I bet she misses it."

Death is a topic that can be difficult to navigate. You never know if the person grieving wants to talk about their deceased loved one or if it's too painful.

I looked to Beau for guidance about how to continue, since he knew his brother better than I did.

Beau chuckled. "Remember that Thanksgiving when she tried changing Bodhi's diaper?"

That made Gabe burst out laughing, which I took as a good sign. "Yes, what a disaster!"

"What happened?"

They proceeded to tell me about how four-year-old Brittany had tried to change her little brother's poopy diaper after dinner without telling anyone. And how Gabe had to pay to have his mom's couch professionally cleaned.

"Well, she hasn't offered to change Jake's pullup, so I think she learned her lesson."

I met Gabe's eyes, and both our smiles fell at the same time.

Awkward.

Just then, Brayden poked his head through the makeshift plastic door.

"Mrs. Wainwri—er, Ms. Kelly? I'm finished."

Thank fuck I had an excuse to get the hell out of there.

"Fantastic! I'll be right there."

I smiled warmly at Beau.

"Thanks again for your help this weekend."

His adorable dimple was on display when he replied, "Of course, my pleasure."

"I, uh," I clumsily gestured with my thumb toward where Brayden sat at the kitchen table now located in the family room. "Better go over his essay with him."

Without waiting for a reply, I spun on my heel and fled.

****

Gabe

"What the hell was that all about?" Beau said softly so only I could hear.

With my voice equally muted, I replied, "Nothing."

"Bullshit. What did you do?"

I shook my head.

"Not here."

We hoisted the sink from the cabinet and walked it out to the truck. The second we set it down, Beau barked, "Start talking."

I let out a big sigh as I leaned against the wall of the box truck, then started talking, like he'd demanded.

"Before you got here Friday, we were flirting. Nothing over-the-top, but we probably would have kissed had you not rang the doorbell when you did."

"I knew it! It was obvious there was something going on between you two. Sorry I cockblocked you."

"It was probably a good thing you did. When I came back inside after walking you out, she basically asked me to join her in the shower—"

My brother interjected, "Nice!"

I ignored his outburst and continued. "I politely turned her down, then left."

Beau blinked at me like I'd just told him I ate boogers for breakfast.

Finally, he burst out, "You're kidding me! Why? Why would you turn her down? Are you stupid?"

"Maybe. But it was the right thing to do."

"*The right thing to do*? How in God's name was that the right thing to do? She's your fucking soulmate, you idiot!"

"Okay, you and Derrick need to stop with that bullshit. We're not soulmates. We're not even compatible. She wants more kids, I don't. No good would come from us sleeping together again."

My brother snorted. "I'm not sure you're doing things right if you think no good comes from sleeping with someone."

"Eat a dick. I don't want to lead her on and hurt her."

"Did she say she wanted to have a baby with *you*, specifically?"

"Well, no."

"It's pretty arrogant of you to assume she wanted anything more than a good time from you, especially since you've been upfront with your feelings. Maybe you're worried about *you* getting hurt."

"Does it matter? Someone is going to get hurt."

"Why? You act like you don't have any say in this, like it's out of your control."

"I can't make her change her mind."

"Maybe not, but you can change yours."

I shook my head.

"You don't get it."

"Explain it to me, then. Because here's how I see it: you found someone you could be happy—really happy—with but you're scared to pursue it because she wants to have kids, and you don't because you haven't gotten over Becky's betrayal or losing Bodhi, or both."

"We spent a weekend together, Beau. I'm not sure how you can make a proclamation that I found someone I could be happy with. Even you could be happy with someone for a weekend."

"So, you're telling me she's not special?"

I opened my mouth to say just that, but the words got caught in my throat.

"I, uh... she's..."

My little brother nodded with a knowing smirk.

"That's what I thought."

"Fuck off."

He threw his head back and let out a loud cackle.

"When 'fuck off' is the only response you can come up with, that's how I know I've won the argument."

I snarled, "Let's go finish up," then stomped back inside.

Beau chased after me and stood on the other side of the sink cabinet as we surveyed how we were going to remove it with the water valves sticking out of the wall.

"Do Britt and Brayden stay overnight with you on Sundays?"

"Not usually. Just Fridays and Saturdays during the school year. Why?"

"Just making conversation."

I eyed Beau with suspicion. Out of the four brothers, he was the last one who would "just make conversation". But he kept a straight face as he studied the remaining cabinet and said, "I think once we unscrew it from the wall, you pull, and I'll make sure the valves clear the cutouts."

"Sounds like a plan."

It didn't take long before we were ready to take out the cabinet. I stood at the front and waited for Beau to give me the signal.

After he tinkered with the hoses, he announced, "Okay, you're good."

I felt more resistance than usual when I tugged and asked, "Are you sure?"

"Yeah. I'm looking right at it! Pull!"

I still felt resistance and paused, but Beau moved next to me and yanked on the wood, and it came free from the wall.

At the same time a geyser shot into the air.

Beau turned to me with a wicked grin as water cascaded down around us and said, "You'll thank me someday."

Chapter Forty-Eight

Gretchen

I heard a commotion in the kitchen, followed by a shout of, "Oh fuck," then the sound of water pouring onto the floor.

As I scrambled to reach the kitchen, Beau stuck his head through the opening in the plastic.

"Do you know where your water shutoff is?"

As a matter of fact, I did know. Back when Troy lived here and we could afford a monthly yard service, the landscaper showed me when he repaired the irrigation system.

"It's on the west side of the house."

Before Beau even stepped back, I heard the door leading to the garage open, and less than a minute later, the water splashing stopped. The sound of the door opening and closing followed soon after.

I didn't even want to look in the kitchen.

Beau's head darted back out from the seam in the plastic barrier.

"Do you have any towels you use for rags?"

"In the cabinet above the washer."

"Thanks."

He disappeared, and I ventured closer to where I could see the distorted image through the plastic of Gabe and Beau throwing towels on the floor, then Beau's floating head appeared again.

"Do you have any buckets? Maybe a mop?"

"Also in the laundry room."

"Got it."

It was almost comical how quickly his face would appear and disappear.

Taking a deep breath, I stepped foot into the kitchen and was met with, "Don't come any further!"

"Can I help?"

"No, we got it," Beau said as he moved the mop along the floor. "But you're going to be without water for at least a few days."

Crap.

"Okay."

Not ideal, but if anything, I knew how to pivot.

"That's gonna make your mornings difficult, huh?"

Morning, night... was there ever a good time to be without water?

"I'll call my parents; they'll let me sleep on their couch."

"Nonsense," Beau replied. "You can stay with Gabe. He's got plenty of room."

Out of the question.

Judging by the look on Gabe's face, he agreed with me.

"No, it's fine. My parents have a crib for Jake and their couch is really comfy."

I wasn't looking forward to the drive in the morning, especially with traffic. West Lancastle had been growing and was busier than our little town. I'd gotten spoiled living so close to the school and Jake's daycare. But I could handle getting up earlier than usual for a few days.

"That's silly. Gabe has plenty of space—he's got two guest rooms, plus a giant playroom in the basement that Jake would love."

"I'm not staying with Gabe."

Finally, the man in question offered his two cents. And it was not what I was expecting.

"Beau's right, you should stay with me. I've got plenty of room. And since I'm the one who screwed up your water; it's the least I can do."

I shook my head as I watched Beau wring the mop into the bucket.

"My parents are in West Lancastle; it's not that far. It's fine."

"Gretchen, I live ten minutes from here. It'd be much more convenient than driving from West Lancastle, especially in the morning."

"I don't mind, honestly. I'm used to the drive."

"I'm afraid I'm going to have to insist."

My hand went to my hip on its own and my eyebrows shot up to my hairline.

"Excuse me? *You're going to have to insist*?"

Beau's grin widened. He was obviously enjoying the show. Meanwhile, Gabe nodded unapologetically as he moved the towels around the floor with his foot.

"Yeah, I am. I'm the one who screwed up, so until your water gets fixed, you're my responsibility."

I scoffed, "I'm not your responsibility."

"You are until you have running water again. So, go pack a bag. As soon as we get this cleaned up, we can head out."

I was just about to let him have it when I noticed Brayden standing outside the plastic doorway, along with Brittany who had Jake planted on her hip. All three were waiting for my response.

"You can sleep in my room if you don't like the guest room bed," Brittany offered.

"Jake needs a crib," I countered. "It's not safe for him to sleep on a bed yet."

End of argument. I win.

But Gabe countered, "I have a brand-new playpen. I bought it when my college roommate was going to bring his family when he visited last summer. It's still in the packaging because he ended up coming alone."

Gabe looked at me with raised brows that seemed to suggest, *what else ya got?*

When I didn't respond, he added, "I can probably get my plumber here tomorrow. It's one night, Gretchen. Do me this kindness; I feel terrible."

I stared at him for a long beat, then finally sighed, "Fine. I'll go pack an overnight bag. But if the plumber can't get here tomorrow, I'm going to my parents."

The arrogant jerk simply replied, "We'll see."

There's Mr. Infuriating.

I should not find his bossiness hot. And yet...

****

Gabe

I motioned to the cabinet, still sitting on the kitchen floor. "Let's get this out of here before the wood warps."

The second the door leading to the house closed behind us, I growled, "What. The. Fuck. Did you just do?"

My cocky little brother replied, "I think it's pretty obvious what I did."

"Do you know how much this is going to cost me?"

We adjusted our hold on the cabinet before walking up the ramp.

"Really?" Beau replied as we set the cupboard down. "You're worried about paying a plumber when you get to have Gretchen staying at your house? I think that's a small price to pay to have your soulmate under your roof for a few days."

"For the last time, she's not my soulmate! This isn't going to end how you think it will."

We hopped off the truck onto her cement driveway, and I slid the ramp into the slot under the truck bed that Beau had custom installed for me.

"I dunno. You were pretty quick to step up and take the blame and insist she stay with you."

Okay, yeah, I did do that.

"What else was I going to do? She doesn't have any water."

"You could have let her go to her parents."

"And add an extra thirty-minute commute to her drive in the morning?" I asked as I pulled the roll door on the truck down and locked it.

"You could have offered to pay for a room at the inn."

The Seaside Inn was the only lodging in town, so everyone just called it "the inn".

Maybe I should have done that.

I shook my head, sputtering, "You volunteered my house! I couldn't exactly back pedal from that without looking like a jerk."

The little prick just shrugged, not remorseful in the least.

"I guess you better make the best of it then."

Yeah, I guess I better.

Chapter Forty-Nine

Gretchen

What the hell am I doing? I reprimanded myself as I picked out what I was wearing to school tomorrow in order to put it in my overnight bag.

The bag that I was taking to Gabe's house.

Because Jake and I were spending the night there.

Because apparently, I'm a masochist.

"Or I don't have a backbone," I muttered out loud while I carefully folded the dress I'd selected.

But I knew that wasn't true. I'd never been a doormat. I wasn't going to Gabe's house because he'd told me to.

No, somewhere deep down, I *wanted* to go. *Why* I wanted to was fodder for my next therapy appointment, but for now, I was going with the masochist angle. It's the only thing that made sense.

Why else would I willingly put myself through the yo-yo of emotions that Gabe wrung out of me?

I'd always considered myself drama-free, but maybe I secretly got off on it.

Whatever it was, one thing was for certain. Gabe Mitchell had turned me into a hot mess.

****

Gabe

Brayden looked over at me from the passenger seat of my truck.

"So, Mrs. Wainwright is staying at our house."

"It's Ms. Kelly, and yes. I mean, I did break her water valve, so it seems only fair. Is that all right?"

"Yeah, it's fine. I just hope no one at school finds out; that would be weird, having a teacher staying with my dad but they're not dating."

Brittany piped up from the back. "I like her. And her little boy."

"They're nice," I concurred.

"And she's pretty, don't you think, Dad?"

She's fucking gorgeous.

I glanced at Britt through the rear-view mirror and lied to my child's face.

"I hadn't noticed."

Brayden whipped his head around to glare at me.

"You said she was pretty."

"When did I say that?"

"When you texted me last month and asked me who my English teacher was because you'd met Ms. Wainwright. And I told you Britt and I would be okay if you asked her out."

Shit, I remember that.

Brittany eagerly agreed. "You should ask her out, Dad."

"She has a little boy!" I protested.

"So? You have us. Lots of families are blended these days," Brayden said, sounding way too mature for my liking.

Brittany put in her two cents.

"You'd be a good dad for Jake, too."

Because I hated the idea of my kids ever having a stepdad who thought he could replace me, I wanted to point out that Jake already had a dad. But that wasn't necessarily true.

Biologically, yes. But what kind of man willingly gives up his parental rights?

The fucking asshole kind.

"Aren't you guys supposed to be jealous of anyone who could take up my time?"

They were quiet as they mulled over my question. Brayden spoke first.

"Maybe if they were our age. But Jake's so much younger, it's not the same. Plus, he's pretty cute."

"Soooo cute!" Britt agreed. "He reminds me of Bodhi."

I felt my spine stiffen. Bodhi was a lot like Bruno from the Disney movie, *Encanto*: we don't talk about him.

Maybe that needed to change.

"Oh yeah? How does he remind you of Bodhi?"

"The way he walks. And how he can't say my name. He kept calling me *Bit-nee*. That's how Bodhi used to say it."

I smiled at the memory I seemed to have forgotten.

"Does it upset you to be reminded of your brother?"

"No, it's kind of nice to remember," she said wistfully as she looked out the window at the passing scenery.

I glanced at Brayden for his opinion.

"What about you? Does Jake remind you of Bodhi?"

He shrugged. "A little. Especially the way he says Britt's name, like she said."

"And does that bother you?"

"Not at all."

It was obvious my kids were one hundred times more well-adjusted than I was. We'd been right to put them in therapy after Bodhi's accident. Begrudgingly, I had to credit Becky for that one. She'd insisted they keep going after the divorce, too.

"I'm glad you can think about your brother with good memories."

"So, are you going to ask her out?" Britt asked with wide eyes and an eager grin.

"I don't think so, kiddo."

My daughter's face fell.

"Why not?"

"She's a lot younger than me. We don't have much in common." I was totally talking out of my ass. "Not to mention, she's a client. Uncle Mav would nail my hide to the wall if I dated a client."

Britt pointed out, "Uncle D dates customers from his bar all the time; what's the difference?"

"How do you know that?"

Brayden rolled his eyes.

"Everybody knows that, Dad."

"Everybody? Who do you know who knows your uncle besides your mom and me?"

"Uncle Beau, Uncle Maverick, Nick..." he sassed.

"And when was the last time you talked to any of them?" Before he could point out the obvious, I quickly interjected, "Besides today."

"We see Uncle Derrick at Brayden's games," Brittany observed. "And Uncle Beau was at the game yesterday."

Dammit, I forgot about that.

These dang kids had me all discombobulated with their "date Gretchen!" talk.

"I can't ask her out, she's a teacher at your school."

Brayden rolled his eyes again.

"So? She's not one of our teachers."

"She's just a friend and client, and that's the end of the subject!"

"Dad?" Britt's voice was small from the backseat.

I felt bad I'd gotten worked up, so I tried to soften my tone.

"Yeah, honey?"

"You know how Mom likes that Shakespeare quote? '*The lady doth protest too much, methinks*'." Her face broke into a big grin. "Well, substitute 'the lady' for 'the dad'."

Brayden snorted.

I scowled.

The only response I could think of was, "You're both grounded."

My daughter was completely unfazed, because she added, "You should order Instacart so you've got food at the house they like."

"They're only staying one night. We can order delivery for dinner, and I have plenty of stuff to make breakfast."

Britt sounded a lot like her mom when she sighed and said, "Okay, if you think that's a good idea..."

"It's fine!"

At least I hoped it was.

I found I wanted to make Gretchen and Jake's stay as comfortable as possible.

I'm so fucked.

Luckily it was only for one night, right?

Chapter Fifty

Gretchen

My GPS told me my destination was on the right, and I muttered, "Wow," out loud when I turned into the drive. "The woodworking business must be good."

The Cape Cod style house was set far back from the road on what was easily three acres. The house itself wasn't obscene or ornate, but everything—from the landscaping to the white paint to the wraparound porch—was perfect, like it belonged in a magazine.

I imagined the inside matched the outside and anxiety bubbled up inside me. My two-year-old was, well, *two*. He could be a walking tornado.

"Jake, Mommy needs you to be a good boy at Mr. Mitchell's house, okay? No messes, baby."

He nodded enthusiastically, but I knew that didn't mean anything.

Why did I agree to this again?

Oh, yeah, I liked flushing the toilet and brushing my teeth with water. Plus, I couldn't afford a hotel.

And Gabe had insisted.

I put my Honda in park in the circular driveway in front of his house but didn't shut the engine off as I debated continuing through and heading to my parents. Or maybe Laura's. My brother probably would make room for us for a few days. *Anywhere* but here.

Just as I put my foot on the brake and put my hand on the gear shift, I noticed Brittany on the front porch waving like a maniac with a big grin on her face. Her stupid, handsome dad stood behind her with a kind smile.

I waved back at Brittany and turned the car off.

This is such a bad idea.

****

Gabe

Britt bounded down the porch steps and opened the back door of the Honda to unbuckle Jake from his car seat while the little boy let out an excited squeal, "Bit-nee!" as he reached for her with both hands.

Gretchen smiled at the scene while she took a small racecar suitcase, a diaper bag, a satchel, and a weekender bag from her trunk.

I followed my daughter down the stairs and told Gretchen, "Let me take those," when she shifted the suitcases to try and adjust the diaper bag on her shoulder.

I looked at her bags in my hand and realized, *She's really going to be staying under my roof.*

And I didn't hate the idea. Not in the slightest. In fact, my dick loved it, and sprang to life to let me know how much.

To my surprise, she released the bags without argument and politely told me, "Thanks," before checking on Jake and Brittany.

"Do you need me to carry him?" she asked Britt.

"No, I've got him!" My eleven-year-old beamed as she held Jake on her hip. I knew she liked how grownup she felt being tasked with caring for the little boy.

Which was why I'd easily agreed when she asked if she could stay at my house that night. The idea of another person being there to make it less awkward between Gretchen and me had also held some appeal.

"Maybe Ms. Kelly can even give me a ride to school tomorrow, since we're going to the same place?"

"Well, I think she has to take Jake to daycare in the morning, so that won't work. But first, you need to make sure your mom is okay with you staying with me. *If* she says yes, I'll take you to school in the morning."

"Or you could take Jake to daycare and Ms. Kelly can take me to school. That's more practical."

"I don't think Ms. Kelly would be on board with that."

And neither would I.

Ever since Bodhi's accident, I rarely let my kids ride with anyone other than me or their mom. And I tried not to transport someone else's child.

Poor Sienna was still in therapy and would only work jobs that she could do from home. She had her groceries delivered, and I don't think she'd been on a date in seven years.

I felt real guilt about that.

If Becky wanted to blame me for something about the accident, that's what it should be about. Her sister was now a recluse, all because I'd asked her to pick up Bodhi.

I'd learned my lesson and wouldn't make the same mistake again.

As Gretchen followed Brittany up the porch steps, I heard my daughter announce, "I'm staying here tonight, so Jake can sleep in my room if you want."

"I thought you said I could sleep in your room," Gretchen teased with a smile.

"That was only if you thought the guest bed was uncomfortable. But since you'll probably sleep in Dad's room anyway, it doesn't matter. His bed is super comfy."

Gretchen's hand went to her chest as she started coughing like she had something in her throat. I felt my eyebrows shoot up, and I heard myself loudly ask the little matchmaker, "What did you say?"

My daughter paused with her hand on the screen door handle and looked back at me.

"What? You even say your bed is comfortable!"

"That's true, but Ms. Kelly isn't going to be sleeping in it!"

Unfortunately.

Britt pulled the door open, and Gretchen held it for her to walk through while she still held Jake.

She waited until I got inside and had set Gretchen's bags down before continuing.

"Oh, I just thought you'd insist she stay in your room like Mom does when Grandma and Grandpa come visit."

Hmm, I wasn't sure I bought that explanation.

"That's because your mom only has a blow-up bed when she has company. I have a real bed."

Actually, two. Four if you counted the pull-out sofa beds in the basement.

I'd never intended to buy a home this big, but it'd checked all the other boxes I'd had. Plus, since it'd been a fixer upper, I'd gotten it for a song.

After letting the kids pick their rooms and converting a bedroom into an office, having two extra bedrooms hadn't been a deal breaker. The housekeeper liked that she could charge me for the square footage without having to clean all of it regularly. She was finally going to earn her money this week.

"Yeah, but Uncle Derrick said it's not very comfortable."

Uncle Derrick had been drunk.

"My college buddies didn't have any complaints last summer."

Britt shrugged. "You also said they sleep on the ground in sleeping bags like animals." She looked at Gretchen. "Do you use a cot when you go camping?"

"I don't think I've ever been."

"You've never been camping?"

My daughter took the words right out of my mouth.

Gretchen shook her head.

"No. We'd stay at my grandparents' cottage on the Cape in the summers when I was a kid but never camped."

"Oh, you've got to go with us this summer. Dad has more camping equipment than anyone. It's like having a home away from home in the middle of the wilderness. Right, Dad?"

I offered an embarrassed smile.

"The perks of having a corporate job with Adventure Gear Sporting Goods before starting my own business."

That seemed to intrigue Gretchen, although I noticed she didn't say anything about camping.

"You were in the corporate world?"

"I started with Adventure Gear when I was a junior in high school. Once I graduated college with a business major, I moved up through the ranks pretty quickly. When Frank's bought the company four years ago, I took the offered buyout and, with the help of my older brother, turned my side business into a fulltime one."

"Wow, I had no idea you once had a desk job. Do you miss it?"

"God, no. Leaving Corporate America was the best decision I've ever made." I ruffled Brittany's hair. "Other than having my kiddos, of course."

Britt rolled her eyes, "Oh, Dad," then told Jake, "Come on, let's go find some toys to play with," and took the little boy toward the family room.

Gretchen met my gaze.

"She's so sweet."

"She loves taking care of Jake. She said he reminds her of Bodhi."

"I'll bet she was a great big sister."

Maybe she could be again.

Whoa, whoa, whoa.

Where the fuck did that come from?

Was I being disloyal to Bodhi for thinking that? Was I trying to replace him with Jake?

With a forced smile, I replied, "She really was."

Gretchen must have sensed my uneasiness because she cocked her head and asked, "Are you sure you're okay with us staying here?"

I took a cleansing breath in through my nose and thought back to the conversation I'd had with Bodhi at the cemetery earlier this week. A sense of peace flowed through me, and I told her unequivocally, "Absolutely. I'm happy you're here. Let me show you the guest room."

Chapter Fifty-One

Gretchen

I'd been right—Gabe's house was beautiful inside, too, although it wasn't as pristine as the outside. It was clean and tidy, but also homey.

I kept a vigilant eye on Jake to make sure he didn't get into anything he wasn't supposed to. Brittany and Brayden were eleven and thirteen, there was no need for the house to be baby-proofed for them.

My little walking wrecking ball, on the other hand...

Gabe noticed my hyper-vigilance and put his hand on my arm.

"Relax. There's nothing he can touch that can't be replaced."

"But I'd rather not have to replace anything."

"Gretchen, between Brayden and Britt and their friends, there have been plenty of kids in this house. We *live* here. This isn't a museum. Stop worrying."

I willed myself to lower my shoulders and offer him a small smile.

"I'll try."

His eyes were kind as he stared at me, and I felt the familiar flutter in my belly. I needed to squash that bullshit immediately. I wasn't making a fool of myself again.

I tucked my hair behind my ear as I cleared my throat and looked away, searching for something to talk about.

I finally asked, "Um, are you hungry?"

"Yeah. What should we order for dinner?"

"We don't have to get delivery; I can make us something."

"You're my guest. I'm not going to ask you to cook."

"You're not asking, I'm offering. Besides, I *enjoy* cooking. I've missed doing it. Jake can be a picky eater, and it's no fun cooking for one."

"Are you sure?"

"Of course. Although let me see what ingredients you have before I get ahead of myself."

"My housekeeper does a good job of making sure my pantry and freezer are stocked, and she tries to have more fruits and veggies when the kids are going to be here, but a lot of times it ends up getting thrown out."

He walked me into his gourmet kitchen. The cabinets were exquisite. If my kitchen ended up half as beautiful as his, I would be a happy woman.

I glanced around the spacious room.

"Any cupboards that are off-limits to open?"

He furrowed his brows. "You can look through every drawer, cupboard, or closet in this whole house. I'm an open book. Although, you go through a thirteen-year-old boy's room at your own risk."

That made me laugh.

"No thank you. I work with thirteen and fourteen-year-olds all day, I know better."

I opened the door to his pantry and found shelves from floor to ceiling that were lined with enough supplies to last a year.

I knew whose house I'd be going to in the event of the apocalypse.

Even though the pantry was as big as Troy's and my first apartment, Gabe's presence behind me left me unnerved.

His tone was hopeful when he asked, "Are there ingredients for lasagna?"

I turned to face him and shook my head.

"I don't think I'm ready to try that again."

His dumb, handsome face fell in disappointment, and I almost reconsidered.

Almost.

A quick survey of the pantry's contents gave me an idea, provided he had hamburger or its vegetarian equivalent.

"I thought I'd make something all four of us would enjoy."

****

Gabe

Having Gretchen cooking in my kitchen made me feel something I hadn't felt in a long time: contentment.

I offered to help more than once, but she shooed me away each time. So, I sat at the island and made small talk while admiring her ass as she flitted about like she belonged there.

"Is there any chance my kitchen is going to turn out as amazing as this one?" she asked as she stirred the hamburger frying on the stove.

"Yours is going to be nice. I think you're going to love it."

"But not like this."

"Well, no, not quite. But to be fair, this kitchen took me almost six months to remodel."

She turned the burner down and looked at me with wide eyes.

"*Six* months? You were without a kitchen for six months?"

"I didn't live here. I rented an apartment while I gutted the place and worked on it nights and weekends for almost a year."

"You outdid yourself, Gabe. Your home is stunning."

I wanted to puff my chest out with pride. It meant a lot that she appreciated my craftsmanship. As I fantasized about pulling her into the pantry for a quickie, I realized I'd never had sex in my own home.

Any hookups I'd had over the years had taken place in hotel rooms, the woman's place, the backseat of my truck, and one bar bathroom.

Not Flannigan's.

I'd never risk pissing Derrick or Maverick off. My days of drinking my favorite tap beer for free would come to a crashing halt.

But I hadn't met anyone I was willing to allow into my space, even for a night.

And now I'd not only welcomed Gretchen in with open arms, but I'd asked her to bring her son along, too. While one of my kids was here.

What the hell is wrong with me?

The difference is, I told myself, I'm not sleeping with her. Yeah, we'd hooked up before, but this had nothing to do with that.

So what if I'd just imagined covering her mouth with my hand as I fucked her from behind in the pantry?

I'm a guy. It didn't mean anything. We fantasize about everything from football to fishing to fucking. It wasn't like I was going to act on it.

It didn't matter how much I liked her being there; I'd put boundaries in place on Friday night for a reason, and I intended to keep them.

No matter how fucking sexy she looked in my kitchen.

Chapter Fifty-Two

Gretchen

"Ms. Kelly, this is really good!" Brittany announced in between bites of the skillet beef macaroni and cheese.

Gabe nodded enthusiastically. "Delicious."

"Thanks. You saw it was pretty simple to make."

He choked out, "*That* was simple?"

I couldn't help but chuckle as I stabbed some pasta with my fork. "Well, yeah."

"It's like a gourmet version of the stuff from a box that Dad makes."

I glanced over at him with a knowing smile, then told Britt, "I'll send your dad the recipe."

Jake happily munched away in the travel booster seat that was pushed up tight against Gabe's kitchen table.

"Is it good, baby?"

He nodded enthusiastically and attempted another bite that ended up on his face before reaching his mouth.

Gabe smiled as he watched Jake, then told me, "I think I have p-u-d-d-i-n-g in the pantry for dessert. Although it's the instant kind in a box, not in a cup."

"I saw that. The instant is better anyway. At least in my opinion. Although, either way, it's going to end up in his hair."

"That's what bathtubs are for."

He needed to keep his kind eyes to himself. I wouldn't be lulled into believing he felt anything for me other than polite indifference.

I tried to keep the conversation light.

"I can't wait for summer at the Cape, and I can just stick him in the outdoor shower."

Brittany sat up straighter. "Oh! Do you have a place there? My Uncle Maverick and Aunt Olivia just bought a summer house on the beach!"

"My parents do. My mom inherited it from my grandparents."

"The one you stayed at when you were a kid?"

"The very same. And now my kids will get to spend their summers there, too."

"How many more kids do you want?"

"Britt—" Gabe warned. "That's not something you ask someone."

"Why not? She said her kidssss," Brittany drew the "S" out. "I was just wondering how many more she was going to have."

I looked at Gabe, who was obviously uncomfortable with the topic, but I decided not to let it go.

"It's a reasonable question, given how I was the one who brought it up. But your dad's right; that's probably not something you should ask someone out of the blue. The answer is, ideally, I'd love three more. But at my age, I'll be happy if I can give Jake at least one little brother or sister."

Brittany gave Gabe a conspiratorial look.

"Do you have anyone in mind to be the father?"

Gabe abruptly pushed his chair back from the table.

"All right! That's enough!"

Both Brittany and Jake stopped eating and stared at Gabe in surprise.

I wrinkled my nose at Brittany and gently shook my head.

"Yeah, that's definitely not something you should ask."

"I'm sorry! I didn't mean to be rude. I just thought maybe—" She trailed off as she stole another glance at her dad, who still scowled.

He pinned her in place with his glare.

"You thought wrong."

I pretended it just dawned on me what she was thinking and let my eyes go big in dramatic fashion.

"Oh, you thought..." I moved my finger back and forth between Gabe and myself, then chuckled. "Oh, no. No. No. No. That would never happen."

****

Gabe

Never?

Why the fuck not?

Wait.

That's exactly what I'd been saying.

Except I didn't like hearing it come out of Gretchen's mouth.

What the hell was wrong with me? A question I'd asked myself more than once today.

"Honey, I explained this already. Ms. Kelly's a client, and a friend, that's it."

My daughter's pursed lips indicated she wasn't convinced, but she remarked, "If you guys say so."

I stole a glimpse at Gretchen, maybe hoping she'd look as unsure as I felt. Instead of any uncertainty though, she nodded her head in confirmation, so I steadfastly replied, "We say so."

An awkward silence overfell us for a beat; even Jake seemed to understand something was amiss because he shared in the quiet while he continued eating. Then suddenly he loudly announced, "I done, Mama!"

She looked at his empty plate.

"Good job, baby! You ate all your dinner!"

"Can we have p-u-d-d-i-n-g now?" Brittany asked hopefully. "I'll make it."

"It's okay with me if it's okay with Ms. Kelly."

Gretchen nodded her head. "Thanks, Brittany," then asked Jake as she cleared his plate, "Do you want some pudding?"

The little boy's eyes lit up, and he bounced in his seat while echoing, "Poo-ding!"

Brittany got up and headed toward the pantry, and I called out, "He likes vanilla!"

Gretchen's snapped her head to stare at me.

"You remembered that?"

"Of course." I winked at her. "And I think we even have bubble bath for when he's done."

Her smile didn't reach her eyes. "I promise, no naked time though."

My mind immediately went to naked time with *her*.

What a shame.

Her brows furrowed as she exclaimed, "What did you say?"

Shit, did I say that out loud? I needed to back pedal—fast.

"He seemed to have so much fun streaking through your house. You said so yourself, it's just something little kids do."

"I'm trying to teach him there's a time and a place for everything, and this is not an appropriate time nor place to do that."

"Why not? I want you to feel at home here."

"You do?"

I answered without hesitation, "Yeah, I do," and found I meant it.

I noticed my daughter pouring milk into a mixing bowl with a big smirk.

Aw, crap.

Chapter Fifty-Three

Gretchen

I think having Brittany around curbed Jake's zest to go streaking through the house after his bath. My little boy might be experiencing his first crush.

When he was dressed in his pajamas, we went to the basement and the giant playroom Beau had mentioned when he invited me to stay at his brother's house—without Gabe's permission, I was certain.

Brittany lay on the couch watching a movie, and she suggested Jake watch it with her. He didn't hesitate to crawl up next to her and use her for a pillow.

And she was such a good sport. I wanted to hug her for how kind she'd been to my son.

Gabe appeared at the bottom of the stairs holding a bottle of white wine, his brows raised in an unspoken question.

I really shouldn't.

I should stay right where I was—on the couch watching *Moana 2* and grading my students' work.

But then the asshole flashed me his pirate grin, and I found myself putting the file folder of quizzes on the coffee table and standing up, as if my body was disconnected from my brain.

I mouthed, "Just one glass," and followed him up the stairs into the kitchen like he was the Pied Piper.

He pulled two wine glasses from the cupboard, opened the bottle, and made two long pours, emptying half the bottle before sticking the cork back inside.

Handing me a glass, he then raised his like he was about to make a toast, but I beat him to it. I didn't want to hear his bullshit about unexpected surprises.

"To a gracious host. Jake and I appreciate your hospitality. Hopefully we'll be out of your hair by tomorrow."

I clinked my glass against his, then took a big drink of wine.

"There's no rush. You're welcome here for as long as it takes."

"Well, you said you could get the plumber there by tomorrow..."

His glass hovered at his lips, and he replied, "I said I'd *try*," before taking a sip.

I narrowed my eyes at him. "Try really hard."

"I will make a call first thing in the morning. I have a guy that I work with a lot, so hopefully I can play the professional courtesy card."

Gabe topped off my glass before I had a chance to protest, then moved into my personal bubble. He was close enough that I could smell his woodsy cologne, and I was instantly transported back to our magical weekend together.

He softly murmured. "But would it be so bad if you and Jake have to stay a few nights?"

"Yes," I whispered. "You're giving me whiplash, Gabe. I can't keep doing this."

He took a step back and rubbed the back of his neck as he leaned against the counter.

"I know; I'm sorry. I tell myself to leave you alone. I can't give you what you want. But when I'm around you, I want to be selfish and take you in my arms and have my way with you.

When you're right in front of me, I don't care that we want different things. I just want you."

I wanted him, too. I was thirty-one, single, and horny, and I knew I'd be safe with Gabe. Not to mention, the sex was fantastic.

Maybe we could temporarily scratch each other's itch.

"I know there's no future with you. That's been established from the start. But what if we..." I searched for a way to say I just wanted to fuck him—no strings attached—without sounding like the harlot I obviously was. "Kept each other company until my Mr. Right or your Mrs. Right comes along? Or until my cabinets are done, whichever comes first. We both know where we stand and what the expiration date is, so there will be no hard feelings when it's over."

Gabe stared at me for a beat before softly uttering, "I don't want to hurt you."

I boldly took a step forward and looked up at him.

"You won't," I replied far more confidently than I felt. "We're two consenting adults just fulfilling a need— temporarily."

He didn't reply right away, and I wanted to punch my own face. When would I ever learn? Hadn't I sworn when a man showed me who he really was, I'd believe him? Why did this particular man make me forget my own rules, and why the hell did I keep setting myself up to let him hurt my feelings and my pride?

Before I could turn and run, I felt his finger trail from my elbow where it stopped to trace circles around the web of my free hand.

"Let's talk more about this later. Say, my room, after the kids have fallen asleep?"

"O—Okay."

He drew my wrist to his mouth and laid soft kisses along the inside, where I was sure he could feel my pulse racing a mile a minute. Of course, the bastard knew that was one of my erogenous zones.

"And you probably shouldn't wear any underwear under your pajamas."

****

Gabe

She swallowed hard before replying with a shaky voice, "I shouldn't?"

"No."

"Wh—why not?"

I continued kissing the inside of her wrists, pausing only to reply, "It'll make it easier for me when I spread your legs and lick your pussy."

"Oh!" She took another gulp of wine with her free hand before adding, "That would make it easier," as she set the glass back on the counter.

I pulled her closer and whispered in her ear, "Do you know what I was thinking about earlier, when we were in the pantry?"

I felt her hair touch my lips as she gently shook her head.

"I thought about pressing your ass against me, with my hand covering your mouth so no one would hear you moan while I fucked you hard from behind. How good your cunt would feel as it spasmed around my cock when you came, then how I'd bury myself deep inside you to shoot my load of cum."

Her "oooh," was so soft, I wouldn't have heard it if she wasn't right next to me.

My fingers slid along her waistband.

"Is your pussy wet for me?"

"No."

I pulled back and looked down at her with an eyebrow raised.

"No? Are you sure?"

'Cuz I was rock hard, and I know she felt it against her stomach.

She mashed her tits against my chest. "Maybe you should check."

Oh, hell yes.

The sound of Brittany's ringtone signaling an incoming text made me jump back like a teenager getting caught feeling up his crush.

The spell was broken, and I instantly found myself questioning if this was a good idea.

Gretchen had suggested we keep each other company— temporarily, and it hadn't taken but a second for my dick to justify why that was the best thing we'd ever heard. I'd acted before my brain could override my impulse.

But I knew if I changed my mind now, I'd seal my fate with her, and I just couldn't bring myself to do that.

"It's a text from Britt," I explained as I pulled my phone from my pocket.

Britt: Jake is asleep. Do you want me to sleep down here tonight with him?

Me: No, you've got school in the morning. You need to sleep in your bed, so you get a good night's rest.

I looked up at Gretchen.

"Jake's asleep. Let me get the playpen set up." Then, to reassure her, and maybe myself, that I hadn't changed my mind, I put my hand on her waist and stroked her hipbone with my thumb. "The sooner we get the kids to bed, the sooner we can meet in my room to *talk about things.*"

She bit her bottom lip as if trying to disguise a smile.

"Good idea."

Chapter Fifty-Four

Gretchen

I don't know how long I stared at my sleeping boy in the playpen before I slipped my black collared sleep shirt over my head. I knew if Jake woke up, he could easily climb out, but at least he'd be safe from rolling off a bed.

It wouldn't be long before he'd be too big for a playpen. Where had the time gone?

Another reminder my baby clock was ticking.

I was playing with fire—being with Gabe again. For all my "no strings attached, you won't hurt me" bravado, deep down I knew my heart would end up broken, one way or another. One day soon I'd either mourn the loss of him or the idea of having more children.

That was a problem for future Gretchen. Tonight's Gretchen was going to enjoy the heck out of being with Gabe and his dirty mouth.

My phone buzzed with a text and my fingers shook slightly as I opened the app.

Gabe: Britt's zonked out, so we can "talk" now. All night if we want. My door's open.

I had to work in the morning. We weren't going to be "talking" all night.

Gabe: And remember—no panties.

His bossiness was hot. As was the memory of why he said not to wear any underwear.

I can do this.

I can sleep with him without getting attached.

This is just sex. Lots of people have friends with benefits.

I guess in my case, it was a cabinet maker with benefits, but close enough.

Pulling my panties off, I tossed them in my weekender bag next to the closet, then paused to take a deep breath with my hand on the doorknob leading to the hall.

Was I nervous or excited?

Maybe a little of both.

I heard my phone buzzing on the bed, so I went back and picked it up.

Gabe: Sweetheart, if you don't get your cute butt in here NOW, I'm going to come get you and haul you back to my room—caveman style.

Caveman style? The thought made butterflies erupt I my belly.

Me: I'd be there already if I hadn't had to go back to retrieve my phone and read your text!

Me: Although, tell me more about this caveman thing.

****

Gabe

My cock was instantly hard after reading her message.

Well, hard*er*.

I'd had a semi since I saw her car in my driveway, but it'd gone full mast the minute she propositioned me in the kitchen. Setting up the playpen while having to adjust myself every few seconds had been tricky.

I'd thought having a task to do would calm things down below the belt, but the idea of having her in my bed tonight overrode everything else in my Neanderthal brain.

And she wanted to know more about "this caveman thing"? I was more than happy to show her my inner barbarian.

But when Gretchen appeared in my bedroom doorway with her hair down around her shoulders, wearing a silky black nightshirt, I wavered between wanting to rip it off her, drag her by her hair to the bed, and hold her down while I fucked her hard, to pulling her in my arms and worshipping every inch of her body before making love to her.

Decisions, decisions.

She tucked her hair behind her ear and didn't move past the threshold, appearing far more timid than she'd been in the kitchen earlier.

I held my hand out and softly commanded, "Come here, sweetheart."

She ventured further into the room and closed the door. I heard the lock click, then she approached me without hesitation.

That's my girl.

When she was within arm's reach, I grasped her wrist and tugged her against my chest, so my arm could wrap around her waist.

Damn, she felt good, and I realized how much I'd missed holding her.

If I were being honest with myself, I'd missed everything about her.

Looking down at her with a smile, I murmured, "Hi."

Her arm slid around my body as she nestled against me and gazed up into my eyes.

"Hi."

I dipped my head and gently touched my lips against hers, and she let out a contented sigh.

It looked like I was going with the worshipping option.

Maybe tomorrow I'd try the caveman approach.

****

Gretchen

Gabe gently broke the kiss and stared down at my face as he stroked my cheek with the backs of his fingertips.

"You're so beautiful."

His touch and his gaze were almost reverent, and it would have been so easy for me to get lost in the moment with him. He was such a good man and a great dad; I knew it wouldn't take much to fall in love with him.

The domesticity of our situation—being in our pajamas with our kids fast asleep in their rooms—messed with my head.

I reminded myself that our arrangement wasn't about sharing a moment, or playing house, or falling in love. It was physical.

Period. The end.

I reached down to lightly squeeze his junk and flirted, "Are you going to tell me more about this caveman style?"

He shook his head. "Not tonight, darlin'. Tonight I want to take my time and show you how much I've missed you."

Nope. Not gonna happen.

I decided honesty was the best course of action, but also didn't want to kill the mood, so I stroked the outline of his cock over his grey pajama pants when I replied, "I think hard and dirty is a better idea. There's less chance of feelings getting involved that way."

"What's wrong with having fee—" He stopped short. "Never mind; you're right."

His fingers slid into my hair, but then he gripped a fistful and harshly held my head in place, so I had no choice but to look at him when he snarled, "You better not have any panties on or they're going to get ripped off you."

Wow! He flipped that switch pretty easily.

That's hot.

Finding his threat sexy, I almost wished I'd left my underwear on.

Using his free hand, he hiked my nightshirt up to my waist and reached between my legs to find no barrier.

"Mmm, you're soaked, darlin'."

He ran the length of his index finger down my slit, making me whimper while he cooed his approval.

"Good girl."

Dammit.

How am I not supposed to not catch feeling when he calls me a good girl?

I realized it didn't matter what our "arrangement" was. Soft and slow or hard and dirty—Gabe Mitchell was going to ruin me.

Chapter Fifty-Five

Gabe

The sexy teacher in my bedroom wanted it hard and dirty... who was I to say no to that?

She was barefoot, dressed only in a nightshirt without panties, just how I'd instructed her.

Her drenched pussy was a nice consequence.

I spun her around and pulled her nightshirt over her head, so she was completely naked. As I snaked one hand around her neck, I reached between her legs with the other and circled her clit with my thumb while I plunged a finger inside her wet channel.

"You like being my good girl and doing what I tell you, don't you?"

Her soft moan was her only reply.

"You like when I'm in control of your body."

I strummed her little pearl as I continued finger fucking her. My hold on her slender neck was firm without applying pressure. Just enough to keep her in the headspace of being dominated.

"This is *my* pussy."

After emphasizing my words with three quick slaps directly to her clit, she moaned, "Oh my god, Gabe, yes!"

I wasn't sure if the "yes" was a shout of pleasure or agreement that her pussy belonged to me. Either way, it didn't matter. Her pussy was *mine.*

With a smile, I moved my hand from her neck to cover her lips.

"I should have had you bring your panties, baby, so I could stick them in your mouth."

Gretchen shook her head no, and I removed my hand to let her speak.

"I wouldn't like that."

I liked that she felt comfortable telling me her likes and dislikes.

"Then it's off the table." I rubbed her pussy and assured her, "The walls in the house are thick so you don't have to worry about the kids hearing us."

She tapped the backs of my fingers. "You should keep your hand on my mouth though, just in case."

I was going to love getting to know all the things that turned her on and made a decision right then to make sure to stretch out our time together for as long as possible.

****

Gretchen

Earlier, when he'd told me his pantry fantasy, I'd wanted to yank him in there right then so we could act it out. But Brittany's text reminded us we should behave like responsible adults, at least until we got the kids in bed.

And now here we were, with his hand covering my mouth as he played my body like an instrument.

My toes curled as the orgasm crept its way up my body.

Suddenly, he released his hold on my face and withdrew his fingers from between my legs, and I let out a disappointed whimper. With a tap to my ass, he said, "I need to taste your pussy when you come, darlin'. Get on the bed and spread your legs."

Gosh, if you say so.

I was disappointed he'd denied me an orgasm, but knew he'd deliver in spades. I eagerly scrambled onto the bed to comply; hopeful he'd tell me again what a good girl I am.

Who knew I had a praise kink?

Maybe it was because Troy neither praised nor appreciated me while we'd been married. When Gabe did, it felt like balm to my soul.

His broad shoulders between my legs made me spread wider to accommodate him.

I could feel his warm breath on my center when he murmured, "Such a pretty, pink, glistening pussy." He took a swipe down the middle with his tongue. "Mmm, so sweet. Get comfortable, sweetheart, because I'm about to devour you."

Holy. Shit.

That was the hottest thing anyone's ever said to me.

Well, aside from the other dirty things that had come out of his mouth.

Okay, the hottest thing he's said to me tonight.

Except I had liked it when he told me I was a good girl. And claimed ownership of my pussy.

Focus, Gretchen!

Gabe quickly got my attention when he sucked my clit between his lips and screwed two fingers inside me.

I clenched his comforter in both hands and arched my back off the bed.

"Oh. My. God. Fuck, that feels good!"

As he took me higher and higher, I released my hold of his bedspread and reached down to massage his scalp. If he stopped again, I'd be able to grip his hair and pull him back on task.

I felt his chest vibrate with a chuckle.

"Don't worry, baby. I've got you. I'm not stopping until you can't take anymore."

That was all the reassurance I needed to fully relax, which he immediately noticed because he rumbled, "That's it. Keep those legs spread, sweetheart, and take it like my good slut."

"Yes! Oh god, yes! I want to be your good whore!"

Oh my gosh! I'm a teacher and a mother! I can't say things like that!

My inner slut whispered, *Oh yes you can, girl. You're safe with him.*

And I knew I was.

I cupped my tits and pressed my pelvis against his mouth while my body temperature spiked.

Gabe rapidly flicked his tongue against my clit and increased the tempo of his fingers. Every muscle of mine went taut, and then suddenly I found my body shuddering uncontrollably from head to toe when the climax wracked through me.

I felt his strong hands hold my hips in place while he continued his attention to my pussy. He kept going until I tried to clamp my legs shut and cried out, "No more! I surrender!"

He looked up at me from where he was situated between my legs, wearing a wicked grin that would melt my panties, if I were wearing any.

"Good. I love it when you surrender to me."

Ruined, I tell ya.

Roo-inned.

But what a ride it'd be while it lasted.

Chapter Fifty-Six

Gabe

"Are we still okay to go without a condom?" I asked as I climbed up her body.

She nodded her head. "My shot is good for another month."

I knew it was risky, not taking my own advice and wrapping my shit up tight, especially with how badly I knew she wanted a baby.

But I trusted her.

And if she ended up pregnant... I guess we'd cross that bridge if we came to it.

We'd cross that bridge if we came to it? Who the fuck are you?

I honestly wasn't sure anymore.

Not like I complained as I slid my cock inside her wet heat, and she wrapped her arms around me.

She felt like heaven, and I never wanted to come back down to earth.

I moved slowly because I knew it wouldn't take much for me to blow my load.

"I've missed you, baby."

"Hard and dirty, remember? No feelings!"

Too late.

I kept that to myself as I plunged deeper inside her heat.

The smell of her shampoo and body lotion and the sound of her arousal and tiny noises filled my senses as I stared down at her while slowly moving in and out of her pussy.

"You are so beautiful."

"Dammit Gabe, fuck me!"

It was hard to say no to that.

I dropped to my knees and gripped her hips; her tits bounced as I pistoned into her.

"You feel so fucking good."

Her pussy seemed to grip my cock. and my spine tingled while my balls drew up. After one last, deep thrust, I held her tight against me as I came so hard I felt lightheaded.

Dropping down so my body covered hers, I carefully distributed my weight in order to not crush her while I held her against me.

Gretchen is here, in my bed.

A smile escaped me as I let out a long, contented sigh.

I love you.

I immediately followed that thought with, *Oh, that's not good.*

****

Gretchen

Gabe came back from the bathroom with a towel and cleaned me up. After he tossed it toward a door that I assumed was his closet, he returned to bed and pulled me into an embrace.

His familiar scent washed over me, and I tried not to be too obvious as I took a deep breath in. Being in his arms made me feel safe. Something I didn't always feel as a single woman, even in my own home in a small town. Probably because I watched too many true-crime mysteries.

We were quiet as we snuggled in our post-coital bliss, and soon I heard soft snoring sounds coming from him. I started to feel drowsy, too, and knew I needed to get up and go back to the guest room where Jake was fast asleep.

As I gently tried to move his arm from around my waist, he immediately tightened his hold and whispered, "Stay with me. Please."

God, I was tempted. I knew I'd sleep soundly next to him. Probably too soundly.

"I can't. If Jake wakes up, he's in a strange place, I need to be there, so he doesn't get scared. Besides the last thing I want is to do the walk of shame in front of Brittany."

"Britt will sleep until I make her get up in the morning. But I understand you need to be there for Jake. I'll pick up a baby monitor tomorrow, so you don't have to worry."

"I have one, but shouldn't I be back in my house tomorrow night?"

He sputtered, "I mean, yeah. Probably. I just thought in case Henry can't get to your house for a couple of days, it'd be good to have."

"Let's see what he says tomorrow, after you play the professional courtesy card."

"Of course."

I swung my feet to the floor and surveyed the room for my nightshirt.

Gabe also got up and put on his pajama pants. They hung low on his hips, and staring at his bare chest made me reconsider leaving.

"You better stop looking at me like that," he growled, "or I'll haul you back to bed for Round Two."

I feigned offense as I pulled the nightshirt over my head.

"How am I looking at you?"

"Like I'm a midnight snack."

Strutting to where he stood by the bed, I threw my arm around his neck and stared into his eyes when I replied, "Oh, baby. You're the whole damn meal."

The bastard grinned at me as he dropped a kiss to my forehead and said, "I know."

****

Gabe

Going back to bed alone, knowing only a wall separated us, was torture.

More than once, I considered plucking her from where she was probably tucked in tight and hauling her back to my bed. I even got up once, but as I approached the door leading to the hall, thought better of it. I took a piss instead before going back to bed alone.

Not tomorrow night. Tomorrow she was falling asleep in my arms, and I was going to hold her all night long. If this thing between us had an expiration date, I wasn't wasting a minute.

Chapter Fifty-Seven

Gabe

The chaos the next morning was a far cry from the way I usually started my day—enjoying a quiet cup of coffee in my breakfast nook overlooking the backyard while I scrolled my phone and caught up on scores from the night before.

In addition to making sure Britt was awake on time for school, something I wasn't accustomed to since she stayed with her mom most school nights, I had to contend with Gretchen rushing around trying to get Jake fed and ready for daycare.

I asked her more than once what I could do to help, but each time she scurried past me, she repeated her mantra, "I got it."

Finally, I grabbed her by the arm to slow her down for five seconds.

"Let me help you. Do you need your lunch packed? Jake's diaper bag packed? His diaper changed?"

She eyed me suspiciously, like she expected me to burst out laughing and say, "Just kidding!" Finally, she replied, "If you could make me a sandwich for lunch and double check there are at least ten pull-up diapers in Jake's diaper bag, I'd appreciate it."

I released her arm and stepped back.

"On it."

She offered me a grateful smile.

"Thank you."

"Of course."

She headed toward the stairs, and I called after her, "PB and J? Turkey and cheese? Ham and cheese?"

She turned around and declared, "Turkey, cheese, and mayo sounds great."

I replied with a wink. "You got it."

A few minutes later, Brittany walked into the kitchen and saw me making Gretchen's sandwich.

She sat down at the kitchen island and poured herself a bowl of cereal.

"Can you make me something, too?"

I paused my careful distribution of mayonnaise so that the entire slice of bread was covered and looked up at her.

"You don't eat cafeteria lunch?"

"Ew, no."

"What do you want?"

She was careful when she poured the milk, so to get just the right amount of milk to cereal ratio. I'd taught her that.

"You know what I like. Surprise me. And Mom always leaves me a little note, too."

I pulled a slice of mozzarella from the deli bag and shot her a look.

"You're lucky you're so cute."

Sporting the trademark Mitchell grin when she took a big spoonful, she mumbled, "I know," around a mouth full of food.

I finished packing Gretchen's lunch under Britt's watchful eye. I forewent adding a heart when I wrote her name on the brown paper bag, then set it on the counter to go in search of the diaper bag.

After ensuring there were a minimum of ten diapers that I assumed her daycare required, I set the bag next to her lunch, along with her satchel and file folder I'd retrieved from the basement, where she'd left them the night before.

My daughter noticed it all as she rinsed her cereal bowl in the sink and commented, "You really like her."

Remembering our conversation in the car yesterday, I hesitated before answering.

"Well, yeah. She's a nice lady."

"I like her, too. She and Jake seemed to fit in well here."

They do, don't they?

I didn't want to give her false hope, so I warned, "Let it go, Britt."

"I'm just saying, we've got plenty of room. I bet it would be easy to turn the guest room into a little ki—"

"*I said, drop it.*"

I rarely had to raise my voice with my kids, and I'd done it twice in less than twenty-four hours. But just like yesterday, my resilient kid was undeterred.

"Okay..." But of course, she didn't drop it. "I've never seen you smile at a woman like you do at her."

"Well, yeah. We've already established I think she's nice."

"Dad," she let out an exasperated sigh. "You don't like *anyone* who isn't family. So, that means you think of her as family."

I didn't have a response to that, so I grumbled, "Go get ready for school."

Damn kids.

They think they're so smart.

Was she right, though?

****

Gretchen

For the first time since I returned to work after maternity leave, I arrived at school *early*.

It had been nice having Gabe's help this morning, and I couldn't help but smile when I put the sack lunch he'd made me into my mini fridge. My normally harried morning had almost felt easy, and I appreciated how he'd been willing to help me.

It was a far cry from how my days had started when Troy and I had been together.

Believe it or not, my mornings had actually gotten easier once he moved out. I didn't have to worry about keeping Jake quiet—not an easy feat with a toddler, for fear of waking my ex. I'd tiptoe around and shush my little boy if he made the slightest noise; I was in a constant state of anxiety.

But, I'd reasoned, it was the least I could do with how much Troy worked all the time. I hadn't been able to fathom working such long hours.

God, I'd been so naïve.

The morning with Gabe gave me a glimpse of what being with a real partner would look like, and I realized I wanted that for me, Jake, and my future children.

A hint of sadness overcame me to know it wouldn't be with Gabe.

As he'd carried Jake to my car he'd already started so it was warm when we got in, I remembered thinking, *so this is what simpatico feels like.*

I could get used to it.

My morning classes breezed by, and I couldn't help but wonder if the way my day had started out had anything to do with it.

So, at lunchtime, when I looked at my phone and saw the message from Gabe, I wasn't too upset.

Gabe: Don't be mad at me, but Henry can't get to your place until Thursday.

I think he might have been worried when I didn't respond right away, because he sent a follow up text an hour later.

Gabe: I tried calling around. No one is available until the end of the week unless I'm willing to pay their emergency rate. Which I'll do if it's that important that you get back to your place. I just thought things went well last night and this morning, so you might be okay waiting.

Gabe: If that's not okay, I'll understand.

Me: No, I don't want you to have to pay an emergency fee. I just don't want to overstay our welcome. I know having a two-year-old underfoot can be a lot.

Especially since your two-year-old died.

He must have read between the lines because he promptly replied.

Gabe: Jake is absolutely not a problem. I promise. I enjoy having him around.

Me: Okay, I'll swing by my house after I pick up Jake from daycare and get a few days' worth of clothes.

Gabe: Don't forget the baby monitor. You're sleeping in my bed tonight.

That bossy, sexy bastard.

The idea made my toes curl. I should find his cockiness infuriating, instead, I thought it was hot.

Still, I responded,

Me: We'll see.

But when I pulled the note from my lunch—which consisted of grapes, pudding, and chips, in addition to my requested sandwich—that read, "You're beautiful," there was no doubt where I'd be sleeping tonight.

****

Gabe

I might have fibbed a little.

I'd asked Henry what his schedule looked like on Thursday and made the appointment then.

But since I never actually asked if he could make it today, I figured I had plausible deniability.

Sort of.

And no, I hadn't tried anyone else.

I would have called Henry back if she'd been mad or insisted on going to her parents.

But she didn't, and I thought that was a good sign.

Chapter Fifty-Eight

Gretchen

I noticed a few things when I pulled up to my house after work.

One, the main garage door was open. And two, the box truck that had been parked in my driveway yesterday was gone. In its place was Gabe's black Ford truck.

"What's he doing here?" I wondered aloud.

I mean, I had a good idea what he was doing—working on the cabinets, but I was surprised he wasn't at his shop doing work that he'd actually get paid in full for. Not that I wasn't paying in full, I reminded myself. It was just going to take time.

I parked in the driveway in order to not obstruct Gabe's path from the cabinets to the house. After getting Jake from his car seat, we went inside through the front door.

Poking my head through the plastic barrier to the kitchen, I paused to take in the sight in front of me before announcing our presence.

Gabe, wearing his black-rimmed glasses and a pencil tucked behind his ear, was concentrating on the level he'd lined up against the wall. It was such a benign scene, yet my heart skipped a beat looking at him.

"Hey! We're here!"

He broke out into a big grin when he saw us standing in the doorway.

"Hi, guys!"

After making a quick mark on the wall, he lifted his glasses onto his head, and came over to kiss me on the cheek and offer a high-five to Jake.

"How was your day?"

"Really good, thanks. And thank you again for making my lunch. I wasn't expecting anything more than a sandwich."

"You're welcome," he replied with a wink. "Didja get my note?"

I couldn't hide my smile.

"I did. That was sweet."

Sweet was putting it mildly. It'd made my whole afternoon.

"Britt said I had to put a note in her lunch, so I thought I'd add one to yours, too."

"Well, I hope she appreciated hers as much as I did mine."

"I'm glad you liked it."

We stood grinning at each other for a beat until Jake broke the spell, asking, "Mouse, mama?"

Gabe made a quizzical brow, so I explained, "His favorite game on the tablet is ABCMouse."

"Ahhh." He directed his attention at Jake. "Why don't you go get your toolset and help me finish up while your mom does a few things."

My son's eyes got wide, and he wiggled his body until I had no choice but to set him down. The minute his feet hit the floor, he took off running toward his room.

"Are you sure you're okay with him 'helping' you?"

I used finger quotes when I said "helping".

"Of course. We got to get him started young."

We do?

I didn't ask that, just said, "Let me go pack a few outfits. It shouldn't take me long."

"Take your time, sweetheart." His mouth turned up in his signature wicked grin. "Maybe pack some lingerie if you have any. And don't forget the baby monitor."

"I don't think you want me to bring any lingerie. The only things I have are what Troy gave me."

"Good, then you won't mind when I rip it off you."

Gulp! No, I would not mind that at all.

"Um, yeah…" I mumbled as I awkwardly gestured with my thumb toward the bedrooms. "Let me go pack," then turned on my heel and made a hasty exit.

I passed Jake in the hall on my way to his room. His eagerness at helping Gabe was palpable as he raised his toy toolbox and proudly proclaimed, "I help!"

I loved how excited he was. The only time he got this animated was when he was going to my mom and dad's.

"I know, baby. You're going to be a great helper!"

He scurried away and I had to stop and think, *what was I doing?*

Oh yeah, packing.

****

Gabe

There was something about seeing Gretchen's Honda in my rearview mirror as she followed me back to my place that made my chest twinge.

Tonight, it was just going to be the three of us; Britt had reluctantly gone back to Becky's. She agreed her mom would not be on board with her staying with me *two* unsanctioned nights. Frankly, I'd been surprised when Becky agreed to let her come last night, but I suspected she was curious about my guests and wanted Brittany to get the scoop and report back.

I knew our daughter was going to give Becky the version that Britt *wanted*, and I found I didn't mind; it was good to keep everyone on their toes. But when Gretchen and my time was up, I wouldn't be offering any explanations about what happened.

Because I'd already told them—*she's just a friend*.

But when she pulled to the front of my house, I thought, *I should make room for her car in the garage.*

That's when I realized, I might have a problem with our expiration date.

I walked to her car and opened up the rear door, planning on grabbing her bag. But I went to the wrong side of the car, and Jake held out his hands and cried, "Mister Mxchshl!"

"Call me Gabe, buddy," I said as I unbuckled his car seat and caught him as he jumped into my arms.

"You got him?" Gretchen asked as she pulled the diaper bag, her work satchel, and purse from the other side of the back seat. How the heck did she manage all that *and* Jake every day?

Single moms were fucking rock stars.

And yes, I'd include Becky in that group. She pissed me off a lot, but I had to admit, she did an amazing job with Brayden and Britt.

"I got him." I motioned to her loaded down arms. "You need me to grab any of that?"

"Nope. Thank you, though."

Then she went to the trunk and took out the suitcases she'd packed, like she was going to haul everything into the house by herself.

Uh, no. Not on my watch.

Still holding Jake, I followed her to the trunk and took the two handles in one hand.

"I got these."

Fortunately, she didn't argue.

They were lighter than I was expecting, and I found myself disappointed about that. It meant she hadn't packed much because she wasn't planning on staying long.

She clicked the Honda's lock and followed me up the porch steps.

I set the bags down, opened the screen door, and punched in the numbers to unlock the door.

"The code is zero, one, one, three."

"That's Jake's birthday!"

Instead of opening the door, I slowly turned around to gape at her dumbfounded.

"That's Bodhi's birthday, too."

✳✳✳✳

Gretchen

I wasn't sure what to say, so I opted for, "Oh."

Did Jake sharing a birthday with his deceased son bother him?

He softly remarked, "That's quite a coincidence, huh?"

I proceeded with caution.

"Yeah, it is. Does that upset you?"

Gabe shook his head and looked at Jake, still in his arms, with a warm smile.

"No. I think it's kind of cool."

He opened the door, then turned back and brought the bags inside, asking Jake as they walked through the threshold, "What should we have for dinner?"

Chapter Fifty-Nine

Gabe

The familiar conflicted feelings had stirred in my gut when Jake had "helped" me clean up while Gretchen packed. It had been just the two of us, and I'd worried maybe he'd be shy without his mom around.

Turns out, he'd been just the opposite.

He was bold and eager, a lot like Bodhi had been. And adorably funny. I'd enjoyed hanging out with him these last few days, and part of me felt guilty about it. Like I was somehow cheating on my son by liking being around another little boy.

Finding out Bodhi and Jake shared a birthday seemed like a sign. But for what exactly, I wasn't sure.

Chapter Sixty

Gretchen

"Did you guys decide what you wanted for dinner?" I asked as I walked into the kitchen after changing into a pair of pink yoga pants and an oversized pink, orange, and teal t-shirt. Gabe had insisted on bringing Jake's racecar suitcase to the guest room, and my pink floral one to his room.

The pantry door was open, and Gabe and Jake were inside perusing the contents.

"Jake wanted fish sticks, but I don't think I have any of those so he's considering spaghetti and mashed potatoes."

I nodded my head like that was a completely normal combination, then suggested, "Or, we could have chicken and mashed potatoes. Or spaghetti and meatballs."

Gabe countered with, "*Or* we could have lasagna?"

I still wasn't willing to chance it.

"It'd take too long. That's more of a weekend meal."

Jake held up a bag of instant potatoes to show me.

"Jake want 'tatoes, Mama!"

"Chicken and mashed potatoes it is."

"What can I do to help?"

I wanted to propose he occupy Jake while I prepared dinner, but I worried his "time with little kids" meter might be pegged. Instead, I suggested, "Can you see what vegetables you have for another side?" while I fished the tablet from my purse and waved it at Jake. My son took it and ran to the adjoining family room to situate himself on the couch.

I didn't even have to set the game up for him, he knew exactly how to get it started. That's how tech-savvy kids were these days.

He wasn't able to use the potty consistently, but he knew how to operate technology.

I couldn't decide if his generation was doomed or advanced.

Gabe stepped out of the pantry holding a can of green beans as I pulled a chicken packet from the freezer.

I didn't love defrosting chicken in the microwave, but when you work all day, some things had to be compromised.

"What else can I do? And I swear if you tell me to open the can and cook them, we're going to have a problem."

"Well, how else are we supposed to eat them?" I teased.

He came up behind me and crowded me into the counter with his hands on my hips. Nuzzling my neck, he murmured, "I can do a lot more than open a can of green beans."

Oh, I know you can.

"Put me to work, sweetheart."

"You worked all day, then went to my house and worked some more, putting up cabinets. You deserve a break."

"You worked all day, too. Maybe we should order takeout."

"I *like* cooking, and honestly, there's not much you can do. I mean, it's thawing chicken in the microwave then baking it in the oven. The mashed potatoes are instant, and the green beans are from a can. It's not a two-person job."

He laid a soft kiss on my neck and subtly ground his cock against my ass while he cupped my boobs in his hands.

"Good, then you won't mind if I distract you."

I decided to fight fire with fire.

"You should probably wait until later. I brought the lingerie."

I pressed my lips together to keep from grinning when his fingers dug into my hipbones, and he softly moaned in my ear, "Fuuuuuck."

I loved having that effect on him. It made me feel beautiful, and maybe a little powerful, too.

****

Gabe

I hadn't been able to keep my hands off Gretchen as she prepared dinner.

I knew I was getting in her way, yet I couldn't find it in me to care. Gretchen Kelly flitting around my kitchen like a domestic goddess who belonged there was my weakness.

But Gretchen Kelly in yoga pants? My kryptonite.

Imagining ripping lingerie off her body later? Quite possibly the death of me.

But what a way to go.

I did make myself useful and set the table while she carefully cut Jake's piece of chicken into small, bite-sized cubes. She did the same with his green beans, before putting a dollop of mashed potatoes on his plate.

"Jake, baby, come wash your hands. It's time to eat."

I expected stalling and bargaining for five more minutes, like my kids had a tendency to do when they were playing video games, but he just set the tablet on the cushion next to him then slid off the couch without argument.

She turned the faucet on and lifted him up so he could wash his hands at the kitchen sink.

Note to self: buy a step stool tomorrow.

Actually, I should probably buy two so there was one in the bathroom, as well.

I gave myself an internal shake.

They're only staying until Thursday!

Okay, Friday, tops, if Henry needed to order a part. Although shipping times varied so I guess it could be Monday, maybe Tuesday.

I decided another week warranted the purchase of stools. I'd pick two up at the hardware store tomorrow.

Gretchen got Jake situated at the table, and I brought him his plate.

"Doesn't this look good, buddy? Your mama is a good cook!"

Jake popped a piece of chicken in his mouth and dramatically nodded while he attempted to put potatoes on his toddler spoon. I looked over at Gretchen when I continued. "She's spoiling me with all these home-cooked meals. I usually have to pick up my dinner."

She set the serving bowls with the side dishes on the table then picked up the platter of chicken. A far cry from when I made the kids dinner and just served everything out of the pots and pans.

"I don't know why you eat out so much. You have a perfectly stocked pantry and freezer," she scolded as she set the chicken on the table.

"You said it yourself; cooking for one is no fun."

"Yes but paying to eat out all the time has got to get expensive."

I watched confused when she picked up my plate and scooped mashed potatoes onto it. I realized what she was doing and before she could fork a piece of chicken, I took the dish out of her hands.

"You don't have to serve me." I nodded to the place setting in front of her. "Make your plate."

She looked surprised but did as I suggested while I continued the conversation and scooped green beans on my dish, then did the same for her.

"I figure with the time I save not cooking, I can stay at work longer, so it evens outs." I tapped my temple. "Guy math."

That made her burst out laughing. God, I loved that sound and was willing to do whatever it took to hear it as often as I could.

Well, except give her the one thing she wanted most.

A baby.

But that wasn't something I was going to worry about tonight.

Chapter Sixty-One

Gretchen

Gabe offered Jake pudding for dessert, so once again, my son went directly from the kitchen table to the bathtub. And, probably because Brittany wasn't here, he decided to streak through the house naked, screeching, "Nakey time!" as he did.

"Good heavens," Gabe declared as Jake ran into the kitchen ahead of me. "It's a streaker! Gretchen! Keep Jake in the bathtub! The naked boy is here, again!"

I came around the corner to watch Jake stop in his tracks and turn to Gabe.

"No, Gabe. I, Jake." He patted his bare chest and repeated, "I, Jake."

"Jake?" Gabe pretended to study the little man's face. "Oh my goodness, it *is* you! Where are your clothes?"

"Right here!" I declared with a fake roar as I held up his pajamas and pull-up diaper.

That elicited a shriek from Jake who took off running around the island.

"Be careful!" I warned. "Stay in the kitchen!"

He did as I said and raced by Gabe, who feigned reaching for the streaking child and missing, much to Jake's delight.

Finally, after five minutes of running around, Jake was tuckered out and allowed me to get him ready for bed.

"Do you want a game or story?" I asked as I zipped up his pjs.

"Story."

"Go pick one out of your bag."

I'd tossed a couple of his favorite books and games in his suitcase while packing, which he'd immediately noticed as I fished his jammies from his bag—right before he'd declared nakey time and took off running.

Gabe chuckled as he hung a dishcloth over the kitchen faucet.

"Damn, I wish I had his energy."

I nodded my agreement. "They say 'youth is wasted on the young' for a reason."

Jake came back with his favorite bear book, and as I reached for it, he pulled it away and announced, "No, Mama. Gabe read."

I winced when I glanced over at Gabe, unsure how he'd react.

To his credit, he came around the island and asked, "What have we got here?" when Jake handed him the story. "*Bradberry Bear Plays Baseball*? Oh, I'll bet this is a good one, come on."

The two sat on the couch, and as Jake gave his rapt attention to Gabe while he told the story—complete with varying voices, I couldn't help but rub the spot where my heart ached in my chest.

****

Gabe

The little dude fell asleep next to me before the story was over, so I carried him to the guest room. While Gretchen quietly plugged in the baby monitor and placed it on a nearby dresser, I gently put Jake in the playpen

The mattress in that thing was thin and flimsy, and I didn't like the idea of him sleeping on it.

I glanced at the queen guest bed and whispered, "Maybe we could put him in the middle of the mattress and line the edges with pillows, like bumpers?"

"It's safer for him to be in the playpen. He's fine there for a few nights."

I made a mental note to pick up a toddler bed and mattress tomorrow, like the one I'd seen in Jake's room at Gretchen's house, along with the stools.

It'd be good to have for company in the future, I reasoned. Never mind that I hadn't used the playpen once until their visit.

When we stepped out of the guest room and closed the door, she quietly whispered, "Thank you for doing that. I'm sorry he put you on the spot."

"He didn't put me on the spot. I enjoyed it. Britt and Brayden haven't wanted me to read them a story in years. It was nice."

"Well, I appreciate it."

With my hand on the small of her back, I directed her toward my bedroom door and leaned down to growl in her ear, "You know what I'm going to appreciate? Seeing you in that lingerie, then ripping it off you."

The corner of her mouth hitched, and she shook her head at me, like I was being silly.

That did nothing to deter my new mission. Instead, I prompted, "Get changed, sweetheart. I'll be in soon."

Not fucking soon enough.

Chapter Sixty-Two

Gretchen

My heart pounded as I pulled the black teddy from my suitcase. It'd been a birthday present from Troy, because you know, *that's* what I'd wanted for my birthday.

Not.

It had been all I could do to smile and thank my ex after unwrapping the box, when what I'd really wanted to do was roll my eyes. I'd given him a list of present ideas and "lacy, black lingerie" had not been on it.

The idea of Gabe tearing it off me, though was hot as hell, and I was wet just thinking about it.

But first, I needed to put it on.

After pulling my t-shirt and bra off, I shimmied out of my pink yoga pants and held the black lace fabric up to my body. I'd received the teddy before I had Jake, so I was worried if it would still fit. How embarrassing would that be, if I couldn't get it over my ass?

I stepped into the lingerie and held my breath as I pulled it up past my thighs. Once it cleared my hips, I thought I was in the clear.

I thought wrong.

I forgot how much bigger my boobs had gotten in the last few years. My tits spilled out of the sheer material, and it took a lot of adjusting to get them tucked in place. But once it was on, I put my hands on my waist and turned from side to side to observe myself in the mirror.

Not bad.

I'd do me.

But just in case Gabe needed more encouragement, I fished the stilettos from my bag and slipped them on.

Should I put on some lipstick?

Run a brush through my hair?

I definitely should brush my teeth.

Walking on the balls of my feet to keep from falling and breaking my neck in my sky-high heels, I clamored into the bathroom to finish getting ready. I knew I didn't have much time before Gabe came back.

I was lying on the bed, trying to figure out a sexy position, when he walked through the door.

Damn, he's handsome.

Too handsome.

Suddenly, I felt very self-conscious about my appearance, and attempted to slip under the covers, but he yanked the comforter from my hand and pulled it to the end of the bed.

"Uh uh. Let me look at you." He took a step back and perused me from head to toe, finally muttering, "Damn, you are gorgeous."

Meanwhile, I'd never wished more in my life to be invisible; something Gabe immediately picked up on.

He stroked my calf and asked, "What's the matter, baby?"

"Can we turn the lights off?"

"Why?"

"I just... I mean, look at me."

"I am, sweetheart. You are fucking hot."

"Are you kidding? I'm not sexy. I look ridiculous in this."

I kicked off my shoes as if to emphasize my point.

Gabe scowled, grabbed my hand, and placed it over the bulge in his jeans.

"Does this feel like I'm kidding? The first time I laid eyes on you, I thought you were the most beautiful woman I'd ever seen. That thought hasn't changed, if anything, it's been reinforced.

"The first night we were together, I kept asking myself how I got such a hot piece of ass to bring me home with her. You. Are. Fucking. Stunning." He traced a finger along the bodice. "But if you feel uncomfortable in this…"

He brought both hands to the fabric at my chest and ripped my teddy right down the middle.

"Problem solved. Now put those heels back on so I can fuck you in them."

Oh dang!

I kind of liked this side of Mr. Infuriating.

****

Gabe

After thoroughly fucking Gretchen before the eleven o'clock news even came on, I knew I was going to sleep like a log when I settled into bed with her snuggled at my side.

Damn, a guy could get used to this.

Yeah, well, don't. This is just temporary—remember?

How could I forget?

But I still had more time with her, and I was going to focus on that, not our expiration date.

Chapter Sixty-Three

Gretchen

It took me a second to figure out where I was when I fumbled around for my phone when the alarm started buzzing.

The blue and grey décor was a far cry from the pink and cream colors of my bedroom. Yet, I felt comfortable as I lay there naked as the day I was born. Probably because I'd gone to sleep with a satisfied smile.

Or maybe it was because Gabe's bed smelled like him, although he was nowhere to be found. His side of the mattress was cool to the touch.

I knew I needed to get up and get going, but I allowed myself a few more minutes to bask in his scent.

"Mama!"

The sound of Jake's voice came through the monitor, and I threw the covers back only to realize I hadn't brought any pajamas or even a robe. I'd been too busy packing something to get ripped off me.

Hussy.

Yeah, so?

I congratulated myself on embracing my sexuality as I dashed into the bathroom to do my business and found a blue robe hanging on a hook on the bathroom door.

Problem solved.

It's going to be a good day.

The idea was reinforced when I brought Jake into the kitchen for breakfast and found Gabe standing bare-chested at the stove in nothing but his pajama pants slung low on his hips. Spatula in hand, he greeted us with a big smile before scooping a pancake from the skillet and adding it to a stack on a nearby plate.

"Good morning! Hope you guys are hungry!"

I situated Jake in his booster chair at the table before stating the obvious.

"You made pancakes?"

Jake clapped his hands with glee and declared, "Pancakes!"

"Yeah. I figured, what little kid doesn't like pancakes?"

The smell wafted to my nose, making my stomach growl and I added, "Or grown woman," as I tightened the belt on the robe and sat down.

Gabe had already put butter and syrup on the table, along with three place settings.

He kissed the top of my head, then set the plate of hotcakes on the table, and moved to sit opposite me.

"These look yummy, huh, baby?" I said to Jake as I put a golden pancake on his plate. He didn't wait for me to add butter or syrup, just picked up the flapjack like a piece of bread and took a bite.

That was probably better. Less chance of him getting syrup in his hair.

"Mmm," he hummed as he chewed.

Gabe chuckled as he buttered his stack.

"I'm glad you like them, little man."

"Thank you for doing this," I told him as I prepared my short stack. "That was really thoughtful. I can't remember the last time I had something on a school day other than coffee and a cold toaster pastry in my car."

"I noticed yesterday you didn't have breakfast."

"I don't usually have time."

"Well, fortunately you've got some help now."

Help.

What a foreign concept.

I knew better than to get used to it.

It didn't mean I couldn't enjoy it while I had it, though.

****

Gabe

It should be scary how easily we fell into a routine over the next few days.

Even with Britt and Brayden coming over after school for my Wednesday evening with them. The five of us clicked effortlessly.

There was friendly banter over dinner—that Gretchen cooked, and Brayden was eager to tell Gretchen about the latest grade he'd gotten in English.

The two of them sat at the dining room table and worked on his homework after dinner while I cleaned the kitchen and Britt and Jake watched a cartoon on TV.

I surveyed the scene as I filled the dishwasher, and the words *familial bliss* popped in my head.

Where the hell did that come from?

I could say with one hundred percent certainty that I'd never—not once—used those words together in a sentence.

But as I watched Gretchen and Brayden huddled together over his book and Jake sprawled against Brittany while she played with his hair, that was the only way to describe it.

We just needed a damn dog to make the picture complete.

Chapter Sixty-Four

Gabe

"Bad news, buddy," Henry said when I answered the phone late Thursday afternoon. "The part I need is on back order. They're telling me middle to late next week at the earliest."

Oh darn.

He added, "I'm really sorry. I checked with every place I could think of, but no one has it in stock."

"I get it. We're dealing with supply chain issues, too. There's not much you can do."

"I'll get a hold of you as soon as I have it in my hands. Like I said, hopefully before the end of next week."

"Sounds good."

I hung up, pleased with myself for having bought the toddler bed and stools. It looked like my guests were going to be staying a little longer.

And I was A-okay with that.

However, I wasn't sure how Gretchen was going to feel about it. Living out of a suitcase for another week probably wasn't her idea of a good time, no matter how hard I tried to make her and Jake feel at home.

I decided to wait until dinner to break the news to her.

****

Gretchen

After the final bell rang, I pulled my phone from my desk drawer to check my messages and found I had three.

One from Laura, one from my mom, and one from Gabe.

As much as I wanted to read Gabe's first, I restrained myself and went in the order they'd been received.

Laura: Girrrrl, I miss you! Can we please get together soon?

Me: I miss you, too! Yes! Let's have dinner next week?

I was hesitant to commit to a specific day because I wasn't sure when I could get back in my house. Fortunately, Gabe had been working on installing the cabinets, so it wouldn't be long after I was back in my house that I'd have my kitchen, and some sense of normalcy, back.

Not that cooking in Gabe's kitchen had been a hardship.

Laura: Let me know when!

Me: I'll text you Monday?

Laura: Yes! Love you, miss you!

Me: Talk soon! Love you, miss you, too!

Next was my mom.

Mom: Just seeing how the kitchen is going! Is it finished yet?

Me: Not yet! I think a few more weeks.

Mom: Keep us posted! We're excited to see it! In the meantime, if you're in need of a sitter anytime soon... we miss our grandson and would love to have him for a night or two.

That made me smile. My parents were the best. God, Jake and I were lucky to have them in our lives.

Me: LOL I'll see what I can do. Talk soon! Love you!

Mom: Talk soon. Love you, too!

Finally, I opened Gabe's message.

Gabe: Do you and Jake want to go to Brayden's game tonight? It starts at 5:30. We can grab a pizza afterwards.

Brayden had mentioned it last night and invited me to go watch him play.

Me: That sounds fun. I'll finish up here, then go grab Jake. Do I need to bring a blanket or anything?

I knew our lacrosse field didn't have bleachers.

Gabe: I'll have chairs for you and Jake. Just bring yourselves.
Me: Thanks. I'll talk to you soon! Love you!

I hit send just as I reread the message and realized what I'd written.
Fuck. Fuck. Fuck.

Chapter Sixty-Five

Gabe

I blinked at what she'd written.

Love you.

Gretchen loves me?

If I were being honest, I think I loved her, too.

I was in the middle of typing back, "love you, too," when my phone rang. It was her.

"Hello?"

"Before you go freaking out, I didn't mean anything by that." She didn't let me get a word in while she continued on. "I'd just got done texting my mom and Laura and had closed with 'love you,' so it was a complete slip of the fingers to type that to you."

Well, that wasn't exactly what I was hoping she'd say. Thank god she'd called before I'd sent my return text.

I forced a chuckle.

"I'm not freaking out. I knew you didn't mean anything by that. We agreed this was just until your Mr. Right or my Mrs. Right came along."

Except, why did it feel like I was talking to my Mrs. Right?

"Or you finished my cabinets," she clarified.

"Right. Whichever comes first."

"Because we want different things."

"Exactly."

I couldn't help but wonder... *did we really though?*

"I'll see you at the game later. Do they have snacks? I think Jake might get a little cranky if he doesn't have something to eat before the game's over."

"They have a snack bar. We'll get him a hot dog or a pretzel."

"Okay." There was a pregnant pause before she asked, "So, we're good, right? You're not freaked out? You know I didn't mean anything by it."

"We're good, sweetheart. I know you don't love me. I'll see you tonight."

****

Gretchen

Except I did love him.

And I had no one to blame but myself when my heart broke into a million pieces.

Chapter Sixty-Six

Gabe

Britt waved at me as I set the cooler and camping chairs down not far from where she sat with her mom. By the time I'd slid the cover off the chair that was universally understood to be *mine*, she stood at my side.

She nodded at the chairs on the ground and her voice squeaked with excitement when she asked, "Are Gretchen and Jake coming, too?"

"They are."

"Awesome! I'll be right back!"

She disappeared only to reappear a few seconds later with her chair that she set next to mine.

"Is it okay if I sit with you guys?"

"Of course, as long as your mom's okay with it."

"She doesn't care."

Yeah, that's what Britt thinks. Hopefully I wouldn't catch hell for it later.

As I set up the next chair, I asked, "How was school?"

She shrugged and pulled the cover from the remaining chair. "It was fine. I'm ready for summer."

"Not much longer. How much time do you have left?"

"Just a little over a month! Twenty-four school days."

"It'll go fast."

We sat down at the same time, and she replied, "I hope so. Do you think Gretchen and Jake will still be at your house by then?"

"No, they should be back in her house by next week."

"Can I stay at your house this weekend then?"

"I don't think your mom would go for that, kiddo."

"Can't you just trade weekends?"

"I don't think—"

She put her hands in a prayer position in front of her chest and gave me her best puppy dog eyes as she begged, "Please? I can help out with Jake. He loves me."

That was true. The little dude seemed to hang on every word she said.

"How do you think your brother's going to feel about switching weekends?"

"He can still come next weekend. He's sleeping over at Will's tomorrow night, and then I think his team is having a big slumber party at the coach's house after their tournament on Saturday."

"Fine, I'll talk to your mom."

"I already asked her. She said yes."

"She said yes? Just like that?"

"Yep."

I narrowed my eyes at my eleven-year-old. I had a hard time believing my ex would acquiesce without so much as an argument.

"I think she wants to be alone with Aaron."

Okay, that made sense.

"I still need to talk to her about it."

My daughter seemed unfazed when she lifted her shoulders. "Okay."

"Bit-nee!"

I looked over to see Jake arching his back, trying to get out of Gretchen's hold as she walked toward us. When she was a few feet away, she relented and put him down, and he came toddling toward us with his arms open and a big smile on his face. He didn't stop until he had his arms wrapped around my daughter's middle.

She hugged him back and exclaimed, "Hey, buddy!" then beamed at me over his head, as if to say, "Told ya he loves me."

I stood to kiss Gretchen's cheek but stopped short when I noticed her pull back and her body go rigid.

Yeah, you're right. Probably not the best place for even innocent PDA.

I nodded subtly to convey I understood but still offered her a smile and wink as I told her, "Have a seat."

She sat in the chair next to me, and I reached down to open the cooler and pull out a water bottle, which I handed to her, and an apple juice bottle that I handed to Jake.

Gretchen's face lit up with a smile. I could become addicted to that smile.

"Thank you!" then she prompted Jake, "What do you say to Gabe?"

"Tank you!"

Just as Britt asked, "Where's mine?" I produced a can of Sprite Zero and gave it to her.

Her sheepish grin when she took it told me she thought I'd forgotten about her.

"Thanks, Dad."

I looked over at Gretchen when I reached back into the cooler for my Coke Zero and saw her watching me with a soft expression. She leaned over and cupped my face while she kissed my cheek, then whispered, "You're pretty great."

Popping the top of my soda as I leaned back in my chair, I murmured, "Yeah, I know," with a cocky grin.

That prompted an eyeroll from her, but she was still smiling.

"I talked to Henry. He was able to make it over to your house today and says it's an easy fix."

"Oh... good. So, we can—"

I cut her off before she finished her question. "Unfortunately, the part is on back order everywhere he checked. He thinks he can have it by Wednesday or Thursday of next week."

She bit the corner of her lip as she digested what I'd just told her.

"I can call my mom and see if we can—"

I interrupted her again.

"Don't be silly. Jake has a bed at my place now, so he's comfortable." I felt the side of my mouth hitch. "And you have a comfortable bed. What's another week?"

****

Gretchen

Right.

What's another week watching him with his kids and my son and falling deeper in love with him? Letting him take care of us.

No problem.

Yeah, sure.

~~

Jake was perched on Gabe's lap with a big smile as Gabe pointed out which player was Brayden.

Brittany chose that opportune time to yell, "Wahoo! Go, Brayden!" and Jake eagerly followed suit with his own encouragement. "Go, Bay-den!"

Brayden didn't look over at us, but he wore a grin as he continued to warm up.

A pretty light-brunette with blonde highlights that framed her face approached us with a tight smile. Judging by Gabe's sigh and "Oh, geez," that he muttered under his breath, I had a pretty good idea who she was.

When she stood in front of us, he looked up and acted like he hadn't noticed her until just that moment.

"Oh, hey! What's up, Becky?" at the same time Brittany called out, "Hey, Mom!"

"I just wanted to come over and meet your guests that Brittany can't stop talking about." She held out her hand. "Hi, I'm Becky. Brayden and Brittany's mom."

I shook her hand and replied with a polite smile, "I'm Gretchen," then tilted my head at my son, still in Gabe's lap. "Jake's mom."

"It's nice to finally meet you. The kids can't say enough good things about you."

I wasn't sure if she was being genuine but then decided to give her the benefit of the doubt until proven otherwise.

"They're awesome kids. You and Gabe are obviously great parents."

She stole a look at Gabe whose chest was doubling as a pillow for Jake, who stared at the woman like he was unsure of her.

"We try."

Gabe replied, "Speaking of Britt... she said you're okay with her switching her weekend so she can come tomorrow night?"

"Yeah, it's no problem."

"But Brayden is still going to come next weekend?"

"Britt can too, if she wants." She cast a quick glance at me then sputtered, "I mean, if that works for you. I know you might have plans."

"Any plans I have with Brayden can include Britt."

"Of course."

The referee blew his whistle to signal the start of the game, so she said, "I better get back to my seat."

"It was nice meeting you."

She nodded her head. "Likewise."

When she was out of earshot, I heard Gabe remark to Brittany, "Well, I'm glad that's out of the way."

****

Gabe

I was replaying our interaction with Becky that went way better than I expected when I heard, "Well, hello, Mrs. Wainwright!"

Aw, fuck.

It was Will's mom, Missy.

"Good to see you, Mrs. Lloyd."

"It's so nice of you to be here! I love it when teachers come to the games!"

Gretchen's, "Go Lancers!" lacked enthusiasm.

Missy seemed to realize Gretchen was sitting with me and moved her finger back and forth between us. "How do you two know each other?"

"Ms. Kelly and her son are staying at my dad's house," Britt oh-so-helpfully supplied.

Missy's eyebrows hiked and her gaze lingered on Jake in my lap. "Oh really? With Mr. Wainwright, too?"

Gretchen's smile was placating. Obviously with Will in her class, she'd had dealings with Missy throughout the year.

"Mr. Wainwright and I are divorced."

Missy's voice went up an octave. "So, you two are dating now?" With her hand on her hip, she narrowed her eyes at me. "I thought you weren't interested in dating anyone."

"We're not dating, Missy."

"So why—"

None of your fucking business.

"It's a long story, but rest assured, I'm still not interested in dating anyone or having children."

"Well, if you change your mind…"

"Your sister is available. Yeah, I know. Thanks."

Missy made a point of looking at Jake when she replied, "And she doesn't have any baggage."

Oh no, you didn't.

I planted a kiss on the crown of Jake's head and gave him a little squeeze.

"Are you hungry, buddy? I brought some snacks for you."

He nodded enthusiastically at the same time Gretchen asked, "You did?"

I reached into the cooler and pulled out two plastic storage containers. One filled with grapes, sliced apples, and orange slices and the other with crackers.

"Of course I did."

Hoping I'd made my point that Jake was not "baggage," I looked at where Missy was still standing and asked, "I'm sorry, did you say something?" as I removed the lids and held onto the containers so Jake could dig in.

With a fake smile plastered on her face, she replied, "No. Just looking forward to having Brayden over tomorrow night."

I'll bet you are.

I was going to have a conversation with my son about how to respond when Missy tried grilling him.

"Thanks for having him. He always has a good time at your house."

"I'm glad. We think of him as our bonus son."

That was a reminder I needed to be civil to this woman since Brayden spent so much time at her house. As annoying as I found her right now, I had to concede she was good to my kid.

"We love Will, too."

Okay lady, how much small talk are we going to make?

Thankfully, the crowd roared, and she realized she'd just missed a big play.

"It was good seeing you, Gabe." She finally acknowledged Gretchen again with a tight smile. "You too, Mrs. Wainwright."

Gretchen mirrored Missy's smile. "Always a pleasure."

Once Missy walked away, I turned to Gretchen.

"I'm so sorry about that."

"I think she was shocked to see me sitting with you."

"She didn't need to be rude."

Gretchen smirked. "She just wanted to make sure you know what a catch her sister is."

"Yeah, that's never going to happen. I don't know why Missy would want to set her sister up with me anyway; she's said her sister is looking to get married and have kids. I've told her I don't want more kids. But she's under the illusion that I'll somehow change my mind."

"You will, Dad," Brittany piped in. "For the right woman."

****

Gretchen

I knew better than to think I was that woman.

~~

As the game drew to a close, I turned to Gabe and said, "Do you want me to bring Brittany home with me tomorrow?"

He furrowed his brow and frowned.

"Hmm."

His response took me by surprise, and I hemmed, "I—I was just trying to save you a trip, but if you don't want me to, I won't be offended."

"Why would you make a special trip, Dad? Ms. Kelly is going to the same place."

He nodded, as if convincing himself.

"You're right—it doesn't make sense for me to make a special trip when you're already there. Thank you."

"You or Becky will just need to call the office tomorrow and give permission for me to drive her."

"I'll take care of it."

Chapter Sixty-Seven

Gretchen

The last bell of the day rang, and Brittany appeared in my doorway as I shut down my computer.

"Hey, kiddo! How was your day?"

"Hi, Ms. Kelly! It was good. I got an A on my math test."

"That's awesome! That calls for a celebration! We should do something special this weekend!"

"Like what?"

"I don't know? Is there something you'd like to do?"

"Maybe we could go bowling?"

"Oh, I haven't been bowling in ages! That sounds fun. We'll talk to your dad about it when we get home and see what he says."

"If you suggest it," she replied confidently, "He'll go for it."

"Oh, honey. You give me too much credit."

"I don't think so. He's letting me ride home with you, and he never lets us ride with anyone but him or Mom. You know, after Bodhi's accident and all, he's paranoid and doesn't trust anyone to drive us."

That explained his hesitation yesterday when I'd offered.

"Wow. I had no idea."

"But he obviously trusts you. You and Jake are special to him. To me, too."

I ruffled her hair.

"You, Brayden, and your dad are special to me, too."

It was crazy how attached I'd already become to them—especially Britt since she'd gone out of her way to spend time with us. But Brayden, too, having gotten to know him during our one-on-one tutoring.

I finished packing up and slung my satchel and purse over my shoulder.

"Come on, let's go get Jake. He's going to lose his mind when he sees you."

****

Gabe

I'd been on edge all afternoon, ever since I called the school to grant permission for Gretchen to take Britt home with her.

The lady on the phone tried to explain that staff couldn't give students rides, so I asked incredulously, "So, you're telling me my girlfriend, who's living in the same house as me, can't have my daughter in the car with her?"

"Oh... well, obviously, that's different. If that's the case, you probably didn't even need to call."

"I think Gretchen just wanted to make sure all her bases were covered."

I'd had a pit in my stomach ever since I hung up, but I wasn't sure if it was because I was worried Gretchen was going to be mad at me for telling one of her coworkers she was my girlfriend, or if I was worried about her driving Britt.

Maybe a little of both.

Or it could be how easily calling her my girlfriend rolled off my tongue.

I noticed the time and texted Britt and asked her to let me know once they got home. I couched it that I'd start that way once I heard from her.

Seconds after I hit send, my phone rang with my daughter's name on the screen.

"Hey, Dad! We just walked in the door! Gretchen wants to know if you're okay with spaghetti and meatballs for dinner."

"Do we have garlic bread, or should I stop on the way home?"

Her voice was muffled when she asked Gretchen about the bread. A few seconds later, she came back on.

"We have some. Gretchen wants to know if you have an ETA when you'll be home."

"I just need to finish installing this cabinet, then I'll head that way. I should be home by six."

I could tell her mouth was away from the receiver when she said, "He says six," then with a stronger voice told me, "We'll see you then!"

Knowing Gretchen was in my house, making dinner for the four of us did something to my insides. Gretchen and Jake fit in so well with my kids, it was like they belonged there.

I'd best remember this thing was temporary.

Chapter Sixty-Eight

Gretchen

Gabe helped me clean up after dinner, then we sat down on the couch with Jake and Brittany while they watched an episode of *Bluey* that Brittany had thoughtfully recorded.

I normally fast-forwarded through commercials at my house, but Gabe had questions, so I muted them while Brittany explained the premise of the show.

Jake tried to help and patted my leg. "Chilli," Bluey's mom's name. Then he patted Gabe's leg and declared, "Bandit," which was the father's name in the show.

Even in the seven-minute segment we'd watched, Gabe had to have figured that out.

My little man then patted his chest and said, "I Bluey," then reached for Brittany's hand and said, "Bit-nee Bingo."

Bingo was Bluey's sister. Bluey was also a girl, a fact that didn't seem to bother Jake for the scenario he was creating.

Oh boy. How the hell am I supposed to handle this?

I decided I'd try to be literal about it.

"No, silly. You're *Jake*!" I tickled his sides as I tried to lighten the mood. "You're a boy, not a puppy! I'm Mama." I pointed to Gabe and continued. "That's Gabe. He's Brittany and Brayden's daddy, not yours. Your daddy's name is Troy," and Gabe scoffed softly.

When I snapped my head to look at Gabe, he murmured, "Sorry," before coughing into his hand.

Jake wasn't to be deterred and patted Gabe's leg again as he proclaimed, "Bandit," then leaned against him to watch the show, like that was the end of the discussion.

I shot Gabe a look over Jake's head and mouthed, "I'm sorry."

Gabe shrugged and situated his arm around Jake's little body curled up next to him before turning his attention back to the TV.

I looked at Jake snuggled against Gabe, with Brittany on the other side of my son and realized I had a problem. It wasn't just my heart that was going to be broken when things came to an end. Our kids were going to suffer, too.

This was going to hurt my boy more than when his dad walked away. Jake hadn't really known Troy since the man was never around. My son hadn't missed him once he was gone, but it was obvious he was starting to care for Gabe and Gabe's kids and would be hurt by their absence.

What had we done?

****

Gabe

Gretchen followed me into the guest room, where I laid a sleeping Jake gently on the toddler bed. I noticed her pink flowery suitcase against the wall and turned to her with a frown.

"Why is that in here?"

"I can't stay in your room with Brittany here, Gabe."

"She sleeps like a log. And so what if she knows you're sleeping in my room?"

"What happens when our time together comes to an end? The kids are going to be confused and hurt. Jake already thinks of you as a father figure; he said as much tonight. He's already had his biological father reject him; what do you think you suddenly disappearing from his life is going to do?" She sank onto the bed and buried her head in her hands, murmuring, "Staying here was such a bad idea."

While I didn't think them staying here had been a bad idea, I had to admit, Jake comparing me to the cartoon dad tonight had made me pause. I thought I'd been doing the right thing by stepping up and being a role model. I hadn't thought he'd think of me as a father figure. I guess I thought he was too young to make that kind of connection. But he had, and while he sat next to me on the couch, I'd kind of felt proud that he thought I was worthy.

But Gretchen pointed out that Jake was going to think he'd been rejected again when she and I finally went our separate ways, and now I felt terrible.

"So, what do we do?"

She let out a long breath. "I don't know. Anything we do now is going to be too little, too late. We can't put the toothpaste back in the tube."

I was relieved she didn't suggest they go to her parents, or that I try to keep my distance.

"Maybe you both could go with me when I work on your cabinets this weekend. And this week, instead of going straight to my house after school, you go to yours for an hour or two."

"That might work. It will get him back in his old routine."

The one that didn't include me.

That stung more than it should.

I reached for her hand.

"Come on, Britt said she'd wait for us to start the movie."

She took my hand, and as we walked down the hall, she murmured, "I think I'm going to go stay at my parents' tomorrow night while you guys go bowling. We haven't visited them in a while."

"Britt's going to be disappointed."

Crushed was more like it. She probably wouldn't want to go.

"I'll feign a family emergency or something."

I didn't love the idea, in fact, I fucking hated it. But decided I was going to choose my battles.

"I'll back you up, whatever you decide."

Chapter Sixty-Nine

Gretchen

"Sweetheart," Gabe whispered in my ear. "It's six a.m."

I'd relented and slept in his room after he promised to set an alarm. Now, warm and cozy nestled against him, I didn't want to leave.

"Fifteen more minutes," I mumbled and snuggled closer.

He chuckled as his arm came around me. "I did wear you out last night."

"Pffft, *I* wore *you* out."

"I don't know... you didn't have to cover my mouth."

"That's because you buried your face in my neck when you came."

"Your neck smells good."

"Well, you know I like it when you cover my mouth, so..."

I had learned to embrace my kinky side with Gabe. I loved that he wanted to know what turned me on. I'd never had a partner who took so much pleasure in getting me off.

Would I ever find that again?

Probably not. I doubted I'd ever find another man like Gabe Mitchell.

With that sad realization, I kissed his chest and rolled out of bed.

~~

I woke again to hot, little boy morning breath as Jake whispered inches from my face, "Mama, I hungry."

I lay there for a few seconds to mentally engage in mom mode before opening my eyes.

"Good morning, baby. Let me go to the bathroom, then I'll make you breakfast."

When I came out of the bathroom, my little man was nowhere to be found, so I wandered toward the kitchen, praying he hadn't tried to help himself to the cereal in the pantry.

Instead, I found him in his booster seat next to Britt, happily munching away on a plain pancake. Meanwhile Gabe looked mouthwatering as he stood, spatula in hand, shirtless at the stove in his blue and green plaid pajama pants.

"Good morning!" I called as I walked in.

Gabe gave me a wink and a smile as he flipped a pancake. "Hey, how'd you sleep?"

I shot him a look and replied, "Great, thanks."

Brittany was all smiles as she popped a forkful of hotcakes dripping with butter and syrup into her mouth. I hoped she slept as soundly as he'd assured me she did.

Jake wore a goofy grin as he loudly proclaimed, "Bandit make pancakes!" before taking another bite.

There he went with the Bandit/dad reference again.

But as I looked around the kitchen, I had to admit, the scene had a familial feel to it.

This was the kind of morning I used to daydream about before I married Troy. I'd wanted what I'd had growing up. The reality, however, had been nothing like what I'd envisioned, and I'd resigned myself to believing that was just a fantasy. No one lived like that anymore.

Apparently, I was wrong.

It wasn't fair.

Gabe set a plate of pancakes in front of me, and I picked up a knife and fork from the pile someone had set down on the table as I replied, "Thank you. This looks great."

My heart skipped a beat when he smiled at me.

"Of course." He shot me a wink and added, "Chilli."

Oh, Gretchen. What have you done. You stupid, stupid girl.

****

Gabe

"Um, I'm sorry but we're not going to be able to make it to bowling tonight," Gretchen said as she stared at the few bites of pancakes remaining on her plate.

Britt's head shot up to stare at her.

"Why?"

"I forgot I told my parents we'd visit them. We're going to spend the night at their house. I'm so sorry I forgot all about it when we talked yesterday."

My daughter dragged the tines of her fork through the syrup on her plate.

"That's okay; we can wait until Sunday. That works out better anyway because Brayden can go with us then."

"Oh—I, I'm not sure what time we'll be back Sunday."

Yeah, that wasn't going to work. I'd give her tonight, maybe she needed a break from me and my kids, but she was the one who'd agreed with Britt to bowling in the first place.

"I thought you were tutoring Brayden Sunday. We can go once you're done."

Brittany chimed in, "Yeah, we're supposed to be celebrating my A, remember?"

Gretchen offered a weary smile.

"Yes, of course. You're right. I'm sorry. We absolutely must celebrate that."

Seeing the smile on my daughter's face made me realize it wasn't just Jake who was going to get hurt when our time was done.

Man, I'd fucked this up.

Chapter Seventy

Gabe

Since Gretchen and Jake were spending the night at Gretchen's parents, Brittany decided to go to a slumber party at her girlfriend's house. Brayden's tournament was out of town, so that left me home alone in the big, quiet house with just my thoughts. Normally, I relished my time alone, but now, that was the last thing I wanted.

My mind had been racing since Gretchen pointed out how upset our kids were going to be when we stopped seeing each other.

The kids, yeah.

Because *I* was totally equipped to handle it.

I wasn't crawling out of my skin because I missed them, and they'd only been gone a few hours.

Not. At. All.

I decided to be productive and go work on Gretchen's cabinets. But I realized that would still give me time alone to think, so I called Beau.

Sure, he'd give me shit, but at least I'd stay out of my head.

"Hey, what are you doing right now?"

"Watching a recording of last night's hockey game, why?"

"The Bruins win."

"I already know that, dickhead. I watch *SportsCenter* in the mornings."

"I'll buy you dinner if you come help me at Gretchen's."

"Dinner, huh? Do I get to pick the place?"

"Within reason."

"Are you going to be stingy?"

"Are you going to be an asshole?"

He didn't even hesitate. "Probably."

Knowing I didn't have much choice, I let out an exasperated sigh.

"Fine, but anything over fifty bucks, you're paying for yourself."

"Seventy-five."

"Sixty."

"Deal. I can meet you at her place in half an hour."

"See you then."

~~

My little brother walked into Gretchen's kitchen and let out a low whistle when he looked around.

"Wow, you've really made a lot of progress."

"It's amazing how much you can get done working just a couple of hours a day over the course of a week."

He ran his hand over one of the cabinets I'd already installed.

"Don't let this go to your head, but you are one talented motherfucker."

"Yeah, no shit. People aren't paying me for my stellar personality."

"Good thing. Otherwise, you'd be broke."

"Or worse, working for you."

"Pffft. You wouldn't last a week."

"You're probably right. I wouldn't be able to stand smelling like oil." I leaned forward and sniffed the air around him. "Even on my days off."

"I doubt if you even know how to change your oil."

I gripped his shoulder with a grin. "That's what I've got you for."

Now that we'd exchanged the required amount of sibling barbs, he looked around again with a thoughtful expression.

"But seriously, this is really coming together nicely. I bet we can finish everything today."

The thought was bittersweet. Fortunately, I still had a few more days since she still didn't have water.

"Well, not everything. We'll need to leave the sink cabinet" I shot him a dirty look as I continued, "until Henry repairs her pipes. But once that's done, she should be ready to come back home."

"When's Henry supposed to get that done?"

"He's waiting on a part, but he thinks Wednesday or Thursday."

His face split into a grin.

"So, she's been at your house almost a week. How's it going? You engaged yet?"

"I think your plan may have backfired, little brother."

He wrinkled his brow.

"Backfired? How?"

"She's staying at her parents tonight, so her son doesn't get too attached to me and the kids. And Britt has liked playing big sister. It's become a whole clusterfuck. We should have just kept it a weekend fling between us and not gotten our families involved."

"It's too late for woulda shoulda couldas. I think it's a good thing."

"How do you figure that?"

"You've learned your families are compatible, so you could blend them together."

"It's a nice fantasy, Beau, but she wants another baby."

"So, give her a baby. Do I need to explain how that works? When a daddy and a mommy love each other very much, they go to bed without any clothes on, and nine months later, they have a baby."

"You're such a dick."

"We already know that. But that doesn't explain why you're making this so complicated."

"I closed that door a long time ago."

"So, open it back up. Or go through a window. Or a wall."

He then broke out in Lil John's *Get Low* song, complete with choreography.

Watching my little brother grab his balls while dancing around the kitchen, I thought, *maybe being alone with my thoughts would have been the better option, after all.*

Chapter Seventy-One

Gretchen

It was bad enough I'd gone and fallen in love with Gabe Mitchell and his kids, I'd let my son do it, too.

He'd talked about "Bandit," Brittany, and even Brayden the entire car ride to my parents' house.

Fortunately, seeing his *daideó* and *mamó,* had been a distraction. But it was only temporary because my mom came into the kitchen where I was grading papers and asked, "So, who are Bandit, Bit-nee, and Bwaydon?"

"He calls Gabe 'Bandit'. You met Gabe. He dropped off my cabinets with his brother when you brought Jake home. Brittany and Brayden are his kids."

"And why is Gabe making pancakes for my grandson?"

"Well... it's a long story."

~~

I spilled my guts to my mom, leaving out the more salacious details, but she got the gist of my dilemma.

"Does it have to be temporary? I mean, it sounds like he's a great guy and you're compatible..."

"It does if you want any more grandchildren. I don't think Andrew and Carrie are going to come through for you, and Gabe doesn't want more kids."

"I'm still holding out hope for your brother and sister. Have you talked about it with him recently? It sounds like he came around with Jake. Maybe he's changed his mind about a baby."

"I mean, I haven't come out and directly asked him, but we have talked about how the kids are going to react when things between us end. I think if he'd changed his mind, he'd have said something."

"Perhaps, but love can be hard to navigate. You might have to put yourself out there and ask him, honey. Let yourself be vulnerable."

"That didn't work out so well for me last time."

"No, but he doesn't sound anything like Troy. Take a chance. What's the worst that could happen?"

"He could tell me he's not interested and break my heart."

"It sounds like your heart's going to be broken either way. At least if you talk to him and tell him how you feel, you'll know you tried."

"Maybe you're right..."

She raised her eyebrows. "Maybe?"

That made me laugh. "Okay, probably." Then my expression grew grim when I thought about putting myself out there to be rejected.

"I think I'd need him to say something before I'd be willing to risk it."

"Love is risky, honey. But when you find the right one, it makes it all worthwhile. The question you have to ask yourself is, *is he the right one?*"

My heart already knew the answer.

Chapter Seventy-Two

Gabe

I couldn't help my smile when I saw Gretchen and Jake come through my front door.

I think a tiny part of me had worried she wouldn't come back. I'm not sure what I would have done had she decided to stay at her parents until she could move back into her house. Fortunately, I didn't have to find out.

"Bit-nee!" Jake squealed as he ran toward her.

She reached down and picked him up and walked him into the family room. "Hey! Did you have fun at your grandma and grandpa's?"

He nodded his head. "Dodo and mamo!"

Brittany looked at Gretchen with a quizzical brow.

"We call my parents, *daideó* and *mamó*. The Irish version of grandma and grandpa."

"That's what my friend Adam calls his grandparents," Brayden offered from where he sat on the couch with an open textbook.

I loved that he'd gotten ready for his tutoring session without any prompting from me.

And I loved that his tutor was finally here.

"How are your mom and dad?" I asked.

"They're great. They love being retired. My dad has time to putz around and my mom goes to Zumba five days a week. She's in better shape than I am! She says she needs to be able to keep up with her grandkids, so it's worth it."

"How many grandkids does she have?"

"Well, just Jake for now."

She left the *until I have more* part unspoken.

"My parents are in Florida, so Britt and Brayden don't get to see them as often as I'd like. But Mav flies down a lot to see them and his son Nash, who's in the Navy in Pensacola., and he says the same thing about them. Mom goes to exercise classes daily at the rec center in their retirement community, and Dad tinkers around the house."

"Must be part of the retirement handbook."

I laughed. "Must be."

I wanted to ask her if she'd slept as shitty as I had. If she'd felt as lonely as I had, but I opted to go with, "I'm glad you made it back safe," as I touched her elbow.

"Thanks. It's really not a bad drive."

In case she had any ideas about staying there this week, I countered with, "Probably not on the weekend, but I've been caught in that morning commute traffic. Not fun."

"I think we're just spoiled, living in Lancastle."

"That's true."

We stared at each other for a beat, as if neither of us knew what to say next.

I did not like this awkward feeling between us one bit.

She looked at my son, still on the couch with his open textbook, and clapped her hands together.

"Whaddya say we move to the dining room table, Brayden?"

I guess I was dismissed.

****

Gretchen

Things between Gabe and me returned to normal once we got to the bowling alley.

I almost intervened when Jake insisted "Bandit" help him find his bowling ball but relented. It was too late to keep Jake from adoring Gabe—it'd already happened.

I knew the feeling.

Halfway through our first game, Brittany, Brayden, and I were cheering on Jake as he pushed his ball down the lane with the bumpers up while Gabe stood close by, when a young woman approached me holding a chubby little girl with a big, pink bow on her head.

It took me a second, but I finally recognized her as one of my former students from my first teaching gig.

"*Michelle?*"

"Hi, Mrs. Wainwright."

"Oh my goodness! You're all grown up!" I offered the baby my fingers, which she dutifully grasped in her fist. "And who is this little cutie?"

"This is my daughter, Lucy."

I shook my head with a soft smile. "You have a daughter. How is that possible? You were just in my seventh-grade class last week!"

She laughed. "I know, right? Now I'm a sophomore at Monroe Community College."

"Time flies," I replied wistfully as I moved my finger in Lucy's hand, so she gripped it harder. The baby gave me a toothless grin, and my heart was in a puddle on the ground.

"What are you studying?"

"I'm hoping to become a nurse, but it's going to be a lot of schooling."

"Yes, but you were a great student. It'll be worth it in the end."

"That's what I keep telling myself." Michelle looked past me at Gabe, Jake, and Britt who were now cheering for Brayden as he took his turn.

"This must be your family."

No. Sadly, it wasn't and never would be.

I pointed to my little towheaded son who was now clapping and jumping up and down after Brayden threw a strike. Gabe was wearing a big grin, but when I caught his eye, it slipped.

"That's my son, Jake. We're here with our friends, Gabe, Brittany, and Brayden."

"I can't wait until she can play."

I stared at her sweet baby and mused, "It'll be here before you know it. Love every second of every stage."

"That's what my mom says, too." She looked over her shoulder and said, "My boyfriend is waiting for me, so I probably should get going. I just wanted to say hi."

"I'm so glad you did." I side-hugged her free shoulder. "It was great seeing you. Congratulations! And good luck in school!"

I returned to the group, and Gabe asked, "Who was that?"

"One of my former students. She was in the first class I ever taught." I looked where she was walking out the door with her boyfriend and baby girl and murmured, "Now she's in college and a mom."

"One of your success stories."

I paused. I hadn't thought of it like that.

"I guess so."

"Ms. Kelly!" Brittany called. "Your turn!"

As I passed her on my way to get my ball, I told her, "When we're not in school, you can call me Gretchen."

She looked pensive as she tried it out. "Okay, Gretchen," then wrinkled her nose. "I think it will take some getting used to."

I laughed and patted her arm. "Maybe we can come up with a nickname."

"How about Chilli?" she said with a smirk.

"Mmm, let's keep thinking."

Although, I probably wouldn't be seeing her outside of school after a few days, so it wouldn't matter anyway.

Chapter Seventy-Three

Gretchen

I could feel Gabe pulling away after he'd watched me with Michelle and Lucy. There were no more stolen looks or discreet touches as we sat next to each other. In fact, he hardly looked at me the rest of the time at the bowling alley.

I'd thought maybe I'd take my mother's advice and talk to him tonight when we were alone. But there was no way I was doing that now. It was obvious he hadn't changed his mind. Especially when I'd said I was going to sleep in the guest room, since Brayden was also staying over, and he didn't argue.

I cried myself to sleep. The writing was on the wall.

He still made those goddamn pancakes in the morning, though. Much to Jake's delight.

The kicker came later that afternoon as I was getting ready to leave school.

Gabe: Hey! Good news! The part for your sink came in early. Your water is officially back on.

I wondered how many strings he had to pull to get that part early and get me out of his house.

Me: That is good news. If it's okay with you, I'm going to swing by your place and get all our stuff before I pick up Jake.

Gabe: I'll come help you.

I wanted to tell him I could handle it, but then realized he was more than likely coming to officially end things without Jake being around. That was probably smart.

Me: Okay, I'll be headed that way shortly.

~~

Gabe's truck was in the drive when I pulled in. My legs felt like they were filled with cement as I walked up the front steps, and I wiped my palms on my pants before opening the door.

Jake's booster seat was already by the door, along with a bag with some of his toys in it.

Gee, talk about *here's your hat. What's your hurry?*

I found Gabe sitting at the kitchen island, staring at his phone.

"Hey," I called from the doorway. Nodding toward the stairs, I told him, "I'm just going to finish packing. I see you've already gathered his toys and stuff from the downstairs."

"I'll check the basement while you do that."

Yes, you wouldn't want me to leave anything behind that you might have to get in touch with me about in the future.

"Sounds good. Thanks."

I willed myself not to cry when I walked in the guest room, but the finality of us leaving, and subsequently Gabe and I being over, was too much. The first tear soon gave way to a second. Then a third.

I heard him coming up the stairs, and quickly swiped at my face, but the tears kept coming anyway. Careful to keep my back to the door, I finished gathering my clothes and stuffed them in my suitcase.

His deep voice came from the threshold. "Need any help?"

Refusing to look up when I opened Jake's racecar suitcase, I tried to keep my tone cheerful.

"Almost done!"

He was quiet as he watched me from the doorway. I could see in my peripheral vision that he was leaning against the door jamb. Still, I wouldn't glance his way, for fear that I'd break into ugly sobs if I met his eyes.

No one wanted to see my ugly sobs. Not even me.

I was more careful with Jake's clothes than I'd been with mine, since Gabe's housekeeper had gone to the trouble of washing and folding them for me.

(Talk about a luxury! It had become my goal in life to make enough money to hire a housekeeper.)

It didn't take long to pack Jake's things, and soon all that was left were my toiletries in the bathroom.

Which meant I was going to have to go past him.

I refolded a few of Jake's shirts to stall for time, until it was painfully obvious there was nothing left for me to do.

With forced levity in my tone I proclaimed, "I just need to get my stuff from the bathroom!"

As I walked past him, he reached for my elbow. The contact felt like electricity pulsing through my veins.

"Can we talk for a minute?"

Oh god, not "the talk".

I tried to act unaffected.

"Yeah, sure."

He took my hand and led me to the edge of the bed, where we sat down at the same time. I kept my hands in my lap and stared at a chip in my nail polish on my index finger as I waited for him to start.

"You are such an amazing woman..."

The minute I heard the words, my ire went through the roof, and I snapped, "Oh, not this speech again!"

He looked taken aback at my outburst.

"What do you mean?"

"You handed me this bullshit the last time you rejected me."

"I'm not rejecting you. We had an agreement that this thing between us was just until your cabinets were finished. And, well, minus a few little things I can probably take care of tomorrow, they're done."

"*They're done?*"

"Yeah, I told you it wouldn't take me that long. I was able to work on them last week and Beau helped me again on Saturday while you were at your parents."

"You said it would take a month, and you finished in a week?"

God, I felt like an idiot. Here I was thinking he'd take his time to draw this out. When in reality, he was really hurrying to get it done so this would be over, and he could move on.

"Technically, it was ten days. And I always tell people longer so they're pleasantly surprised when I'm done sooner than they expected."

My voice dripped with derision. "Lucky me."

"Look, I know you're hurt right now, but I promise you, one day when you're happily married again, holding your new baby, you'll be glad we stuck to our agreement to end things."

"I don't understand, Gabe. I know you care about me. Why are you doing this?"

I hated the desperation in my voice. Back in college, I swore I'd never beg a man to be with me, and so far, I never had—not even Troy, but I was bordering on it with Gabe.

"Sweetheart..." he took a deep breath then gave me a sad smile. "I *do* care about you. I care enough about you to let you go because I can't give you what you want. It took me a long time to come to terms with the fact that I wasn't going to have more kids, and now that I have... well, the idea of bringing another child into this world terrifies me. I just couldn't do it. And that's not fair to you. The longer we're together, the harder it's going to hurt."

I felt my spine stiffen.

"Oh, so this is all for my benefit?"

"You're not the only one getting hurt in this."

That took the wind out of my sails.

"Right, the kids."

I hated that he threw my words from the other night back at me.

"This hurts me, too, darlin'."

So don't do it!

But even as I thought it, I knew he was right. I would thank him some day.

Just not today.

I grabbed his hand and squeezed.

"Me, too."

~~

I finished packing my toiletries, and he walked me to the door.

I wanted to make a dramatic exit, but it was somewhat hindered when I tried to maneuver the suitcases, booster seat, and bag of toys.

Gabe took the booster seat from me, then reached for the suitcase handles.

"Let me help you."

And that's all it took to make me start crying again.

****

Gabe

The night before, I'd laid in bed staring at the ceiling, unable to sleep. Gretchen was back under my roof, so that brought me some comfort. But she wasn't in my bed, hence the reason I'd been wide awake at three a.m.

I knew letting her go was the right thing to do, but my heart wasn't happy about it.

No, more than my heart wasn't happy. My soul felt like it was being crushed into a million pieces.

Still, it'd seemed like a sign that I was making the right decision when Henry called to tell me he'd got the part that morning and could be at Gretchen's house later that day.

Now as she stood in front of me outside her car with tears streaming down her face, I didn't know what the right thing to do was. Was I making a mistake?

I wiped her tears with my thumbs and whispered, "I'm sorry, sweetheart. You have no idea how sorry."

She offered me a weak smile through watery eyes, and I repeated myself. "One day you'll see we made the right decision."

When she was with someone new.

I hated the idea more than I could even express.

I found myself continuing, "And I know you probably don't want to be friends, but I'm hoping we can at least be friend*ly* when you're tutoring Brayden. And I'd love to be able to see Jake every now and then."

"Of course we can be friendly."

"Can I take you and Jake to dinner tonight?"

"I don't think that's a good idea, do you?"

"I mean, I don't want to just disappear on him."

That'd been another thing that had kept me up last night. The idea of Jake thinking I bailed on him really bothered me.

"Kids are resilient. He'll be okay."

"That's not what you said the other day."

She stared up at me with those big blue eyes that had mesmerized me from the start.

"What other choice is there, Gabe?" She pulled her neck back as she searched my eyes. "Have you changed your mind about having a baby?"

"No."

She gave me a sad smile. "Neither have I."

I guess this is it then.

Neither of us said it, but it hung in the air like a dark cloud over us.

I opened my arms, and she stepped into my embrace. As I held her tight, I tried to memorize everything about the moment. How perfectly her body fit against mine, the scent of her shampoo, how soft her hair was when I laid my cheek on top of her head.

I never wanted the hug to end. Maybe she didn't either, because she wasn't in a hurry to step away.

Finally, she released her hold on me and murmured, "I have to pick up Jake from daycare, or they'll charge me a late fee."

I stepped back and nodded.

"I can come by tomorrow and make the finishing touches on the cabinets."

"Why don't you wait until Wednesday's tutoring session with Brayden."

"Is it okay if Britt comes, too?"

"I was hoping you'd suggest that."

I couldn't resist kissing her forehead, then opened her car door for her.

"Take care, sweetheart."

She slid behind the wheel.

"You, too."

I closed her door, then she was gone. And she'd taken my heart with her.

Chapter Seventy-Four

Gretchen

I bawled my eyes out on the drive to daycare; I actually had to pull over into a strip mall parking lot and sob for a good five minutes.

After glancing at the clock on the dash, I knew I needed to pull myself together and pick up Jake, so I willed myself to calm the fuck down. After a few deep cleansing breaths, I got back on the road.

I may have overcompensated in the cheery department to mask how devastated I felt.

"Hey, baby! Guess what? We get to go back to our house! Isn't that awesome?"

My little boy held his hands out and asked, "Bandit's house?"

"We don't have to stay at Gabe's anymore. We get to go home!"

Yippee.

"No, Mama. Bandit's house."

"No, we're not staying at Gabe's anymore. Our kitchen is all done. I'm so excited to see it! It's going to be so pretty!"

At least I hoped it was. I hadn't actually seen it yet.

Judging by Jake's scowl, he couldn't give a shit less about how pretty the kitchen was going to look, but he didn't argue anymore.

My breath caught in my throat when we walked into the house through the garage door.

The kitchen was beyond anything I could have imagined. It was absolutely stunning. Like, be-featured-in-a-magazine worthy.

Even Jake agreed.

"Wow, Mama."

"I know. Isn't it so pretty? Gabe did this."

Tears welled up in my eyes, and I quickly dashed them away, but they threatened to keep falling.

I handed Jake my tablet and said, "Why don't you play mouse, while Mommy unpacks the car."

Once I was back in the garage, I sat in the passenger seat and grabbed some napkins from the Honda's glove box. Burying my face in the stack, I allowed myself another few minutes to cry until the napkins were falling apart in my hands.

Then I pulled my shoulders back, let out a deep breath, and got the rest of our things from the trunk.

"What should we make for dinner?" I called when I walked back into the kitchen.

I wasn't excited about our prospects since I hadn't been to the grocery store in almost two weeks. We probably didn't even have milk that wasn't expired.

"Mac 'n cheese!"

I'd been afraid he'd say something that required milk.

"How about fish sticks and fries, baby?"

He shook his head and repeated, "Mac 'n cheese!"

Crap.

"We don't have—"

Just then the doorbell rang, and Jake quickly set the tablet aside, slid off the couch, and raced toward the front door, exclaiming, "Bandit's here!"

I dashed after him and grabbed him just before he reached the door.

"Little kids don't answer the door," I reminded him, then called, "Who is it?"

"Instacart. I have a delivery from Gabe Mitchell."

Jake clapped his hands and called, "Bandit!" while tears filled my eyes yet again.

****

Gabe

I couldn't help but grin when the ringtone for her text messages alerted.

Gretchen: Okay, a couple of things...

One: You were right. My kitchen looks incredible. Better than I could have ever imagined. Thank you.

Two: That was really thoughtful to send me some groceries.

BUT

You can't keep taking care of us.

My first instinct was, *Wanna bet?* But I knew she was right. Still, I wasn't going to apologize for it.

Me: I just wanted to make sure you had something for dinner and breakfast. You've been gone from your house a while.

Gretchen: I know, but you didn't have to do that. We would have figured something out.

Me: Well, now you've got choices.

Just say "thank you," sweetheart and go make Jake dinner.

Gretchen: Thank you.

Fuck, I missed them already, and it hadn't been more than ninety minutes since she left my house.

I was so screwed.

I needed a damn drink.

Chapter Seventy-Five

Gretchen

A box of pancake mix was included in the Instacart delivery that Gabe had sent over. I guess he wanted to make sure Jake got pancakes in the morning, even if he wasn't going to be the one to make them.

After tossing and turning all night, in between bouts of tears, I finally gave up on sleep and got up before the alarm. Jake's breakfast routine was going to be continued.

Except my pancakes didn't taste the same as Gabe's, and Jake only ate half of his.

Nothing was the same.

Instead of sleeping soundly all night, I hardly slept at all. Jake didn't dance happily in his chair as he munched on his pancake. I didn't leave the house relaxed, with plenty of time to spare because I had someone helping me.

In fact, I was late for work and forgot my damn lunch, and I probably passed my stressful mood onto my kid and students.

I was grateful to Gabe, though.

He'd shown me what life with a good partner could be like. Now I just needed to find said partner.

I knew that was going to be easier said than done. The Gabe Mitchells of the world were a rare breed. I had a feeling I was going to have to settle for close enough.

Jake was quiet in the backseat as I drove home from daycare. I knew he missed Gabe as much as I did.

"Hey, baby..." I said as I looked at him in my rearview mirror. "What do you say we get McDonald's for dinner tonight? You can have a Happy Meal!"

Yeah, I was bribing my kid to be happy with a Happy Meal. I know, cliché.

If only they had Happy Meals for adults.

"They do," Laura said with a laugh when I lamented my pathetic life observation to her on the phone after Jake went to bed. "It's called wine."

"I think it's going to take a lot of wine to get over Gabe. And tissues."

"Lucky for you I have a Wine Depot membership. But the tissues you'll have to get on your own."

On my own. Story of my life.

~~

I woke up exhausted Wednesday morning and it hit me why I'd been able to sleep so soundly at Gabe's. As a single mom, I could never fully let my guard down. Even in my own home. I felt like I had to be on high alert all the time.

I always made sure to check all the locks on the doors and windows every night before bed and would wake to the slightest creak the house made.

With Gabe, I hadn't had to do that. He'd made me feel safe and protected. Kind of like how I'd felt growing up. I'd never worried as a kid because I thought there wasn't anything my dad couldn't handle.

That's what being with Gabe felt like. There wasn't anything he couldn't handle.

I don't think I'd ever felt that sense of peace with Troy. Which meant Jake probably hadn't either. He'd had that with Gabe.

Annnnd I was crying again.

****

Gabe

When you're thirty-nine, you don't spring out of bed and head to work after a night of drinking like you did when you're in your early twenties.

Something I learned the hard way—two mornings in a row.

But getting drunk was the only way I could tolerate sitting in the quiet of my big, empty house all alone.

Fortunately, I got to see Gretchen and Jake that night. I was going on forty-eight hours of no contact with her, and I'd fucking hated every second.

Then I received a text from Britt.

Britt: Brayden's staying home from school. He has a fever and was throwing up all night.

Fuck.

Me: How are you feeling?

Britt: Fine so far. Mom is busy disinfecting the house.

I should probably have my housekeeper do the same to mine. I also needed to let Gretchen know Brayden wouldn't be coming to tutoring tonight.

I wondered if she'd be okay if I still came.

Me: Fingers crossed you don't get sick, too.

Britt: Should I stay home tonight? I don't want to get Jake sick.

Oh, yeah. I hadn't told the kids yet that Gretchen and Jake were gone.

Time to rip the band-aid off.

Me: Gretchen's water was fixed. They were able to go back home.

Britt sent back a string of crying emojis.

Me: We'll still be able to see them when Brayden goes to tutoring.

Britt: That's like once a week for a few hours and every other weekend, Dad! Not to mention summer is coming, and Brayden won't get tutored at all!!

Tell me something I don't know, kid.

Me: Well, next fall, Brayden won't have lacrosse, so it will be twice a week and every other weekend.

Britt: Big whoop.

Me: It's the best I can do, kiddo.

She didn't respond.

I fired off a text to Gretchen, hoping she'd get it during her lunch hour.

Me: Hey. I hope all is well in your world.

I wrote out "I miss you," then erased it before continuing.

Brayden is sick with a stomach bug, so we'll have to cancel tutoring tonight.

She replied right away.

Gretchen: Yeah, that's going around right now. I hope he's okay!

Me: I think he will be once it runs its course.

Gretchen: Thanks for letting me know. Please tell him I hope he feels better soon. We can have extra sessions next week to help get him caught up on his missed work and prepare for finals.

Me: I can still come by tonight though and finish the kitchen.

The dots indicating she was replying started and stopped, started and stopped, and finally her message came.

Gretchen: Let's just wait until next week.

I was afraid she'd say that.
Didn't she know *I* needed to see her and Jake?

Me: It's no problem for me to come. I hate the idea of your kitchen not being perfect. We guarantee perfect.

No, we didn't. But she didn't know that.

Me: Plus, I'd love to see you and Jake.

Again, with the dots starting and stopping.

Gretchen: I think we should wait. I don't want to confuse Jake any more than he probably already is.

It felt like all the air left my lungs, but I managed to reply.

Me: I understand. I'll be in touch about next week. But don't hesitate to reach out if you need anything.

Gretchen: Will do.

It seemed Gretchen was already back to normal. Me, on the other hand... I was far from "normal" and wondered if I'd ever feel that way again.

****

Gretchen

It'd taken every ounce of strength I had to turn down Gabe's offer to come over that night.

I missed him with every fiber of my being.

But I thought if he showed up without the kids, Jake might get confused. I think my son had a basic understanding that I was helping Brayden, but if Gabe came by himself, Jake might get the wrong idea.

Hell, *I* might get the wrong idea.

So, when the doorbell rang that night at seven-thirty, after I'd put Jake to bed, my heart skipped a beat. Gabe knew Jake's bedtime, maybe he was coming by to see me.

As I put my hand on the doorknob, a thought popped in my head.

He knows Jake's in bed. He wouldn't risk waking him up by ringing the doorbell.

I looked out the window and instead of a black, Ford 150 in my drive, there sat Troy's red two-door Jaguar. The one a car seat wouldn't fit in.

What the hell? Why is he here?

My emotions went from nervous excitement thinking Gabe was at my door to dread now that I knew who it really was.

I slowly unlocked the door and found my ex-husband, in one of his fitted black suits with his red tie loosened, sporting a tan like he'd just come back from a vacation in the Bahamas.

I swear to God, you better not be here to ask about lowering your child support.

"Hey, Gretch," he said with a sheepish smile.

I nodded my head. "Troy."

He didn't say anything else, just stared at me until I finally asked, "What are you doing here?"

"Can I come in?"

Against my better judgment, I opened the door and allowed him inside.

Chapter Seventy-Six

Gretchen

We sat in the formal living room that, as far as I was concerned, was a waste of space. Back when we'd been married, I'd had plans to knock some walls down once the kitchen was finished.

It looked like I was going to have to just change the furniture and décor if I wanted a different use for the room now. But who knew when that would be in my budget.

Troy sat on the edge of the loveseat and flashed his toothy smile that I used to find so handsome. I'd always thought he was sexy in his suit, but apparently work boots and tool belts were my real weakness because I felt nothing as I looked at him.

He reached for my left hand and caressed my empty ring finger.

"It's weird to see you without my ring on your hand."

I snatched my hand back and absentmindedly rubbed the digit as if trying to cancel out his touch.

"Speaking of that, can you tell me where you bought it? I'd like to see if they'll buy it back."

"You want to hock your wedding ring?"

Duh.

"It's not doing me any good sitting in my jewelry box, and I have bills to pay, Troy."

He glanced at the ground and murmured, "What would you say about me moving back?" before looking up at me expectantly. "You wouldn't have to struggle to pay your bills anymore. I could take care of you and Jake."

I gave my head a little shake and closed my eyes tight as I replayed his words in my head to make sure I wasn't hearing things.

"*What?* Are you kidding? I'd say, Cora would have a problem with that."

"We broke up. When she realized I wasn't going to marry her, she filed a sexual harassment suit against me with HR, and they fired me."

Gee, who knew banging your subordinate wasn't allowed?

"*They fired you?* So, that's what this is about. You're broke."

"I'm not broke, I got hired the next day by Dylan and Associates making more money."

I made a mental note of that for the next child support adjustment hearing.

He clasped his hands between his legs and leaned forward.

"I miss you, Gretch. I miss our little family. I fucked up, but it didn't take me long to realize Cora could never be you."

My head was whirling. Was I in the *Twilight Zone?* He couldn't possibly think I'd take him back.

I wracked my brain for something to say, and he continued.

"Give me another chance, Gretch. Let me come home and be your husband again. Jake needs his father."

Now he's worried about my son needing a dad?!

I gave him my patient smile—the one I usually reserved for belligerent seventh graders or their parents.

"You're right, Jake does need a dad. And I'm glad you're interested in getting to know your son. But we don't need to be together for you to do that. I wouldn't keep you from seeing him. In fact, I'd love to set a schedule for you to spend time together."

****

Gabe

Derrick looked over at me as I sat down at the bar.

"What are you doing here on a Wednesday?"

"I was tired of getting drunk at home alone."

He pulled out a mug from the freezer but stopped short before pulling the tap.

"You've been getting drunk—alone—at home?"

I snarled, "Yeah, so?" and he pulled the lever to start the flow of beer.

"Wanna tell me what's going on?"

"Beau is an asshole, that's what's going on."

He put a bar coaster down, then set the draft on top of it.

"We all know that. I'm going to need some context."

I gave him the abbreviated version of what had transpired over the last ten days, then added, "And I thought I'd show up to her house tonight, anyway, but there was a red Jag F-Type in her drive."

"So? That could be anyone."

I took a long pull, then set my mug down with a thud.

"Please. She's got a dude over. We haven't even been broken up forty-eight hours, and she's already dating someone else."

"But you just said she was supposed to tutor Brayden tonight. I doubt she made plans with such short notice."

I dropped my head onto my forearms on the bar.

"Even worse—it's a booty call!"

Derrick made a show of looking at his watch.

"At eight o'clock?"

"It could happen! She's gotta work in the morning."

My little brother pursed his lips and rolled his eyes.

"I seriously doubt that. You're getting yourself all worked up over something you don't even know is real. I think the better question is, why do you care? You don't want to be with her, remember? Or is this a case of *I don't want her, but I don't want anyone else to have her either*?"

"I do want her!"

He crossed his arms and glared at me.

"So, what are you gonna do about it?"

I took another drink and grumbled, "Not a goddamn thing. Just drink and be miserable."

Derrick nodded to my near-empty glass.

"You're off to a good start."

Chapter Seventy-Seven

Gretchen

"Troy said *what*?" Laura screeched as she picked her martini glass up from the lacquered high-top table where we were perched in Louie's Bar and Pub. One of the few alternatives to Flannigan's available in Lancastle, although the Sunday crowd was thin compared to the cars in Flannigan's parking lot.

I did *not* look for a black F150 when we drove by.

"He said he knows he has his work cut out for him, but he's going to win me back."

"Did you laugh in his face? Please tell me you laughed in his face."

"No, I didn't laugh in his face."

"You should have," she grumbled. "So, what *did* you say?"

"That if he's serious about having a relationship with Jake, I'm all for it."

"Really?"

"Jake needs his dad in his life."

She set her glass down and cocked her head at me.

"Does he really need *Troy*, though?"

I slumped back in my bar stool in defeat. I'd been wrestling with that same question.

"You should have seen him with Gabe. He ate up his attention."

"Yeah, well so did you, that doesn't mean you should accept any ol' man in your life just because you have a history with him. You need someone special who's worthy of you and Jake."

"I'm thirty-one, Laura. I don't think I have the luxury of being too picky."

"Well, you sure as hell aren't going to allow yourself to get treated like crap."

"I'm not getting back together with Troy. And honestly, I haven't heard from him since Wednesday, so I'm not expecting him to pursue a relationship with Jake."

"Good. He's a deadbeat, babe. He signed away his rights to his son. Who does that?"

I shrugged. "He seemed remorseful about that."

"And yet, you said so yourself, he hasn't followed up about seeing him again."

"I know."

"Are you sure there's no chance you and Gabe are going to get back together?"

I felt my eyes tear up and shook my head sadly.

"Positive. I haven't heard from him either. Brayden was the one who texted me about tutoring this week."

"I thought you said Gabe had to make some finishing touches on your kitchen?"

"I'm sure he'll work on it this week sometime. I'm tutoring Brayden Wednesday and Thursday with our final session of the year on Sunday."

My friend studied my face in the neon glow of the lights reflecting off the bar mirror.

"You need to try online dating."

****

Gabe

"Five nights in a row! This must be a Mitchell Brother record!" Dan, Derrick's bartender and right-hand man, called when I took my usual seat at the bar.

He grinned when he tossed a coaster in front of me. "Even Beau isn't in here that much."

"It's either this place or stay home and type out text messages I'm never going to send."

That'd been my daytime habit all weekend.

"Why don't you just make up with her?"

"Because we want different things."

"Sounds like you need to move on, then."

Yeah, that wasn't going to happen anytime soon.

I tried to keep the snarl out of my tone when I replied, "Thanks for the advice. How about a beer?"

Dan showed why he was a good bartender, because he nodded and said, "Coming right up."

Chapter Seventy-Eight

Gabe

Monday morning, I decided I couldn't keep showing up to the shop bleary-eyed with the stench of alcohol seeping from my pores.

I was the owner of a successful business—I needed to step up and start acting like it.

So, Monday and Tuesday, instead of going home and drinking to keep my mind off Gretchen, I stayed at the shop and worked until I was ready to drop from exhaustion.

That way avoiding my feelings was at least making me money, and I wasn't racking up ride share charges.

Wednesday morning, I woke up feeling energized. I was going to see Gretchen for the first time in nine days.

Nine, painfully long days.

The hours seemed to drag until finally it was time to pick Brayden up from lacrosse practice and Britt from Becky's. My daughter had jumped at the chance to "watch" Jake while I put the final trim on Gretchen's cabinets and Gretchen tutored her brother.

"I wonder how they've been," Britt mused on our drive.

Brayden responded, "I've seen Ms. Kelly in the hall. To be honest, she looks tired."

I knew the feeling.

"I'm sure the end of the year is as stressful for teachers as it is for students."

"Yeah, maybe," Brayden murmured as he looked out the window.

Britt chimed in from the backseat. "What's your excuse, Dad?"

I caught her eye in the rearview mirror. "What are you talking about?"

Her mouth turned up in a devilish grin.

"Why do you look so tired?"

Little shit.

"I've been working a lot. I got a little behind when I was installing Gretchen's cabinets."

"Well, I'm excited to see them."

"The cabinets or Gretchen and Jake?"

"I guess both. Although I meant Gretchen and Jake."

Me too.

I didn't say that out loud, but I was excited.

Until I pulled up to her house and saw the same red Jaguar from last week sitting in her driveway.

****

Gretchen

I left work the soonest I thought I could without being hauled in front of Samantha McClung, then hustled to pick up Jake.

I wanted to make sure the house was tidy, Jake's hands, face, and diaper were clean, and there was no mascara smudged under my eyes and my hair was brushed. Okay, I'd put on a coat of lipstick, too.

I wasn't about to open the door looking like a woman who'd been pining over the man on the other side of my threshold. Even though that's exactly what I'd been doing.

But he hadn't bothered to call or text, so there was no way I was going to let on how miserable I'd been.

I decided not to tell Jake they were coming, just in case it fell through.

I'd certainly never said anything about his dad wanting to see him. Partly because Jake probably had no idea who Troy even was, but in the event he did, I didn't have a lot of faith my ex would follow through with seeing him.

Especially since Troy had yet to reach out to schedule a time to come over.

It was probably just as well.

I didn't want Troy floating in and out of Jake's life.

But if he really was serious, I was all for the two having a relationship. Maybe we'd even get to a point where we'd share custody.

Yeah, talk about putting the cart before the horse.

The guy hasn't even called back. Slow your roll, Gretchen.

I think I just wanted Jake to have a father-figure in his life. He hadn't stopped asking about Gabe, so I knew it was important.

The doorbell rang, and Jake streaked toward the door squealing, "Bandit's here!"

I wasn't sure how he knew, or if it was just wishful thinking on his part.

Except it wasn't Gabe and his kids standing on my porch when I opened the door.

I adjusted Jake on my hip and stammered, "Wh—what are you doing here, Troy?"

He stepped inside without being invited.

"I wanted to see you, Gretch." With his arms extended, he made his eyes wide and his voice go up an octave when he said, "Hey, Jakester! Come here and say hi to your dad!"

Jake buried his face in my shoulder, refusing to look at Troy, and the man dropped his arms to his sides with a scowl.

I tried to keep my tone even when I said, "This isn't a good time. I've got a tutoring client who'll be here any minute."

"Well, let me take Jake while you work."

"No, Troy. I told you to call and schedule something. You can't just show up unannounced and expect to take Jake. It doesn't work that way."

His lips were set in a firm line when he bit out, "Fine."

I opened the door wider and reiterated. "Call me and we'll set up a time to get together. Maybe we could meet up at the park or something."

"How about we take Jake to Mickey's Friday night?"

I glanced at my watch. Gabe and the kids were going to be here any minute. I knew if I told Troy no, he'd argue and wouldn't leave, so I found myself saying, "Fine."

His face broke into a wide grin.

"I'll pick you up at five-thirty. Maybe after we finish at Mickey's, we can drop Jake off at your parents' so we have some alone time to... talk." He waggled his brows at me with a salacious grin.

Yeah, that was never going to happen.

"My parents are out of town."

I think he recognized he was pushing his luck, because he mumbled, "Oh, okay," as he stepped out the door. He added, "I'll see you Friday," and without a word to Jake, he headed toward his car.

Chapter Seventy-Nine

Gabe

My daughter's voice had a hint of awe in it as we approached Gretchen's drive.

"Ooh, look at that car!"

I'd rather smash its tail lights.

"Dad! You missed Gretchen's house!" Britt cried as I drove on by.

"What?" I feigned looking around in confusion. "I did?"

Yet, I kept on driving.

"Yeah. It was back there where the cool car was parked."

"Huh. The car must have confused me; all these houses look alike."

I mean, they *kind of* had at first, but after visiting a few times the differences were obvious. Still, it was the best I could come up with on the fly.

I don't know why I'd kept going when I saw the red car in her driveway, because I wanted to know who the fuck the owner was and why he—or she—seemed to be at Gretchen's house all the time.

Then it hit me, *maybe Laura got a new car.*

Oh my god. That was it! Laura got a new car!

Jesus, I was being a little bitch over nothing. And worse, Derrick had been right.

At the end of the street, I turned right to circle around the block. This time when we pulled up, the Jag was gone.

"I wonder whose car that was," Brayden asked as I put the truck in park where the Jag had been three minutes ago.

"Probably her friend, Laura's."

The kids didn't wait for me as I got my toolbox from the truck bed and continued up the walk to her house.

They were already inside, with Jake draped around Britt's middle, when I entered. But the second the little guy saw me, he squealed, "Bandit!" and went limp so Brittany had no choice but to put him down. Once on his feet, he ran toward me with his arms wide, and I set my toolbox down and scooped him up in one fell swoop.

He wrapped his little hands around my neck as he chastised, "Where been?"

"I've been working, buddy! How've you been?"

He jabbered animatedly, of which I understood about two words, but I thought my response of, "Oh my! Really?" was appropriate, because he nodded and continued.

My reply of, "Wow!" seemed to satisfy him.

I noticed Brayden unpacking his backpack at her dining room table and Britt declared, "It wasn't her friend's car. It was Jake's dad's."

When the little man heard "Jake's dad," he tightened his hold on my neck and put his head on my shoulder. I gave him a squeeze in return even as I felt my blood pressure spike.

What the fuck had that asshole been doing here? He gave up his right to spend time with Gretchen and Jake.

I looked over at Gretchen with raised eyebrows.

"Oh yeah?"

Her shoulders lifted. "He wants to spend time with Jake."

What a bunch of bullshit.

I had to consciously will my face not to convey what I was thinking.

Instead, I replied. "Huh. I hope that works out."

But I'd bet my mortgage it wouldn't. And why the hell was she allowing it?

It seemed like there was more to the story.

"I do, too," she said softly.

Then it hit me, and I blurted out, "Are you getting back together with him?"

Her gaze snapped to mine, and she forcefully replied, "No!" then dialed it back. "He just stopped in to talk about a schedule for him to spend time with Jake."

Yeah, sure. A schedule, my ass.

I wanted to shake her. She was worried Jake would be confused about *me*? What about that loser?

"Hey, bud, go get your toolbox so you can help me in the kitchen."

Jake's eyes got big, and a grin spread across his face. I set him down, and he tore down the hall toward the stairs.

I looked over at Brittany and said, "Can you help him?"

She knew something was up, but did as I asked, then I grabbed Gretchen's elbow and pulled her into the kitchen.

"Are you seriously considering letting this guy back in your life?"

"He's Jake's dad. Jake needs his father."

What could I say to that? I had no right to an opinion. Yet, I voiced mine anyway.

"This is a mistake, Gretchen."

"I appreciate your concern. But we're not your problem to worry about."

She was right, of course. It didn't mean I liked it. In fact, I fucking hated it.

****

Gretchen

"You feeling better?" I asked Brayden as I sat kitty-corner from him at my dining room table.

"Yeah, but now I have a ton of homework to catch up on, *and* I've got to get ready for finals next week."

"Well, fortunately, we're meeting tonight, tomorrow, and Sunday. We'll get you caught up and ready for finals."

"How are you with World History and Geography?"

"I'm certified to teach it..."

He pulled out a folder and said, "Can we start with that?"

~~

As I helped Brayden finish his Renaissance worksheet, he quietly said, "So, you and my dad."

Shit.

I wasn't sure how to respond, so I went with the obvious.

"Your dad is a great man."

"Does that mean you're...?"

I set my pencil down and looked him in the eye.

"Your dad and I are at different stages in life. His chicks will be flying the coop before he knows it, while one of mine just hatched, with hopefully more on the way."

Keeping with my analogy, he replied with a grin, "I think my dad would be a great rooster for your chicks."

Me, too.

Of course I couldn't share that with him.

"You know I adore you, but this isn't a conversation we should be having."

"I just see how much he cares about you. We want him to be happy, you know? He was happy when you and Jake were staying with him."

This kid was going to make me break down crying.

"He was a very gracious host."

"Don't you think—"

I cut him off by handing him a practice test for a World History quiz I knew he had on Friday. One of the perks of tutoring at the school on Tuesdays.

With a smirk, I said, "You've got fifteen minutes," as I stood up and set the timer on my watch.

I debated whether to go into the kitchen. Things between Gabe and I were tense. Although I wasn't sure why he cared about Troy seeing Jake.

The sound of my son's giggles compelled me to see what was going on.

I walked in just as Jake slapped Gabe's shoulder and said, "Oh, Bandit," while wearing a big grin.

Britt had a pair of safety goggles on top of her head, and a drill on the counter nearby, while she concentrated on the level she had lined against the wall.

I loved that Gabe didn't care about gender roles and was teaching his daughter how to do his job. All while making my child laugh.

I wanted to blame him for hurting me, but I couldn't. He'd never lied to me. I bore the responsibility for letting my heart get involved when I'd told him I wouldn't.

But now my kid's heart was involved, too.

It was painfully obvious Jake needed his dad.

God, I hoped Troy stepped up.

"Whatcha guys doing?"

Gabe's smile fell when he saw me.

Ouch.

Britt answered, "Dad's teaching me how to put trim up, and Jake is helping."

Jake proudly patted his chest and proclaimed, "I help, Mama!"

"That's great. Are you doing a good job, baby?"

Gabe answered on my son's behalf.

"Of course he is! When he's not laughing!"

He then grabbed Jake's sides and tickled him, causing my son to shriek in delight.

I both loved and hated watching the three of them interact. Their rapport was bittersweet.

It hurt knowing after this week, this was all going to end.

Damn, I wished things could have turned out differently between Gabe and me.

Maybe in another life.

Even though the timer on my watch hadn't gone off yet, I looked at it and murmured, "I better get back to Brayden."

He nodded his head with a sad smile, but otherwise, didn't say a word as I made a hasty retreat back to the dining room.

I hated how things were now between us, but sadly, I knew that was going to be our new normal.

Chapter Eighty

Gretchen

On Thursday, Jake must have had a rough day at daycare, because he fell asleep on the couch right after dinner. So, a little before six, the time we'd scheduled for Brayden's tutoring session, I kept an eye out for Gabe's truck in order to open the door to keep them from ringing the doorbell. I was surprised to find Britt and Brayden walking up the drive while Gabe waved at me from the cab of his truck, then pulled out of my driveway.

"Your dad's not staying?"

Britt remarked, "He said he'd be back in an hour," as she walked through the door.

"Oh."

Apparently, our days of spending any time together were over.

It was probably just as well.

But it didn't mean it still didn't sting.

I thought we'd agreed we'd at least be friend*ly*?

I tried to school my expression when Brayden followed, but I don't think I hid my hurt feelings fast enough, because he offered, "He had some errands to run that couldn't wait," with a sheepish expression.

I knew he was lying but wanted to hug him for trying to spare my feelings.

"My cabinets took up a lot of his free time lately, I'm sure he's behind on a lot of things."

"Bit-nee! Bwaydon!"

Jake slid off the couch still bleary-eyed and ran toward our visitors, then stopped short, looked around, and held his hands out in a questioning manner.

"Where Bandit?"

"Gabe has to work, baby."

Fortunately, Gabe's kids were an acceptable substitute because he didn't question it further.

Thirty minutes later, the doorbell rang, and Jake's eyes lit up as he squealed, "Bandit!" and raced toward the door.

I know the feeling, baby.

"Stop!" I commanded from my spot next to Brayden at the dining room table. "Do little kids answer the door?"

He danced in place, antsy to see Gabe, but dutifully replied, "No."

Britt asked, "Can I answer the door?"

I nodded with a solemn smile. "You may answer the door," then braced myself to see the sexy carpenter.

We only had one more tutoring session before summer, and I wouldn't see him for three months.

As much as I hated the idea, I admitted, it was probably for the best. It might give my heart some time to heal.

I heard Britt call, "Uh, Ms. Kelly?"

Followed by a voice I recognized snarl, "Her name is *Mrs.* Wainwright."

Son of a bitch.

I slid my chair away from the table and told Brayden, "Keep working; I'll be right back."

Troy stood in the foyer glaring at me, while Brittany held Jake protectively on her hip out of arm's reach from him.

I didn't want to have a faceoff in front of the kids, so I grabbed Troy's elbow, stepped to the side, and harshly whispered, "What are you doing here, Troy?"

"I thought I'd stop and see you guys. I told you, I'm going to get my little family back, Gretch."

I ignored the part where he said he was going to get us back. That wasn't happening.

"And I told you yesterday that you can't just show up unannounced. I'm *working*."

"How was I supposed to know that?"

"You weren't. Hence, the reason you call and schedule something in advance."

"I'm not going to make an appointment to see my son, Gretch."

His ballsiness took me aback.

"Actually, if you want to see him at all, yes you will."

I didn't want to get in a pissing contest with him, so I tried to soften my tone. "If I know you're coming, I can get him ready to see you."

"I don't care what he's wearing."

I took a deep breath through my nose and willed myself to remain calm.

"*Mentally*. Get him ready mentally."

His scowl indicated he did not like the idea of Jake having to mentally prepare to see his dad.

"As far as he's concerned, you're a stranger. He doesn't know you anymore, Troy."

He announced, "There's no time like the present," and barged past me.

"Hey, Jakester!" He held out his hands, like that was supposed to make him more welcoming as he approached where Brittany had moved Jake into the family room. "Come here and see your dad."

Jake clung to Britt's leg and looked the other way, and I noticed Troy's face had turned red. I wasn't in the mood for this shit.

"Now is not the time. I have clients," I hissed.

He looked over at Brayden, who was now watching the scene intently, then at Britt, then back at me.

"Fine," he bit out. "I'll pick you up tomorrow at five-thirty," then spun on the ball of his heel and stormed toward the front door but paused to look at me over his shoulder.

"I'm going to prove myself worthy again, Gretch. You'll see."

I didn't respond, just stayed frozen in place until he closed the door then turned to the kids and offered an apologetic smile. Their brows were marred with worry.

"I'm so sorry, guys."

Britt came over and wrapped her arms around my middle.

"It's not your fault."

****

Gabe

I sat at my brother's bar, nursing a beer while I waited for Brayden's tutoring session to end.

A pretty brunette sat down at the next barstool and proceeded to flirt with me, complete with pawing my chest and rubbing her tits against my arm while Derrick looked on with an amused grin.

I wasn't the least bit interested but figured it would help pass the time until I could pick the kids up.

My phone buzzed in my pocket with multiple incoming text messages.

Britt: Dad, you need to come NOW! Gretchen's ex-husband is here and acting like a jerk.

Brayden: Are you close by? We have a situation.

I was out of my seat in an instant, mumbling, "I gotta go," and headed toward the door without waiting to hear the woman's response.

I typed out a text on my way to my truck.

Me: Be right there.

I received a reply instantly.

Britt: You don't have to come right away. Everything's okay. He left.

I didn't give a shit. The fucker could come back.

Me: I don't care. I'll be there in five minutes.

****

Gretchen

I apologized again to Gabe's kids. They were gracious and awesome with their response, and I loved them a little more than I already did.

Britt turned on an episode of Bluey, and she and Jake got comfortable on the couch, while Brayden turned his attention back to the homework in front of him.

I put my hand on Brayden's shoulder and said, "Let's finish this and call it a night. We'll review for finals on Sunday."

He nodded. "Okay, that sounds like a good idea."

We'd barely gotten started when a loud knock came from my front door, followed by the doorbell.

I let out a big sigh and said, "I'm so sorry guys," as I stood up.

Britt looked over at me and replied sheepishly, "I think it's Dad."

That'd been a pretty aggressive knock.

"Really?"

"Yeah, he texted a few minutes ago and said he was on his way."

I peeked through the window and saw Gabe's black Ford, then opened the door.

He had a lot of nerve showing up to my house looking as good as he did in those jeans and black polo.

"Hi," I said with a welcoming smile and stepped aside. "Come in. We're almost done. Maybe fifteen more minutes."

I could feel the annoyance vibrating off him when he stepped inside without so much as a word to me as he looked around.

Jake noticed Gabe, and exclaimed, "Bandit!" before running to greet him.

A genuine smile spread across Gabe's face, and he knelt down to embrace my son. My breath caught in my throat at how much the two obviously cared about each other.

"Hey, kiddo. Whatcha doing?"

"Watching Bluey." Jake reached for Gabe's hand. "Come on." Gabe followed him into the family room without argument and without another glance my way.

Chapter Eighty-One

Gabe

I hugged Jake, thanked Gretchen for helping Brayden—I still needed to be polite in front of the kids, then went out to the truck and waited for Brittany and Brayden to come out.

I watched Britt give Jake a hug on the porch, then Gretchen. Then Brayden and Jake did some weird handshake, and finally my son wrapped Gretchen in an embrace that lasted a while.

I could see her lips moving as she hugged him back, and finally he pulled away with a smile and a nod and turned to follow Britt toward my truck.

Gretchen tried to discreetly wipe her cheeks as she watched the two go.

Our eyes locked and after a beat, she gave me a sad smile and wave.

I knew she was saying goodbye.

And I hated it with every cell in my body, so I refused to wave back. I just offered a fake smile in return that morphed into a real one when Britt opened the rear passenger door.

"Hey!"

My daughter barely looked at me when she got in and grumbled, "Hey."

Brayden mirrored his sister's long face when he got in the front passenger seat and shut the door.

"You guys ready?"

Brayden responded with a clipped, "Yep," as he looked out the windshield at Gretchen and Jake going inside the house before putting on his seatbelt.

I backed out of the drive and didn't say anything until we exited her community.

"How'd tutoring go?"

"Fine."

I wasn't keen on his one-word answer, so I tried engaging him again.

"Do you think it's helped? Are you ready for finals?"

He shrugged, still not looking my way.

"My grades are up, and we've got Sunday to get ready for finals."

"So, do you—"

"You should have seen what a jerk Gretchen's ex-husband was," Britt lamented from the backseat, effectively cutting me off. "She kept telling him he couldn't just drop in whenever he wanted, but it was like he didn't even care what she had to say."

Brayden sat up straighter in the passenger seat and puffed out his chest. "I thought I was going to have to ask him to leave."

I hated that my son was put in that position, but I was proud of him for being willing to help Gretchen and step up.

"I should have waited in the truck in her driveway."

Brittany demanded, "Why would you do that and not just come in?"

"We thought it was best if I started to limit my time with Jake. She's worried he's going to get confused."

"About what?"

"Well, he does call me Bandit. And now that his dad is coming around..."

Brayden grumbled, "You're a way better father than her ex, that's for sure."

"But I'm not Jake's father"

Brayden abruptly turned his body in his seat toward me and burst out, "Why are you letting her asshole ex-husband get her back? She and Jake belong with us."

I didn't chastise him about his language, just asked, "Why do you think he's trying to get her back?"

"He said so! He said he's going to prove himself and get his 'little family' back."

He did what, now?

I gripped the steering wheel tighter as I choked out, "Well, I know she wants to have more children."

"She shouldn't be having kids with someone she's worried how Jake is going to act around."

"How do you know she's worried about that?"

"She said so! She told her friend on the phone they're going to Mickey's tomorrow, and she said she was nervous Troy was going to rush Jake into liking him. And she hoped Troy wouldn't get mad if he didn't right away."

"You can't *make* a two-year old like you."

"Dad?" Britt asked from the back.

"Yeah?"

"Shouldn't a two-year-old already like his dad?"

"You'd think so, huh?"

"He likes you."

I thought about how happy Jake always was to see me and couldn't help but smile.

My eleven-year-old got it. Why hadn't I?

"I like him, too."

Brayden asked, "What about Gretchen?"

I let out a long sigh.

"That's a little more complicated."

"Why? You love her, don't you?"

There was no point in denying it with these two.

"Yes."

Britt's voice was urgent. "So, get her back, Dad! They belong with us!"

I shook my head. "She wants more kids."

"Mom told us you always said you wanted a basketball team."

Yeah, I had said that. More than once. But that was a long time ago.

"I think that dream died with Bodhi, guys."

My too-wise-for-his-own-good teenager remarked, "Maybe it didn't die; maybe it was just delayed until you found Gretchen and Jake."

Britt piped up, "They need us, Dad. And we need them."

I shook my head.

"It's not that simple, kiddo."

"I can't believe you're just going to give up," Brayden groused.

I couldn't either. But I knew it was for the best, at least for her.

Chapter Eighty-Two

Gabe

I'd dropped the kids off at Becky's and headed back to Flannigan's. I'd been in a bad mood since Gretchen and Jake moved out of my house, but knowing her ex was trying to get her back had put me in a downright rotten one.

I think I was pissed at myself, too.

Gretchen and Jake had helped heal a part of me that had been broken for a long time. But I was still too big of a chicken shit to put my fear aside and be the man she needed.

Now she was probably going to get back together with her loser ex and it was killing me.

Kinda like what this headache was doing to me now.

That's what I got for trying to numb my pain with alcohol.

I rolled out of bed and went in search of water and pain reliever when the smell of bacon hit me, followed by a sense of panic.

Had I brought someone home last night?

I distinctly remembered the brunette lighting up when I returned. But just like before, I'd had no interest.

At least I thought I hadn't.

I glanced down, relieved to find I had my boxer briefs on.

With quiet steps, I made my way into the kitchen to find Beau in the clothes he'd worn to the bar last night, turning bacon strips in the pan on the stove.

"What the hell are you doing here?" I grumbled as I opened the cupboard that housed the bottle of pain reliever.

"Well, good morning to you, too. I'm making breakfast; what's it look like?"

"Why are you doing it in my kitchen?"

"I figured you were going to need a ride to pick up your truck this morning, since I brought your drunk ass home last night. It just seemed easier to sleep here."

Okay, that made sense.

Still, I replied, "Hmph," while I poured myself a cup of coffee.

Which didn't bother Beau one bit.

"Why don't you make us some toast while I fry up some eggs?"

I didn't do as he asked, just washed the medicine down with coffee.

Bits and pieces of the previous night started to come back to me as I leaned against the counter and took another long sip of caffeine.

"Did I...?"

"Threaten to kick my ass because I took your keys and phone away from you? Yeah." He pointed to where my cell sat charging on the counter. "I even plugged your phone in for you. You're welcome."

"Why did you take my phone?"

"Because you were trying to call Gretchen. You kept going on about how you couldn't believe she was going to get back together with her ex. And how you were going to go over to the dude's house and run over his Jag with your truck. I guess in your drunken state, you thought Freddie had somehow transformed into a monster truck."

I recalled having that thought as I'd sat at the bar.

"I didn't call her, though, did I?"

"Not for lack of trying. You even tried to get the cute brunette who was hitting on you to lend you her phone when I took yours. Fortunately, you didn't have Gretchen's number memorized."

I winced at the picture my brother painted.

"Not my finest moment."

He slid a plate of bacon and eggs in front of me.

"Can I ask you something?" He didn't wait for me to affirmatively reply before continuing. "Why are you doing this to yourself? You two belong together. Everyone knows it. Hell, *you* know it, or you wouldn't be this torn up about her."

"She wants—"

"I swear to God, if you come at me with this baby bullshit, I'm pouring ketchup on your eggs. Give her a goddamn kid, for fuck's sake."

I glared at him as I bit off a hunk of bacon and chewed aggressively.

He continued. "Or don't and become a miserable drunk."

I washed down the bacon with another swig of coffee.

"Have a kid with her or become an alcoholic. Those are my choices?"

Beau put two pieces of bread in the toaster and pushed the lever.

"At the rate you're going? Yeah. Those seem to be your only choices."

I think I was most pissed that I couldn't even argue with him.

Chapter Eighty-Three

Gretchen

Jake clung to me as we observed the flashing lights and flurry of activity of the kid-themed restaurant. I knew the cacophony of kids' screams, laughter, and temper tantrums, mixed with the beeps, buzzes, and whirring sounds of the numerous games made it hard for him to hear me when I said, "It's okay, baby. This is going to be fun!"

Troy held out his hands. "Come on, Jakester! Let's get some tokens so we can play a game!"

My little boy only buried his head in my shoulder. His grip around my neck was ironclad, like he was worried I was going to make him go with Troy.

"Maybe we should find a booth and order some food first. That way he can just watch until he's more comfortable."

I could tell by Troy's scowl that he didn't like the idea, but he murmured, "Yeah, sure." His tone dripped with disdain when he continued, "Pick out where to sit, since I'll probably get that wrong, too."

"You haven't gotten anything wrong, Troy."

Other than abandoning your family.

"It's going to take some time for him to get to know you again."

I tried not to flinch when he stroked my arm.

"I know. I'm just anxious to have our family back together."

That's not happening.

With a fake smile plastered to my face, I nodded, then turned to scope out an empty booth among the gold-colored ones that looked like they hadn't been updated since the seventies. All while I tried to adjust Jake's body, the diaper bag slung over one shoulder, and my purse over the other.

If Troy noticed me struggling, he didn't acknowledge it.

"Where do you want to sit?"

I nodded toward the closest empty booth. None of the seats had padding, probably so they could be hosed down easier at the end of the night. At least, I hope they got cleaned. I couldn't imagine how many germs were floating through this place with all the kids running around.

"How about there?"

"Cool."

He headed to the table without looking back, leaving me to juggle Jake and the bags while I picked up a brown booster seat from the stack at the wall.

Not that I wasn't used to handling everything on my own, I'd just gotten spoiled having Gabe around who insisted on helping me with everything.

I dropped my bags on the left side of the bench and put the child's seat down on the right side before plopping Jake in and scooching him toward the wall. Then I picked up my purse and the diaper bag and set them on the other side of me as I got situated next to Jake.

My ex plucked the laminated menu tent from the end of the table and perused it while I fished out disinfecting wipes from the diaper bag and wiped down the sides of the booster chair and the table. The last thing I needed was for Jake to get sick when I had to administer final exams next week.

Troy proclaimed, "Oh good, they have beer."

Whew. I wouldn't want you to have to go a whole evening with your child without having a beer.

My smile was tight when I asked, "What kind of juice do they have?"

"Since when do you drink juice?"

I stopped what I was doing and scowled in disbelief.

"For Jake."

I couldn't bring myself to call him "our" son yet.

"Oh, yeah. Of course." He flipped the menu over. "It looks like they have apple and orange juice or milk—whole, two percent, and chocolate."

Hearing that, Jake clapped. "Choco milk, Mama! Pweez!"

I smiled at his enthusiasm. "Okay, baby. You can have chocolate milk."

Troy didn't even acknowledge Jake, just glanced around and wondered out loud, "Do they have servers or are we supposed to order at the counter?"

"I'm not sure."

Just as I was about to suggest Troy go find out, a young woman appeared at our table dressed in a red and white striped retro uniform with the top three buttons undone. She appeared to be in her late teens/early twenties, and I noticed Troy's gaze fixated on her boobs popping out of her uniform.

"Hi! Welcome to Mickey's! My name's Christine and I'll be helping ya out today. Are you ready to order?"

Troy flashed a smile that I'm sure he thought was charming, but frankly, I thought it came off as lecherous.

"Hey there, Christine. What pizza specials do you have that include beer?"

She shook her head. "We don't have any; you have to order beer separately."

He raked his gaze back down to her boobs, then to her face again. "But I can order it from you, right? So, you'll get the gratuity?"

At the mention of gratuity, she giggled, causing her boobs to jiggle. "Of course."

Troy didn't even look our way when he asked, "Do any of the pizzas come with tokens?"

She leaned forward, conveniently giving Troy a better view of her twins when she grabbed the menu he'd just been reading to point out the different options. Troy sat rapt listening to her, like the fucker didn't know how to read.

"We'll go with the Number Three."

Christine stood up straight to pull her order pad and pen from her apron pocket.

"What kind of pizza?"

"Supreme."

I scoffed. "Jake won't eat anything but cheese."

You'd know that if you'd ever been around.

"I'm not eating a plain pizza." He offered Christine a smile. "I'm a man—I eat meat."

It took everything in me not to roll my eyes. There was more to being a man than eating meat. I knew a certain cabinet maker who could give him some pointers on the subject.

"Fine," I replied through gritted teeth. "Get a pepperoni and I'll pick them off for him."

I don't know if Troy did as I asked, because I heard Jake squeal, "Bandit!" before sliding out of his booster seat and landing under the table. He then took off running before I registered what was happening.

The bags next to me prohibited me from easily sprinting after him, and I noticed his little arms stretched out wide before he was picked up by a man who looked an awful lot like Gabe. I had to squint to make sure it really was him, and not my imagination.

But as if I'd conjured him up, he was there—in the flesh.

My little guy was talking a mile a minute, with both his hands on Gabe's cheeks to make sure he had the man's full attention. They seemed to be wearing matching grins.

Brittany and Brayden flanked them on either side.

That's my family.

I felt so sure about it that it didn't even freak me out. I'd rather Jake be my only kid and be with Gabe than have another child and end up with a loser like Troy.

I didn't need to have another baby. Jake, Brayden, and Brittany were all I needed, as long as I had Gabe by my side.

I knew I wasn't Brayden and Brittany's mom, but I'd come to love them, and I knew they cared about me and Jake.

"Who the fuck is that, and why is he holding my son?"

I realized I was smiling from ear to ear when I replied, "That's Gabe Mitchell. He made the kitchen cabinets you *had* to have."

I realized how fortunate I was that Troy had insisted on those darn cabinets.

****

Gabe

 Oh, fuck no. They're mine.

 That'd been my immediate reaction when I saw Gretchen and Jake in the booth with that asshole.

 While I'd talked with Beau that morning, I realized he was right—as much as that'd pained me. I loved her more than my fear.

 For the first time in seven years, I allowed myself to consider what having another kid might look like.

 It looked like Jake.

 And however many more little Gretchens she wanted.

 It'd been confirmed when my little man caught sight of me and slipped out of his booster chair to make a mad dash my way.

 The look on the fucker's face, along with Gretchen's bright smile, when I scooped Jake up in my arms had felt immensely satisfying.

 The four of us approached the booth where they were seated.

 I opened with, "Look who I found!" the same time Jake asked, loudly, "Mama and Jake at your house?"

 "That'd be fun, huh, buddy?"

 He nodded solemnly and added a lot of gibberish along with a very clear, "Pancakes!"

That made me laugh out loud.

"I'll definitely make you pancakes again."

Troy scowled and looked at Gretchen.

"What is he talking about? Why is the *cabinet maker* making my son pancakes?"

I answered for her.

"Because Jake likes pancakes for breakfast, that's why."

"And how the fuck do you know that?"

I lightly cover Jake's ears with my hands and admonished, "Language!"

It seemed to have the intended effect, because the dude's face got red, so I went in for another jab.

"I think the bigger question is, why don't *you* know that?"

"That's none of your business."

I handed Jake to Britt and murmured, "Why don't you guys go find a game he wants to play," then took a step closer to the booth.

I could tell by the way Brayden stood up taller that he wanted to stay and give the guy a piece of his mind, but he reluctantly turned and followed his sister.

"You see, that's where you're wrong. Gretchen and Jake are my business."

She squeaked, "We are?"

Our eyes met, and I took another few steps until I was in front of her. "Yeah, sweetheart. You are. If that's okay with you."

Her eyes filled with tears, and she nodded her head.

"More than okay."

Reaching for her hand, I pulled her from the booth and into my arms at the same time I heard Troy exclaim, "You gotta be fucking kidding me! I'm out of here."

Neither of us even acknowledged him as I wiped the tears from her cheeks with my thumbs and stole a kiss right there in the middle of Mickey's.

"I love you, sweetheart."

"I love you, too."

"I want to marry you and have babies with you."

This was so not the place to be quasi-proposing, but it couldn't wait.

"I don't need another child. You, Jake, Brittany, and Brayden are my family."

"You're right, we are. But I know you want more kids, and I want to be the man to give them to you. I want to give you everything."

"*Everything?*" she teased with a grin.

"Every damn thing you want. Making you happy makes me happy."

"*You* make me happy. The fact that you care so much about my son makes me happy."

"I love your son. I want him to be *our* son someday soon."

Her fingers skimmed the hair along my neck.

"I want that, too." Her grin grew wider. "Bandit."

I mirrored her smile, "Come on, Chilli. Let's go find—"

Before I could finish my thought, the kids swarmed us. Brayden and Britt hugged Gretchen while I picked up Jake.

"I'm so happy!" Brittany exclaimed with a big, goofy grin.

Me, too, kiddo. Me too.

****

Gretchen

Gabe and I sat down in the booth while the kids went to spend their tokens.

Christine looked confused when she brought the drinks, but Gabe told her to leave them, then ordered two more pizzas—one cheese, and drinks for his kids.

With a smirk, he took a pull of Troy's beer, then set it down and declared, "You're too far away, sweetheart. Come here."

I didn't hesitate to move to his side of the booth.

He slid his arm around my shoulder and murmured, "That's better."

My heart felt like it was going to burst, and I wondered if it was possible to die from happiness.

He took my hand and said, "I have something very important to ask you."

My breath caught in my throat, and I whispered, "Okay."

"Will you and Jake come home with me tonight?"

I immediately replied. "Yes."

"And never leave?"

I hesitated. Not because I didn't want that, but I was scared this was too good to be true. It was all happening so fast.

He must have taken my hesitation to mean something else, because he pressed on.

"You and Jake healed a place inside my heart that I was afraid could never heal. The kids were right—I *need* you. I need you if I want any chance of happiness in my life."

"I need you, too."

The corner of his mouth lifted.

"Good," then he stole a quick kiss before nuzzling my neck and whispering, "I have one more important question."

"Okay?"

"Will you make lasagna now?"

****

Gabe

She made the lasagna, and it's now one of our family's favorites.

Epilogue

Gretchen

To say the kids were thrilled Gabe and I were together would be an understatement.

It warmed my heart how easily Brittany and Brayden took on the role as Jake's older siblings, and how happy Jake was to let them.

We even got a dog from the shelter that Jake named Bluey.

We decided to sell my house since Jake and I had moved into Gabe's place. It was bigger and had room for all of us, with the ability to add more bedrooms, should we ever need more.

"Oh, we're going to need more," Gabe assured me with a wink.

The question was no longer if, but when.

I was due for another birth control shot, and we'd been discussing if I should get one more before we started trying.

We'd boxed the last of what I was moving and made one final pass through the house, pausing in the kitchen to admire Gabe's work one last time.

"I almost hate to leave them," I said wistfully as I traced my fingertips along the grain of the drawers. "They're what brought us together."

He grabbed me by the waist and hoisted me onto the counter with a devilish grin.

"I know another way they could always be a part of us."

I cocked my head. "What do you mean?"

He bunched my sundress up to my waist, slid my panties to the side, and ran his finger down my already-damp seam.

"I'm saying I want to make a baby right here on this countertop."

I unbuttoned his jeans and pulled down his zipper, then reached inside his waistband to stroke his hard cock.

"Well, handsome, I want that, too."

His face split in a cocky grin.

"Handsome? I thought I was infuriating?"

"Shut up, and fuck me, Mr. Infuriating."

****

Want more of Gabe and Gretchen?
Sign up for my newsletter to receive their bonus story!
https://dl.bookfunnel.com/txy24cpwuo

Look for Beau's story in *Mr. Inappropriate*!
https://books2read.com/MrInappropriate

Thank you

Thank you for reading *Mr. Infuriating*!

I'm so excited about this new series and look forward to bringing you all the Mitchell men (Maverick's sons included), as well as Dan the Bartender!

I hope you enjoyed the book and will consider leaving me a review wherever you purchased it. And, if it's not too much trouble, Goodreads and/or BookBub? (And even if you didn't like the story, I'd be grateful if you left your [gentle] thoughts.)

Don't forget to sign up for my newsletter to get tons of bonus content for *free*, plus be the first to know about cover reveals, contests, excerpts, and more!

https://www.subscribepage.com/TessSummersNewsletter

xoxo,

Tess

Acknowledgments

Maggie Ryan: I sound like a broken record, but I adore you! I'm so grateful for all the care you give my books, and how you never fail to lift me up with your words of encouragement. Thank you for being my editor!

A.L. Jackson and Renee Rose: You are my tribe, and I'm so lucky to call you my friends. I don't know what I'd do without you both. Thank you for all your feedback and helping make this book that much better!

Mr. Summers: Thanks for always taking such good care of me and our kids. You are the perfect example of how I wanted Gabe to be. I love you to Pluto and back.

Kae Popp: Thank you for everything you do for me to make my life easier. I appreciate you more than I can express!

My Rocky Point Posse—Anne Fitzsimmons, Marty Wenzel, and Megan Appelt: Thanks for listening to me as I worked through this story! I love you ladies! "Fireball!"

My extended family: Thank you for continuing to support and encourage me on this wonderful journey. I love you all!

Lastly, to my readers: I continue to pinch myself every day that you read my books. Thank you for helping make my dreams come true.

Click here (https://BookHip.com/TQWAFTV) for a free, standalone short story!

Breakfast Is Served

She doesn't do sleepovers, let alone relationships. He's going to try and change that.

Lauren's business is her baby—she doesn't have time for relationships. So after a fundraiser when she goes home with her best friend's boss and she's still there in the morning, that's a problem. She doesn't do breakfast with her one-night stands—ever.

Not returning his calls seems like the safest bet. Better not to start something she can't finish.

Except Tristan didn't build one of the most successful law firms in the state by not going after what he wants. And what he wants is Lauren in his bed every night and her in his arms every morning.

More from Tess Summers:

San Diego Social Scene

Operation Sex Kitten: (Ava and Travis)

https://tesssummersauthor.com/operation-sex-kitten

The General's Desire: (Brenna and Ron)

https://tesssummersauthor.com/the-generals-desire

Playing Dirty: (Cassie and Luke)

https://tesssummersauthor.com/playing-dirty

Cinderella and the Marine: (Cooper and Katie)

https://tesssummersauthor.com/cinderella-and-the-marine-1

The Heiress and the Mechanic: (Harper and Ben)

https://tesssummersauthor.com/heiress-%26-the-mechanic

The Playboy and the SWAT Princess (Maddie and Craig)

https://www.amazon.com/dp/B0CWRQ9PZC

Burning Her Resolve: (Grace and Ryan)

https://tesssummersauthor.com/burning-her-resolve-1

This Is It: (Paige and Grant)

https://tesssummersauthor.com/this-is-it

Sloane: (Ashley and Sloane)

https://tesssummersauthor.com/sloane

Agents of Ensenada

Ignition: (Kennedy and Dante prequel)

https://tesssummersauthor.com/ignition-1

Inferno: (Kennedy and Dante)

https://tesssummersauthor.com/inferno

Combustion: (Reagan and Mason)

https://tesssummersauthor.com/combustion-1

Reignited: (Taren and Jacob)

https://tesssummersauthor.com/reignited

Flashpoint: (Sophia and Ramon)

https://tesssummersauthor.com/flashpoint

Boston's Elite series

Wicked Hot Silver Fox

https://tesssummersauthor.com/wicked-hot-silver-fox-1

Wicked Hot Doctor

https://tesssummersauthor.com/wicked-hot-doctor-1

Wicked Hot Medicine

https://tesssummersauthor.com/wicked-hot-medicine

Wicked Hot Baby Daddy

https://tesssummersauthor.com/wicked-hot-baby-daddy

Wicked Bad Decisions

https://tesssummersauthor.com/wicked-bad-decisions-1

Wicked Little Secret

https://tesssummersauthor.com/wicked-little-secret-1

Wicked Grumpy Heart Doc

https://tesssummersauthor.com/wicked-grumpy-heart-doc

Wicked Little Thief

https://tesssummersauthor.com/wicked-little-thief

About the Author

Tess Summers is a former businesswoman and teacher who always loved writing but never seemed to have time to sit down and write a short story, let alone a novel. Now battling MS, her life changed dramatically, and she has finally slowed down enough to start writing all the stories she's been wanting to tell, including the fun and sexy ones!

Married over twenty-six years with three grown children, Tess is a former dog foster mom who ended up failing and adopting them instead. She and her husband (and their six dogs) split their time between the desert of Arizona and the lakes of Michigan, so she's always in a climate that's not too hot and not too cold, but just right!

Contact Me!

Sign up for my newsletter: BookHip.com/SNGBXD
Email: TessSummersAuthor@yahoo.com
Visit my website: www.TessSummersAuthor.com
Facebook: http://facebook.com/TessSummersAuthor
My FB Group: Tess Summers Sizzling Playhouse
TikTok: https://www.tiktok.com/@tesssummersauthor
Instagram: https://www.instagram.com/tesssummers/
Amazon: https://amzn.to/2MHHhdK
BookBub https://www.bookbub.com/profile/tess-summers
Goodreads - https://www.goodreads.com/TessSummers